The Know How Book of Experiments

Heather Amery

Illustrated by Colin King

Contents

Educational Consultants:

Frank Blackwell
Patrick Eve
Evelyn Bourne

First published in 1977
Usborne Publishing Ltd
Usborne House, 83-85 Saffron Hill,
London EC1N 8RT, England

© Usborne Publishing Ltd 1989, 1977

Printed in Italy

About This Book

This book is for everyone who likes finding out about things, why they work and why they happen. It is full of experiments to discover the secrets of ordinary things, such as clouds and rain, plants and noises, as well as extraordinary things, such as rainbows and lightning.

There is always a reason why things happen in the way they do. But the reasons are not always simple and easy to understand. Even scientists cannot explain everything and there are still some mysteries to be solved.

All the experiments are absolutely safe to do, although some may surprise you and some are a bit messy. Some are very quick but others take quite a long time to work, so you will have to be very patient. When you have done the experiments, you may be able to think of some of your own to try.

For the experiments you will need paper, jars, bottles, balloons, big baking trays, plastic bags, string and plasticine. You can probably find them, as well as glue, sticky tape and scissors, at home.

This is Professor Bumble and his team

2

Amazing Ping Pong Ball

Here is some real science magic. Try these two experiments on your friends and surprise them. You need a drinking straw with a bend in it and a very small funnel. Or you can make your own. And you need lots of puff.

You will need

a ping pong ball
a piece of paper about 20 cm long and 10 cm wide
a circle of thin cardboard about 10 cm across
a bit of drinking straw, about 4 cm long
glue, sticky tape and scissors

TAKE A DEEP BREATH AND BLOW FOR AS LONG AS YOU CAN.

Hold the ping pong ball above the end of the straw. Take a deep breath and blow hard. Let go of the ball and it will stay there.

Put the ping pong ball into the funnel. Blow hard, pointing the funnel up. Keep blowing and point it down. The ball will stay in it.

1 Making a Tube

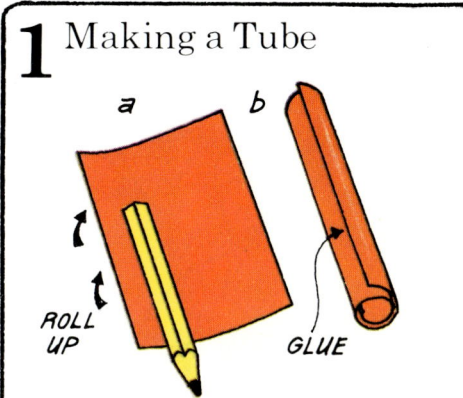

ROLL UP
GLUE

Put a pencil down on the edge of the piece of paper (a). Roll up the paper round it. Stick the edge with glue to make a long tube (b). Shake out the pencil.

2

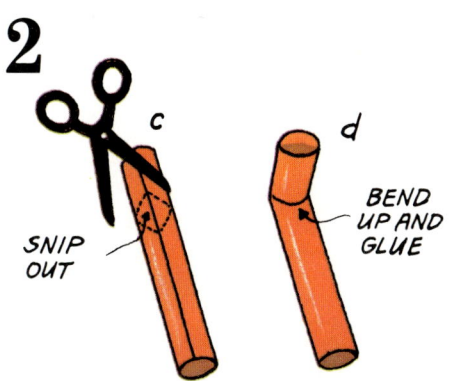

SNIP OUT
BEND UP AND GLUE

Make a small snip in the tube, near one end (c). Then make another snip to cut out a V-shaped bit. Bend up the end, like this, and spread glue round the join (d). Leave to dry.

Making a Funnel

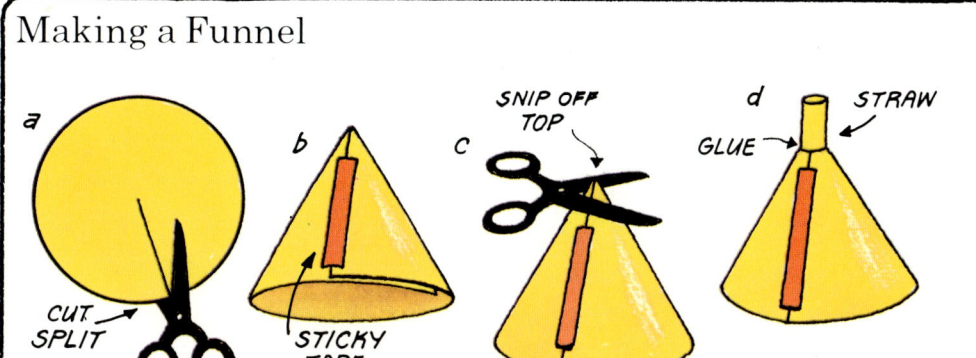

CUT SPLIT
STICKY TAPE
SNIP OFF TOP
GLUE
STRAW

Cut a slit from the edge of the cardboard circle to the middle (a). Curl the circle up to make a cone (b). Stick the edges, inside and outside, with tape.

Snip the top off the cone (c), to make a small hole in it. Push the bit of straw through the hole so it just goes down inside (d). Glue it to the cone. Leave to dry.

Why It Works

SLOW MOVING AIR
FAST MOVING AIR
FAST MOVING AIR
SLOW MOVING AIR

Fast moving air has less push or pressure than slow moving air. When you blow, air under the ball moves more slowly than air above it. This means there is more pressure upwards and the ball stays in the funnel.

Did You Know?

SLOW MOVING AIR
FAST MOVING AIR
SLOW MOVING AIR

Aircraft wings are curved on the top. When a plane is flying, air on top moves faster than air underneath and has less pressure. The slower air underneath has more push and helps to lift the plane and hold it up.

Bubble Boat

Make this boat and it will bubble its way round the bath under its own power. If you bend the tube at the back to one side, you can make the boat go round a corner.

You will need
a plastic bottle with a top
baking soda (this is used in cooking)
vinegar
thin paper or a paper tissue
plastic drinking straw or empty ink tube from an old ball-point pen
plasticine and scissors

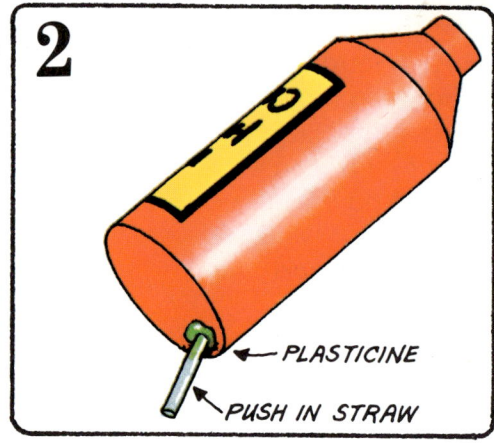

1
PLASTIC BOTTLE
MAKE SMALL HOLE

With scissors, make a small hole in the bottom of the plastic bottle, close to the edge.

2
PLASTICINE
PUSH IN STRAW

Push the plastic straw through the hole until only about 1 cm sticks out. Press the straw down a little. Press plasticine round it to keep it in place and fill up the hole.

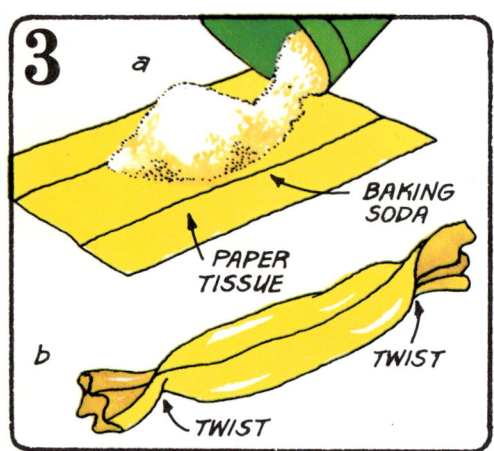

3
a
BAKING SODA
PAPER TISSUE
b
TWIST
TWIST

Shake some baking soda on to a paper tissue or piece of paper (a). Wrap the paper round the soda and twist the ends, like this (b).

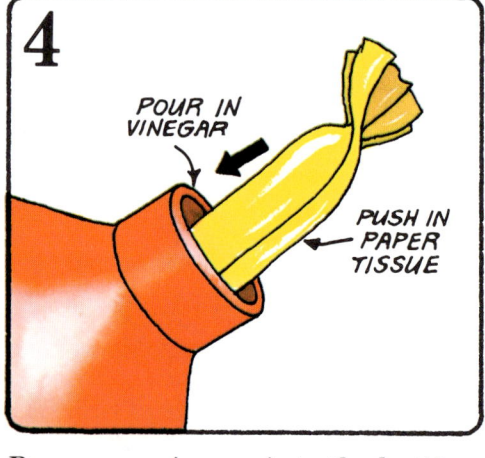

4
POUR IN VINEGAR
PUSH IN PAPER TISSUE

Pour some vinegar into the bottle. Push in the paper with the soda. Put the top on as quickly as you can. Put the bottle gently into a bath of water and let go.

Why It Works

When the paper gets wet in the vinegar, it untwists. The soda and vinegar mix together and make a lot of gas and foam. The gas goes out through the plastic straw and pushes the boat along.

PUT THE BOAT IN THE BATH AND IT WILL GO ALONG BY ITSELF.

Gas Cannon

Try making this bottle cannon and wait for the cork to blow out with a pop. You need baking soda which you may find in the kitchen cupboard, or you can buy it at a grocery shop.

You will need
a small glass bottle with a
  tightly fitting cork
baking soda
vinegar
piece of paper
water

SODA

Put some baking soda into the bottle. A good way to do this is to use a creased piece of paper and slide it in, like this.

VINEGAR

WET CORK

Dip the cork in water to make it very wet. Pour some vinegar into the bottle and push in the cork as quickly as you can. Stand back and wait for the cork to pop out.

HOLD ON AND WAIT FOR THE CORK TO BLOW OUT.

Why It Works

Baking soda is a chemical, called sodium bicarbonate. When it mixes with vinegar, it makes a gas called carbon dioxide. This gas pushes the cork out of the bottle.

Did You Know?

Most explosives work because a special mixture of chemicals makes a huge amount of gas very quickly. The blast of gas blows things up with a bang.

Some rockets work in the same way. The fuel in them makes a great blast of gas. This spurts out the end of the rocket and pushes it up and along in space.

Magic Balloon Bottle

Set up this bottle experiment and amaze your friends. You can make it go on working as long as you like by just putting the bottle into hot water and then into cold water and then back again into the hot.

You will need
a bottle—any sort will do
a balloon
scissors
a bowl of hot water from the hot tap
a bowl of very cold water

Fill the bottle with hot water from the hot tap. Leave it for a few minutes to warm the bottle. Pour out the water.

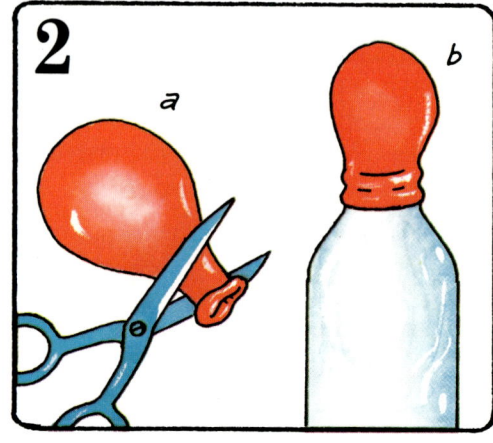

Cut the neck off the balloon (a). Stretch the balloon over the top of the bottle and pull it down (b). Stand the bottle in the bowl of cold water. Now watch.

DON'T POKE IT. IT WILL WORK BY ITSELF.

Why It Works

When you warm the bottle with hot water, the air in the bottle is warmed. When air is warmed it gets bigger. This is called expansion. When you cool the bottle with cold water, the air in it is cooled and gets smaller. This is called contraction. As the air gets smaller, the air outside pushes the balloon into the bottle. If you warm up the bottle again, the air inside expands and pushes the balloon out again.

Did You Know?

DENT

WARM WATER

If you have a ping pong ball with a dent in it, you can get it out. Put the ball in warm water. The air inside will expand and push out the dent.

A hot-air balloon floats up when the burner in the basket heats air in the balloon. This is because the air expands, some escapes and the rest weighs less.

Bottle Fountain

Here is another surprise to puzzle your friends. You will have to tell them why it works because they will never guess.

You will need

a small bottle with a screw-on
   top
a plastic drinking straw
plasticine
a pin or needle
poster paint or ink
a bowl of very hot water

Take the top off the bottle. Make a hole in the top with scissors, pressing downwards, like this. Half fill the bottle with cold water.

Pour a few drops of poster paint or ink into the water in the bottle. Screw the top on very tightly.

Push the straw through the hole. Press plasticine round it to seal up the hole. Put a plug of plasticine in the end of the straw. Poke a hole in it with a pin or needle.

Put the bottle in a bowl and fill it up with very hot water from the hot faucet. Wait a while for the fountain to work.

Why It Works

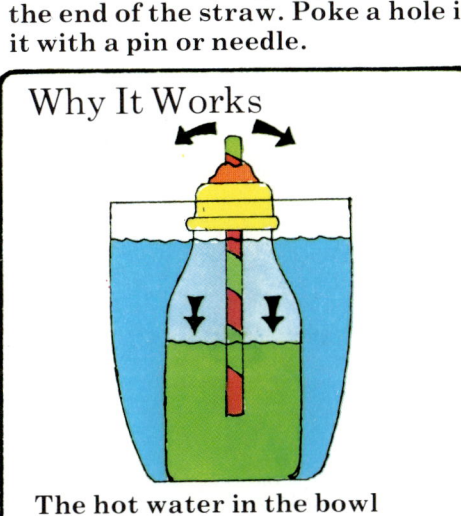

The hot water in the bowl warms the air in the bottle. When the air is warmed it expands and pushes the water up the straw and out in a spray.

THE BOTTLE MAKES A GOOD FOUNTAIN.

Grow Your Own Crystals

You can grow crystals by stirring salt, sugar or washing soda into very hot water. Leave them to grow in a warm place and every day you will see a few more until there are lots clinging together in a lump.

You will need
a clean glass jar
a long piece of thread
a paper clip
washing soda (you may find it in your kitchen or you can buy it at a grocery shop)
very hot water from the tap
a pencil

Put a spoon into the jar to stop the hot water cracking it. Run the hot tap a little and then fill up the jar with water.

Put several teaspoons of washing soda into the water and stir until it has all disappeared. Put in more soda and stir again.

Stand the jar in a bowl of very hot water to keep the water in the jar hot. Spoon in more soda and stir again. Stir in soda until no more will disappear in the water.

Tie a paper clip on to one end of a piece of thread. Tie the other end round a pencil. Drop the clip into the jar. Wind the thread round the pencil until the clip hangs like this.

Try mixing a few drops of poster paint or ink in the water to make coloured crystals.

Did You Know?

Lots of things, such as sugar, salt, sand and precious stones are crystals. Each crystal has its own shape. You can see them with a magnifying glass.

LEAVE THE JAR FOR A FEW DAYS AND THE CRYSTALS WILL GROW BIGGER AND BIGGER.

Crystal Columns

Here is a way to make pillars of soda grow up and down until they meet in the middle. It takes several days to work so you will have to be patient.

You will need
2 glass jars
washing soda and a spoon
4 lengths of wool, each about 35 cm long, twisted together to make a thick string
hot water from the hot tap
a large, old plate

1
a   b   WASHING SODA

Fill two jars with very hot water. Stir in lots of washing soda. Go on stirring it in until no more will disappear in the water.

2
WOOL
PLATE

Put the two jars somewhere warm where they will not be moved. Put the plate in between them. Drop the ends of the wool into the jars so the wool hangs over the plate.

AFTER A FEW DAYS, THE COLUMNS WILL MEET IN THE MIDDLE.

Why It Works

Water and soda from the jars goes along the wool and drips off the middle. As it drips, the water turns into tiny drops, so small you cannot see them, in the air. The soda is left in a hard drip.

Did You Know?

The pillars in caves, called stalagmites and stalactites, are made in the same way as the soda column. Water, with lime from limestone rocks, drips from the ceiling. As the water goes into the air, it leaves the lime behind which builds up over hundreds of years, very, very slowly.

The stalagmites are the ones growing up from the floor. The stalactites grow down from the ceiling.

Air is Everywhere

You cannot see air but it fills nearly every space and crack in the world. When anything looks empty, it is really full of air. Air is a gas which you cannot feel except when the wind blows or when you breathe in and out. There is a thick layer of air all round the earth. This layer has a lot of weight and pushes on everything around us.

You will need

2 glasses and a bowl of water
a thin piece of wood, about 45 cm long and about 4 cm wide
2 sheets of a large newspaper
a hammer or mallet

1 PUSH GLASS DOWN

An empty glass looks as if it has nothing in it. To show it is full of air, hold it down in a bowl of water, like this. The air keeps nearly all the water out.

2

Now tilt the glass a little. The air bubbles up through the water and the water fills the glass. Try catching the air in a filled glass under the water, like this.

3 NEWSPAPER WOOD

Put the thin piece of wood on the table, with a bit sticking over the edge. Spread out two sheets of newspaper over it. Smooth them down so they are very flat.

NOW HIT THE WOOD AS HARD AS YOU CAN.

Did You Know?

The pressure in your body equals the air pressure pushing all over you. Men on the moon or in space, where there is no air, have to wear suits with pressure in them.

Why It Works

AIR PRESSING ON PAPER

When you hit the wood, the air pressing down on the newspaper is too heavy to be lifted up, so the wood breaks. The push of air round us is called atmospheric pressure.

Hit the thin piece of wood very hard with a hammer or mallet. Do it quickly and the wood snaps.
If you just press down on the bit of wood, the newspaper will lift up as the air gets in under the paper. So give the wood a good bang.

Is Air Heavy?

Here is a good way to find out if air weighs anything. It is difficult to take all the air out of a tin or bottle without special equipment but you can do it with balloons.

You will need
a thin stick, about 60 cm long
2 balloons, which are the same size and shape
3 pieces of string, each about 30 cm long
a pin

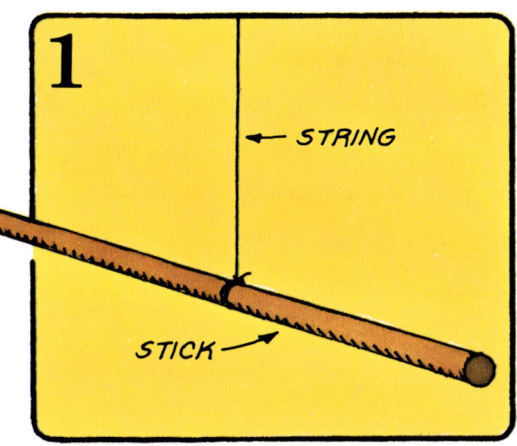

Tie the end of one string tightly to the middle of the stick. Hang the stick up by the other end. Slide the string along the stick until it hangs exactly level.

Blow up one balloon and tie the neck with a second string. Blow up the second balloon until it is about the same size as the first. Tie the neck with a third string.

Tie a balloon on to each end of the stick. Slide the strings along the stick until the stick hangs exactly level again. Now prick one balloon with a pin and watch.

NOW BURST THE OTHER BALLOON AND SEE WHAT HAPPENS.

Did You Know?

If you weighed a bottle which holds one litre of air and then took all the air out and weighed it again, the bottle with air would weigh one gram more than the bottle without.

Why It Works

When you burst one balloon, all the air comes out. The other balloon with air in weighs more than the empty one, so the stick goes down.

Now burst the other balloon and the stick will become level again.

Can You Believe Your Eyes?

If you can see something, then you know it is real—unless it is magic, of course. Here are a few ways to test whether your eyes are telling you the truth or if they sometimes deceive you. Try these tricks yourself and then ask other people to do them. You will need a ruler to check the answers. You may be in for a few surprises. Keep a score of the ones you get right.

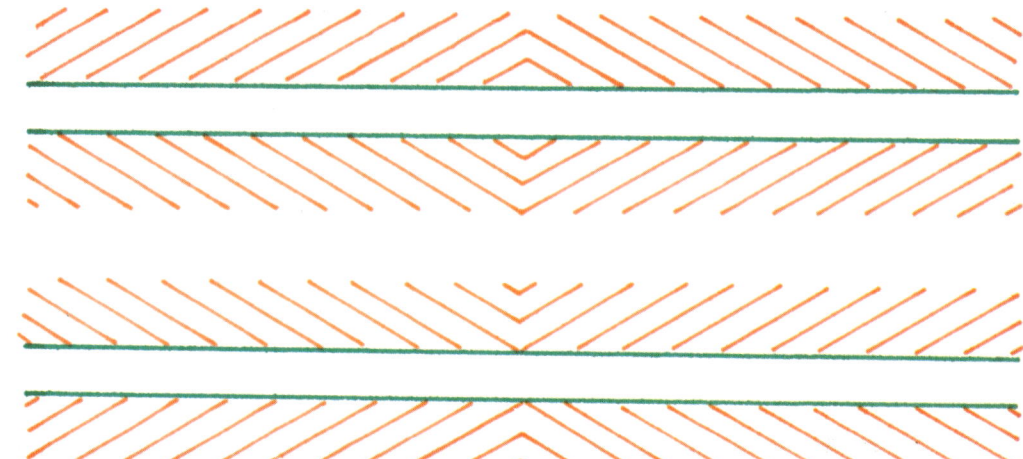

Are all the green lines straight or do they bend a bit? Do the top ones get wider at each end? Do the underneath ones get wider in the middle? To find out, put the edge of a ruler along each green line.

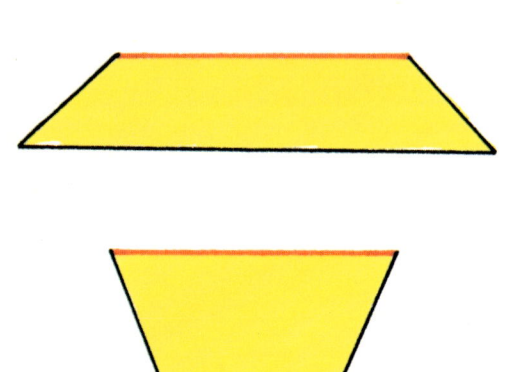

Look at these two shapes. Is the top red line longer than the lower red line? Measure them with a ruler to find the answer.

USE A RULER TO MEASURE ALL THE LINES.

Are these two red lines the same length? Use a ruler to find out.

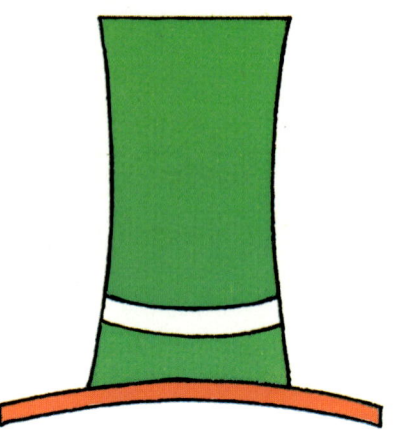

This is a funny hat but is it as high as the brim is wide?

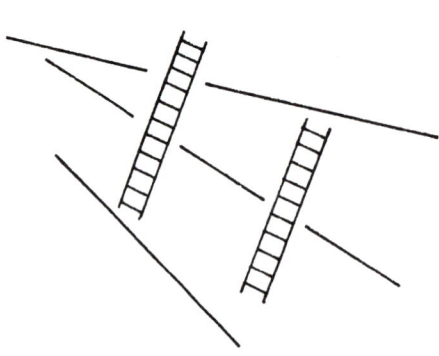

Which of these two ladders is the longer one; or are they both the same length?

Why It Works

When we look at things, our brains are sometimes fooled by them. These things are called optical illusions which means we see things which are not really true.

When you look at the green lines at the top of this page, your eyes are misled by the red lines, so the green lines look bent. It is the same with all the other tricks. When you measure them with a ruler, you find all the lines are the same length. How many did you get right?

Eye Tricks

Here are some more tricks to play with your eyes. Try them yourself first. Then tell other people how to do them but don't tell what they will see so they get a surprise. You can always pretend it is a bit of magic that only you can do.

For the Hole in Your Hand trick you need a paper or cardboard tube. You can make one out of a sheet of paper.

How Many Fingers?

Hold one finger of each hand up in front of your eyes, about 20 cm away from your face. Stare at something beyond your fingers, not at them.

You Will See

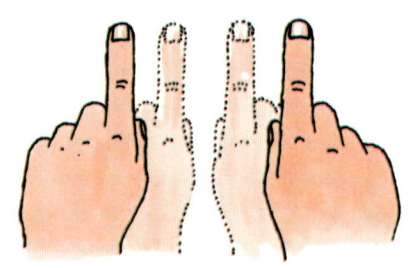

If you stare hard, you will see three or four ghostly fingers in front of your eyes. Look at your two fingers and the other two will disappear.

Floating Finger

STARE HARD JUST BEYOND YOUR FINGERS.

Hold one finger of each hand up in front of your eyes, like this. Stare hard between them.

You Will See

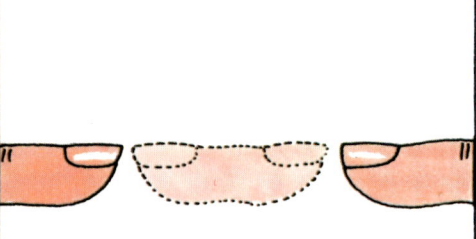

If you stare hard at the gap between your fingers, you will see a short finger appear between them. The odd thing about it is that it has a nail on each end.

Why It Works

You see four fingers in the How Many Fingers? trick because you are looking beyond your fingers. So you see two fingers with each eye, making four in all. With the Floating Finger trick, the two extra fingers overlap to make an extra finger in the middle. You see a hole in your hand because one eye is looking down the tube and the other is looking at your hand. These two views mix together so you see a hand with a hole in it. They all work because you have two eyes.

Hole in Your Hand

LOOK DOWN THE TUBE AND KEEP THE OTHER EYE OPEN.

Hold a tube up to your right eye. Hold your left hand up beside the tube, like this. Stare very hard down the tube.

Making a Tube

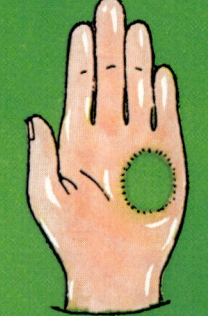

ROLL UP

30 cm

21 cm

Make a tube by rolling up a sheet of stiff paper, about 30 cm long and 20 cm wide. Stick the edge with sticky tape or glue.

You Will See

Stare hard down the tube with your right eye, keeping your left eye open. You can see your hand and then you will see a hole you can look through.

Seeing the Invisible

You cannot see noises—even nice ones like music or nasty ones like the screeching of car brakes—but you hear them all the time. There is always noise of some sort and, if you listen hard, you can always hear something. Here are two ways to find out about noise.

You will need
a thin plastic bag
a big tin or bowl
a rubber band
bits of paper and some sugar
a big spoon and a baking tray
a wine glass
a piece of silver foil and thread

BANG THE TRAY AS HARD AS YOU CAN. WATCH THE SUGAR JUMP!

1 Jumping Paper

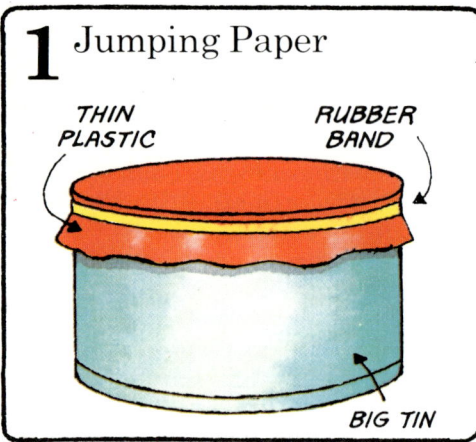

THIN PLASTIC
RUBBER BAND
BIG TIN

Cut along one side and the bottom of a plastic bag. Spread it tightly over the top of a big tin or bowl. Stretch a rubber band round the tin or bowl to make a drum.

2

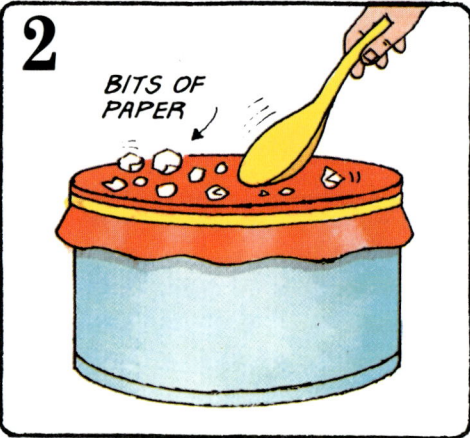

BITS OF PAPER

Tear up a piece of paper into very small bits. Put them on top of the drum. Tap the drum with a spoon. and the bits of paper will jump.

3 Jumping Sugar

BAKING TRAY
SUGAR

Sprinkle some sugar on top of the drum. Hold the baking tray close to the drum. Hit the tray hard with a big spoon. Watch carefully and you will see the sugar jump.

1 Jumping Ball

THREAD
TAPE
SILVER FOIL

Put a wine glass down on a table but don't use one of the best ones. Scrunch up a bit of foil into a ball. Stick a piece of thread, about 30 cm long, to it with tape.

2

WINE GLASS

Hold up the thread so the foil ball just hangs against the edge of the glass, like this. Tap the glass gently with a pencil and the ball will jump away.

Why It Works

When you hit the drum, tray or glass, they all waggle when they make a noise. This waggle is called vibration and makes the paper, sugar and foil ball jump about. When anything vibrates it makes the air round it vibrate. The air then carries the vibration from the thing to your ears so you hear a noise.
You can sometimes feel sound with your fingers. If you put your hand lightly on a radio or record player which is on very loud, you can feel it vibrating.

High and Low Notes

When you play a tune on a musical instrument, you have to make different notes. If the instrument has strings, you press them with your fingers. If it is an instrument you blow, you put your fingers over the holes to play a tune. Here are two ways to find out about music—even if you cannot play anything.

You will need
a wooden ruler
a rubber band
2 pencils

VERY BIG INSTRUMENTS MAKE LOW NOTES. LITTLE ONES MAKE HIGH NOTES.

1 Noisy Ruler

PULL DOWN AND LET GO

Put a ruler on a table, with most of it over the edge, like this. Hold the part on the table down with a book. Pull the other end down and let it go. It makes a low twang.

2

PULL DOWN AND LET GO

Push the ruler in under the book a bit and pull it down again. It makes a higher twang. Push it in a bit more and the noise gets higher. You can see the ruler waggling.

1 Ruler Guitar

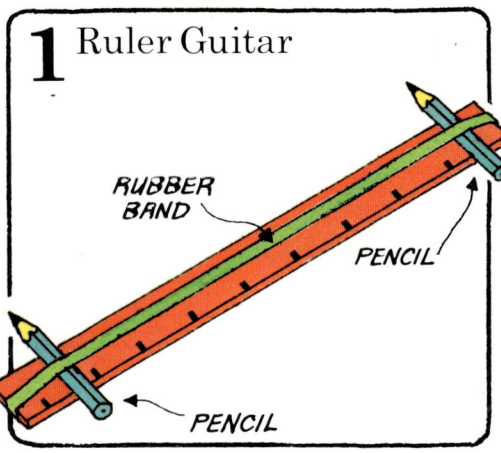

RUBBER BAND

PENCIL

PENCIL

Stretch a long rubber band over a ruler, like this. Push a pencil under the band at one end and a second pencil under the band at the other end.

Why It Works

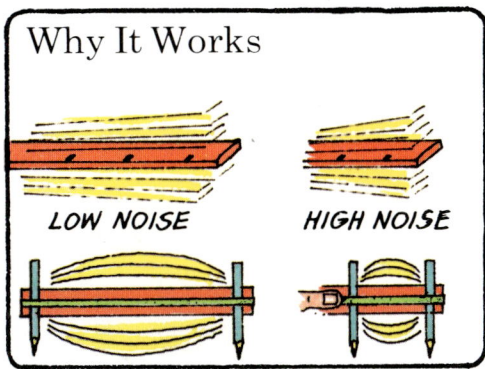

LOW NOISE   HIGH NOISE

When a ruler or band is long, it vibrates slowly and makes a low noise. When it is short, it vibrates quickly and makes high noises. High and low sounds depend on how fast things vibrate.

2

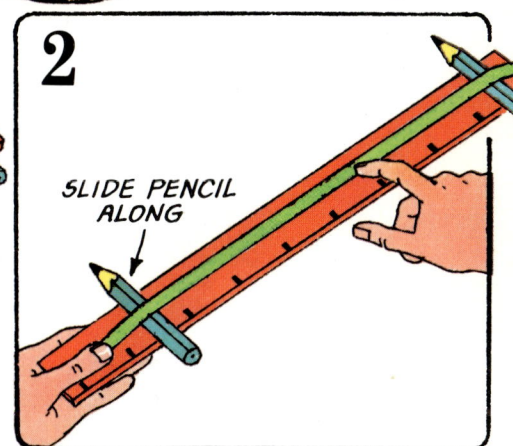

SLIDE PENCIL ALONG

Pluck the band with one finger. Push one pencil along the ruler a bit and pluck the band again. It will make a higher note. You can play a tune—very slowly.

Did You Know?

Players of string instruments press the strings to shorten them and make higher notes. They tighten or loosen the strings before they play. Tight strings vibrate more quickly and make higher notes.

Water Tricks

All light—light from the sun, from electric light and from fires—usually travels in straight lines. If it could go round corners, there would be no shadows when the sun shines or shadows in a room. But light does strange things when it goes through the air and then through water. Here are some ways to find out what it does.

You will need
a glass of water and a straw or a pencil
a bowl of water and a coin

THE STRAW LOOKS QUITE STRAIGHT FROM HERE.

Put a straw or a pencil into a glass of water. Hold the glass up level with your eyes and the straw or pencil will look broken.

1 Magic Coin

DROP IN COIN

Drop a small coin into a china or plastic bowl. Tilt the bowl until you cannot quite see the coin over the edge.

2

WATER

Hold the bowl in exactly the same position so you still cannot quite see the coin. Pour water slowly into the bowl and the coin will gradually reappear.

Moving Coin

MOVE UP AND DOWN

Now hold the bowl up so you can see the coin. Move the bowl slowly up and down, staring at the coin. As you watch, it seems to move up and down in the bowl.

Why It Works

Light going through air and then through water at an angle, bends as it goes into water and out again. This makes the straw look broken and the coin reappear in the bowl.

Did You Know?

A boy standing on a river bank, trying to catch a fish in the water, may miss the fish, unless he knows about light and water. The fish will look higher up in the water than it really is. This is because the light beams the boy sees have been bent by the water. The river will also look much shallower than it is.

Light Tricks

When you look down at a pool of still water you can see your own face in it. The water acts like a mirror. Before people knew how to make mirrors, they used bowls of water instead. If you could look up from underneath the water, the top of it would also act like a mirror. Try these ways of finding out about water.

You will need
a glass, water and a coin
a square glass or clear plastic container
water and a teaspoon of milk
a sheet of paper and a book
a torch

One or Two Coins?

Drop a small coin in a glass with water, about 2 cm deep, in it. Hold the glass up in front of your eyes. You will see a big coin on the bottom and a small one just above it in the water.

I CAN SEE ONLY ONE COIN. HOW MANY CAN YOU SEE?

1 Bouncing Beam
PAPER
WATER
TORCH

Stand the square container, full of water, on a book. Prop up a sheet of paper at one end. Draw the curtains or switch off the light. Shine a torch like this.

2
PAPER
WATER

Shine the torch straight through and the beam comes out in a straight line. Shine the torch at an angle and the beam comes out at an angle on the paper.

3
MILK

To see the beam more clearly, stir a teaspoon of milk into the water. Then try shining the torch through the water from lots of different angles to see how the beam bends.

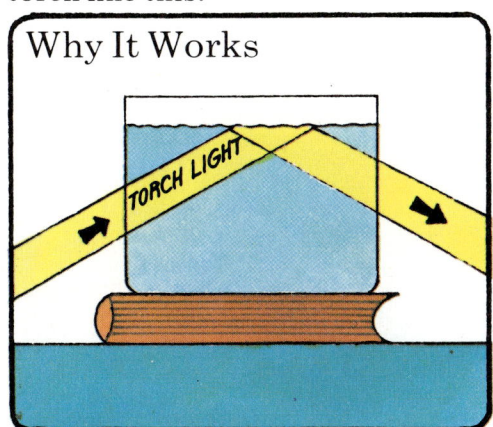

Why It Works

TORCH LIGHT

When light shines straight into water, it goes in a straight line. When a beam hits the top of the water at an angle, it is bounced back at an angle by the water.

Did You Know?

LAYER OF WARM AIR
LAYER OF HOT AIR
SUNLIGHT

On a very hot day, you sometimes see puddles on a road. When you get near, they vanish. These are called mirages and are seen in deserts. The man in this picture gets light from the sky. It is bent by a layer of hot air on the ground. He sees a reflection of sky and clouds on the ground, which looks like pools of blue water.

What Makes a Rainbow?

Look for rainbows in the sky when the sun is shining and it is raining at the same time. You can also see rainbows in the spray from garden hoses,

THE COLOURS OF A RAINBOW ARE ALWAYS IN THE SAME ORDER.

fountains and waterfalls. But to see rainbows, you have to stand with your back to the sun and facing the raindrops.

How to Make a Rainbow

WATER MIRROR BOWL

You will have to do this on a sunny day. Fill a small bowl with water. Put a small mirror into the bowl so that the sun shines on to it.

Hold up a sheet of white paper so the sun shining on the mirror reflects on to the paper. Hold the paper as still as you can and you will see rainbow colours.

Why It Works

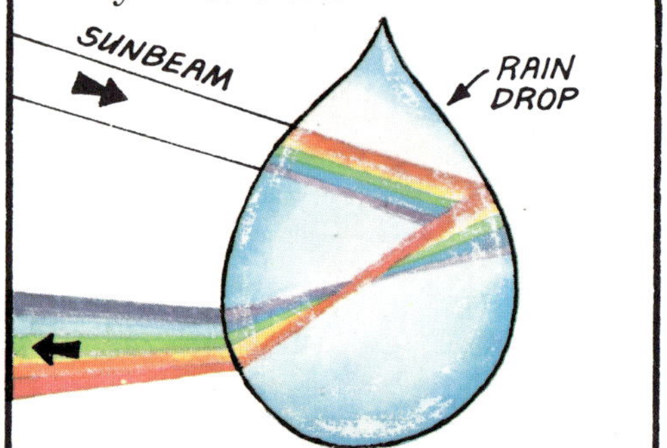

SUNBEAM RAIN DROP

When sunlight goes through a water drop, it is split up into seven main colours, like this. That is why you see a rainbow when the sun shines on lots of drops of water.

Rainbow Colours in Glass

White light shining through glass with sharp angles in it is split up into colours. You can see some colours in precious stones, like diamonds, and in cut glass.

The best shape of glass for making colours is one like a tent, called a prism. The coloured light coming out of one prism is turned into white light by another.

Did You Know?

If you were in the cockpit of a plane flying towards a rain storm, with the sun behind you, you would see a moving rainbow. It would be a circle.

18

Disappearing Colours

You can make colours appear and disappear. Paint a circle with the seven colours of the rainbow and spin it very fast. Watch to see what happens.

THESE ARE THE MAIN COLOURS YOU SEE IN A RAINBOW.

The colours you see in a rainbow are called a spectrum. They are red, orange, yellow, green, blue, indigo and violet. There are lots of shades in between them.

You can paint the whirler just red, yellow, green and blue, if you like. The coloured squares on the outside of this one blur into the colours of the rainbow.

1 Coloured Whirler

DRAW ROUND

Put a cup down on a thick piece of cardboard and draw round it. Cut round the line with scissors to make a neat circle.

2

PAINT COLOURS

Draw six lines from the middle of the circle to the outside edge to make seven sections. Paint each section a colour of the rainbow, like the picture on the left.

Why It Works

When the Whirler spins very fast, our eyes see the colours but they get mixed up in our brains. Our brains tell us the Whirler looks a greyish white.

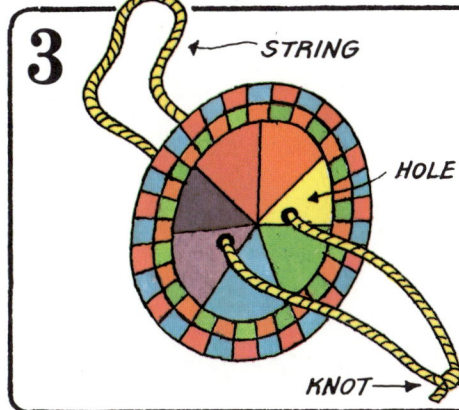

3

STRING

HOLE

KNOT

Make two holes in the circle, about 1 cm apart, like this. Push the ends of a piece of string, about a metre long, through the holes. Tie the ends in a knot.

4

FLIP TO WIND

Hold the loops of string like this. Flip the circle round to twist up the string. Pull your hands apart and then let the string go slack. This will make the Whirler spin.

What Makes a Thunderstorm?

The different sorts of clouds you see in the sky mean that different sorts of weather are coming. When you see huge, tall clouds, like puffy castles, they may mean a thunderstorm is on its way, with flashes of lightning. A flash is a huge, hot electric spark. You can make a little one safely at home, but it may make your fingers prick and tingle a bit.

THOSE BIG CLOUDS MAY MEAN A THUNDERSTORM IS COMING.

1 Making a Spark

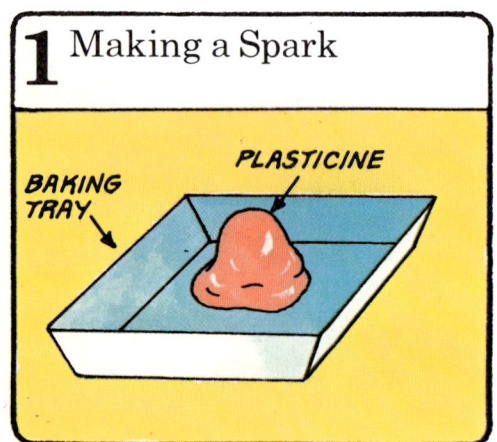

BAKING TRAY

PLASTICINE

Press a large lump of plasticine on to the middle of a very big baking tray or small tin tray. Press it hard so it sticks well.

2

PLASTIC BAG

RUB HARD

Put the tray down on a very large, thick plastic or polythene bag. A rubbish bag is good for this. Hold the plasticine lump and rub the tray round and round on the bag.

3

LIFT UP TRAY

TIN LID

Pick up the tray by the plasticine. Hold something metal, such as a tin lid, close to one corner. You will see a big spark jump from the tray to the tin especially in a dark room.

Why It Works

When you rub the tray on the bag, it makes electricity, called static electricity. When there is enough, there is a spark. Static electricity builds up in clouds before a thunderstorm.

Did You Know?

Most lightning flashes jump from one cloud to another. A few strike the earth and may do damage. Tall buildings have lightning conductors to carry the electricity safely down into the ground.

The thunder you hear after a flash is made by lightning. The spark heats the air round it and the air expands very quickly. This sets off a giant wave of air which makes the thunder you hear.

Why is a Sunset Red?

When the sun first rises in the morning, the sky often looks red, especially if there are a few clouds about. During the day, when the sun is overhead, it looks yellow and the sky looks blue. When the sun sets, it may turn a fiery red and the sky pink. Do they really change colour or just look as if they do? Here is a way to find out.

THE SUN IS BRIGHT RED NOW IT IS SO LOW ON THE SEA.

1

WATER

TORCH

Fill a clean glass jar with cold water. Stir in one teaspoonful of milk. Hold a torch to the side of the jar, like this, in a dark room. The water looks blue.

2

Now move the torch round so it is shining through the jar at you, like this. The light from the torch looks yellow, like the sun during the day.

3

MILK AND WATER

Stir in two more teaspoonfuls of milk. Hold the torch to the side of the jar. The water still looks blue. Hold it so it shines at you and the water looks pink.

Why It Works

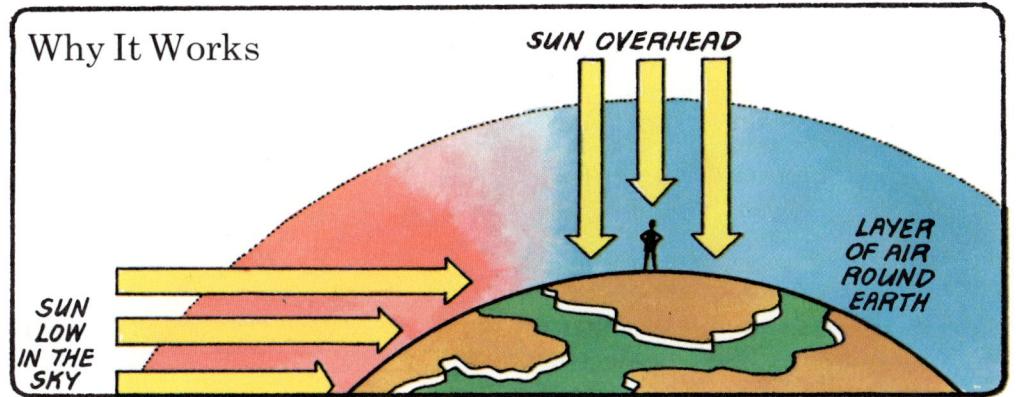

SUN OVERHEAD

SUN LOW IN THE SKY

LAYER OF AIR ROUND EARTH

The Earth is wrapped in a blanket of air which is full of bits of dust and water drops too small to see. The dust and water drops, like the milk in the glass of water, scatter the blue part of sunlight to make the sky look blue. When the sun is low in the sky, it looks red because its light has to go further through the air and only the red part of it comes through to your eyes.

Did You Know?

If you looked out of a window in a space ship, the sky would look black and you would see stars in the day. This is because there is no dusty air in space to break up white light into its colours.

Rubbing and Warming

Have you ever noticed that things get warm when you rub them? On cold days, people rub their hands together or rub their hands on their sleeves to warm them. Try it and your hands will soon warm up. There are lots of things which get warm and even very hot when they are rubbed. Here are a few for you to try. There are lots more you can probably think of yourself.

Try rubbing two dry sticks or bits of wood together as hard as you can. After about 20 rubs, feel the wood. It will be quite warm.

Rub two pieces of metal, such as flat tin lids, together. Rub a piece of wood with sandpaper. Feel the metal and wood after a minute or two and they will be quite hot.

RUB HARD AND THEN FEEL HOW WARM IT IS.

When you ride a bicycle and brake hard, the brake blocks rub on the wheel to slow you down. Try braking while riding quite slowly. Then feel the brake blocks.

Scuff your shoes hard across the floor. Then feel the bottoms of your shoes. Try rubbing your bare foot hard on a carpet. It will soon feel quite warm.

Why It Works

Most things have rough surfaces. You can see they are rough if you look at them closely or with a magnifying glass—your hands, wood and metal. When they move against each other, the roughness slows down the movement. This is called friction. The rougher two things are, the harder you have to work to move them. The work is turned into heat and the things become hot.

Did You Know?

Car tyres warm up because of the friction between them and the road. After a long journey, they may be too hot to touch. This warms the road too. Ice on roads melts if lots of cars go over it.

When a spacecraft returns to Earth, friction between it and the air makes it very hot. Its special shape and shield of special materials stop men inside from being burnt up.

Slipping and Gripping

The rough surfaces of lots of things are useful because they grip together and stop slipping. Your shoes grip a slippery floor. Bicycle brake blocks are made of special material to grip the wheel rim. Car tyres have ridges in them to help grip the road. But this grip is a nuisance when we want things to slide easily. Slippery oil is poured into machines so the moving bits slide over each other. Here are some ways to make things slip about very easily.

SHOES WITH SMOOTH SOLES SLIDE MORE EASILY THAN ROUGH SOLES.

The rough soles of your shoes stop you from slipping. You slide on ice because the pressure of your shoes melts the ice a little. You slide on a very thin sheet of water which then freezes again.

1

SOAP
RUB HARD

Find two dry sticks or bits of wood. Rub a piece of soap over one of them. Now rub the sticks together. They will slide over each other and stay cool.

2

WOOD

WATER

Put a small block of wood on a table. Give it a knock to make it slide (a). Pour a little soapy water on the table (b). Knock the block again to see what happens.

3

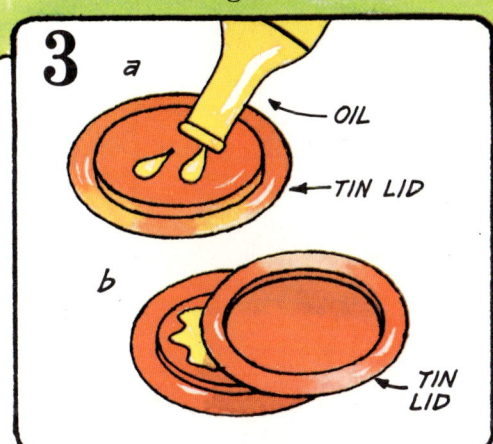

OIL
TIN LID
TIN LID

Pour a little oil on a flat tin lid. Any oil, such as cooking oil, will do. Rub the lid with another lid. You can feel the lids slide easily over each other on the oil.

Why It Works

Oil is poured on the moving bits of machines to keep them slightly apart. They slide over each other on a layer of slippery oil without touching, and do not get hot. This is called lubrication.

Did You Know?

Cars skid on greasy, wet or icy roads because grease, water or ice makes a layer between the tyres and the road. The tyres cannot grip so the car skids.

All machines with parts which slide over each other need oil or grease lubrication. Without it, they would rub and could get so hot they would melt.

Bottle Volcano

Here is a surprising trick to try with two bottles of water—one warm and the other cold.

You will need
2 clean glass bottles—ones with wide necks are best
cold water and warm water from the hot tap
a small square of cardboard
a few drops of ink or water paint.

1 Fill one bottle with cold water and the other with warm water from the tap. Pour a few drops of ink or paint into the bottle with the warm water to colour it.

2 Put the square of cardboard over the top of the bottle with coloured water. Hold it on with one hand (a). Still holding it, turn the bottle over with the other hand (b).

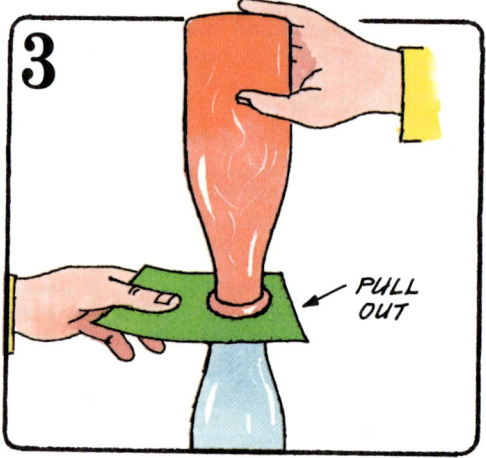

3 Put the bottle with coloured water on top of the other bottle, like this. They must be exactly on top of each other. Hold the top bottle and pull out the cardboard.

4 Hold both bottles like this. Turn them up the other way, without letting the tops slide apart and the water run out. Now watch.

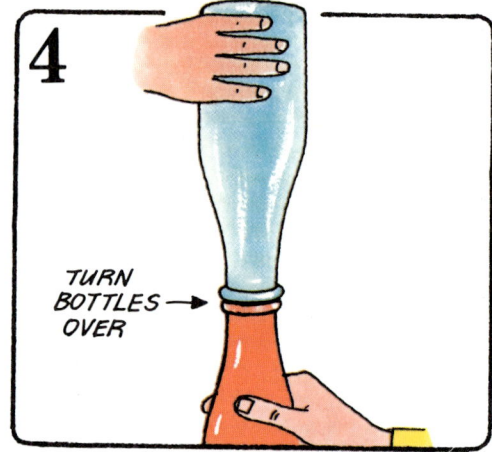

Why It Works

Warm water is lighter than cold water so it floats on the top of cold water, like this. When you turn the bottles over, so the cold is on the top, it sinks down and pushes the warm, coloured water up.

Did You Know?

At the North and South Poles the very cold weather cools the top of the sea. The cold water sinks down, pushing up water from the bottom. Scientists think this may cause ocean currents.

Strong Ice

When water cools down and freezes into ice, something strange happens to it. For these experiments, you have to use the freezing compartment of a refrigerator. Use a plastic pot or a tin. Do not use glass or it will crack.

You will need
a small plastic pot with a lid
a small, clean tin with a lid
3 pencils
a bottle top
sticky tape
a refrigerator

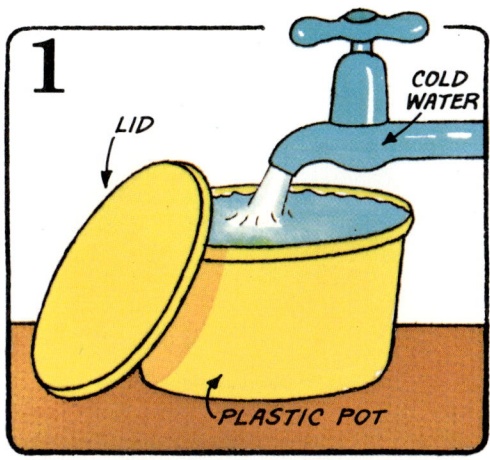

1

Fill the plastic pot right to the top with cold water. Press on the lid. Put the pot in the freezing compartment of a refrigerator. Leave it for about eight hours.

2

Take out the pot. When the water has turned to ice, it lifts up the lid and pushes it off the pot. You may find the sides have been pushed out a bit too.

3

Fill a tin up to the top with cold water. Press on the lid as hard as you can, without spilling the water.

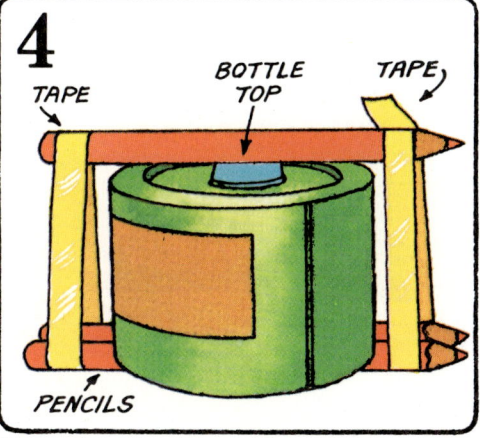

4

Put a bottle top on the lid. Put two pencils under the tin and one on the bottle top. Wind sticky tape round the pencils, like this. Freeze for about eight hours.

Why It Works

When water cools and turns into ice it gets bigger and pushes outwards. It presses so hard that it breaks water pipes on the outside of houses in freezing weather.

Did You Know?

When rain runs into tiny cracks in rocks on mountains and then freezes into ice, the ice pushes so hard it splits the rock. That is why some mountain tops are covered with sharp, broken rocks.

WHEN WATER FREEZES IT GETS BIGGER AND BREAKS VERY STRONG THINGS.

When the tin has been in the freezing compartment for about eight hours, have a look at it. You will find the lid has been pushed up by the ice and broken the pencil. The sides may have been pushed out as well.

Ups and Downs of Plants

If you plant a seed upside down, does it grow upside down? Or does it turn itself round and grow the right way? Try growing some beans or peas to find out what happens to the roots and stems.

You will need

6 beans or peas (the kind sold for growing, not for eating)

some earth—the sort sold in bags called potting compost is best)

a pot or bowl

a little plastic bottle

black paper, a rubber band and scissors

Fill the bowl or pot with earth or compost. Press it down with your fingers. Fill the bowl with water and wait until it has sunk into the earth.

Press the beans or peas into the earth. Put the bowl in a warm, light place and wait for the seeds to sprout. They will take about a week to split and grow.

When the seeds have sprouted, cut the top and bottom off a small plastic bottle. It should be big enough to slip a bean or pea in easily with room to spare.

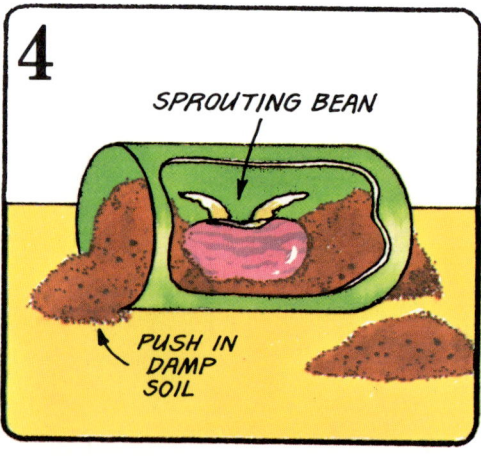

Push one bean or pea into the bottle. Push damp earth in at each end. Pack it well round the seed. Drip on a little water at each end.

Wrap a bit of black paper round the bottle, leaving the ends open. Keep it in place with a rubber band. Put the bottle in a warm, light place. Look at it every day.

TURN THE BOTTLE FOR A DAY AND THE SHOOTS WILL GROW THE OTHER WAY.

When two shoots come out of the bottle, one grows up and has tiny green leaves. The other, the white root, grows down. Turn the bottle over for a day and a night. The shoots will grow the other way.

Why It Works

Whichever way you plant seeds, the stems will always grow up to the light. The roots always grow down into the earth for water and food.

Waterways of Plants

All plants need water to keep alive and to grow. They get the water through their roots and it goes up their stems. Plants also give out water through their leaves in such tiny drops you cannot see them. Try these experiments with plants.

You will need
a stick of fresh celery
a table knife
ink or water paint
a bush or branch of a tree
   growing out of doors
a plastic bag
a piece of string

1 Sucking up Water

Slice a bit off the end of the stick of celery. Put the stick in a jar with a little water. Pour in some ink. Stand the jar in a warm, light place for a day.

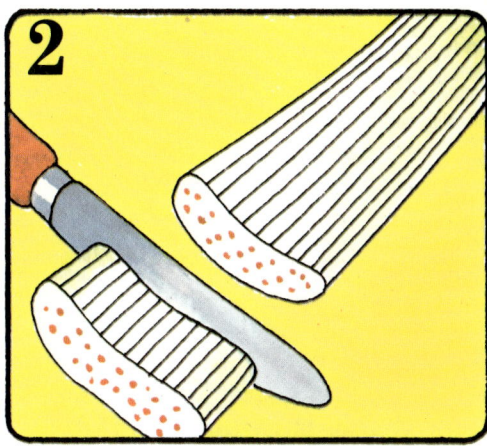

2

Wash the end of the celery stick in clean water. Slice the stem about every 3 cm. Look at each cut. You can see dots where the stem has taken up the coloured water.

1 Breathing Out Water

PLASTIC BAG

STRING

Put a plastic bag over a small branch of leaves on a bush or small tree in a sunny place. Tie it on with string, like this. Leave it for two or three days.

2

Look at the bag every day and you will see drops of water on the inside of the bag. If the days are very hot, quite a lot of water will collect in the bag.

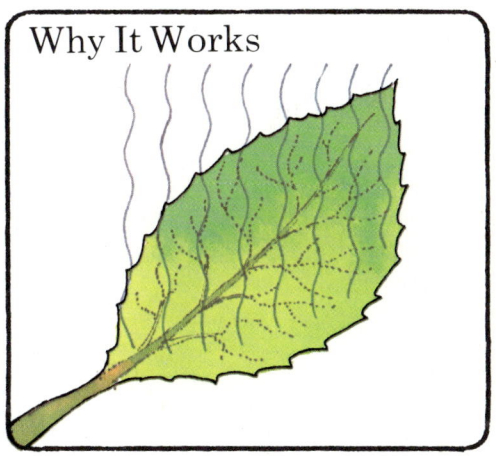

Why It Works

The leaves of plants have very tiny holes all over them. On hot days, tiny drops of water come out from these holes into the air. These collect on the inside of the bag.

Did You Know?

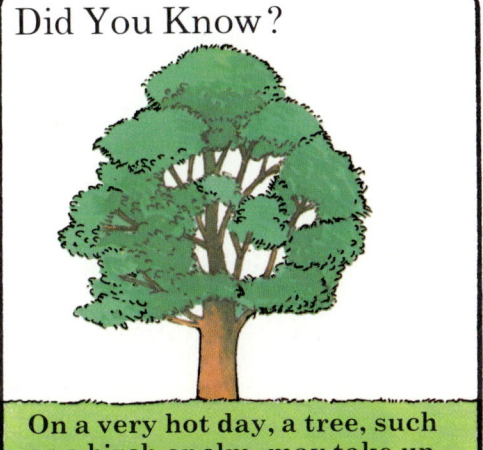

On a very hot day, a tree, such as a birch or elm, may take up as much as 50 large buckets of water. This comes out invisibly through its leaves into the air.

YOU CAN CHANGE THE COLOUR OF A FLOWER WITH A LITTLE INK.

Try tying a plastic bag round a plant indoors. Water it and stand it on a windowsill in the sun.

Try putting a white flower stem in coloured water. The petals will soon show the colour of the water.

Where Do Clouds Come From?

After a shower of rain, all the water on the roads, the grass, the houses and even your clothes, slowly dries up and disappears. The puddles get smaller and smaller until they vanish. The water disappears much more quickly when the weather is hot and sunny. When it is cold and damp, the wet things take much longer to dry. But where does the water go? And where do the rain clouds come from? How does all that water get into the sky to make rain? Here are ways to find out.

ON HOT, SUNNY DAYS, PUDDLES DRY UP VERY QUICKLY.

1 Water Into Air

Put a big plate on a sunny windowsill. Pour some cold water on to the plate. Leave it for three hours. Look at it often and you will see the water disappears.

2

Put two plates in a sunny place. Pour about half a cup of water on to each one. Shade one with a book, like this. Look at them after an hour or two to see what happens.

Why It Works

When water dries up, it turns into tiny drops, so small you cannot see them. This is called evaporation. The water drops go into the air. This damp air, called water vapour, rises. On warm days, it rises all the time, taking the vapour up to the sky. In the sky it is much cooler than down on the ground. The tiny drops of water join up to make bigger drops. These make the clouds you see in the sky.

Warm Air Goes Up

Cut a few strips of the thinnest paper you can find. Tissue paper or thin cellophane work well. Hold them over a radiator or room heater and they flutter upwards.

Did You Know?

On warm days, the water in clouds falls as rain. It runs into ponds, lakes, rivers and then to the sea. Water from all wet things, even clothes on a washing line, goes up into the air. In warm weather it goes up to make more clouds which may rain again.

Why Does It Rain?

Try these experiments and find out how water comes from warm damp air.

IT IS RAINING HERE BUT IT IS SNOWING HIGH ON THE MOUNTAINS.

1 Water from Air — COLD PLATE

HOT WATER

Fill a bowl with water from the hot tap. Hold a cold plate over the bowl for about a minute. Turn the plate over. It is covered with tiny drops of water.

2

MIRROR

Hold a mirror close to your mouth and breathe hard on it. Or breathe on a window pane on a cold day. Soon the glass clouds up with tiny drops of water.

3

ICE CUBES

SHINY TIN

Find a clean tin which is shiny on the outside. Fill the tin with ice cubes. After a few minutes, the outside of the tin will be covered with water drops.

Why It Works

When warm air, with lots of water vapour in it, touches something cold, the tiny water drops collect into big drops and you can see them. This is called condensation. When warm air, with lots of water vapour, rises up to meet cold air in the sky, the tiny drops of water collect round specks of dust in the air. As more collect, they make a cloud. If there is enough water in low clouds, it falls as rain.

Dew

The water drops you see on grass and leaves on some mornings are water from the air. During the night the ground gets cold and water vapour collects into drops.

Frost

The white frost you see on a very cold morning on grass or windows is frozen dew. The water which collects on the ground and glass freezes into white ice.

Snow

When air very high in the sky cools quickly, the water in it freezes into crystals and falls as snow. You can see the snow crystals with a magnifying glass.

Water Turbine

Make this Turbine and hold it under a running tap. It will spin round and round as the water spurts out. If you hold the string between your fingers, so it can turn too, the Turbine will spin as long as there is water in it.

You will need

an empty plastic or polythene
    bottle
a pencil
a short bit of string, about 15 cm
    long and a long, thin string,
    about 30 cm long
scissors

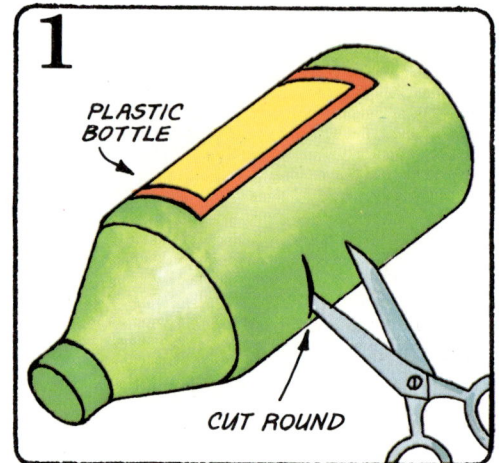

1

PLASTIC BOTTLE

CUT ROUND

Push one blade of the scissors into the bottle, near the top, like this. Snip all the way round to cut the top off.

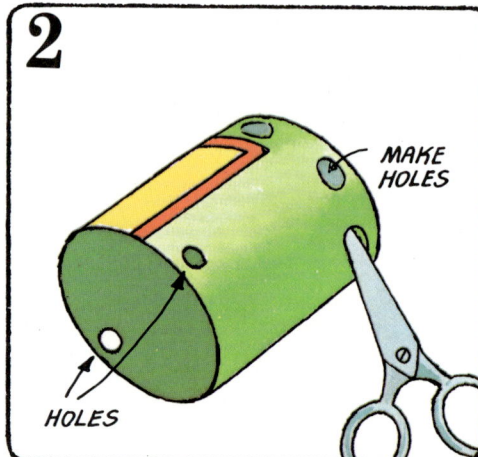

2

MAKE HOLES

HOLES

Make eight holes in the side of the bottle, near the bottom, with scissors. Space them out evenly. Make two holes in the top of the bottle, one on each side.

3

PUSH IN AND PRESS DOWN

Push the point of a pencil into a bottom hole in the bottle. Press the pencil down until it is against the side of the bottle. Do the same with each hole to slant them.

4

KNOT

KNOT

PENCIL

Tie the ends of the short string to the holes in the top of the bottle. Tie the long string to the middle of the short bit. Tie a pencil to the other end, like this.

Turn on the cold tap and hold the bottle, by the string or pencil, under it. As it fills up, the water squirts out the sides and the bottle spins round and round.

HOLD THE TURBINE UNDER A RUNNING TAP TO MAKE IT WORK.

Why It Works

When water squirts out of the holes, it comes out sideways. The jets push the bottle away and make it spin round in the opposite direction.

Spin Drier

Spin this little Drier and it will whizz all the water out of wet cloth or wet paper towels. It will not make them completely dry but it will get rid of a lot of water. It is best to do this experiment out of doors where it does not matter if things get wet.

You will need
a plastic bottle
a pencil
a cotton reel
scissors
string

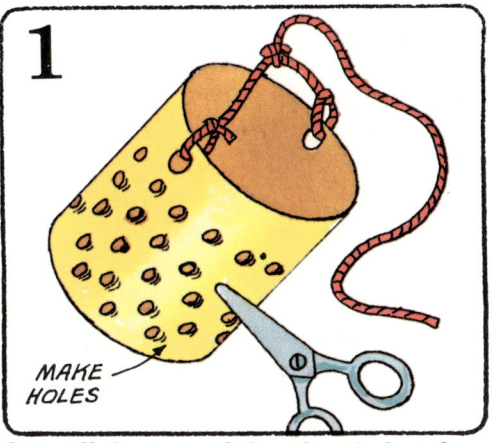

1

MAKE HOLES

Cut off the top of the plastic bottle and tie on strings in the same way as pictures 1 and 2 for the Water Turbine. Poke lots of holes in the bottle with scissors.

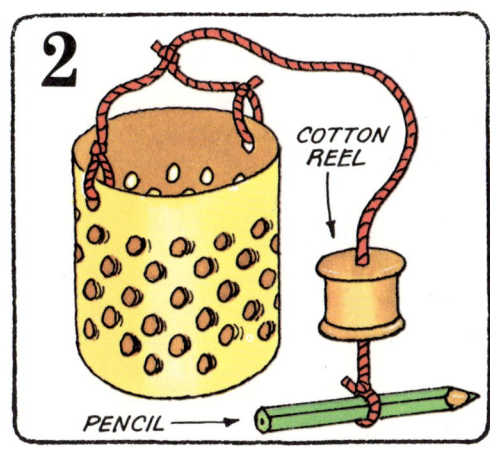

2

COTTON REEL

PENCIL

Slide a cotton reel on to the long string on the bottle. Tie a pencil to the end of the string.

3

WET CLOTH OR PAPER TOWELS

Push bits of wet cloth or wet paper towels into the bottle. Press them down gently. Do not pack them in too tightly.

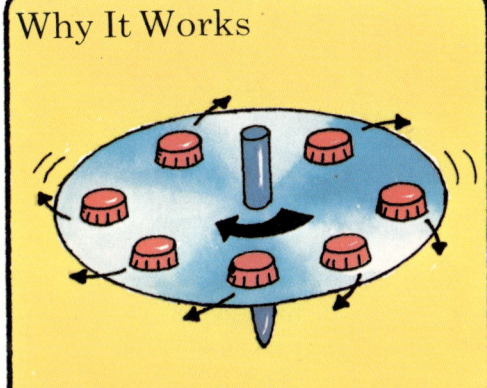

Why It Works

When anything, like this big top, spins things on it are flung off. This is called centrifugal force. When the Drier spins, the water is flung out through the holes.

If you have one, tie the string to the end of an egg whisk. Wind the handle as fast as you can to spin the Drier. As it spins, water will come out of the holes.

Hold the cotton reel in one hand. Wind the pencil round and round as fast as you can with the other hand, like this.

Did You Know?

Electric spin driers and washing machines work in the same way as your drier. They whizz round very fast and the water in the wet clothes flies out the holes in the drum.

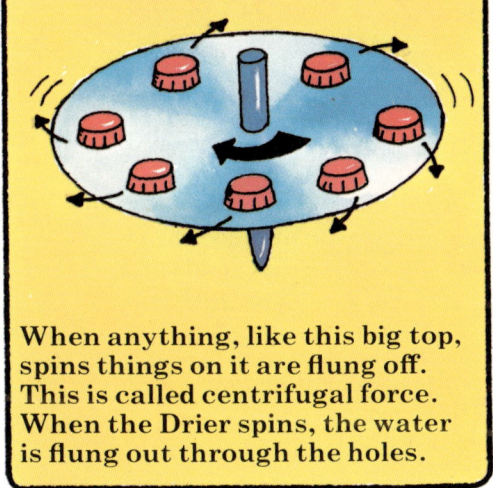

SPIN THE DRIER AS FAST AS YOU CAN.

Science Words

Atmospheric Pressure
This is the pressure of air all round us. At sea level, it is nearly three kilograms per square centimetre but gets less as you go up hills or up in the air. You do not feel this pressure on you because there is equal pressure in your body pushing outwards. The cabins of high-flying aircraft have pressurized air in them. Without this, the passengers would feel very uncomfortable and their noses and ears might bleed.

Carbon Dioxide
This is a gas which is made when you mix together vinegar and baking soda. There are lots of other ways of making it. Carbon dioxide is put into some drinks, such as coco-cola and lemonade, to make them fizzy.

Contraction
This means shrinking or getting smaller. Things such as metal, air and water contract when they are cooled. A steel bridge, 1½ kilometres long, may be as much as a metre shorter on a very cold day than on a hot day.

Condensation
This is the tiny drops of water you see on cold things, such as the bathroom walls when you run the hot tap, or mist on windows on a cold day. Tiny drops of water in warm air, too small to see, condense on something cold and collect into big drops.

Expansion
This means swelling or getting bigger. Lots of things, such as air, metal and water expand when they are warmed. Bridges and railway lines are a bit longer on hot days than on cold ones. Even tall buildings grow a little. The Empire State Building in New York is about 15 cm taller on a hot summer day than on a cold winter day.

Friction
When two things are rubbed together, the rougher they are the more difficult it is for them to slide over each other. This resistance is called friction.

Lubrication
This means putting something, such as oil or grease, on a machine to stop the moving bits rubbing together. The oil keeps the bits slightly apart so they slide easily over each other. If a machine runs without oil, the bits grate together and may get so hot that they melt and stick to each other.

Optical Illusion
This is something you see but which is not really there. Or it may be something which looks different from the way it really is. You see illusions either because your eyes are tricked by them or because what your eyes see is real but the message they give your brain gets muddled up.

Sodium Bicarbonate
This is the chemical name for baking soda. When sodium bicarbonate is stirred into cakes or pastry and then cooked, it gives off carbon dioxide gas. The gas bubbles up through the cake or pastry and makes it light to eat.

Spectrum
This is the name of the seven main colours you see in a rainbow. They are red, orange, yellow, green, blue, indigo and violet. You see these colours when ordinary light, which looks white, is split up into the colours it is made of. When lights of all these colours are shone on the same spot, the spot looks white.

Vibration
This means that something wiggles up and down or backwards and forwards very fast. It may be too fast for you to see it. When anything vibrates you hear a noise, unless the vibration is too small. If you touch anything which is making a noise or music gently with your fingers, you may feel it vibrate.

Water Vapour
When water dries up, it goes into the air in tiny drops, so small you cannot see them. This is called water vapour. Warm, dry air can take up more water than cold damp air. Wet things dry more quickly on warm, dry days than on cold or damp days.

Going Further

If you would like to try more experiments, here are some books about science with experiments in them.

The Young Scientist Book of Jets
 by Mark Hewish (Usborne)

The Young Scientist Book of Spaceflight
 by Ken Gatland (Usborne)

The Young Scientist Book of Electricity
 by Phil Chapman (Usborne)

The Young Scientist Book of the Undersea
 by Christopher Pick (Usborne)

The Young Scientist Book of Stars and Planets
 by Christopher Maynard (Usborne)

The Book of Experiments
 by Leonard de Vries (Carousel Books)

Experiments with Everyday Objects
 by Kevin Goldstein-Jackson (Souvenir Press)

Fun with Chemistry
 by Mae and Ira Freeman (Kaye and Ward)

The KnowHow Book of Spycraft

First published in 1975
by Usborne Publishing Ltd
Usborne House
83-85 Saffron Hill, London EC1N 8RT

©Usborne Publishing Ltd 1989, 1975

The name Usborne and the device  are
Trade Marks of Usborne Publishing Ltd.

This abridged edition contains
the best projects from the
original 48-page version.

Printed in Italy

About This Book

This book is all about keeping
secrets. It shows you how to set
up secret meeting places and a
secret post office and how to
disguise your messages. It shows
you lots of secret codes and
signals.

On the first page you will meet
the Black Hat Spy. Watch out
for the tricks he plays in *Spy*

Trick – these are things real
spies have done. You can see
what equipment a spy uses and
how he hides it quickly in an
emergency.

There are messages in code all
through the book. See if you can
work them out – you can check
your answers on page 32.

The KnowHow Book of Spycraft

Falcon Travis and Judy Hindley

Illustrated by Colin King
Designed by John Jamieson

Contents

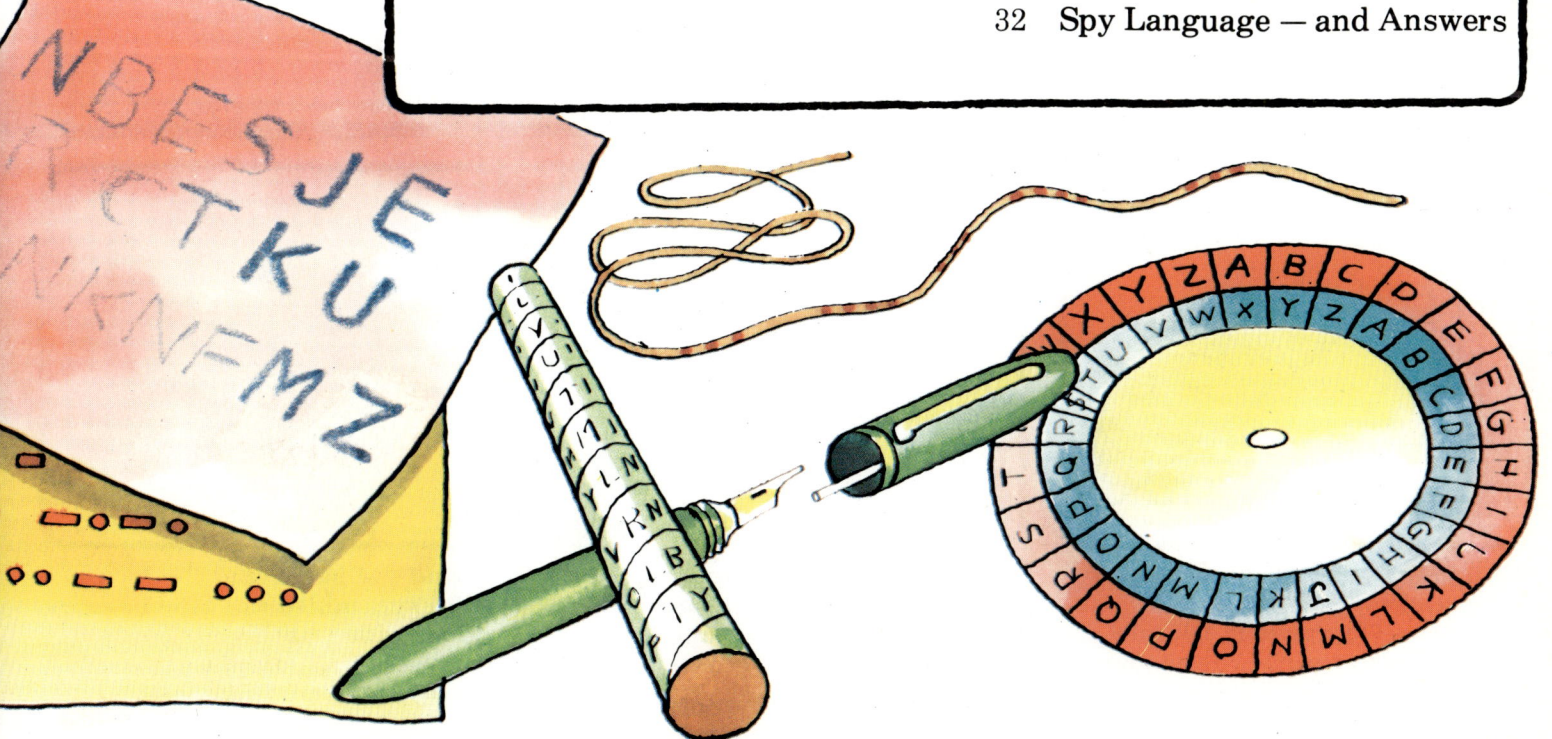

Carrying Secret Messages

One of the first spy tricks you should learn is how to deliver a secret message. Don't attract your enemy's attention by carrying a satchel or holding suspicious-looking papers. With the Stick Scrambler shown below you can encode a message on a paper strip that is easy to hide. See the chart for the methods used by Black Hat Spy for hiding messages.

Practise removing the message with a quick and casual-looking movement – as though you are just hooking your thumb in your pocket or taking a pebble from your shoe. If you hide the message in a pen or hat you can pretend to leave it somewhere by accident, and then your spy-friend can pick it up.

On the following pages you will find more details on where to hide your messages and how to pass them secretly to other spies.

Spy Language – A spy-friend is called a contact. A spy who carries messages is a courier. A spy who holds messages to be picked up is a 'letter-box'.

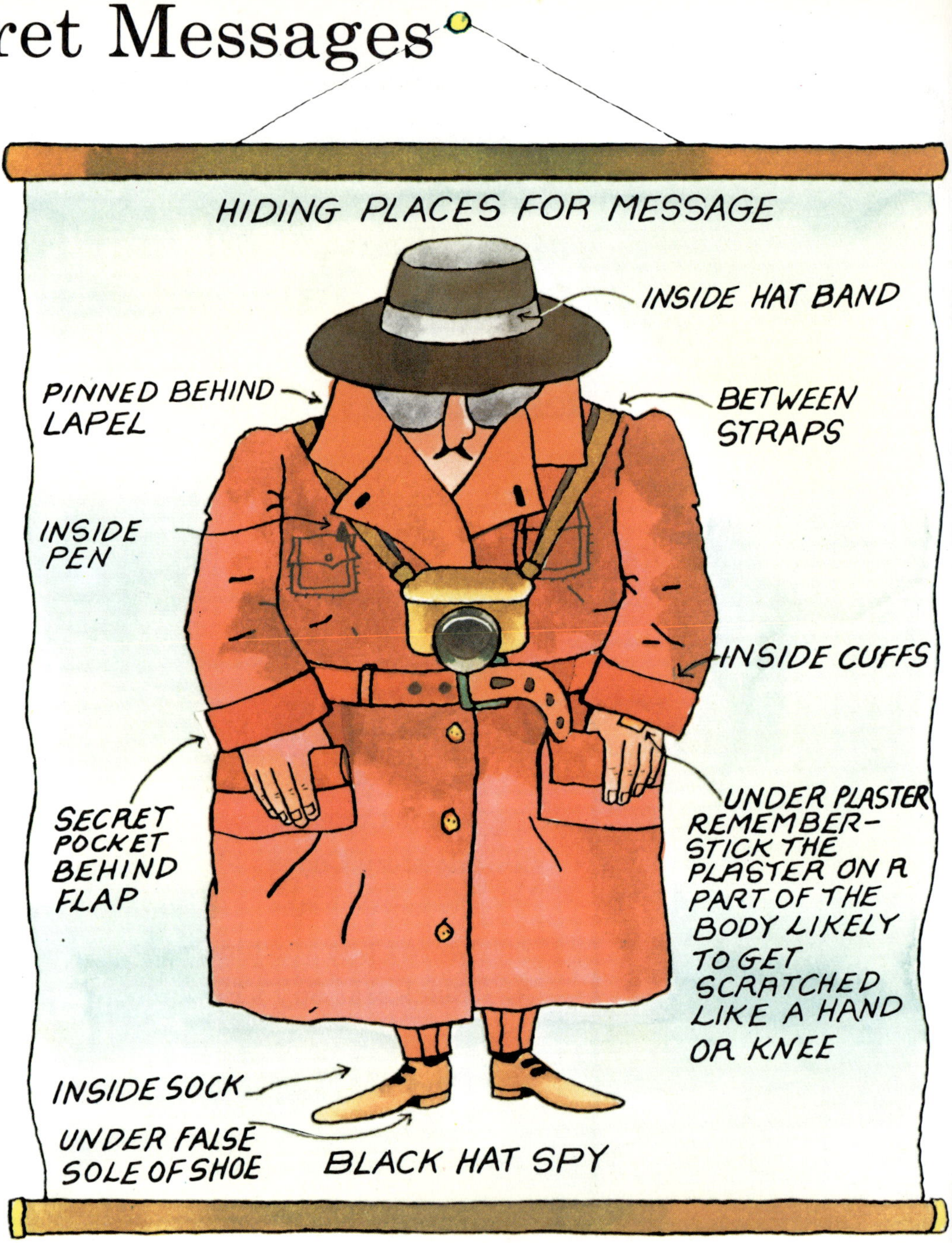

HIDING PLACES FOR MESSAGE

INSIDE HAT BAND

PINNED BEHIND LAPEL

BETWEEN STRAPS

INSIDE PEN

INSIDE CUFFS

SECRET POCKET BEHIND FLAP

UNDER PLASTER
REMEMBER – STICK THE PLASTER ON A PART OF THE BODY LIKELY TO GET SCRATCHED LIKE A HAND OR KNEE

INSIDE SOCK

UNDER FALSE SOLE OF SHOE

BLACK HAT SPY

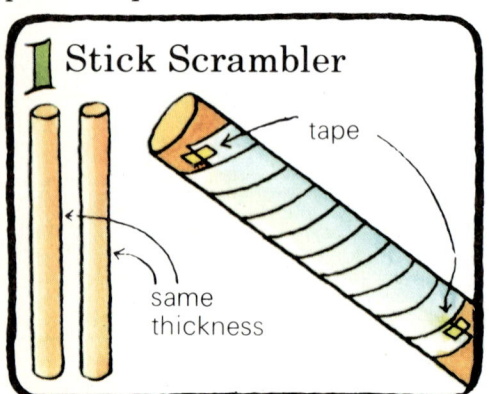

1 Stick Scrambler

tape

same thickness

Both you and your contact must have sticks of just the same thickness. (Try pencils.) Wind a strip of paper tightly round your stick. Fasten it with sticky tape.

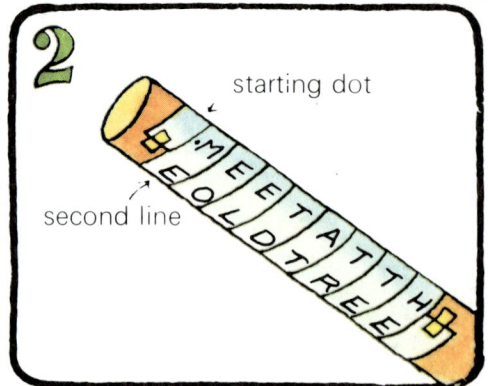

starting dot

second line

Write a message on the strip, like this. Make a dot beside the first letter to show your contact where the message starts. Turn the stick to add more lines.

Unwind the paper and the letters will be scrambled up. The message will be hidden until your contact winds the strip round a stick of exactly the same thickness.

1 False Sole

Put your shoe on a piece of light cardboard, such as a piece of cereal package and draw around it.

2

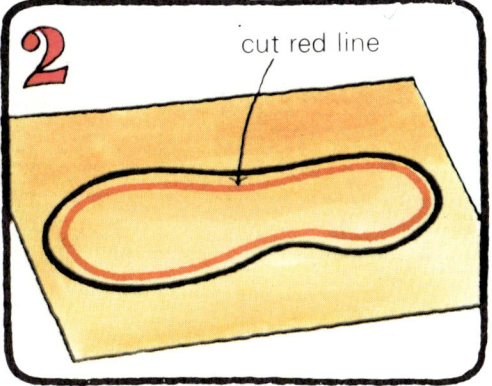

cut red line

Cut just inside this line to make a false sole that will fit inside your shoe.

3

put message here

Slip the message between the real sole and the false sole as shown. Use this method if you think you might be stopped and searched by enemies.

1 Secret Pocket

Cut off a corner of a tea-bag and empty out the tea. Make tabs of sticky tape.

2

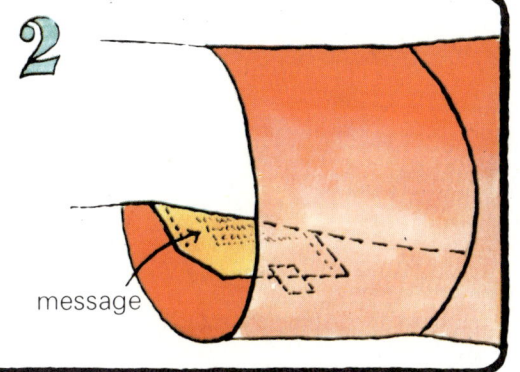

message

Stick the tea-bag in a hidden place, like the inside of a cap or sleeve. Fold the message very small and tuck it inside.

Spy Trick

THE SPY IS SEEN STANDING BESIDE THIS WALL. HE SEEMS TO BE INNOCENTLY READING A NEWSPAPER BUT IS HE?

1 Pen Message

message

Write the message on a small strip of paper. Roll the strip very tightly and keep it in the top of a pen.

2

message

Or unscrew a cartridge pen and wind the message strip around the ink cartridge. Then screw the pen together again.

SECRETLY, HE IS HIDING A ROLLED PAPER MESSAGE IN A CRACK IN THE WALL. LATER HIS CONTACT WILL PICK IT UP. TURN THE PAGE TO FIND MORE SPY TRICKS. ➡➡

Spy Post Office

A park is a good place to set up a secret post office. Spies often meet or leave messages in parks because you can wander or dawdle in a park without looking too suspicious. Most parks have open places where you can have a good look round to see if you're being followed. And your meetings with other spies can look very innocent and accidental. Follow the spy in the picture here to see some of the ways a spy post office works.

You can hide messages in all kinds of places if you make sure your contact knows where to look. But if you bury the message, put it in a small tin, like an elastoplast tin, or in a bottle, so that it won't get rain-soaked or chewed up by a nosey animal.

Spy Language – A place where you leave messages is called a 'drop'.

When on spy business, a good spy tries not to be seen twice in the same spot. Can you work out how a spy could get to all the message spots in the picture without re-tracing his steps? Clue – the letters on the picture spell the name of a car. Join them up correctly to find the trail.

THE SPY'S CONTACT IS THE MAN SELLING NEWSPAPERS. THE SPY BUYS A PAPER AND FINDS A MESSAGE TUCKED INSIDE.

THE SPY STOPS TO PICK A FLOWER NEAR THE RABBIT HOLE. HE SLIPS HIS OTHER HAND INTO THE RABBIT HOLE AND TAKES OUT A TINY BOTTLE WITH A MESSAGE INSIDE.

THE SPY PICKS UP A NEWSPAPER LYING ON THIS BENCH. THE WORDS UNDERLINED IN THE LEFT-HAND COLUMN ON PAGE 12 ARE A SECRET MESSAGE.

THE SPY FINDS MESSAGE PUSHE. INTO A CRACK IN THIS W

Whispering Wood

THE SPY STOPS AND PRETENDS TO SMELL THE FLOWERS. HE FINDS THE MESSAGE IN A SMALL BOTTLE PUSHED INTO THE SOIL.

V

THE SPY PICKS UP THIS UMBRELLA AND TAKES IT HOME. WHEN HE IS ALONE HE UNSCREWS THE HANDLE AND FINDS A MESSAGE INSIDE.

G

THE SPY KNEELS BY THIS TREE AND PRETENDS TO TIE HIS SHOE LACE. HE FINDS THE MESSAGE UNDERNEATH A TREE ROOT.

E

L

THE SPY SITS DOWN ON THIS BENCH AND FINDS A MESSAGE STUCK UNDER THE BENCH WITH A DRAWING PIN.

N

THE SPY PRETENDS TO STUMBLE AGAINST THIS LOG. HE STOOPS TO RUB HIS SHIN AND PULLS OUT A MESSAGE FROM BENEATH THE LOG.

O

HERE THE SPY MEETS A MAN WALKING A DOG. THE SPY SCRATCHES THE DOG'S HEAD AND FINDS A MESSAGE UNDER THE DOG'S COLLAR.

7

Quick Codes

You can make some very quick and easy codes just by making a few small changes in your messages. The best example is the Word-Split Code. Just split the words in a different way to make the message look completely different. For instance, the message 'We trail spies' can be changed to 'Wet rails pies.' In the code message all the letters are the same – only the spacing between the letters has been changed.

You can make other good codes by changing round the message letters in simple ways or adding dummy letters to the message. On the right you will find examples of these codes and clues on how to break each kind of code.

Find the Master Spy

The people you see in the picture below are QZ spies. Each has a message for you in one of the six codes shown on the right. Begin with the message at Start – each decoded message will lead you to another contact. Break all the codes to find which of your contacts was actually the Master Spy of the QZ Spy Ring.

Breaking the Codes

Try these methods on each message to work out which code was used.

1   Try joining the first code word to one or two letters of the second code word.
2   Spell the first few code words backwards.
3   Take away the first letter of each code word and see if the remaining letters make words.
4   Take away the last letter of each code word and see if the remaining letters make words.
5   Exchange the last letter of each code word with the first letter of the next code word.

1 Word-Split
WE/T RAIL/S PIES
First word Second word Third word

To break the code, join the letters in a different way.

2 Backwards Words
EW LIART SEIPS
Spell each word backwards

To break the code, spell each code word backwards.

3 Backwards Sentences
SEIPS LIART EW
Spell sentence backwards

To break the code, spell the sentence backwards.

4 Dummy First Letter
ØWET BRAI XLSP XIES
Take away first letter

To break the code, cross out the first letter of each 4-letter code word. Join up the remaining letters into words.

5 Dummy Last Letter
WETX RAIX LSPX IESX
Take away last letter

To break the code, cross out the last letter of each 4-letter code work. Join up the remaining letters into words.

6 Exchanged Letters
WETA RILP SIES
Exchange first and last letters

To break the code, exchange the last letter of each 4-letter code word with the first letter of the next.

9

Mystery Codes

The mysterious papers Black Hat is examining are coded messages. These pages show the key to each of them. Can you decode them?

Music Code

The key to the music code is at the right. It shows which note stands for each letter of the alphabet and for each of the numbers from one to nine. Use O for nought.

Match Black Hat's message notes with those in the key to find the letter that each note stands for. (The first letter of the message is W).

A dot marks the end of a word.

Pig-Pen Code

This mysterious-looking code is very easy to use. To make the key, first draw the patterns shown here.

Railfence Code

To encode a message, first write the letters in an up-and-down pattern, on two lines. Add a null (extra letter) if needed to make both lines the same length.

Now write out the letters of the first line, then the letters of the second line. Put them in groups, like words. Make sure your contact knows how to decode this.

To decode a railfence message, first count out the first half of the message. Write it out with big spaces between the letters.

10

Key to Music Code

Now write in the letters of the alphabet like this. The pattern of lines or of lines and dots next to each letter is used to stand for that letter.

GERMANY =

This example shows how the password 'Germany' looks in Pig-Pen. Now see if you can work out the secret message Black Hat has found.

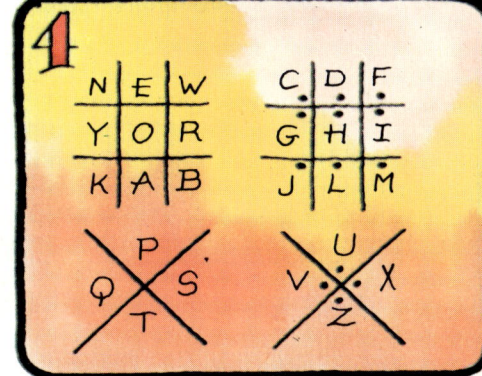

To make a more secret Pig-Pen key, write the alphabet in a different order. Start with a keyword (a word with all-different letters). Then add the rest of the alphabet.

HIDE THIS MESSAGE X

add second half

Now put the letters of the second half one by one into the spaces, like this. Try this method on the secret message that Black Hat is looking at.

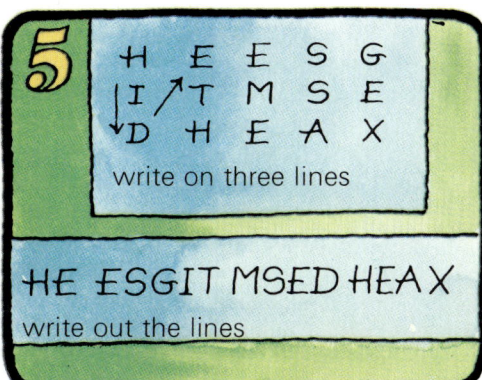

HE ESGIT MSED HEAX

write on three lines

HE ESGIT MSED HEAX

write out the lines

To change the code, write the letters in an up-and-down pattern on three lines, like this. Then write out the letters from each line, as before.

find three equal groups
5 letters 5 letters 5 letters

HE ESGIT MSED HEAX

read down

To decode the message your contact must count out three equal groups of letters and write them in three lines again. Then he can read down each group of three.

Code Machines

With these machines you can encode and decode messages very quickly. The code strip shown below is easy to make. Use it to match the plain alphabet with a code alphabet that starts and finishes at a different letter. For example, start the code alphabet at B. Then change each plain letter for the one that follows it in the alphabet. Change the Z's to A's.

PTMVA HNM YHK LMKT GZXK PBMA UETV DATM

To make a code wheel, trace the pattern on page 13. Trace it carefully so that the alphabets line up when you spin the dial.

This message is written in Code T. Match A with T on a code machine to break the code.

When you send messages, be sure your contact knows which code alphabet you have used.

Code Strip

plain alphabet

code strip → A B C D E F G H I J K L M N O P Q R S T U V W X Y Z

A B C D E F G H I J K L M N O P Q R S T U V W X Y Z A B C D E F G H I J K L M N O P Q R S T U V W X Y Z

code G alphabet

plain language — PARIS

code G — VGXOY

Mark a strip of paper into 26 spaces, one cm wide. Write the alphabet neatly in the spaces. Then mark 52 spaces, one cm wide, on a strip twice as long.

Write the alphabet twice in the spaces of the long strip, as shown above. Slide the short strip over the long strip to match the plain alphabet with a code alphabet.

For example, slide the short strip so that A stands over G to make Code G. Then match each plain letter with the letter beneath it on the code strip.

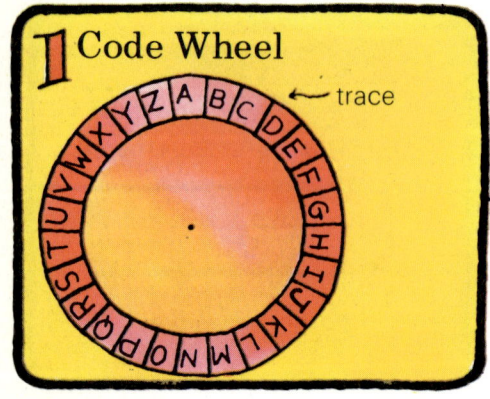

1 Code Wheel

trace

Trace the red wheel from the pattern at the right. Trace the lines very carefully and mark the centre dot.

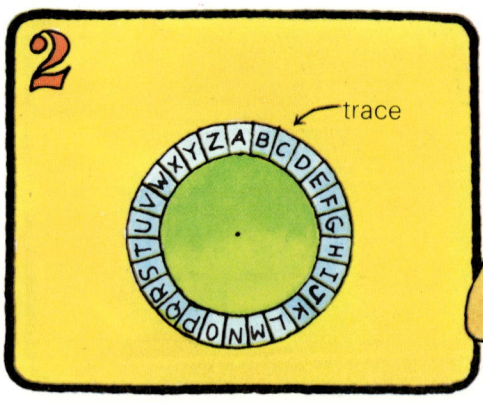

2

trace

Trace the blue wheel in the same way. Print one letter of the alphabet in each border space, on both wheels. Cut out the wheels.

3

Draw and cut out a wheel from light card (like a cereal package) and glue each paper wheel to a card wheel.

Top Secret

This is how to use two code alphabets. First print the message. Then print the names of the alphabets over and over to mark each plain letter. Set the code strip or wheel at P and encode all the letters marked P. Set it at Q to encode the rest. Tell your contact to decode with PQ.

	PQP	QPQPQ	PQP	QPQPQ	PQP
message	WHO	WEARS	THE	BLACK	HAT
code P	L D	T G	I T	A R	W I
code Q	X	M Q I	X	R Q A	Q
code PQ	LXD	MTQGI	IXT	RAQRA	WQI

Code Wheel Pattern

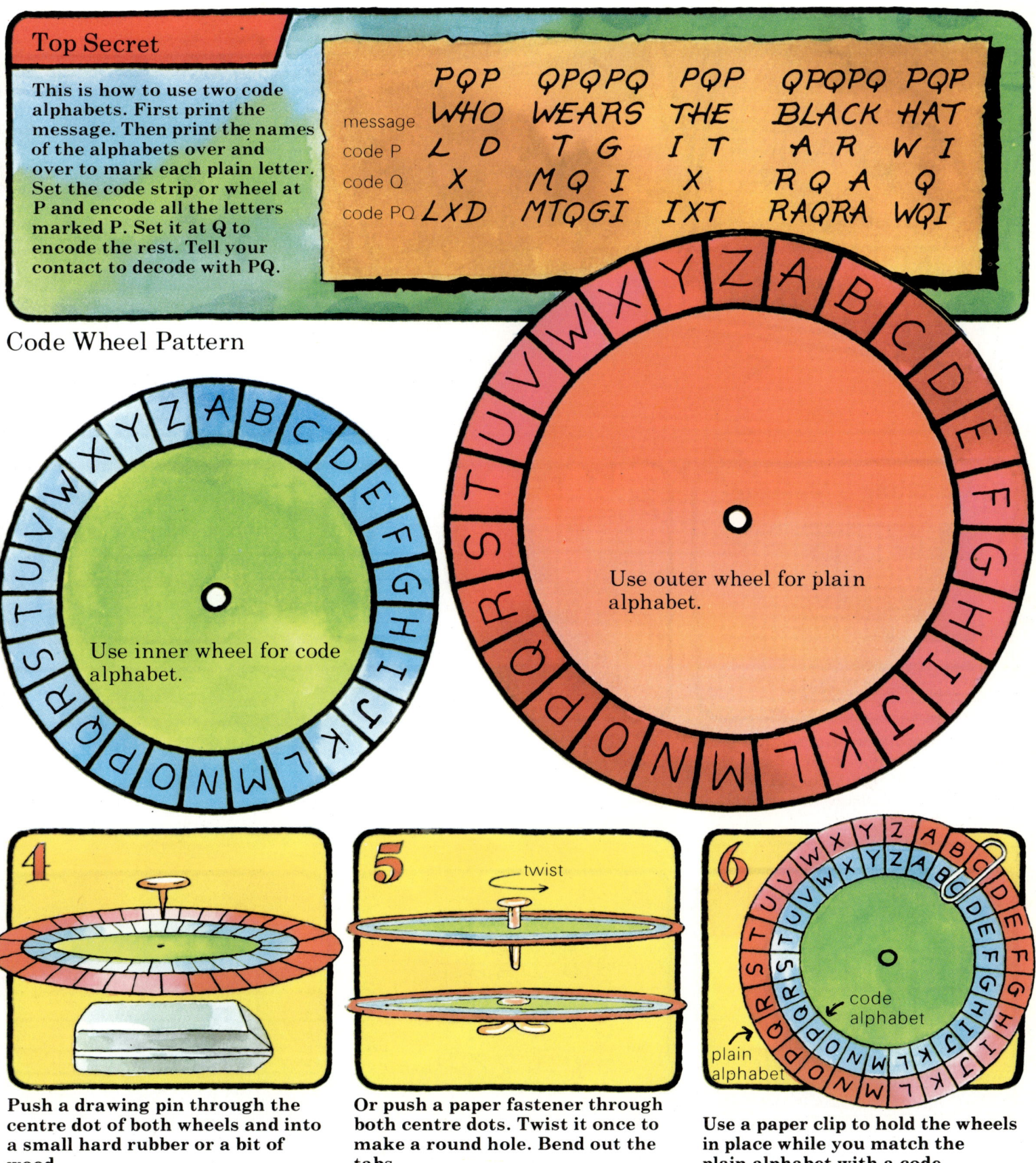

Use inner wheel for code alphabet.

Use outer wheel for plain alphabet.

4 Push a drawing pin through the centre dot of both wheels and into a small hard rubber or a bit of wood.

5 twist

Or push a paper fastener through both centre dots. Twist it once to make a round hole. Bend out the tabs.

6 code alphabet

plain alphabet

Use a paper clip to hold the wheels in place while you match the plain alphabet with a code alphabet. Be sure to tell your contact which one you have used.

More Code Machines

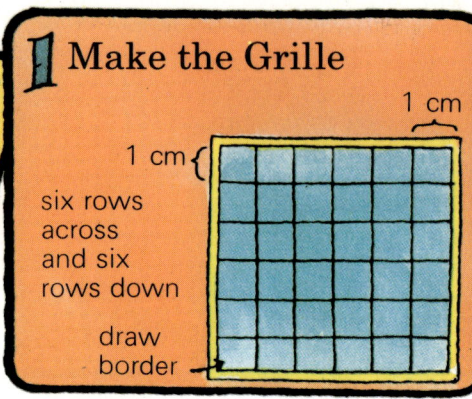

Use a code grille to reveal the hidden message.

1 Make the Grille

1 cm

1 cm

six rows across and six rows down

draw border

Use light card, like a cereal box, and draw a square like this. Draw lines about one cm apart, as shown, and draw a border round the square. Cut round the border.

1 Encoding a Message

THIS IS HOW

mark corner

Place the grille on some paper. Draw round one corner of the grille to mark its place. Print one letter of the message in each space as shown.

2

first turn

TO USE THE S-

Now give the grille one turn clockwise so that the top edge becomes the right side. Match a corner with the corner mark. Fill the spaces with letters.

3

-ECRET CODE

second turn

Give another clockwise turn so that the top edge becomes the bottom edge. Match the corner with the corner mark and fill the spaces with letters.

4

GRILLE (XYZ)

third turn

Turn again to make the top edge become the left side. Fill the rest of the spaces with letters. Add extra letters if needed to fill all the spaces.

5

TEGTOC
HUIRRI
LESTES
CLIEST
HHEOXD
OYESWZ

When you lift the grille the message will look like this. Write it in a line, like this: Tegtoc huirri lestes cliest hheoxd oyeswz.

Decoding a Message

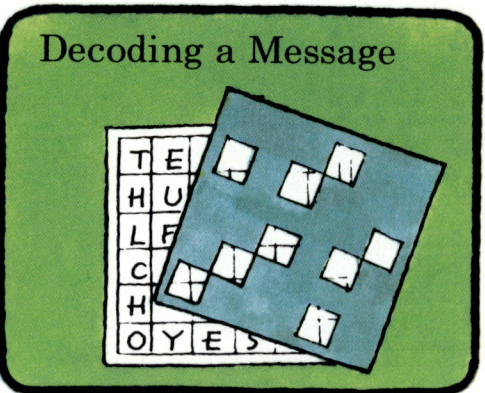

First print the message in squares that match the grille. Place the grille over the message with the coloured edge at the top. Turn it to show all the letters.

Cut out the squares marked with an x. Colour the top edge. Make an exact copy of the grille for your contact.

To cut out a small square, first push the tip of your scissors through the centre of the square, as shown.

make hole

Then make snips from the centre to the corners, like this. Fold back the four triangles and cut them off.

corners

Back-to-Front Grille

top edge

front

Here is a different pattern. Hold the grille as shown to begin. For the second step give two clockwise turns so the top edge is at the bottom.

top edge

back

For the third step turn the grille over. For the fourth step give two clockwise turns again, so that the top edge is at the bottom.

Super Code Grille

Trace this pattern to make a 144-letter code grille. With this code machine you can write a secret message almost as fast as an ordinary letter.

Black Hat Spy's Equipment . . .

Here is Black Hat in his attic den, surrounded by spy equipment. (You may recognize many of his tools – other pages in the book show how to make them.) Black Hat has just noticed that someone is climbing towards the attic on a ladder. It may be the window-cleaner – but it may be a spycatcher in disguise. In the next few minutes Black Hat must find a way to hide all the evidence that he is a spy. How can he do it?

On the right you can see how the spy den will look in just five minutes. Can you work out any of the tricks that Black Hat uses to hide his spy equipment? The answers are on the next page, upside-down.

AERIAL →

TUNER →

THE SPY DOES NOT KNOW HIS ROOM IS 'BUGGED'

PEN BARREL TWO LENSES

SHORT WAVE RADIO FOR SENDING SPY MESSAGES

MICRODOT READER – THE TWO LENSES IN THE BARREL OF THE PEN CAN MAGNIFY THE DOT 200 TIMES

MICRODOT-MAGNIFIED 200 TIMES TO SEE SECRET MESSAGE

CODE WHEEL (SEE PAGE 141)

HOLLOW RING WITH MINIATURE TAPE RECORDER

BOTTLE OF INVISIBLE INK

CODE BOOK-LIKE A FOREIGN DICTIONARY, WITH A SIGN OR NUMBER FOR EACH WORD OR MESSAGE THE SPIES MIGHT WANT TO SEND ALWAYS VERY TINY.

SPY MAPS

and How He Hides It Away

5 MINUTES LATER

Where is Black Hat's Spy equipment now? Turn the page upside-down to check your answers.

Bottle of invisible ink – inside teapot spout.

Microdot – on the side of the envelope that is turned down. A microdot has a special shine that a spycatcher might notice.

Microdot reader in pen barrel – put together as pen.

Code book – hidden in teapot inside small plastic bag with elastic band around it.

Hollow ring – on Black Hat's finger.

Radio – behind sliding panel disguised as book shelf. The books at the left end are real books. Those at the right are just pieces of book-cover stuck to the panel.

Code Wheel – hidden under lid of sugar bowl.

Binoculars – hidden under tea-cosy.

Maps – pushed into sleeves of coat, which are tucked into pockets to keep maps from sliding out.

Invisible Writing

A message in secret ink is usually written on the back of an ordinary letter or in the blank spaces between the lines and along the sides.

You will need

a piece of white candle and some fine powder for wax writing. You can use powdered instant coffee, chalk scrapings or even fine earth in an emergency

ink or paint and a brush or sponge to make the water message appear

a potato for the potato inkwell

some paper – use thin paper for the water mark

To make a pen that doesn't leave deep scratch marks, sharpen one end of a used match with a pencil sharpener, sandpaper or a nail file.

Remember – always mark the message to show your contact how to develop it (make it appear).

Marks to use are:

wx for a wax message

wm for a water message

h for a message that must be heated

× on the message side of the paper

sign for wax message

Know How
Spycatcher Club
Box (WX) 123

Dear Member,
To send a really secret message, use invisible writing and a code. Can you decode the password written between these lines? (Pig-Pen Code, page 138) Red chalk dust was used to make it appear. Notice the phoney address – the letters WX are really a sign that the true message was written with wax.

1 Potato Inkwell

Hold the potato like this and cut off both ends with a table knife, as shown.

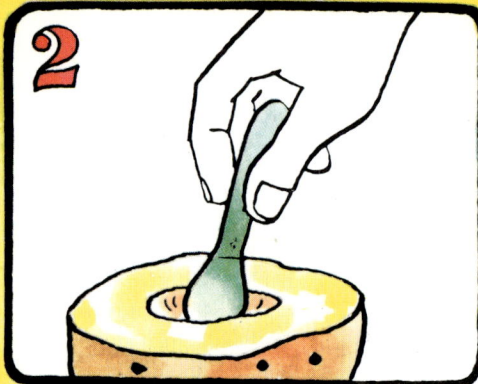

2

Stand the potato on one end. Scoop a hole in the top with a spoon.

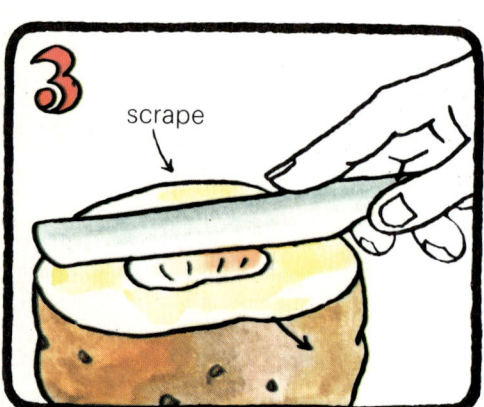

3

scrape

Now use the blade of the table knife to scrape and squeeze the juice from the cut top of the potato into the hole.

4

Dip the sharpened end of a used match into the potato ink to write the message. When the 'ink' dries, the message will be invisible.

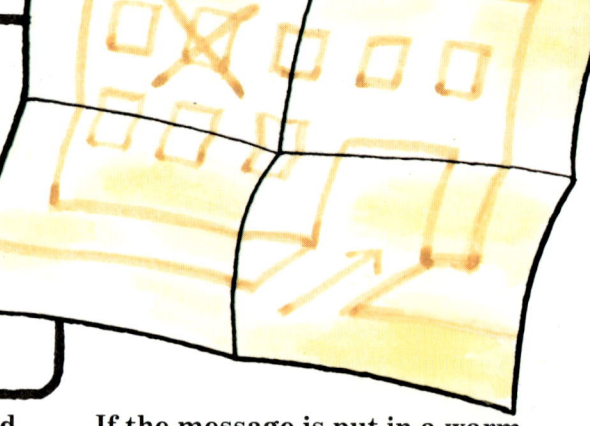

If the message is put in a warm oven (250°) it will look like this. Make other 'inks' with lemon juice, milk, onion juice or coca-cola.

1 Water Writing

dry paper
write firmly
wet paper

Wet some paper thoroughly. Lay it on a smooth, hard surface. Cover it with dry paper and write firmly. The message will appear on the wet paper when it is held to the light.

The message will vanish when the paper dries and reappear whenever it is wet. Your contact can brush it with watery ink or paint to make it permanent.

You can make water-mark messages on dry paper with a matchstick dipped in slightly soapy water. The soapy shine will help you see what you are doing.

1 Wax Writing

paper with waxed underside
write firmly
plain paper

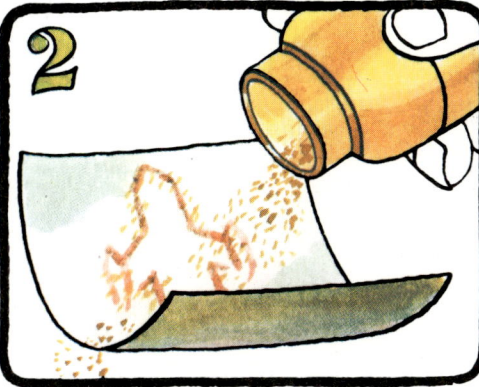

Wax some paper by rubbing it with white candle. Then lay the waxed side on plain paper. Write firmly to print the message in wax marks on the plain paper.

Your contact should sprinkle the message paper with powdered instant coffee or chalk scrapings or some fine dust.

When he gives the paper a gentle shake the powder will stick to the message and slide off the rest of the paper.

Spy Trick

BLACK HAT HAD JUST ARRIVED IN THE COUNTRY. AT THE AIRPORT HE WAS STOPPED AND SEARCHED, BUT WAS FOUND TO BE CARRYING ONLY...A SEWING KIT...

THE SPY WAS ALLOWED TO GO. AFTER ALL, A FEW NEEDLES AND COTTON CAN'T BE MUCH HELP TO THE ENEMY... OR CAN THEY?

ALONE IN HIS ROOM, THE SPY DREW THE COTTON OVER A HOT LIGHT BULB, AND TINY DOTS OF INVISIBLE INK APPEARED ALONG IT. TURN THE PAGE TO SEE HOW TO USE A DOT CODE. ➡

Dot Code Messages

Dear Grandma
How are you? It is
very nice in the country.
Arthur got chased by a ~~ce~~
cow today. Albert got
chased by a lot of bees. I am
having a good time in the
country.   Love
*   Frances*
*   P.S. Here is Albert being*
chased by the bees.

| A | B | C | D | E | F | G | H | I | J | K | L | M | N | O | P | Q | R | S | T | U | V | W | X | Y | Z |

This letter is really a secret spy message. Each bee in the picture stands for one letter of the message. To find the message, first trace the code strip below the picture. Hold the strip with its end right at the edge of the picture and slide it slowly down the page to match each bee with a letter. (The top bee stands for H.)

In this code each letter is made by dotting a piece of paper or a piece of string in a special place. A string message is easy to hide – you could even tie it round a parcel. And the dots on a piece of paper can be disguised inside a picture.

To encode a message you need a paper strip carefully printed with the alphabet. To decode the message your contact needs a strip just like yours. For extra secrecy use a keyword to scramble the letters of the alphabet.

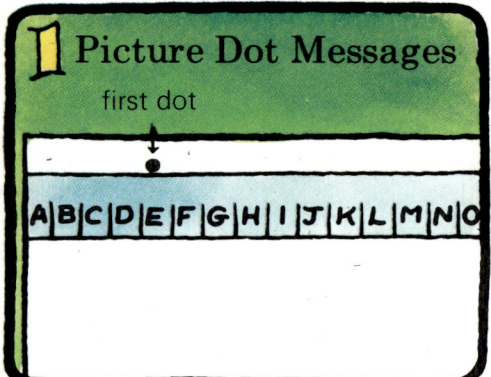

1 Picture Dot Messages

first dot

| A | B | C | D | E | F | G | H | I | J | K | L | M | N | O |

On this code strip you needn't leave space at start. Hold the strip near the top of a piece of paper. Put a dot over the first letter of the message.

1 Disguising the Dots

You can disguise the dot message as a picture. For example, you could turn the dots into birds, like this.

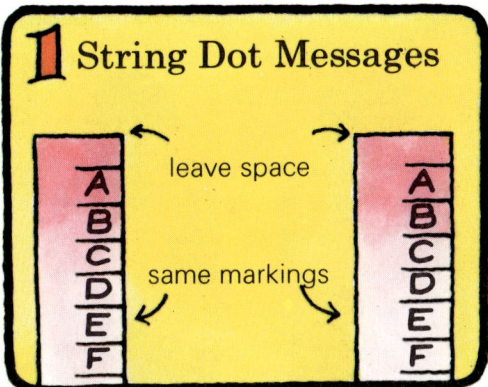

1 String Dot Messages

Mark a strip of paper into 27 spaces about one cm wide. Tell your contact to mark his strip the same way. Leave a space and write the alphabet as shown.

Make a starting dot at the end of a piece of string. Hold the string along the strip like this and dot it with ink at the first letter of the message.

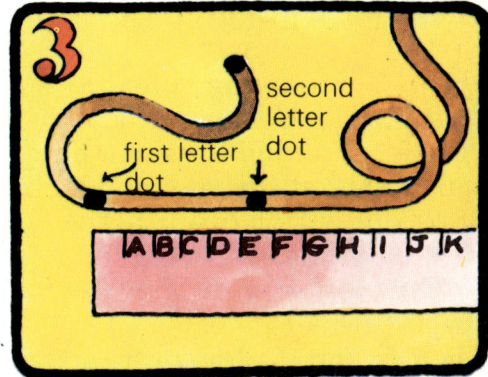

Move the first dot to the starting point and make a second dot at the second letter of the message. Move each dot to Start before you make the next dot.

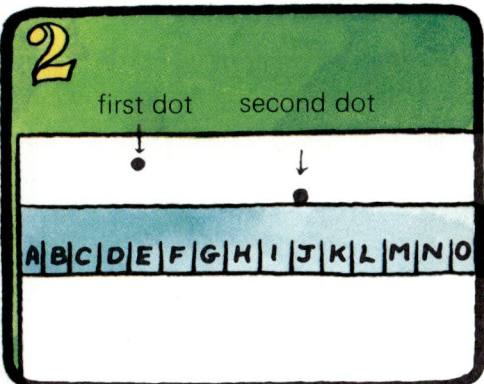

Move the strip down slightly and put a second dot over the second letter of the message. Continue to move the strip down to make each new dot.

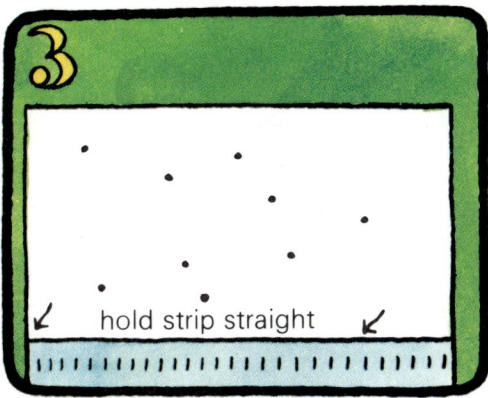

To decode the message your contact moves his strip down the page and 'reads' each dot. He must hold the strip very straight, with its end at the paper edge.

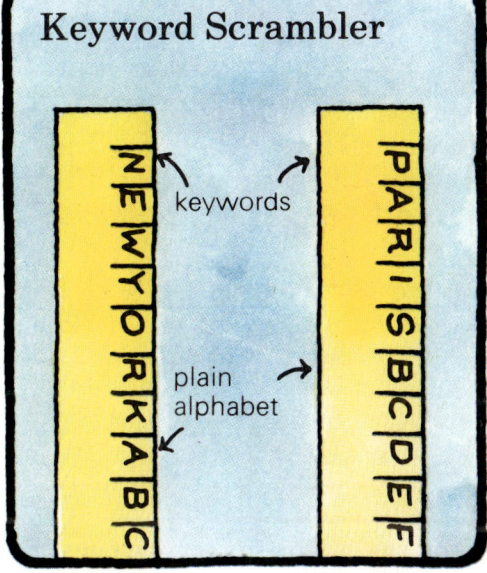

Keyword Scrambler

Suppose a lot of people know how to use the ordinary code strip. To keep them from reading your messages make a special strip that only you and your contact know about. Choose a word with all-different letters, like those above. This will be your keyword. Write the letters of this word in the first spaces of the code strip. Then write in the alphabet as before, skipping the letters you have already used.

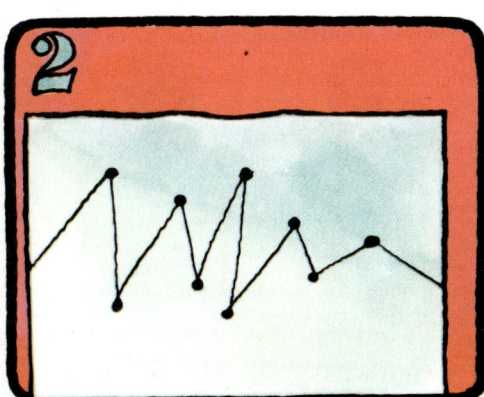

Or the dots could become points on a jagged line, to look like part of a chart.

You could even disguise the message as a board game. The snake's eyes here are the same dots.

Quick Disguises

These quick disguises can help you fool your enemy. If your enemy is following you at a distance he will keep track of you by watching for something special about the way you look. Start out with a disguise that will catch his eye. Wear a bright scarf or a sling or use a special walk (see below). Then go into a shop or duck into a doorway and come out without it. Your enemy will be left wondering where you've gone.

Spy Language – Following is called 'shadowing' or 'tailing'. The person who does it is a 'tail' or 'shadow'.

Change Your Walk
A good spy trick is to pretend to have a stiff leg or a limp. But you might forget your stiff leg, or start limping on the wrong foot. Here are some ways to make sure you remember.
1 To make yourself limp, put a small stone in one shoe.
2 For a stiff leg, put a ruler at the back of one knee and tie it on with a scarf or string. Then you won't be able to bend it. Wear long trousers or a very long skirt to hide the ruler.

Arm in Sling

You will need a helper to put your arm in a sling. Use a big scarf or piece of cloth folded like this. Hold your arm across it and put a corner round your neck.

Lift the bottom corner and knot it to the piece round your neck. Then pin the side corner over your elbow, as shown.

One-Armed Spy

arm inside coat

sleeve in pocket

Wear your coat like this to look as though you only have one arm. Put one arm into a sleeve. Tuck the other sleeve into a pocket. Button the coat with one arm inside.

Two-Way Scarf

knot thread

take out pins after stitching

To make a quick-change scarf you will need two scarves the same size and shape but different colours. Pin them together like this and stitch around all four sides.

Change Your Shape

1

put on towel

with disguise

without disguise

hat and towel in bag

To raise your shoulders, lay a small towel behind your neck, like this. Then put a coat on over it. This will help you look like an older person with muscular shoulders.

To change your back view even more wear a hat or scarf as well. Take a folded carrier bag in your pocket. Later you can carry the hat and towel in the bag.

2

To make yourself look fatter, tie a small cushion round your middle. Button a coat on over it, or wear a very big jersey.

Change Your Looks

If your enemy knows you and is watching for you, try these tricks.

White Hair

Put talcum powder on your hair and eyebrows to whiten them. If you are fair they will go white and if you are dark they will go grey. Do just the front if you wear a hat.

Hair Combed Wrong Way

Comb your hair a different way. Slick it back or part it in a different place. If you have a fringe, comb it to the side.

Changed Eyebrows

Cover your eyebrows by rubbing bits of damp, soft soap into them. It might help to use face powder over the soap. Then draw new eyebrows with black crayon.

Face Colours

To make your face paler, rub some talcum powder on it. Rub it in gently and don't use too much. Use cocoa powder to make your face look browner.

Missing Tooth

From a distance, a blacked-out tooth looks like a gap. First wipe the tooth dry. Then rub black crayon over it.

5 O'clock Shadow

Mix daubs of blue and black paint with some face cream, like Pond's Cold Cream. Rub a little on your face like this, to look as though you need a shave.

Lumpy Face

Put small wads of cotton wool between your teeth and cheeks. Stick in lots to make fat cheeks. To make lumpy jowls just put them next to your lower teeth.

Wrinkle Lines

Draw wrinkle lines with a soft pencil, like a pencil marked 3B or 4B. Smile very hard, then wrinkle your forehead to see where the lines should go.

Spotting Clues

A spy must be very good at spotting clues. He has to get information from little signs and marks that other people would not notice. This page shows how to get information from footprints and from car and cycle tracks. This can be very useful if you lose sight of someone you are following. Sometimes the person you are following may disguise himself. Watch out for clues that can help you see through the disguise. Try the Spy Test below to see how good you are at spotting this kind of clue.

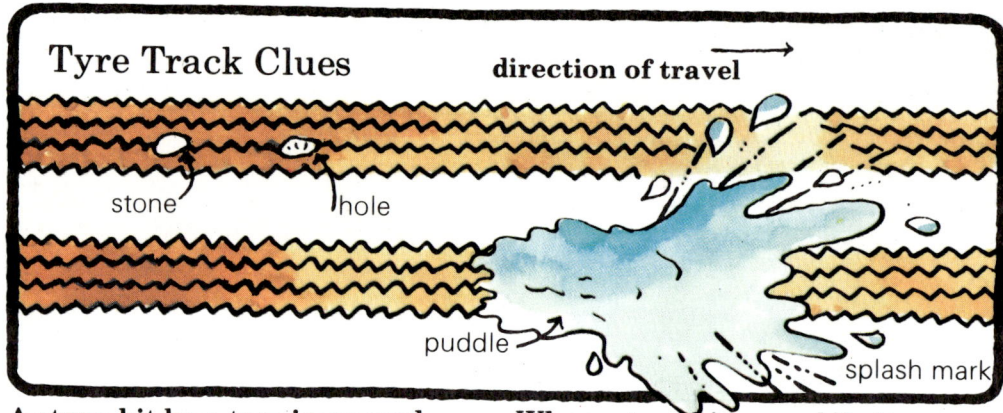

Tyre Track Clues

direction of travel →

stone

hole

puddle

splash mark

A stone hit by a tyre is pressed down to make a hole and then kicked back. The marks left in the road show the direction in which the tyre was travelling.

When a tyre hits a puddle it splashes the oil or water forwards. Look for the splash-mark to work out which way the tyre was going.

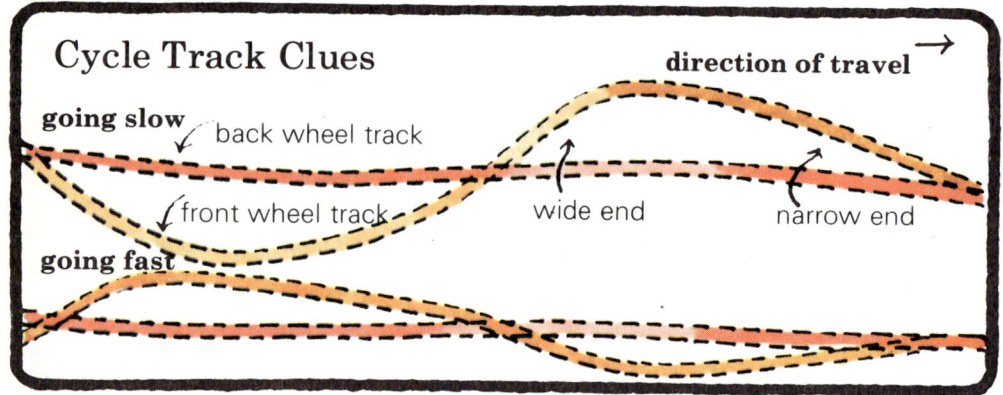

Cycle Track Clues

direction of travel →

going slow
back wheel track
front wheel track
wide end
narrow end
going fast

The front wheel of a cycle makes a loopy track, because the cyclist has to keep turning it to keep his balance. He turns less when going fast and makes smaller loops.

After turning the wheel, the cyclist straightens it, so the loops are always wider at one end than at the other. The narrow end points out where he is heading.

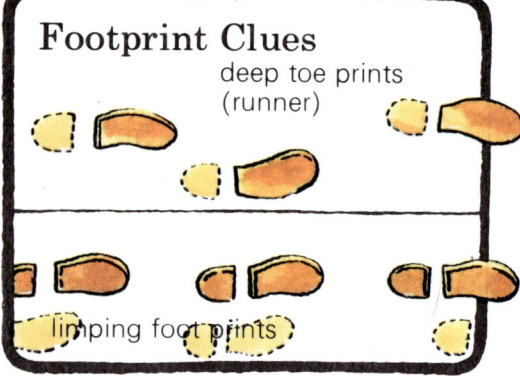

Footprint Clues

deep toe prints (runner)

limping foot prints

If the person you are trailing is running, look for a deep toe print and light heel print. If he is limping, look for a deep footprint and then a light footprint.

Spy Test

SPY Z KNOWS A LOT OF DISGUISE TRICKS, BUT HE FORGETS TO HIDE ONE CLUE. READ ON AND SEE IF YOU CAN SPOT IT.

BLACK HAT HAS JUST SPOTTED SPY Z NEAR THE PALM HOTEL

AS SPY Z ENTERS THE HOTEL AND CALLS THE LIFT, BLACK HAT IS WATCHING. NOW IS HIS CHANCE TO SEE WHERE SPY Z HIDES OUT.

WHEN SPY Z ENTERS THE LIFT BLACK HAT RUNS UPSTEARS..

SLAM

Trapping Spies

Suppose you think that your enemy is getting into your secret hiding places. Set up one of the spy traps on this page and the intruder will be tricked into making a noise or leaving a clue that shows someone has been there. Door Trap No. 2 is particularly useful. Made with flour, it will leave a mark on anyone who who goes through the door.

You can make another good noise trap by sprinkling sugar on the floor. But people in socks or rubber soles can avoid this trap.

Hallway Trap

Tape a thin black thread from wall to wall, like this. Anyone who walks past this spot will make the thread fall down.

Desk Trap

clue mark

Spread some papers in a careless-looking way. Draw a tiny line that runs across two of them, like this. The smallest movement of the papers will break the line.

Door Trap No. 1

glued hair
(glue it low down or high up)

Glue a hair across the opening crack, like this. Check later – if someone has gone through the door, the hair will come unglued. Use the same trap on a drawer.

Door Trap No. 2

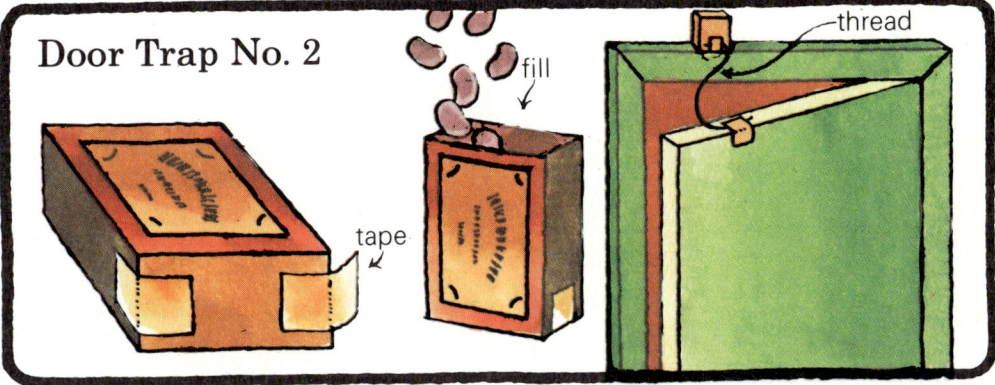

fill

tape

thread

Tape a bit of cardboard to one end of the cover of a matchbox to make a small, narrow box. Fill it with beans (for noise trap) or with flour (for marking trap).

Tape one end of a thread to the box. Then prop it on a door frame. Tape the thread to the door, like this, and close the door. If anyone opens it, the box will fall.

...AND REACHES THE FIRST FLOOR LANDING JUST IN TIME TO SEE A SECOND PERSON ENTER THE LIFT.

ON THE NEXT FLOOR, TWO MEN GET OUT. THIS IS THE TOP FLOOR — ONE OF THEM MUST BE SPY Z IN DISGUISE.

BLACK HAT FOLLOWS THE TWO MEN DOWN THE HALL. AS THEY TAKE OUT THEIR KEYS HE SEES THE CLUE THAT HE'S BEEN WAITING FOR. DO YOU?
(SEE PAGE 31 TO FIND THE ANSWER)

Secret Telephone Messages

BLACK HAT PICKS UP THE TELEPHONE AND SAYS..

ZABI DAKIDO KUKADA BUKON OZO BUBIDU KOBA BI BAGU-BE

The code spoken by Black Hat is made by using the alphabet box on the next page. Each plain letter is replaced by two of the code letters in the frame. The code can be spoken because one of the two letters is always a vowel (a, e, i, o or u). Your contact should write down the code message as he hears it and decode it later.

Remember – be sure that you and your contact agree on how to say the vowels, or he may write down the wrong letter.

THE ENEMY, LISTENING, IS BEWILDERED..

1 Encode your Message

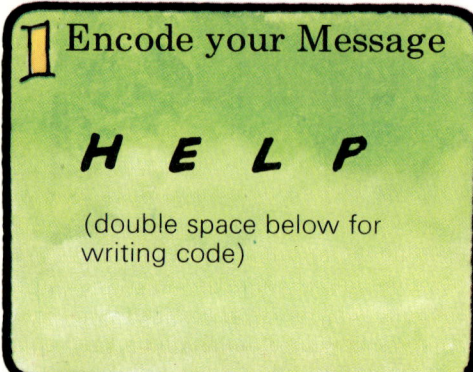

H E L P

(double space below for writing code)

Print the plain message neatly. Leave space between each letter and between each line of letters.

2

H E L P
DO ZI NO GU

Replace each plain letter with the code letter on its row and the code letter on its column. Use strips of paper to line them up.

1 Extra Security

	B	D	K	G	Z	N
I	L	A	Z	Y	B	O
O	N	E	S	C	D	F
U	G	H	I	J	K	M
A	P	Q	R	T	U	V
E	W	X				

Remember that you can scramble the alphabet by starting with a keyword (a word with all-different letters). Then add the rest of the letters.

1 Disguise Your Voice

To change your voice on the telephone, hold your mouth in a funny shape while you speak. For example, try to speak while holding a pencil in your teeth.

2

Now purse your lips as though you were going to whistle. Hold that shape while you speak. Try to speak in a normal voice and see what happens.

3

Now try a few more experiments. Try to speak while smiling very hard, as shown, or frowning.

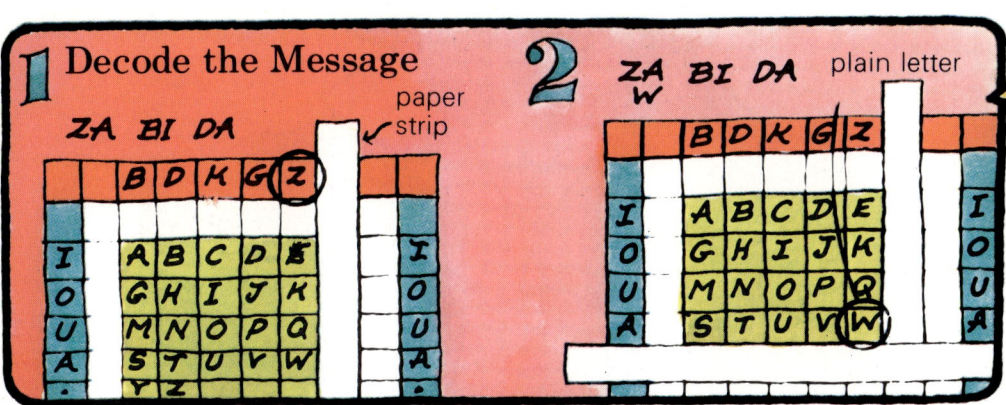

1 Decode the Message

ZA BI DA

paper strip

Write out Black Hat's message in pairs of letters. The first code letter is in one of the red squares that mark the columns. Mark the column with a paper strip.

2

ZA BI DA   plain letter

You will find the second code letter in one of the blue squares that mark rows. Mark the row with a paper strip. The plain letter is where the two strips of paper meet.

SEVERAL MINUTES LATER COMES THE ANSWER..

KO ZODUZIZA KODA DADOZI BUKONOZO KOBA BAKUKANU

2

changeable letters

Or use different code letters to mark the columns. You can use any letters except vowels (the letters that mark the rows).

4

Now try holding your nose while you practise the methods shown. You will find that your voice is completely different.

Alphabet Box

CODE LETTERS		B	D	K	G	Z	N		
I		A	B	C	D	E	F		I
O		G	H	I	J	K	L		O
U		M	N	O	P	Q	R		U
A		S	T	U	V	W	X		A
E		Y	Z						E
		B	D	K	G	Z	N		

Make the code for each plain letter with one letter from a red square and one letter from a blue square.

The picture shows how to encode the letter K. It doesn't matter whether you say OZ or ZO.

Silent Signals

If you and your contact can see each other but cannot speak or get close enough to pass a message, signal with the Silent Alphabet shown on the page on the right. Or blink the Morse **Code (see page 30) as shown** below. In a crowded room or busy street you and your contact can send quick messages or warnings with Silent Hand and Leg Signals.

Silent Hand and Leg Signals

1 One hand in pocket – yes.
2 Two hands in pockets – no.
3 Scratching head – can you meet me at the hiding place?
4 Scratching back of neck – be careful. You are being watched.
5 Crossing legs – leave your message at the 'drop'.
6 Both hands behind back – I cannot pass the message now.
7 Scratching ear – I will telephone you later.
8 Standing on one leg – I'm going home now.

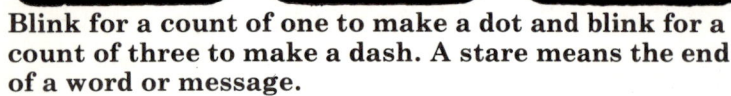

Morse Blink Signals

Blink for a count of one to make a dot and blink for a count of three to make a dash. A stare means the end of a word or message.

Morse Wink Signals

Wink to make a dot and blink to make a dash. A stare means the end of a word or message.

Silent Alphabet

On this page you can see how to make the letters of the alphabet with your hands. The pictures show how the hand signals should look to your contact. Don't practise in front of a mirror – the reflected signals will be the wrong way round. You and your contact should practise the signals together.

At the bottom of the page you will find some quick signs to make to answer questions or to tell your contact whether or not you understand his message.

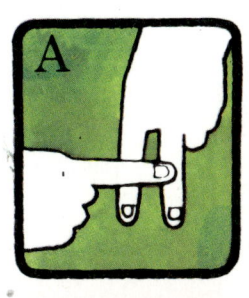 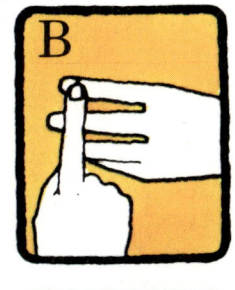 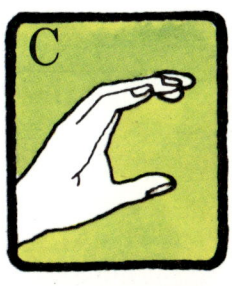 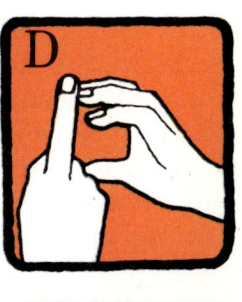

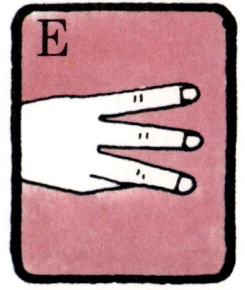   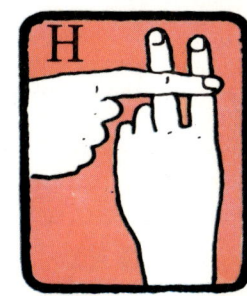

 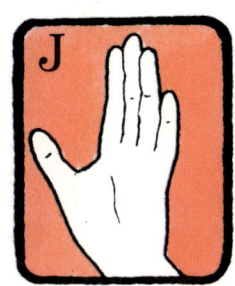  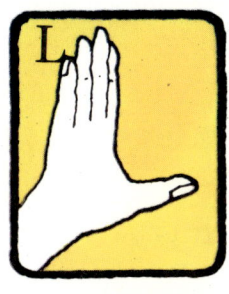 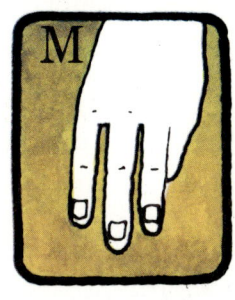 

 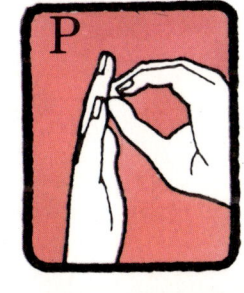   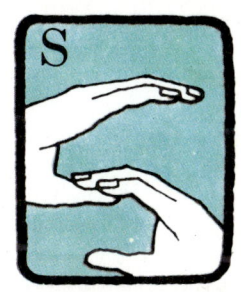 

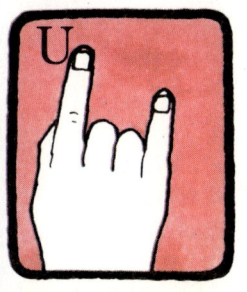 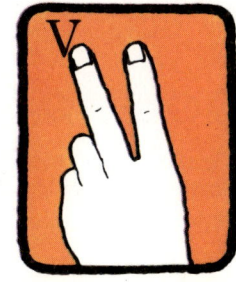 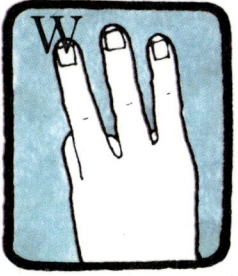  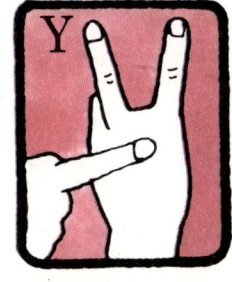 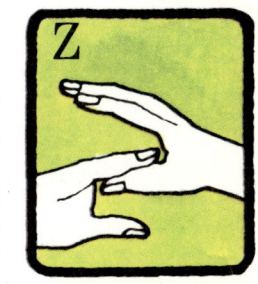

Quick Signs

Yes

No

Understood

Not Understood

Repeat

Morse Code

Morse is a particularly useful code because it can be sent in so many different ways. You can signal it with a buzzer or a whistle or by flashing a torch on a dark night. Morse can also be tapped out or blinked with your eyes. This page shows the Morse code alphabet.

In this code a dot (·) stands for a short signal and a dash (−) stands for a long signal. To time the signals correctly, remember that a dash is always three times as long as a dot. For example, you should flash your torch for a count of one to make a dot and for a count of three to make a dash.

Don't run letters or words together. Between two letters, wait for a count of three. Between two words, wait for a count of five.

Use the extra signals shown below to make sure that your contact is ready to receive your message and that he understands it.

Morse Alphabet

A ·−	H ····	O −−−	V ···−
B −···	I ··	P ·−−·	W ·−−
C −·−·	J ·−−−	Q −−·−	X −··−
D −··	K −·−	R ·−·	Y −·−−
E ·	L ·−··	S ···	Z −−··
F ··−·	M −−	T −	full stop ·−·−·−
G −−·	N −·	U ··−	question mark ··−−··

Sender's Signals

·−·−
This means 'I'm about to send a message'. Wait for the receiver to signal 'ready' before you start.

··−
This means 'end of message'. If the receiver answers 'not understood', repeat the message.

······
This means 'mistake'. When you have mis-spelled a word, repeat the word.

Receiver's Signals

·−
This means 'ready to receive'. At the end of a message it means 'message understood'.

·····
This means 'not ready to receive'. At the end of a message it means 'message not understood'.

Quick Signal Code

This is a special code to use for signalling if you don't have time to learn the whole Morse or semaphore alphabet. With this code you can send any message with just six signals.

The code is made with an alphabet box, like the one used for secret telephone messages (pages 26-27). Each plain letter is replaced by the two code letters that line up with it in the frame of the box. But this time there are just six different code letters in the frame. They are written in capitals at the side and in small letters at the top of the box. The code pair should start with a capital. For example, the code pair used for R is Oi.

Learn the Morse or semaphore signals for the six letters used. Encode the message before you start signalling. Your contact should write down the code message as he receives it and decode it later.

To make the code more secret, start the plain alphabet with a keyword, like 'crazy'. Then add the other letters of the alphabet.

Telephone Messages
You can read off the code pairs like this. Say 'adle' for A, 'eedle' for E, 'idle' for I, 'odle' for O, 'yewdle' for U, and 'wydle' for Y.

If you turn the coded message into Morse you can read it out by saying 'iddy' for a dot and 'umpty' for a dash. Remember to wait for a count of three between two letters. Between two words, wait for a count of five.

Alphabet Box

CODE→LETTERS↓	e	a	i	o	u
E	A	B	C	D	E
A	F	G	H	I	J
I	K	L	M	N	O
O	P	Q	R	S	T
U	U	V	W	X	Y
Y	Z				

Replace each plain letter with the capital letter on its row and the small letter on its column.

Always start with a capital. For example, the code pair for R is Oi.

Break the Code

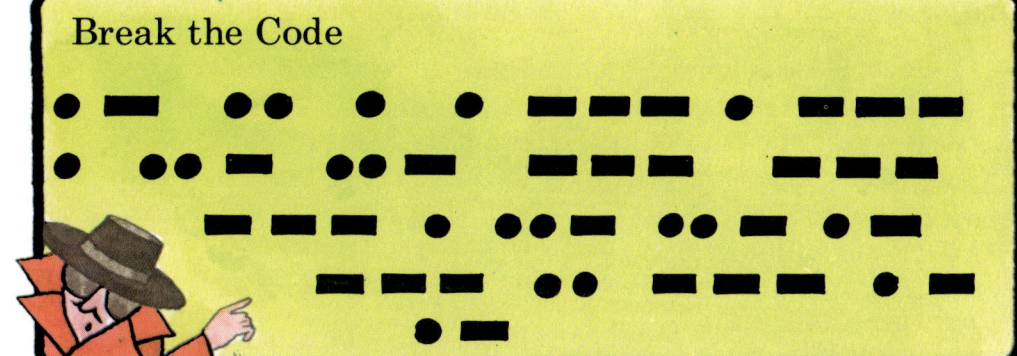

Here is a message Black Hat has just encoded, ready for signalling. Can you break the code?

Remember – the first letter of each code pair comes from the side of the box.

Spy Language

bug – a very small microphone hidden in a room so that people talking in that room can be overheard by the enemy.

contact – a spy friend, particularly one you meet by arrangement.

courier – a spy who carries secret messages or who carries orders from master spy to spy.

dead – 'Victor is dead' means 'Victor has been caught by the enemy'.

dead-letter box – hiding place for secret messages.

drop – hiding place for secret messages.

ill – 'Victor is ill' means 'Victor is being watched by the enemy'.

letter-box – a person who holds secret messages for spies to pick up.

master spy – head of a spy ring.

plain language – a message is in plain language when it has not been encoded.

shadow – someone who is following or 'shadowing' another person.

spy ring – a group of spies who work together. The master spy gives the orders, the couriers carry the orders to the spies, and the spies carry out the orders.

tail – someone who is following or 'tailing' another person.

Answers

Pages 2-3 — There are four secret passwords on these pages They are 'Washington', 'Madrid', 'Paris' and 'Bologna'. Can you find them? (Use pig-pen and a code wheel.)

Pages 6-7 — The clue to the Spy Post Office Trail is 'Volkswagen'.

Pages 8-9 — Here is what the Quick Code Messages say:

At start – 'Meet girl in red hat at clock tower.'
At clock tower – 'Talk about roses to flower seller at fountain.'
At fountain – 'Ask man at statue for light for cigar.'
At statue – 'Stand near church door till old man arrives.'
At church – 'Wait under tree for lady with white cat.'
At tree – 'Man with arm in sling waits on bridge.'
At bridge – 'Buy a dictionary at the book stall and open at page 10.'
At book stall – 'Master Spy was the one you last met.'

Page 10 — The music code message says, 'We leave tonight.' The pig-pen code message says, 'Send new code immediately.' The railfence code says, 'Change the password.'

Page 12 — The message in Code T says, 'Watch out for stranger with black hat.'

Page 14 — The code grille message says, 'Light in east top window means all is lost.'

Page 18 — The password between the lines is 'Coca-Cola'.

Page 20 — The message made by the bees is 'Help is on the way.'

Pages 24-25 — The first few pictures show that the spy is left-handed. The left-handed man in the last picture is the spy, wearing a disguise.

Pages 26-27 — Black Hat is saying, 'Watch out – milkman is a spy.' His contact answers, 'I knew it – the milk is sour.'

The KnowHow Book of
DETECTION

First published in 1978
by Usborne Publishing Ltd
Usborne House
83-85 Saffron Hill, London EC1N 8RT

© Usborne Publishing Ltd 1990, 1978

The name Usborne and the device   are
Trade Marks of Usborne Publishing Ltd.

Printed in Italy

Lettering by J.G. McPherson

MEET SHAMUS

THIS IS DETECTIVE INSPECTOR SHAMUS, HEAD OF FUZZVILLE C.I.D. (CRIMINAL INVESTIGATION DEPARTMENT). HIS LEGENDARY PATIENCE, KNOWLEDGE OF CRIME AND CRIMINALS, AND KEEN EYE FOR DETAIL ARE THE KEYS TO HIS SUCCESS.

OLD BILL...

THIS IS DETECTIVE CONSTABLE WILLIAM WATSON ('OLD BILL'). HE HAS JUST HUNG UP HIS HELMET TO JOIN THE C.I.D. AS A DETECTIVE. HIS OVER-ENTHUSIASM SOMETIMES LEADS TO DISASTER...

AND THE FLAT MAN

THIS IS WEEDY WEEKY—KNOWN AS 'THE FLAT MAN' TO POLICE OF A DOZEN COUNTRIES. USUALLY HE WORKS ALONE BUT THIS TIME HE SEEMS TO HAVE AN ACCOMPLICE... A PARTNER IN CRIME.

READ THEIR STORY TO WATCH A DETECTIVE TEAM AT WORK...AND LEARN HOW TO FOLLOW IN THEIR FOOTSTEPS.

How to Use This Book

A good detective needs special skills, lots of training—and imagination. In this book there is a mystery story to test your imagination. There are also puzzles to solve and projects to teach you skills, like finding a get away car.

Try some of the puzzles as you read the story. See if you can solve the mystery Shamus faces on page 27. Then go back and try the projects.

As you know, a detective is a plain-clothes policeman. After becoming a detective he wears no uniform and works only on solving crimes.

But before this he may spend years as a patrolman—directing traffic, walking his beat, and helping ordinary people in emergencies. This is how he learns to be observant, to think logically, and to keep cool in emergencies.

It takes experience to learn these things, but there are special skills that help a lot. In this book we have given you some tips on these, too.

Our story is set in England, but detective work is very much the same in every country. All over the world the police co-operate—as you can see when you read about Interpol. The fight against crime is international.

The KnowHow Book of Detection

Judy Hindley
and
Donald Rumbelow
(City of London Police
Chairman, British Crime Writers Association, 1978)

Illustrated by Colin King

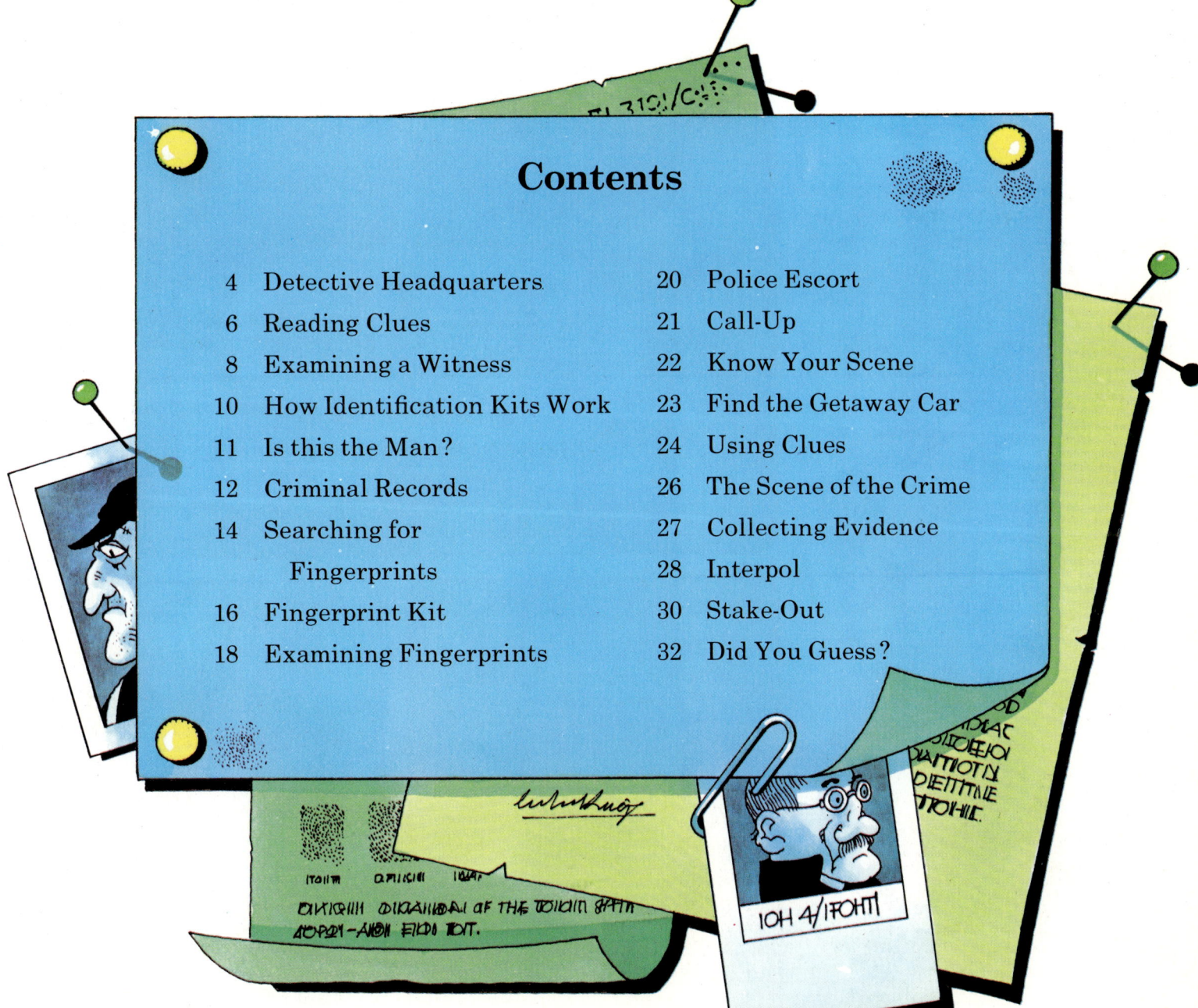

Contents

Detective Headquarters

As a detective, the first thing you must do is set up headquarters (H.Q.). This is where you will keep your reports, your criminal records, your maps of the neighbourhood—all the information you will need in order to act quickly when the time is ripe.

A good detective needs a lot of information. He may spend hours walking slowly round his neighbourhood, getting to know his ground. But he spends even more time at his desk at H.Q., sifting through reports and carefully piecing together tiny facts and clues.

His office may look dusty (police stations never close) but his paperwork must always be in perfect order. He may have twenty cases going at once and he may get new information on any of them. He must be sure each new report is added. Information is his chief weapon in the battle against crime.

Look around the picture on the right to see what you need to set up headquarters. Below you can see the first thing you need—a warrant card.

Warrant Card

A warrant card is a policeman's identity card.

THIS IS FUZZVILLE H.Q.—IT'S BEEN A SLOW DAY—AND DETECTIVE-INSPECTOR SHAMUS IS GETTING RESTLESS.

SHAMUS

BOX FILE

NOTEBOOK

DESK DIARY

IT'S JUST TOO QUIET, BILL. ALL THE VILLAINS SEEM TO HAVE GONE UNDERGROUND ...OR STRAIGHT. I DON'T KNOW WHAT TO MAKE OF IT!

NOT EVEN AN ESCAPED MOUSE IN SIGHT

WARRANT CARD

BACK VIEW

TAPE

PIN

Making a Warrant Card

Cut out a neat piece of white cardboard (or cereal packet with white paper glued over it). Glue on to it a good head-and-shoulders photograph of yourself. Print on it your name and the words 'Warrant Card' and sign it in ink.

If possible, cover the card with see-through plastic. Stick a safety pin on the back with sticky tape and pin it behind your lapel. Then you can flip back your lapel and show it to identify yourself.

Box File

D.I. BLOGGS

A box file is just a handy container for information on the cases you are investigating. Use it to carry things like photographs, reports and statements made by witnesses.

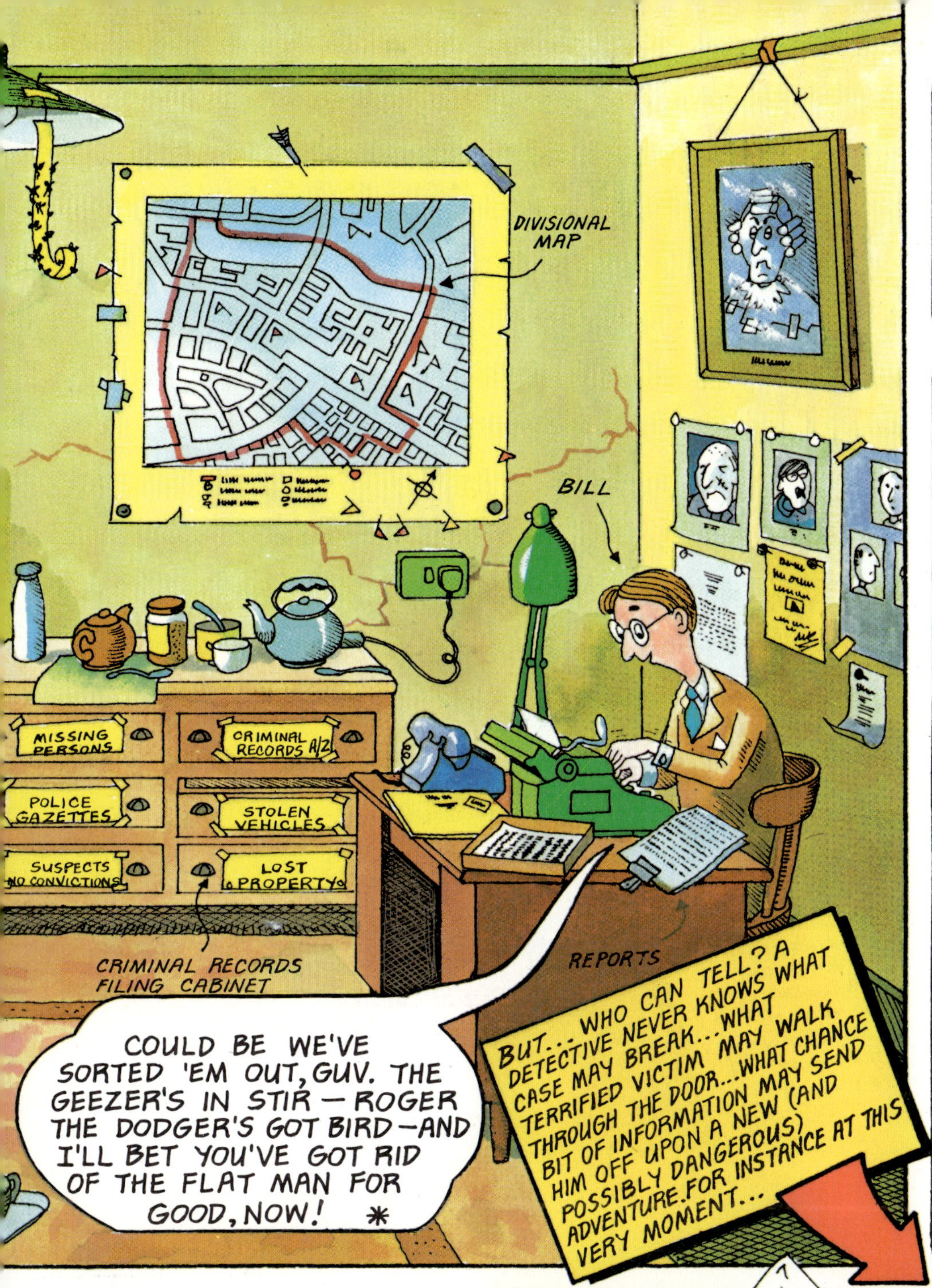

DIVISIONAL MAP
BILL
MISSING PERSONS
CRIMINAL RECORDS A/Z
POLICE GAZETTES
STOLEN VEHICLES
SUSPECTS NO CONVICTIONS
LOST PROPERTY
CRIMINAL RECORDS FILING CABINET
REPORTS
COULD BE WE'VE SORTED 'EM OUT, GUV. THE GEEZER'S IN STIR — ROGER THE DODGER'S GOT BIRD — AND I'LL BET YOU'VE GOT RID OF THE FLAT MAN FOR GOOD, NOW! ✱
BUT... WHO CAN TELL? A DETECTIVE NEVER KNOWS WHAT CASE MAY BREAK... WHAT TERRIFIED VICTIM MAY WALK THROUGH THE DOOR... WHAT CHANCE BIT OF INFORMATION MAY SEND HIM OFF UPON A NEW (AND POSSIBLY DANGEROUS) ADVENTURE. FOR INSTANCE AT THIS VERY MOMENT...

✱ Detective Language

Villain—a criminal
Stir—in prison
Bird—a prison sentence
Gone straight—now honest, stopped commiting crimes.

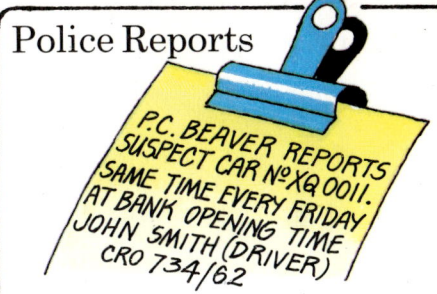

Police Reports

P.C. BEAVER REPORTS
SUSPECT CAR Nº XQ 0011.
SAME TIME EVERY FRIDAY
AT BANK OPENING TIME
JOHN SMITH (DRIVER)
CRO 734/62

All policemen make reports on the information they gather. They clip or 'spike' the reports together, for the person who collects them (known as the collator).

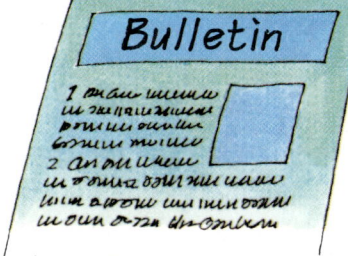

Bulletin

The collator puts all the reports into a kind of news-sheet. Then each policeman can find out what is happening all over his area.

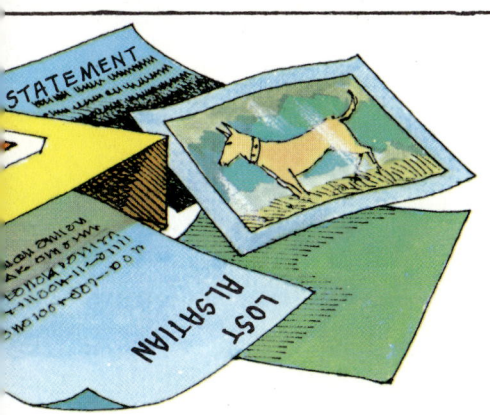

STATEMENT
LOST ALSATIAN

A cereal packet makes an excellent box file. Just be sure to label it with your name along one side, as shown.

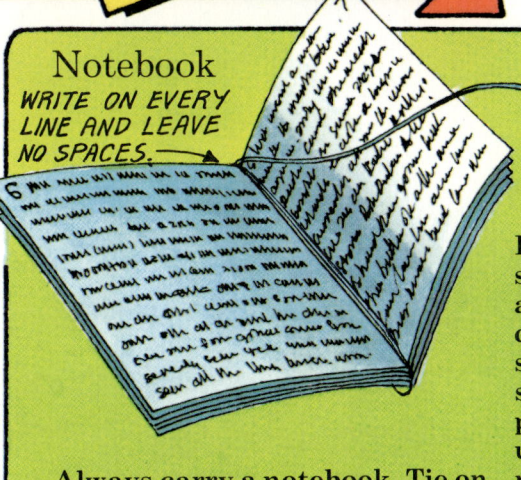

Notebook

WRITE ON EVERY LINE AND LEAVE NO SPACES.

Always carry a notebook. Tie on a pencil with some string, like this. Use it to write down useful information.

For example, make notes of suspicious things, like a car always parked by a bank just at closing time. And try taking statements from people who have seen accidents. Remember—a policeman's notebook may be used in court as evidence. There must be no rubbing out. Each page must be numbered. Leave no gaps in the writing, even for paragraphs.

Reading Clues

LOOK AT THAT...A WOMAN I MIGHT HAVE SEEN ANY DAY RIGHT HERE IN FUZZVILLE... AND IT APPEARS THAT SHE MAY BE A RUSSIAN PRINCESS. AH WELL...LIFE IS REALLY STRANGER THAN FICTION..!

TRUE STORY by SAMANTHA JONES

Overnight Millionairess?

Fuzzville jeweller recognizes local woman's diamond as part of famous Wozinsky fortune. Can she prove her claim to the rest of the fortune?

The WOZINSKY DIAMOND

What is the Story of the Fuzzville Heiress?

A clue is anything that helps you discover new information. It may be very small—a thread, a hair, a shiny screw on an old car number plate. A good detective can get lots of information from tiny details. Try this puzzle to test your skill at reading clues.

Shamus has just learned that a Fuzzville woman may be the long-lost heiress to the Wozinsky fortune. Where did the fortune come from? Why didn't she know about it sooner?

The pictures in the magazine show several clues to the Fuzzville woman's story. Study them carefully, noticing things like flags and buildings. (There is one clue you will find in almost every picture.)

Try to work out the story the pictures tell. Turn the page upside-down to find the answer.

Answer

Olga was the only child of the Wozinskys, a wealthy Russian family. (Notice the flag and jewels in the first picture.) Their lives were threatened by a revolution in Russia. Olga's mother, disguised as a peasant, asked a visiting English army officer to protect Olga. When she heard his train was wrecked she believed Olga had died. He adopted Olga, not realizing who she really was—until her diamond brooch was recognized as possibly linking her to the Wozinskys and their fortune.

7

Examining a Witness

A person who has witnessed a crime is often confused and panicky. At first, it may seem impossible to get any facts from him. One of your most important jobs is to calm him down—only then will he remember what he knows.

Always start by getting the main facts—the very simple things, like the time and place.

These facts will identify your witness if the case comes to court.

Day of the week
Date
Time
Place
Name of the witness
Address
Telephone number
Occupation

These are the most important things you need to know. Going through the list will help to calm your witness. Knowing the list will help you to keep cool.

Never rely on your memory—write down everything your witness says. (Here, Bill is taking notes while Shamus questions Olga).

Now go on to get a description of the case. Ask your witness how he heard of the case, or why he found himself at the scene. Ask him what action he took. Again, write it all down.

When you ask for a description of a place or person, your witness may not know where to start. Help him by asking questions, as Shamus does on the right.

Again, start with simple things like height and weight and get him to compare the person with himself or you. Whenever you can, use examples to jog his memory.

YES, MAURICE HERE — MAURICE WAS *SO* UPSET.

CAN YOU DESCRIBE THE MAN? YOU HAD A GOOD LOOK AT HIM?

HEAVENS, NO... I WAS TOO CONCERNED WITH MAURICE. HE'S STILL OVERWROUGHT, POOR DARLING... HE HAS *SUCH* A SENSITIVE NATURE...

BUT DETECTIVE INSPECTOR SHAMUS HAS FACED THIS KIND OF THING BEFORE.

DEAR LADY, YOU REMEMBER MORE THAN YOU THINK. GO SLOWLY — TODAY IS THURSDAY, MAY 16TH. THE TIME WAS —

GRADUALLY, SHAMUS CALMS THE DISTRAUGHT PRINCESS... AND LITTLE BY LITTLE, PRECIOUS FACTS BEGIN TO COME TO LIGHT...

WHEN YOU ANSWERED THE DOOR, DID YOU LOOK UP INTO HIS FACE? OR DOWN?

NOW LET ME THINK. THERE WAS A CUT ON HIS CHIN — YES, I LOOKED UP.

SLOWLY, WITH INFINITE PATIENCE SHAMUS ESTABLISHES THAT THE VISITOR WAS TALL... VERY TALL. A LEAN, SCOWLING MAN WITH THICK, GREY HAIR...

YACKETY YACKETY YACKETY

AND...

YOU MENTIONED HANGING UP A HAT. COULD YOU DESCRIBE IT? WOULD YOU SAY IT WAS OLD?

NEW? — NO...

— YES!

BROWN? — OH NO!

GREY? — YES —

AND COME TO THINK OF IT, I HAD A QUICK PEEK AT THE LABEL —

THE MAN HAD WORN A BRAND-NEW HAT... SO LARGE IT MIGHT HAVE BEEN BOUGHT TO FIT OVER A THICK GREY WIG...

MOST INTERESTING! BUT LET US LOOK THROUGH THE FILES... PERHAPS YOU CAN IDENTIFY YOUR MAN.

AND TOMORROW, WE'LL GO TO THE BANK WITH THAT VALUABLE ALBUM AND THE DIAMOND.

CERTAINLY, INSPECTOR... CERTAINLY..!

LET'S MAKE A START, THEN!

9

How Identification Kits Work

The identification kit used by police works by building up layers of see-through photographs. Each shows just one feature, such as the chin or nose. It is chosen to match what the witness remembers. The layers can be slid up and down to change the face even more, as the witness remembers details.

In a photofit kit there may be hundreds of chins or noses to choose from, so they are sorted into groups. For example, there may be groups of square jaws or long noses. There are groups of close-together eyes, as well as eyes of different shapes, sizes and colours. There are also lots of different hats and hair styles.

But even one set of features can make several faces, if you squash them close or pull them far apart. Try making the kit shown here, and see what happens when you juggle the bits around. If you have read Olga's description in the story above, you may find a picture of the Flat Man . . . .

Hair and Features

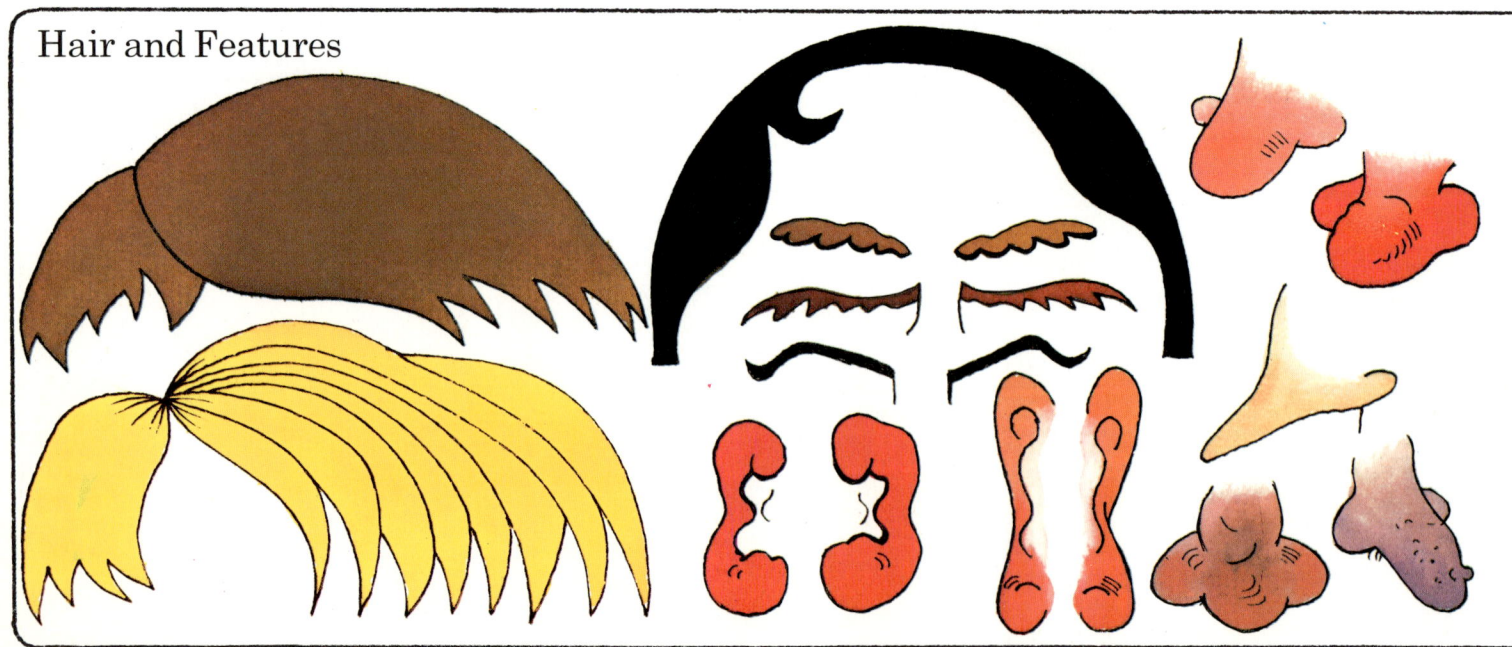

Is this the Man?

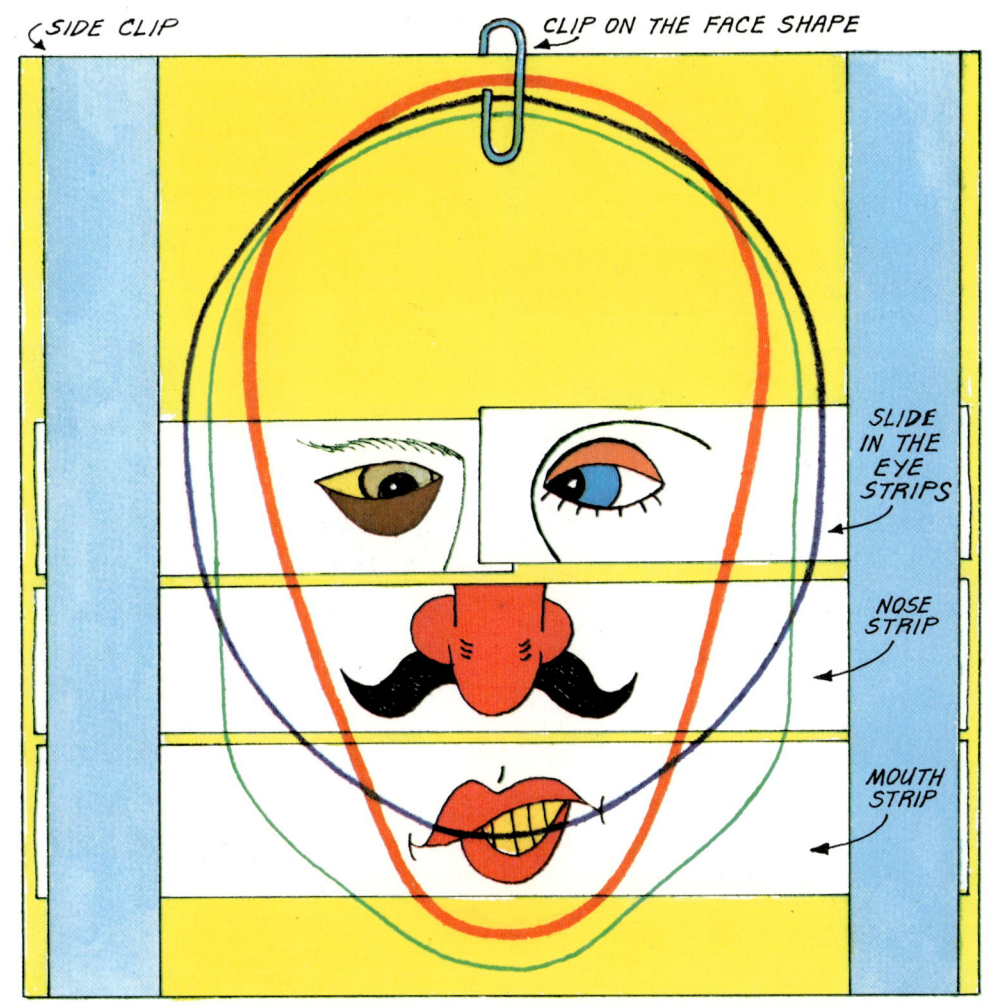

SIDE CLIP

CLIP ON THE FACE SHAPE

SLIDE IN THE EYE STRIPS

NOSE STRIP

MOUTH STRIP

Identi-Fit Kit

You will need
white card
thin paper or tracing paper
strips of stiff paper for the side clips
scissors, glue, pencil and rubber
four or five paper clips

Cut out a piece of card like the one shown on the left. Cut two strips of stiff paper, about 2cm wide and 4cm longer than the square. These are the side clips.

Glue one end of each side clip to the back of the card. When the glue is dry, fold round and glue the other end, pulling it tight. Hold it in place with a paper clip.

To make a face shape, trace the red outline on to a piece of paper about as big as the card. Trace the green and blue outlines separately to make two more shapes. Then trace the bits shown below on strips of paper at least as wide as the card and about 2cm deep.

To use the kit, clip a face shape over the square and try out different features by sliding them under the side clips. Trace over the whole face on a fresh piece of tracing paper to make a record for your criminal files.

Each of these coloured lines is the outline of a face. Trace the one that seems most like the face Olga describes. Trace some noses, mouths and eyes from the bits shown below, and try them on the face. Then turn the page to check your identifit against a genuine picture of the Flat Man.

HAT SHAPES

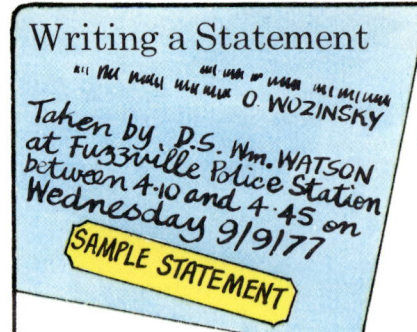

Keeping Records

As soon as you start working on a case, start keeping records. For example, when you are questioning a witness, you or an assistant should take notes. They may help show if the witness is confused, or lying. When the witness has remembered all he can, he should write a statement, as shown here.

Keep all your notes, papers and evidence together in a box file. Label each item with the case number. Remember, it's important to have all the details at your finger-tips.

Writing a Statement

In a statement, the witness should write down exactly what he knows about the case and sign his name, leaving no spaces where words could be added later. Sign your name, too.

Using Case Numbers

If your first case turns up in 1979, its case number will be 1/79. Give each case its own number and use this number on all reports, papers and evidence.

Criminal Records

What Shamus has just found is the Flat Man's criminal record —the papers that describe him and give details of all his criminal activities. Here is the first page.

A record like this is started for each criminal as soon as he is arrested. You can use this form as a model for your own files—just copy the printed part. Page 16 tells how to take fingerprints.

Every suspect is given a number when he is first arrested. This is shown on all his records. The number here shows that the Flat Man was the 883rd criminal in Fuzzville (FV) and was first convicted in 1957.

CRIMINAL RECORD

CRO FV 883/57

883/57   883/57

NAME: Weedy Weeky (BELIEVED FALSE)
D.O.B.: August 23 1937
ALIAS(ES): The Flat Man
DESCRIPTION:
OCCUPATION: Pilot, Racing Driver
HEIGHT: 6'3"   BUILD: Slim
EYES: Grey   COMPLEXION: Sallow   HAIR: Black (Dyed)   MARKS: Scars

PRINTS TAKEN BY INEXPERIENCED OFFICER... SMUDGED BECAUSE TOO MUCH INK WAS USED

FINGERPRINTS
LEFT HAND
THUMB   1   2   3   4

RIGHT HAND
THUMB   1   2   3   4

HABITS

PROPERTY: Gold Pencil, Crowbar, Sausage,
COURT: Fuzzville Mansi
DETAILS CIRCULATED

More Detective Language

Alias—false name
Charge—the particular crime or offence for which the criminal was arrested.
D.O.B.—date of birth

M.O.—(Modus Operandi) the way a particular criminal works. A criminal usually sticks to the same kind of crime and does it the same way. If he lies, he usually sticks to the same story.

The M.O. may help a detective to identify him.
Property—things the criminal was carrying, or things in his pockets when arrested.

13

Searching for Fingerprints

The skin of your fingertips has a pattern of ridges which is special for each person. If you press them on an ink pad and then on paper, you can see the print left by these ridges. The oily sweat on your skin can print the patterns, too. It leaves good prints on polished things like glass or silver—though you need a fingerprint kit to see the details. (The next pages show you how to make one.)

Fingerprints can help you work out who has been at the scene of a crime—but there are tricks to searching for them.

First, when you search a room be careful not to leave your own prints. Avoid touching anything, even the door, with your fingertips. Do not think it will be safe if you wear gloves—this can make you careless. Gloved fingers can smudge good prints, and a split in the glove may let the fingerprint through. (This happens to criminals, too.)

Stop and look about when you enter the room. Then search it carefully and thoroughly. Go over it in a circle (clockwise or anti-clockwise) to make sure you've covered every spot. Make notes of all the places where you see finger-shaped smudges, or where you guess you might find prints. Later you can use your fingerprint kit to develop them (make them show up) and put them in your files.

Follow Detective Shamus round this picture to see how and where to look for fingerprints. Move anti-clockwise, along the path shown by the arrows.

Print-Hunting Practice

A normal fingerprint is just a delicate grease-mark. Usually it takes a slanting light to show it up. You may get the right light by stooping and bending your head, but often you need to pick things up.

Practise examining things without using your fingertips. Use tweezers to lift small things and use a pencil to open and close drawers. Always start at the bottom and work up—then you needn't close each drawer to examine the next one.

To lift a cup or glass, put your fingers inside, as Shamus does. Then open your hand so that it presses against the sides. (Be sure to practise on a plastic cup or tumbler!)

Be careful to touch things as little as possible. Notice how Shamus uses rulers to close a window. The only point touched is the inside corner of the frame—a place where you would never find a print. You can use this trick to open a window too. Always push into the corner—not straight up or down—and push both corners.

With practice you will find lots of ways to move things without touching them. Pencils and tweezers are useful, but you may want to invent your own tools too—like loops of wire, or hooks for lifting things.

Work with a friend to exchange ideas and have contests. Go round a room together and see who is the first to find a fingerprint in each part of it.

Keep in mind the likely spots, like T.V. knobs and light switches. Smooth, polished things show the best prints.

FOR AN INSTANT, A FAMILIAR SILHOUETTE FLICKERS IN THE LIGHTS OF A PASSING CAR. BUT AS SHAMUS LEANS OUT INTO THE DARKNESS, THE DOORBELL RINGS...

BRRRR

Fingerprint Kit

Here is what you need for a fingerprint kit. Notice the special powders used to develop prints. Use them when you search for fingerprints.

For practice, try developing your own prints. First rub your fingertips in your hair to make them oily. Then press them firmly on white paper. Use pencil powder to develop them.

AND HE TURNS TO SEE PRINCESS OLGA WITH A STRANGER...

INSPECTOR, MEET MY NEW FRIEND!

THIS IS SAMANTHA JONES, WHO WROTE THE MAGAZINE STORY... SHE KNOWS EVERYTHING ABOUT ME!

HERE ARE YOUR PHOTOGRAPHS, BUT YOU NEVER GAVE ME THE ALBUM.

OH, I PROMISED NOT TO LET IT GO. WE'RE GOING TO POP IT SAFELY IN THE BANK TOMORROW MORNING AREN'T WE, INSPECTOR?

FUZZVILLE BANK?

YES... JUST UNTIL I GO TO SWITZERLAND.

SHAMUS RETURNS TO WORK FEELING TROUBLED BY THIS INTERRUPTION. BUT THERE IS A JOB TO DO... HE FEELS SURE THAT SOMEWHERE IN THIS ROOM HE WILL FIND A TELL-TALE FINGERPRINT...

Use pencil lead to make dark powder. First, grind off as much wood as possible. Then, holding the pencil over some paper, carefully grind just the tip. Press it gently against the blade of the sharpener. Pour the powder into a container – you only need a bit.

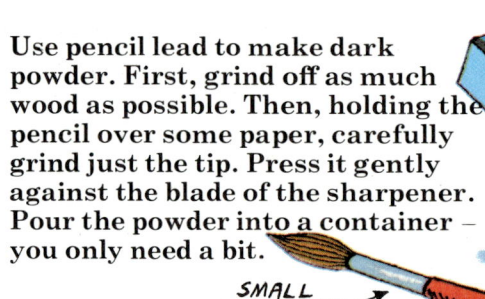

STAMP PAD

SMALL CLEAN DRY PAINTBRUSH

LEAD PENCIL

ROLL OF WIDE STRONG STICKY TAPE

SHARPENER

PAINT PAD

TA PO

SCISSORS

ENVELOPES TO HOLD POWDERS. FOLD SEVERAL TIMES AND FASTEN WITH PAPERCLIPS

PRINTS ON FILE
Elmer T. Bloggs
Aliases used: NONE
LEFT HAND
THUMB 1 2 3 4

To take a print, first 'ink' the finger on a stamp or paint pad, rolling it from side to side. Then press it firmly on the album and roll it from side to side again. Label each set of prints as shown.

When you find prints, you can develop them, lift them and put them in the album. Label to show when and where you found them.

Make an album from a scrapbook. Start by taking prints from all your family—then search for prints to develop and compare. The next pages show how to examine them.

If you don't have a stamp pad, make a paint pad. Use a piece of soft cloth, folded several times. Pour on thick poster paint until the pad is soaked. To take a print, press the finger very lightly on the pad and roll it from side to side.

ECT PRINTS
ce:– and time: 10:00am APRIL 26TH 1978
TOP AND SIDES OF T.V. SET IN FRONT LIVING ROOM IN HOME OF DOCTOR WEIGHT, 48 HOLMES DRIVE, CAMBRIDGE.

① ②

② ③
①

WHERE DISCOVERED ON T.V.

FINGERPRINT ALBUM

MAGNIFYING GLASS

1 Developing Prints

LEAD POWDER HERE

TALCUM HERE

Use talcum powder on dark things and pencil lead on light things. Dip the brush in and gently shake off any extra powder.

2

Brush the powder very lightly from side to side over the spot where you expect to find a print. Be sure to cover a fairly big area.

3

Clean the brush by blowing it or wiping with a tissue. Then carefully brush the loose powder away from the print.

1 Lifting Prints

PRESS FIRMLY

Unroll a length of tape and press it carefully on to the developed print. Then cut the tape.

2

Press down hard on the print and rub it well with your fingernail or a paper clip. This brings the pattern of powder on to the tape.

3

If you peel off the tape carefully, the print will come up, too. You will see it again when you stick the tape down again. Always stick talcum prints on darkish paper.

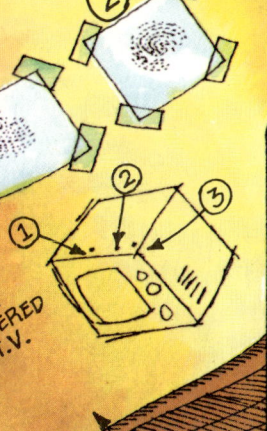
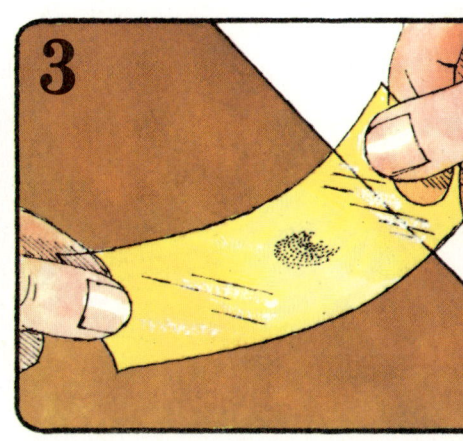

Examining Fingerprints

A fingerprint is one of the most deadly clues a criminal can leave.

First of all, each fingerprint is unique. The tiny ridges of skin on a fingertip make a pattern that is different from any other in the world. Even identical twins have different fingerprints.

Second, your fingerprints never change. No matter how old you become, no matter how well disguised you are, your prints reveal your true identity.

Some criminals have tried to burn away their prints, but when the skin grew back, the patterns came to light again . . . .

Try examining some fingerprints yourself—the main shapes of fingerprints are shown below. On the right, you can see how Detective Shamus examines the prints left by the Flat Man in Princess Olga's flat. Could you identify the Flat Man's fingerprints? The puzzle at the bottom of the page is a chance to try.

ARCH

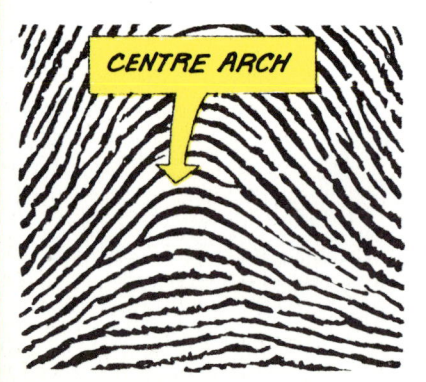

This pattern is called an arch, because the shape in the middle is like an arch. The ridges round it are arch-shaped too.

LOOP

The centre line in a loop is shaped a bit like a hairpin. When you find a loop, you will always find another shape called a delta. The ridges repeat until they get to the delta.

Matching Fingerprints

Take prints of your family and sort them into groups like these—arches, loops, whorls and mixed. (Police files use these groups.) Then find and develop a print from somewhere in your house. See if you can work out whose it is.

Get paper and pencil for taking notes, a metal pointer or sharp pencil for counting ridges and, if you can, a magnifying glass that magnifies 2 times.

Now go to work on the subject print like this:

1. Decide which group the print belongs in (arch, whorl, loop or mixed).
2. Check for identifying marks like cuts and scars.
3. Match the deltas, or any other small shapes you notice.
4. Count the lines (or ridges) between these shapes, to see if the number is the same.

When counting, always start at the centre shape and work outwards until you reach a new shape or odd-looking ridge. Make a quick sketch of it. Then go back to the centre and work outwards in a new direction. Always follow a pattern (clockwise or anti-clockwise) and keep notes as you work. The notes might look like this:

1. Whorl.
2. Small cut lower left.
3. 34 lines between right-hand edge of whorl and the next shape. (Draw the shape.)

WHORL

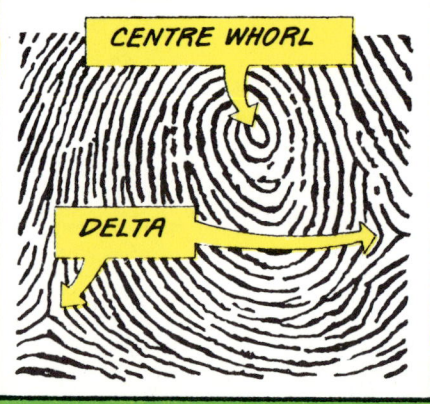

A pattern with a line that curls up in the middle is called a whorl. It may be circular or long. It always has two deltas, one each side.

MIXED

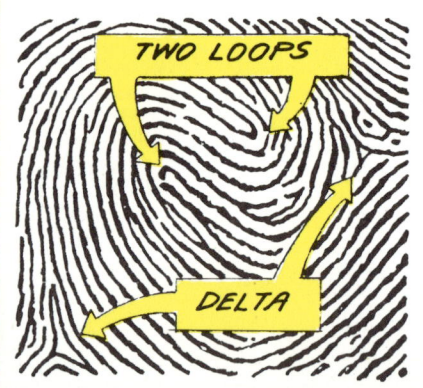

There are many kinds of mixtures. One of the commonest is a double-loop. The line right in the centre bends back upon itself.

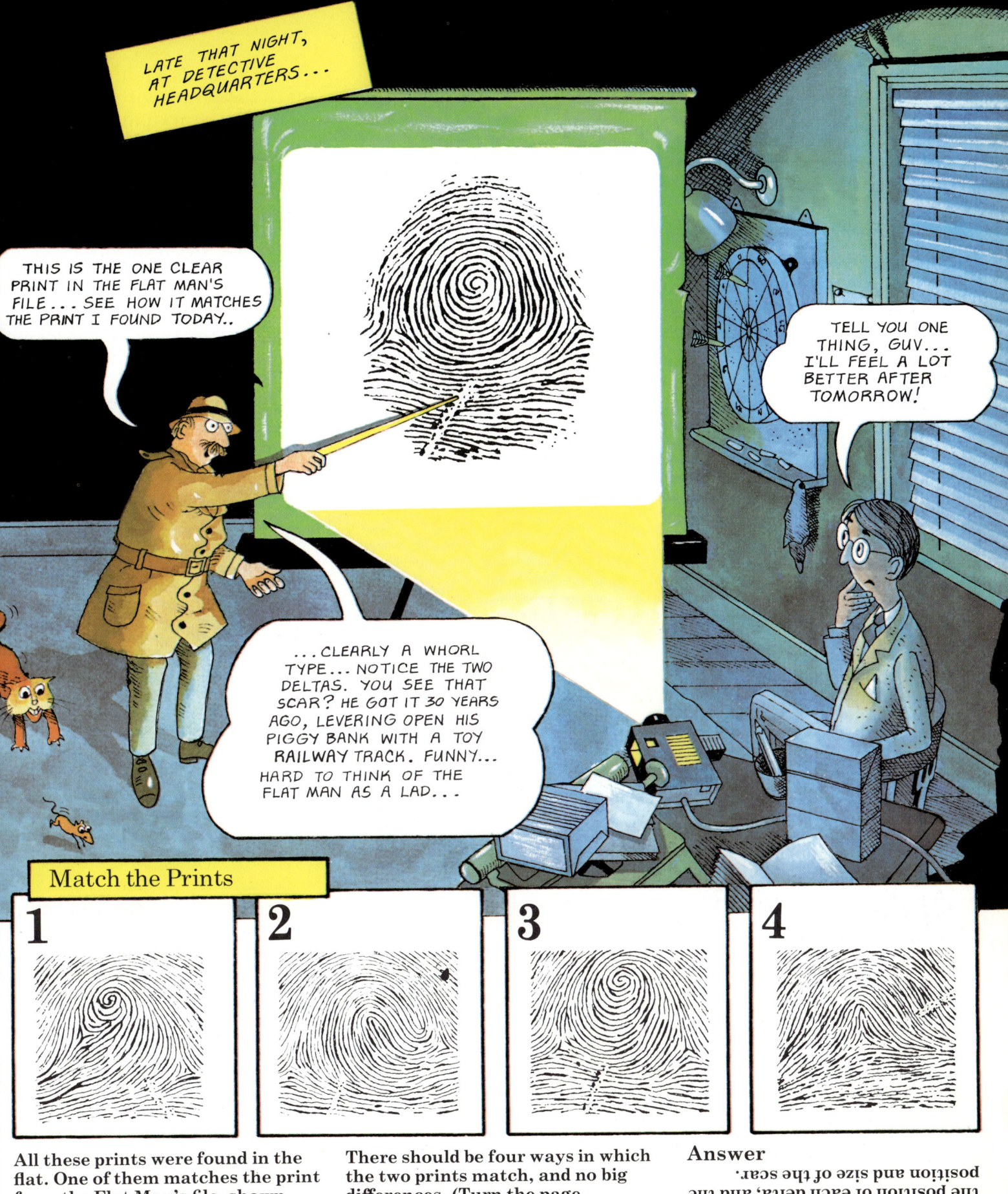

Police Escort

Police are often asked to protect valuable things or Very Important People (sometimes called V.I.P.s) as they are taken from place to place. This is called an 'escort'. The police stay close to the V.I.P., ready to shield him from attack and get him clear of danger.

It may take years of practice to get a feel for all the places where danger might be lurking, and the kinds of ordinary-looking event which may really be the start of a clever attack. However, it will help if you remember these main points:

1. Two people make a good escort team—one to walk just ahead of the V.I.P., one behind.
2. Be specially cautious at corners and points where you can't see the route ahead.
3. Steer clear of possible hiding places like doorways.
4. Stay alert at all times.

Escort Practice

For escort practice, you need at least three people. One is the detective, one is the criminal, and one is the V.I.P.

Pin some paper to the V.I.P.'s shoulder to make a target. The criminal needs a felt pen to mark the target with. Plan a route with start and finish points. Give the criminal five minutes to hide himself along the route. Then as the escort walks past, the criminal tries to mark the V.I.P.'s paper badge. The detective can stop him by shouting 'Criminal Alert!' before he strikes. He must hide again after each try, whether he strikes or is caught. (This can be a game if you take turns. The detective whose V.I.P. gets the least shoulder marks from Start to Finish is the winner.)

Call-Up

As a detective, there may be times when you need help fast. This is when you use a radio call-up.

Every policeman has a two-way radio which links him to radio control (the operator shown in the centre, below). With the flick of a switch, he can use his radio to contact control. If he says 'Emergency!' control stops all other calls to take his message.

Control can broadcast calls for help to every police radio in the area.

Your radio calls should be short and clear. Begin with the code for control (FV for Fuzzville) and give your number or name and rank. For instance, 'FV from 663, a message, 663 over.' (The word 'over' means you have finished speaking.) In a crisis, start by saying 'emergency'.

When spelling names or giving car numbers, it may be hard to say the letters clearly. Use the international call-up alphabet shown on the right. In this, an easy-to-hear word stands for each letter.

Call-Up Alphabet

A — Alpha	N — November
B — Bravo	O — Oscar
C — Charlie	P — Papa
D — Delta	Q — Quebec
E — Echo	R — Rome
F — Foxtrot	S — Sierra
G — Golf	T — Tango
H — Hotel	U — Uncle
I — India	V — Victor
J — Juliet	W — Whisky
K — Kilo	X — Xray
L — Lima	Y — Yankee
M — Mike	Z — Zebra

Using this alphabet, the car number 'JFB 3H' is 'Juliet Foxtrot Bravo 3 Hotel'.

21

Know Your Scene

You must know your neighbourhood thoroughly to set up a road-block. You must know the times and places where traffic might be heavy and where the criminals might slip the net (like motorway entrances). You must know every one-way road and short-cut, to plan where your team should be waiting.

Once a call-up starts, you should be able to seal off the area in minutes.

Unfortunately, experienced criminals expect this—and plan for it. A criminal usually tries to dump his getaway car, and switch to a different kind of car or transport, before he hits the road-block.

But the abandoned car may hold a vital clue, like a set of fingerprints—or it may help pinpoint the criminal's whereabouts. The sooner you find it, the more useful it is.

When you are searching for a getaway car, try to put yourself into the criminal's place. What do you think his final destination is—a river, an airport, a motorway? What dangers must he avoid, like crowds and traffic? Where might he find a spot to switch his car without being seen?

A good map of your neighbourhood is all-important. Below you can see how to prepare it.

Preparing a Map

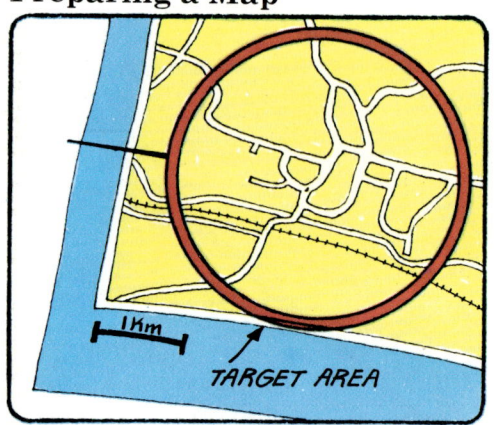

First get a street plan of your area. Try the local library, a bus station or an estate agent's. Mark in red the main target for criminal attack—the bank or the jeweller.

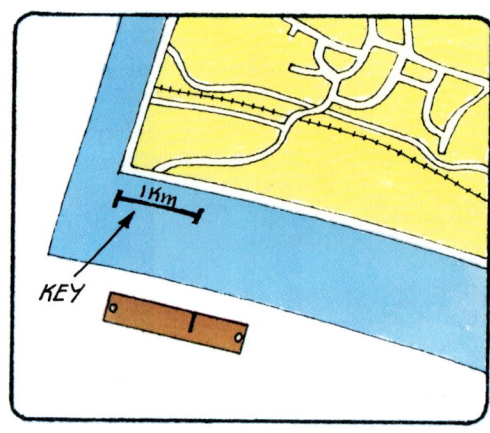

Use the 'key' or 'legend' in the corner of the map to measure a strip of cardboard that stands for 2 km. Make a small hole at each end of the strip.

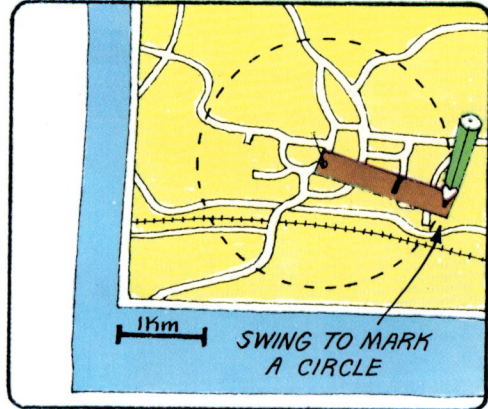

Stick a pin through one hole in to the 'target' area. Stick a pencil through the other hole. Swing it to make a circle. This shows where your road-block should be set up.

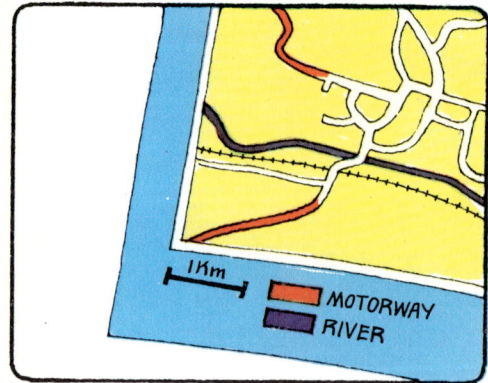

Use coloured pencils to mark points the criminals might head for, like motorways, rivers and roads that lead to airports. Then glue the map to a piece of card.

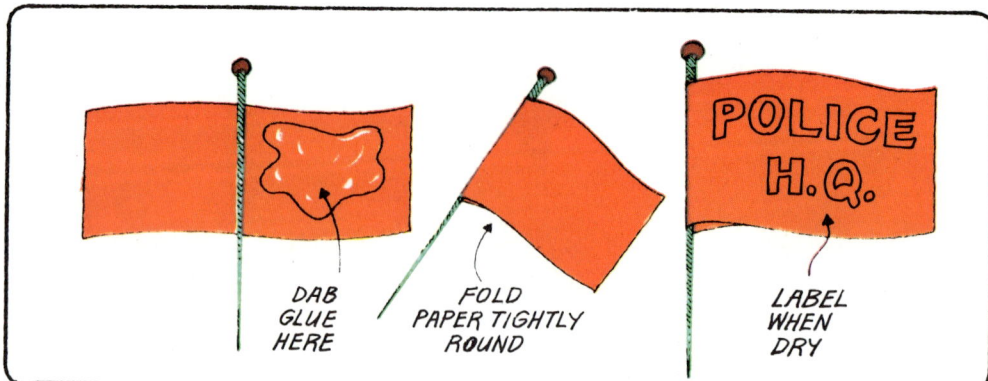

Make flags, like these, to mark all the spots you may need to know in an emergency—like your local hospital, police and fire stations. Mark all the phone boxes—you never know when you'll need one.

Then search your neighbourhood for spots to dump a getaway car, like old yards and warehouses. Look for taxi-ranks or railway stations; the criminal may need them if his car-swap fails. Mark these, too.

Find the Getaway Car

Now that the alarm has been given, the Fuzzville police are looking for the Maserooni J8. They have a description of the car and the criminals and the car number plate. In any case, a Maserooni is hard to miss. But this, of course, is part of the Flat Man's plan.

Like all experienced criminals, the Flat Man knows he must dump his getaway car very fast. Knowing the car will have been spotted, heading east for the M10, he is now heading back towards the bank.

Below you can see the area inside the road-block. Somewhere in this area the Flat Man must get rid of the Maserooni and begin the next stage of his getaway. Can you work out where and how he will do it? (Page 32 shows the answer.)

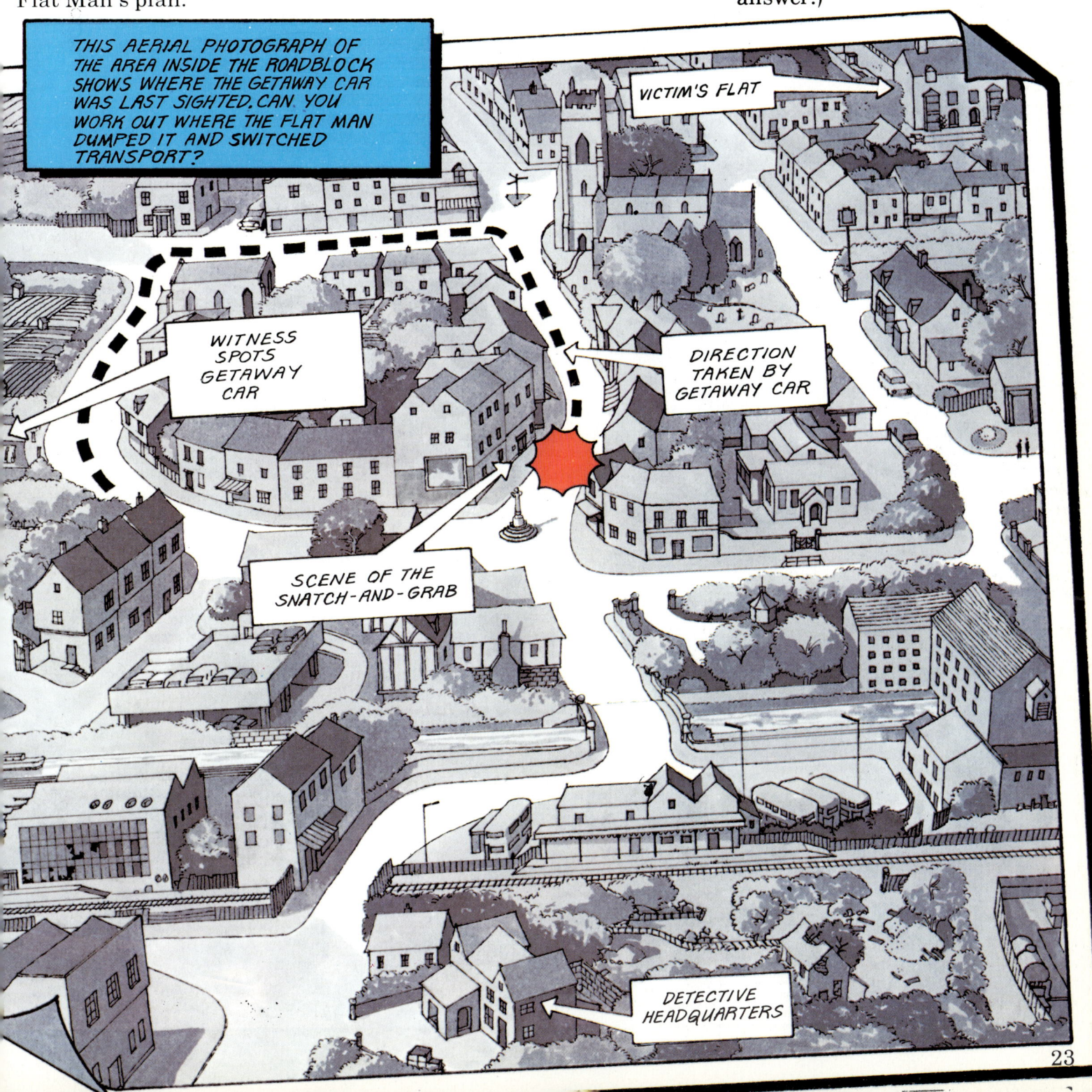

THIS AERIAL PHOTOGRAPH OF THE AREA INSIDE THE ROADBLOCK SHOWS WHERE THE GETAWAY CAR WAS LAST SIGHTED. CAN YOU WORK OUT WHERE THE FLAT MAN DUMPED IT AND SWITCHED TRANSPORT?

VICTIM'S FLAT

WITNESS SPOTS GETAWAY CAR

DIRECTION TAKEN BY GETAWAY CAR

SCENE OF THE SNATCH-AND-GRAB

DETECTIVE HEADQUARTERS

23

Using Clues

Even the most experienced criminal often gives himself away by tiny clues left at the scene of the crime. Some clues may give you a good idea of who (or where) the criminal is. (This is called a 'lead'.) Clues may also be used as evidence (to help prove your case in a law court.)

Anything the criminal left or marked or disturbed may turn out to be an important clue—if you know how to use it. Keep each clue in a plastic bag and label it. (The police make plaster casts of things like teethmarks and footprints.) Follow Bill round the laboratory on the right to see some of the ways science can help.

POLICE PHOTOGRAPH TAKEN AT THE SCENE OF THE CRIME

Find the Clues

The villains who snatched Olga's valuables have left at least four clues at the scene of the crime. Can you find them?

Answers

1. Wig (one of the criminal's hairs may have stuck to it)
2. Cap (same reason—the criminal may have worn it on his real hair)
3. Footprint (see below on what footprints can show)
4. Plank (see what the plank shows on the right)

Reading Footprints

To get clues from footprints, you need to study how they are made. Practice with several pairs of shoes, like those shown below. Try to work with friends who are bigger, smaller or a different weight, so you can compare prints and test each other.

Work on damp sand or fine, damp earth and rake or smooth it before you start. Be very careful not to pack it down.

First walk on it normally, in different pairs of shoes. Measure each sole and compare it to its print. Then try running and limping in the same shoes and see where the shoe presses down. Try a standing jump to see where your toes dig in. Notice what happens if you are carrying a heavy load.

Notice that a new shoe may print the maker's name or trademark. This may help you solve a case.

The maker of the shoes will have a list of stockists (shops that sell his shoes). You can go round to the nearby stockists and question them. If you know the brand and size, a shop assistant may still remember the people who bought them. This could help narrow down your list of suspects.

Remember, even the size of the print may tell you something important about who made it.

Compare these Shoes and Shoe-Prints

HIGH HEEL

SHOE WITH HEEL

SMOOTH-SOLED SANDAL

RUNNING SHOE

WALKING BOOT

GUM BOOT

OLD SHOE WITH WORN HEEL AND SOLE

SMALL NEW SHOE

LARGE NEW SHOE

NOTICE HOW THE SHAPE CHANGES AS THE SHOE GETS OLD.

SMALL OLD SHOE

LARGE OLD SHOE

SMALL NEW SHOE

LARGE NEW SHOE

AS SHAMUS DIRECTS OPERATIONS AT THE SCENE OF THE SNATCH, HE KEEPS IN TOUCH WITH RADIO CONTROL. AT LAST...

THEY GOT AWAY, GUV... WE FOUND THE CAR. THEIR BOILER SUITS WERE INSIDE.

I'LL TAKE A LOOK AT THE GETAWAY CAR... YOU TAKE THIS LOT TO THE LAB, BILL.

IN FUZZVILLE'S FORENSIC SCIENCE LABORATORY...

RUSH JOB I'M AFRAID!

AGAIN? YOUR GOVERNOR SENT SOME PACKETS FROM THE FLAT LAST NIGHT.

RIGHT, LADS... PRIORITY CRIME. STOP EVERYTHING AND START ON THIS LOT!

HAVE YOU GOT ANYTHING FROM LAST NIGHT?

OH YES... THE LADS HAVE BEEN BUSY.

FANCY A SANDWICH?

WE GOT A GOOD CAST OF THE BITES.

PLASTER CAST

THE TEETHMARKS ARE DEFINITELY THE FLAT MAN'S. H'MMM... CLEVER OF SHAMUS TO SPOT HIS M.O.!*

FLAT MAN'S DENTAL CHART

*M.O.— MODUS OPERANDI (THE FLAT MAN IS A NERVOUS NIBBLER.)

BILL WATCHES EAGERLY AS THE WORK BEGINS...

AS THE CRIMINAL'S CAP IS CAREFULLY UNSTITCHED (A HAIR COULD BE INSIDE.)

AS THE WIG IS EXAMINED FOR ANY LOOSE HAIRS THAT MAY BELONG TO THE CRIMINAL...

AS EACH HAIR IS MOUNTED BETWEEN GLASS SLIDES, TO GO UNDER A MICROSCOPE...

AND EVEN THE PLANK IS THOROUGHLY CHECKED...

LOOK AT THIS SMEAR OF PAINT. I'LL BET IT'S MEANT TO HIDE SOMETHING!

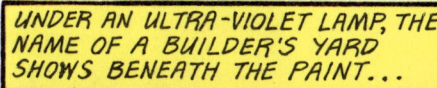

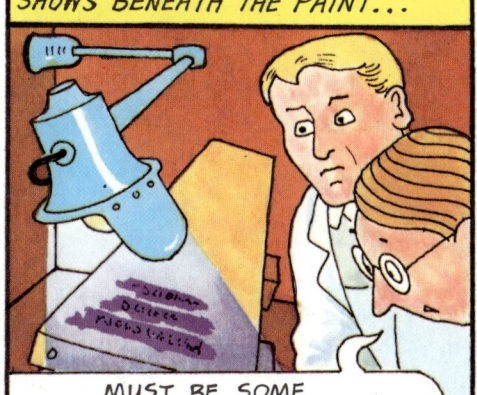

UNDER AN ULTRA-VIOLET LAMP, THE NAME OF A BUILDER'S YARD SHOWS BENEATH THE PAINT...

MUST BE SOME **REASON** WHY IT WAS PAINTED OUT. ANOTHER LEAD..?

AT LAST, BILL RETURNS TO H.Q. WITH THE REPORTS. BUT HIS DAY ISN'T OVER YET...

Come to Olga's flat there's been a break-in Shamus

25

The Scene of the Crime

Try to keep calm when you face the confusion left at the scene of a crime. A lot may depend on what you notice and what you do. Keep these rules in mind.

1 Look First—Don't Touch

Don't touch anything until the scene has been examined and dusted for fingerprints.

2 Follow a Method

Make your examination step-by-step. Look for fingerprints first. Use your kit to pick up any prints you find. Then, slowly circle the room again. Look for anything the criminal might have touched or left.

3 Use Your Notebook

Write down everything interesting you see. Don't leave out any detail that might be useful. Remember that what you notice and write down may be used as evidence.

4 Clues and Evidence

The next page shows tips on gathering evidence.

5 Take Full Statements

Ask victims and witnesses to tell you everything they can (see page 8)and write it down. Take the full name and address of any person mentioned.

Remember, it may be a long time until your case goes to court. Your notebook must give a complete picture of what happened today.

6 Search Thoroughly

Now it doesn't matter if you disturb things. Look everywhere —even in dustbins and drain-pipes—for anything the criminal might have left. (Even the stub of a train ticket might give you an important lead.)

7 Work out a Story

From the start, try to work out what happened, to get an idea of what to look for.

Collecting Evidence

Which ball broke the window? The position of the evidence may give you a clue. (Check your answer on page 32).

BALL № 1
2M. FROM DOOR
1·8M. FROM NORTH WALL.

BALL № 2
2·7M. FROM EAST WALL.
3·5M. S.W. OF TREE.

BROKEN GLASS SCATTERED AS FAR AS 1M. INSIDE OF DOOR.

Put each piece of evidence in a plastic bag. Don't touch it—use tweezers. Or push it on to some card, then into the bag.

Before you remove the evidence, take a photograph or make a sketch to show where you found it. The exact position may be vital.

Give at least two measurements, as shown, to pinpoint a position. Measure from things, like walls or trees, that stay in the same spot.

Label the bag to show the case-number and your name. Later you can examine the evidence more thoroughly.

SAFE?

I NEVER DREAMED THEY'D LOOK UNDER THE MATTRESS!

WELL, THE STORY'S CLEAR ENOUGH! WHILE THE PRINCESS WAS HELPING US AT H.Q. THEY ABANDONED THE GETAWAY CAR, BROKE INTO THE FLAT, AND GOT THE DIAMOND. THE EARTH UNDER THE WINDOW IS COVERED WITH FOOTPRINTS. AND WE FOUND A TRACE OF PAINT ON THE CARPET. IF MY HUNCH IS RIGHT IT'LL TIE IN WITH THIS MORNING'S JOB!

BUT WE KNOW IT'S THE FLAT MAN... DON'T WE?

I'M NOT SO SURE, JUST TAKE A LOOK AT THIS!

BUT THIS IS AMATEUR STUFF! THIS LOT OF DRAWERS WAS OPENED TOP TO BOTTOM... THE FLAT MAN DOESN'T OPERATE LIKE THAT.

RIGHT! AND THE PRINCESS CLAIMS THAT CLOTHES ARE MISSING. NOTICE THE OPENED PERFUME BOTTLES... LONG BLONDE HAIR IN THE COMB... AND UNDER THE LEFT-HAND SET OF DRAWERS WE FOUND...

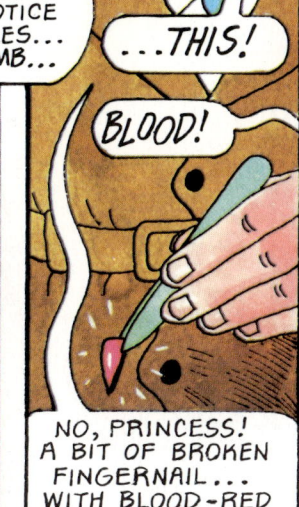

...THIS!

BLOOD!

NO, PRINCESS! A BIT OF BROKEN FINGERNAIL... WITH BLOOD-RED VARNISH!

IF IT'S THE FLAT MAN, HE MUST HAVE AN ACCOMPLICE! WE KNOW IT'S AN AMATEUR, AND PROBABLY A WOMAN.

BUT WHO? AND WHY?

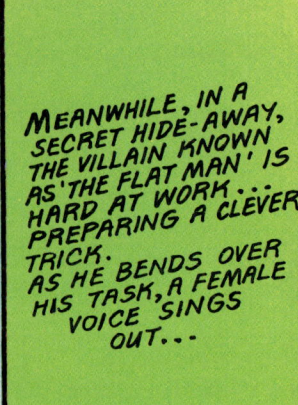

MEANWHILE, IN A SECRET HIDE-AWAY, THE VILLAIN KNOWN AS 'THE FLAT MAN' IS HARD AT WORK PREPARING A CLEVER TRICK. AS HE BENDS OVER HIS TASK, A FEMALE VOICE SINGS OUT...

♫ HAVE YOU UNSTITCHED THE PAGE?

WOZINSKY FAMILY ALBUM

YEAH... ALMOST!

♫ HAND IT OVER. I'LL KEEP IT IN MY HANDBAG...JUST IN CASE.

HOW ABOUT THE FORGERY?

♫ I'M JUST DABBING ON SOME PHONEY FINGERPRINTS..!

♫ WELL?

I DON'T LIKE IT, BABE... BEFORE THIS, I ALWAYS WORKED ALONE.

AH, BUT YOU NEED ME—DON'T YOU. COULD YOU IMPERSONATE * THE PRINCESS?

*IMPERSONATE—TRY TO LOOK AND ACT LIKE A CERTAIN PERSON.

NOW THEN, STITCH THIS PHONEY PAGE IN THE ALBUM, AND WE'LL BE READY!

IS THE HELICOPTER READY?

YEAH, THE COPTER'S WAITING!

WE'VE GOT IT ALL! FORGED PASSPORT...THE ALBUM WITH THE DOCTORED PAGE...THE DIAMOND...AND TOMORROW..

...THE WOZINSKY FORTUNE!

WHO IS THIS WOMAN?

28

MEANWHILE, AT FUZZVILLE DETECTIVE HEADQUARTERS...

WHOEVER THE VILLAINS ARE THEY'LL SOON BE HEADING FOR SWITZERLAND TO CLAIM THE FORTUNE. WE'VE GOT TO STOP THEM.

INTERPOL!

RIGHT AGAIN, OLD BILL. GET ME PARIS HEADQUARTERS.

Interpol

Many dangerous criminals roam from country to country in their search for riches—and their flight from detection. They try to escape to places where they are unknown.

They can only be stopped if the police of different countries band together, exchanging help and information. This is the purpose of the International Criminal Police Organization—known as Interpol.

Over 100 countries belong to Interpol. Each country is ready to share its information with the rest and take up the hunt when a criminal is thought to have crossed its borders. Each helps pay for special services like news bulletins and telephone links.

Interpol has its headquarters in Paris. It has its own laboratories to test for counterfeits and forgeries. Once a year it holds a meeting, where police sent from each country discuss crime problems shared by all.

But Interpol does its most vital work through its telex and telephone services. In minutes they can link police a thousand miles apart—and start tightening the net around a criminal.

WITHIN MINUTES A CALL GOES OUT FROM LONDON TO PARIS...

THEN FROM PARIS TO EVERY COUNTRY ON THE SWISS BORDER. SOON THE POLICE OF EACH COUNTRY HAVE A DESCRIPTION OF THE CRIMINALS.

WHILE THE FAMOUS OLD SWISS BANK THAT GUARDS THE WOZINSKY FORTUNE IS IMMEDIATELY PUT ON THE ALERT.

SHAMUS HIMSELF WARNS THE MANAGER OF THE SWISS BANK...

BE ON YOUR GUARD FOR IMPOSTERS!

BUT, MONSIEUR SHAMUS, I HAVE JUST HAD A CALL FROM PRINCESS OLGA. SHE IS ARRIVING TOMORROW MORNING AT 11.00.

THIS IS SERIOUS...IT MUST BE THE FLAT MAN'S ACCOMPLICE. SHE'LL BE STAKING HER CLAIM IN LESS THAN 15 HOURS.

OH! IT'S TOO DREADFUL! AND ONLY TODAY MY PASSPORT FINALLY ARRIVED!

BUT THAT'S A PIECE OF LUCK. YOU'RE COMING WITH US...TO SWITZERLAND.

THAT. NIGHT...

I TELL YOU, BILL... THIS TIME I'M GOING TO TRAP THEM.

YOU MEAN...A STAKE OUT?

Stake-Out

A stake-out is a police trap. It is set up when detectives know a certain target will be attacked. They plan things so that the villains can get into the trap without spotting the detectives —but can't get out.

Detectives near the target may be disguised as shop assistants or bank clerks. Those outside are disguised as shoppers, window-cleaners—even tramps. Hidden all round are unmarked police cars and motor bikes.

One detective acts as 'eyes'. Usually he watches from some point like an upper window. He radios news of the villain's movements to the other detectives and signals when it's time to spring the trap.

BY MID-MORNING THEY ARRIVE AT THE SWISS BANK...

DON'T BE LONG, BILL...JUST GIVE HIM A QUICK WALK ROUND THE BLOCK!

...WHERE THE MANAGER AWAITS THEM IN THE VAULTS.

THIS IS THE REAL PRINCESS!

SUCH ELEGANCE ...TRULY, HER BLUE BLOOD SHOWS!

WE HAVE ONLY AN HOUR TO PREPARE. WHEN THE IMPOSTER ARRIVES, PRETEND TO BELIEVE HER STORY. IT'S HER ACCOMPLICE I WANT... WE MUSTN'T SPRING THE TRAP 'TIL WE'VE GOT THEM BOTH!

BUT THE STAKE-OUT PLANS ARE DOOMED. AT THAT VERY MOMENT A CAR WITH TWO FAMILIAR PASSENGERS IS DRAWING UP...AS ALWAYS, THE FLAT MAN IS AT LEAST ONE STEP AHEAD.

IT'S THE SECURITY OFFICER. THE FAKE PRINCESS HAS ARRIVED!

QUICK...THE EMERGENCY STAIRS. WE'LL HAVE TO MANAGE WITHOUT OLD BILL!

THIS WAY, PRINCESS. WE'LL HIDE IN THE FOYER.

I AM OLGA... HEIRESS TO THE WOZINSKY FORTUNE.

DO YOU HAVE PROOF?

OF COURSE...THIS DIAMOND...AND THE OLD FAMILY ALBUM WITH MY FINGERPRINTS.

VERY GOOD! BUT WE MUST COMPARE YOUR FINGERPRINTS WITH THE ALBUM. A MERE FORMALITY...

AND SO...

PRINCESS OLGA CLAIMS THE WOZINSKY FORTUNE...

AND DEVOTES HERSELF TO REWARDING HER FAITHFUL COMPANION.

WON'T YOU HAVE JUST ONE MORE SAUSAGE, DARLING?

PERHAPS I CAN SELL THE STORY!

SAMANTHA JONES, FORMERLY OF THE PICTURE NEWS, IS JAILED FOR HER PART IN THE ATTEMPTED FRAUD.

AND D.I. SHAMUS AND D.C. WILLIAM WATSON TAKE UP THEIR DUTIES AGAIN AT FUZZVILLE POLICE H.Q.

WELL GUV, I GUESS IT'S BACK TO THE QUIET LIFE..!

I WONDER...

H'MMM..!

AS FOR THE NOTORIOUS WEEDY WEEKY (ALIAS 'THE FLAT MAN') WHO CAN TELL....?

Did You Guess?

One of the people who knew most about Olga's claim to the fortune—who had an introduction to Olga and a chance to get hold of photographs to help forge identification papers—was the writer of the magazine story. This, as you may remember, was Samantha Jones.

The opportunity was immediately clear to the Flat Man, who read the story in the Picture News. He contacted Samantha and helped her plan the fraud. Through her friendship with Olga, he learned what he needed to know about Olga's plans and movements.

He helped Samantha steal the diamond and the old family album, so they could take out the page showing Olga's baby fingerprints—and put in a phoney page with Samantha's fingerprints. With these they could have claimed the fortune—if they had not been outwitted by D.I. Shamus.

Helping Police

Remember—information is the key to crime-fighting.

Practise describing people you see, making quick notes on their main features and what they wear. Learn to recognize different kinds of car and to memorize car numbers quickly.

Most important, learn how to telephone emergency services, like the police. If you see a crime or accident, phone the police immediately

DON'T TAKE RISKS— NEVER TRY TO STOP A CRIMINAL!

Answers

Page 23 The car-swap took place at the two-storey car park near the bank.

Page 27 The direction in which the broken glass fell shows that the window was probably broken by a ball thrown in from the garden when the door was closed.

The KnowHow Book of
Batteries and Magnets

Additional projects:
Neil Thompson

Models for photography:
Lynda Bland

Photographs:
George Pennington

Educational Advisers:
Frank Blackwell and Sally Chaplin

First published in 1975 by Usborne Publishing Ltd
Usborne House, 83-85 Saffron Hill,
London EC1N 8RT, England

© Usborne Publishing Ltd 1989, 1975

**This edition contains the
best projects from the
original 48-page version.**

Printed in Belgium.

About This Book

This is a book about lots of games and models which work with a battery or a magnet. They are all quite simple to make if you look at the pictures and read the instructions carefully. The measurements given are only a guide. You can make them any size you like.

For the games and models, you will need a magnet, a battery, a few torch bulbs and some pieces of flex and wire. There is a Shopping List **on page 8** to show you what to ask for. You can probably find pieces of cardboard and boxes at home.

In the pictures the flex to be joined up is coloured red to make it very clear. When it is finished with, it is white again. When you make the games and models, you can cover them with coloured paper as you go along, or paint them when they are finished.

Batteries will last quite a long time if you switch the lights or electro-magnets off when you are not playing with them. When a battery is worn out, throw it away at once, or it may leak and spoil the model or game.

Warning

All the projects in this book are absolutely safe if you always use a 4·5 volt battery. NEVER play with electricity from the mains.

The KnowHow Book of Batteries and Magnets

Heather Amery and Angela Littler

Illustrated by Zena Flax and Pierre Davies
Designed by John Jamieson and Jim Laidlaw

Contents

Lots of Tricks with Magnets

You cannot see why a magnet works but you can have lots of fun picking up and moving things with it. Buy a strong horseshoe or bar magnet and find out what it will do. The stronger the magnet the more it will pick up. Remember to treat your magnet gently. If you drop or bang it, it will lose some of its magnetism. Keep magnets away from your watch or it may be damaged and stop working properly.

The Paper Clip Trick

Try this trick and puzzle your friends. The paper clip will hang in the air for as long as you like to leave it. It looks like magic but the paper clip is held up by a magnet in a matchbox.

You will need
a small horseshoe magnet
a matchbox
a long piece of thin thread
a paper clip
sticky tape and scissors

1 Paper Clip Trick

Put the magnet in a matchbox like this. Hold the box against the edge of a shelf and stick it in place with tape.

Magnetizing Things

Make another magnet by stroking a needle eight or nine times with a magnet. Always stroke it in the same direction. Then try picking up a pin with the needle.

Magnetic Chains

Pick up a paper clip with a magnet. Then try to make a chain by sticking more clips to the first one. The stronger the magnet, the longer will be the chain.

Try picking up lots of things with a magnet and find out what will stick to it. Or try sticking a small magnet to big things.

Find out if a magnet will work through paper, cardboard and wood. Hold a magnet underneath and try moving pins and nails on top.

Stick one end of a long piece of thread to the shelf below with tape. Hook a paper clip on to the thread and hold it up to the matchbox. Let go when it sticks.

Pull the free end of the thread down very gently until the paper clip is floating just below the matchbox. Stick the thread down with tape to the shelf below.

If anyone thinks the paper clip is held up by a thread or wire, pass a piece of cardboard between the clip and the matchbox.

Making a Compass

The earth is a huge magnet. That is why a compass needle always points to the North Pole. Make your own compass and it will swing to the North.

You will need
a horseshoe magnet
3 needles
a small strip of paper
some plasticine
sticky tape and scissors

1 A Compass

Hold a needle by the eye and stroke it gently about six times with a magnet. Always move the magnet in the same direction.

2

Stroke a second needle in the same way. Fold the strip of paper in half and stick the needles to it with tape, like this. Both needles must point the same way.

Dry Fingers

Take a paper clip out of a glass of water without getting your fingers wet. Hold a magnet to the outside of a glass and slide the clip up the glass.

3

Push a third needle into a small lump of plasticine. Balance the paper on top so it can swing. Mark the needle eye end with an S and the point end with an N.

4

If you want to take the compass out of doors, hang the paper by a thread. Tie the thread to a pencil and drop the paper into a glass jar, like this.

Going Fishing

Make this fishing game and have races to see who can pick up the most fish as quickly as possible. The more magnets you have, the more people can play the game.

You will need
several small horseshoe
  magnets
the same number of pieces of
  string as magnets
the same number of thin
  wooden rods or sticks
large paper clips
kitchen foil and sticky tape

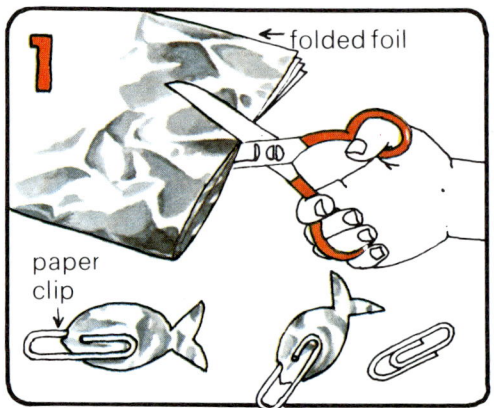

Cut some fish shapes out of kitchen foil. If you fold the foil, you can cut out several at a time. Slide a paper clip on to each fish shape.

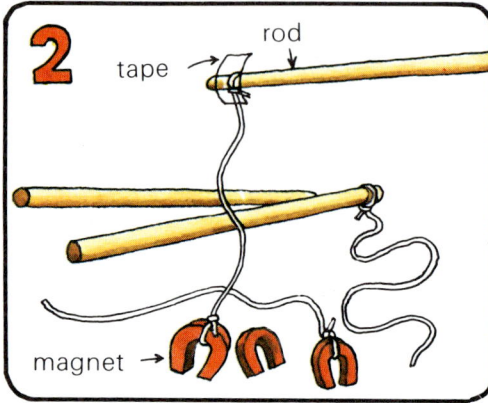

Tie a magnet on the end of each piece of string. Tie the other end of the string to one end of a stick. Keep it in place with sticky tape.

Put the foil fish in a bowl of water. Catch the fish by picking them up with the magnet hook on the fishing line.

If two players catch the same fish, they take it off their magnet hooks and put it back in the bowl. The player with the most fish at the end of the game is the winner.

1 Dry Fly Fishing

Instead of making foil fish, cut some fish out of coloured paper. Write a number on each one and slide on a paper clip.

Put the fish in a dry bowl and catch the fish with the magnet hooks. Each player adds up the numbers on the caught fish. The one with the highest score wins.

Racing Cork Boats

Make these cork boats and float them on a tray of water. Colour the paper sails if you want to. Each player holds a stick with a magnet under the tray and moves a boat across the water. Then you can have boat races.

You will need
several corks
some paper clips
some sewing needles
some nails
a plastic tray
horseshoe magnets
thin wooden sticks or rods
paper and sticky tape

Bend up one end of each paper clip and push an end into the side of each cork.

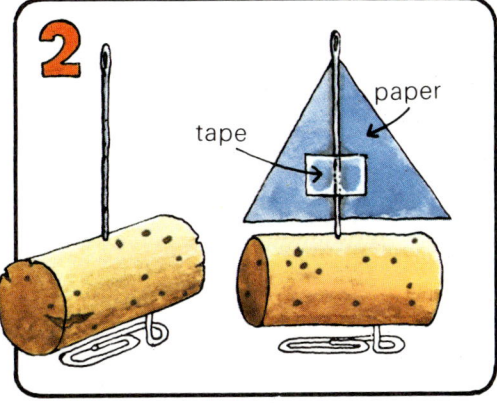

Push a needle into the other side of each cork. Cut out little triangles of paper and stick them like sails to the needles in the corks.

Put the tray on two piles of books, making sure it is level. Pour in water until it is about 3 cm deep. Float the boats and the buoy on the water.

Put a magnet on one end of each wooden rod and stick it firmly in position with tape.

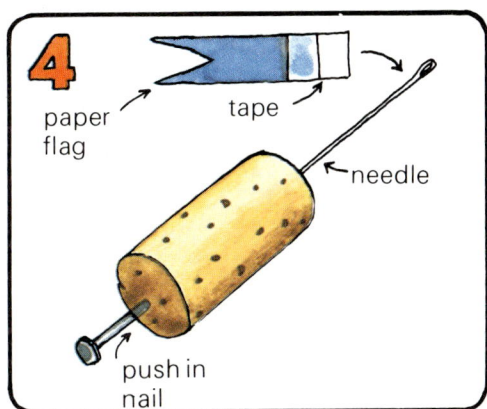

Make a cork buoy to race the boats round. Push a nail into one end of the cork and a needle in the other. Cut out a little paper flag and stick it to the needle with tape.

Batteries and Circuits

Shopping List

These are the things you will need to make the games and models in this book. You can buy most of them at a hardware store or an electrical shop.

Batteries
The strength of a battery is measured in volts. Use a 4·5 volt battery, like one of these. It will last longer.

Flex
This is wire covered with plastic. If you cannot buy the single-strand flex, get the two-stranded sort and pull it apart. Or buy the flat kind and split it down the middle.

Florists' wire
This is thin, bendy wire without any covering on it.

Glazed copper wire
This is shiny copper wire coated with varnish. It is used to make electro-magnets.

Bulbs
Buy 2·5 or 3·5 volt torch bulbs. A 2·5 volt bulb will give a brighter light but a 3·5 volt bulb will last longer.

Bulb holder
Small screwdriver
Horseshoe magnet
Iron bolt or big iron nail for an
    electro-magnet
Paper clips and paper fasteners

You will also need
kitchen foil, cardboard boxes, cardboard, paper, pins, needles, sticky tape, pencils, a ruler, ball point pens, poster paint, cotton reels and scissors.

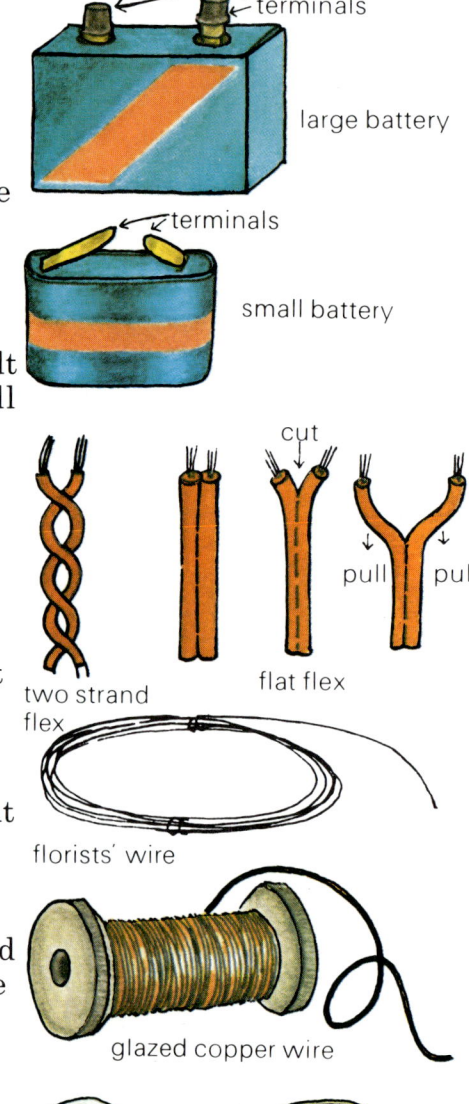

terminals
large battery
terminals
small battery

cut
two strand flex
flat flex
pull pull

florists' wire

glazed copper wire

bulb
bulb holder

small screwdriver

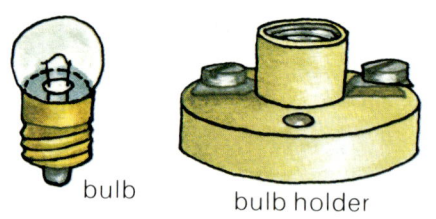

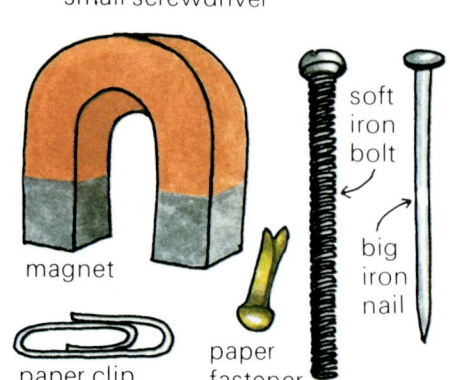

magnet
soft iron bolt
big iron nail

paper clip
paper fastener

1 Preparing the Flex

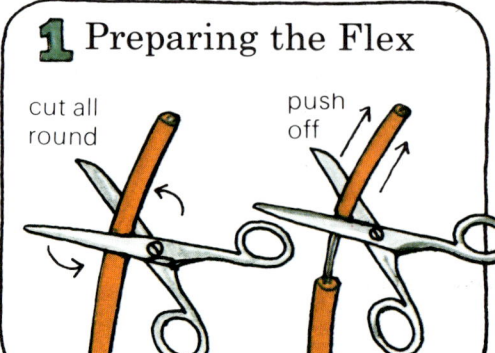

cut all round
push off

Strip about 3 cm of plastic covering off the ends of each piece of flex before using it. Be careful not to cut through the wires.

1 Wiring up a Bulb Ho

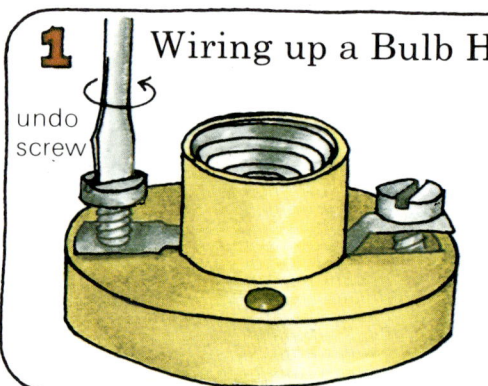

undo screw

Put the end of a screwdriver in the slot on one of the screws. Give it a few turns, this way, but do not take the screw out. Undo the other screw.

1 Battery and Bulb Holder

unwind this way

Bend one end of a piece of flex on the bulb holder into a hook. Undo a terminal on the battery and hook the flex on. Do up the terminal tightly.

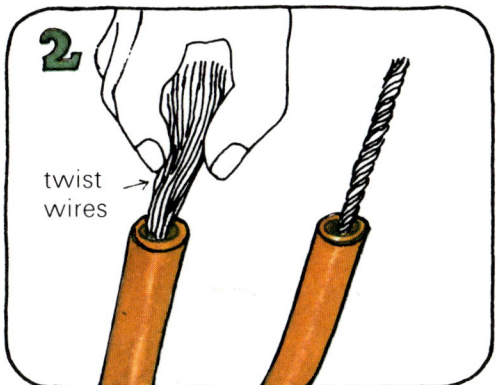

2

twist wires

If your flex has bundles of little wires inside the plastic, twist them together to make a neat end, like this.

1 Wiring a Battery

bend   turn this way to undo

Unwind the two terminals on the battery, giving each one a few turns, like this. Bend the bare wires at the ends of two pieces of flex into small hooks.

2

turn this way to do up

Hook a piece of flex on to one terminal and tighten the terminal, turning it this way. Hook the other flex on to the second terminal and do it up.

2

tighten screw

3

screw in bulb

Make small loops at the ends of two pieces of flex. Hook a loop round each screw. Push the flex round with the screwdriver to make a small circle.

Do both screws up tightly, turning the screwdriver like this. Screws always do up this way. Put in the bulb, turning it this way.

Danger

The electricity used in your house runs along wires like electricity from a battery. But there is so much electricity in these wires that they are VERY DANGEROUS. Never play with them. Leave all electric plugs, sockets, fires and machines well alone. Always use a battery to work your models and games.

2

tighten this way

Make a hook on the end of the other flex and hook it on to the second terminal. The light will go on. To make it stay on, do up the terminal.

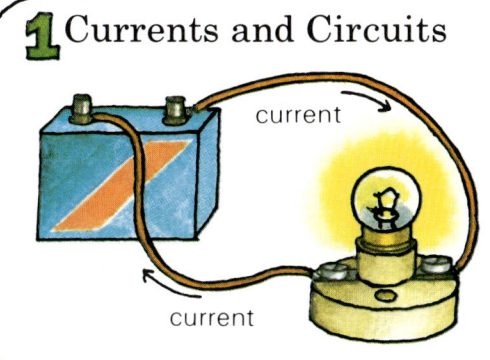

1 Currents and Circuits

current

current

The light goes on when the electric current from the battery runs along the flex, through the bulb and back to the battery. Its path is called a circuit.

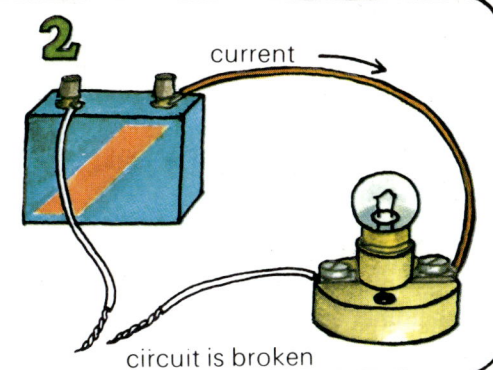

2

current

circuit is broken

If the flex is cut, the circuit is broken and the light will not go on. If the cut wires touch, the circuit is complete and the bulb will light up.

Bulb Holders and Switches

Making the KnowHow Bulb Holder

Make this KnowHow bulb holder and use it for the models and games in this book.

You will need
a matchbox
a large paperclip
a piece of kitchen foil
2 paper fasteners
2 pieces of flex, with stripped
    ends (see page 8)
a 3·5 volt bulb
scissors

1 KnowHow Bulb Holder

small hole   large hole

Take the tray out of the matchbox. Make a small hole in the top of the box. Put a paper clip over it and push a paper fastener through. Make a larger hole, like this.

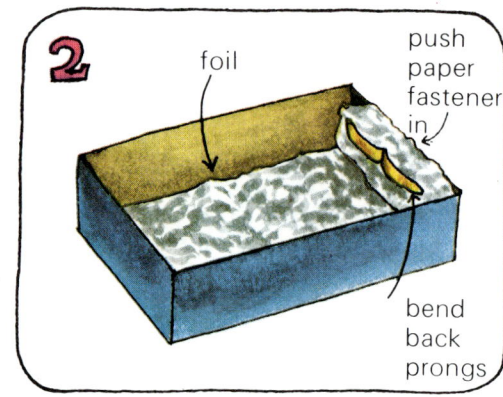

2

foil   push paper fastener in

bend back prongs

Line the bottom and one end of the tray with foil. Push a paper fastener through the lined end and bend back the prongs.

Making the KnowHow Switch

This useful KnowHow switch is simple and easy to make.

You will need
a small piece of cardboard
    (about 5 cm by 5 cm)
2 paper fasteners
a large paper clip
3 pieces of flex with stripped
    ends (see page 8)
a KnowHow bulb holder with a
    3·5 bulb
a 4·5 volt battery

1 KnowHow Switch

push through

Make a small hole in a piece of cardboard. Hold one end of the paper clip over the hole and push a paper fastener through. Bend back the ends underneath.

2

push through

Make another hole at the other end of the paper clip and push a paper fastener through. Bend back the ends but do not let them touch the other fastener.

Which Bulbs Will Light Up?

Answers on page 32

1   2   3   4   5

3 turn bulb this way

Push the tray into the matchbox. Screw the bulb through the paper clip into the hole. The bottom of the bulb must touch the foil inside the box.

4

Wind the end of one piece of flex round the paper fastener on top of the box. Wind the other piece round the fastener on the side of the box.

5

Join the end of each piece of flex from the bulb holder to a terminal on the battery to make the bulb light up.

3

Turn the cardboard over and wind an end of one piece of flex round one fastener. Wind one end of another flex round the second paper fastener.

4

Join the free end of one flex to a battery terminal. Wind the end of the other flex round a fastener on the bulb holder.

5 on

Join one end of a third flex to the free battery terminal. Wind the other end round the free fastener on the bulb holder. Switch on like this.

Quick Switch and Holder

Here is an easy way to make a quick switch. Or you can tape the ends of the cardboard down and turn it into a bulb holder.
You will need
a strip of cardboard about 15 cm long and 5 cm wide
a piece of foil about 5 cm square
2 pieces of flex with stripped ends (see page 8)
a 3·5 volt bulb
a 4·5 volt battery
sticky tape and scissors

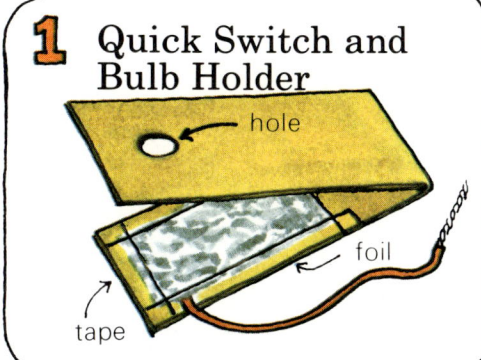

1 Quick Switch and Bulb Holder

hole

foil

tape

Make a hole in the cardboard at one end. Fold it in half. Put the flex on the cardboard, like this. Put the foil over it and stick down the edges with tape.

2 wind flex round bulb

press down

Push the bulb through the hole. Wind one end of the second piece of flex round the bulb. Join the free ends of the flex to the two battery terminals.

Making a Lighthouse

You will need

a round bulb holder and a 3·5
  volt bulb
a piece of thin cardboard, about
  20 cm long and 10 cm wide
3 pieces of flex about 30 cm
  long, with stripped ends (see
  page 8)
a KnowHow switch (see page 10)
plasticine and coloured paper
a very small glass or plastic jar
sticky tape, glue and scissors

Join the end of a piece of flex
to each of the two screws on the
bulb holder.

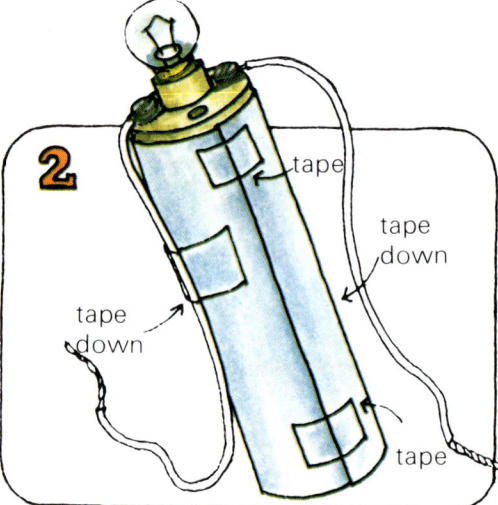

Roll the piece of cardboard round
the bulb holder, with the flex on
the outside, like this. Stick the
roll with the tape and then tape the
flex to the tube.

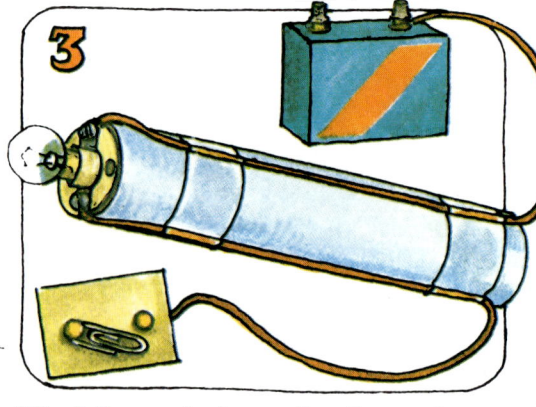

Wind the end of one flex from the
bulb holder round one of the
fasteners on the KnowHow switch.
Join the other bulb holder flex
to a battery terminal.

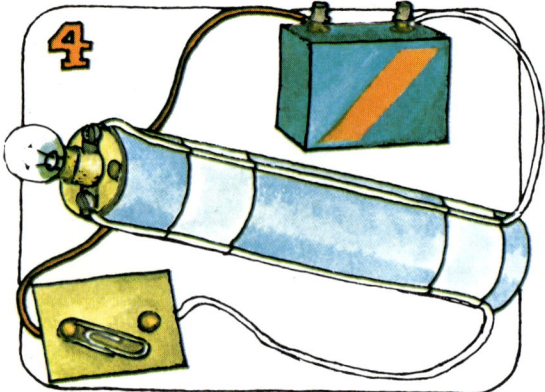

Wind a new piece of flex round
the free fastener on the switch.
Join the other end of the flex
to the second battery terminal.

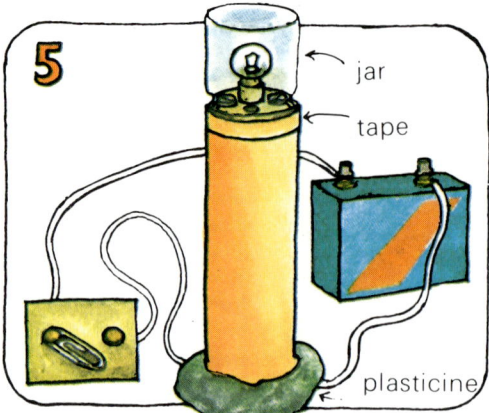

Cover the cardboard with paper
and glue it down. Stand the tube
upright and press plasticine
round the base. Put a jar over
the bulb and stick it with tape.

If the Light won't go on

Check that the flex is tightly
wound round the battery terminals,
that you have made a proper
circuit, that no bare wires are
touching each other.

Making a Lantern

Here is another idea for using a simple circuit.

You will need
a small square cardboard box
a KnowHow bulb holder (see
   page 10) and a 3.5 volt bulb
a KnowHow switch (see page 10)
a 4.5 volt battery
2 pieces of flex, about 50 cm
   long with stripped ends (see
   page 8)
1 piece of flex, about 10 cm long,
   with stripped ends
a stick about 30 cm long
coloured cellophane
sticky tape and glue
scissors

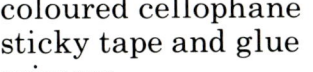

1

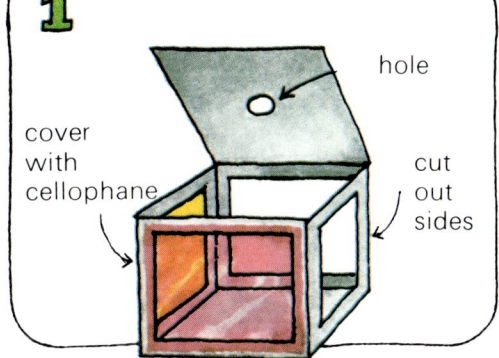

Cut a large square hole in each
side of the box. Make a hole in
the lid, big enough for two
pieces of flex to go through. Glue
cellophane over the box sides.

2

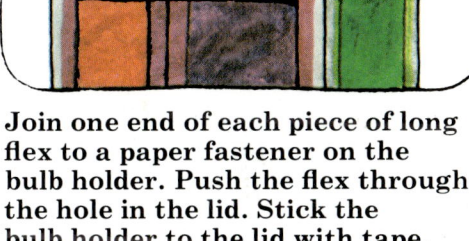

Join one end of each piece of long
flex to a paper fastener on the
bulb holder. Push the flex through
the hole in the lid. Stick the
bulb holder to the lid with tape.

3

Close the lid and tape it down.
Put the flex on the end of the
stick and keep it in place with
tape. Tape the flex down the stick
to the other end.

4

Join an end of one flex on the
stick to a battery terminal. Join
the other flex to one fastener on
the KnowHow switch.

5

Wind one end of a new short piece
of flex round the free fastener
on the switch. Join the other end
to the second battery terminal.
Now switch on the lantern.

KnowHow Night Light

Making a Night Light

You will need

a small cardboard box, a little
  bigger than the battery
a KnowHow bulb holder with a
  3·5 volt bulb
a 4·5 volt battery
3 pieces of flex with stripped
  ends (see page 8)
2 paper fasteners
1 paper clip
a sheet of paper
sticky tape, glue and scissors

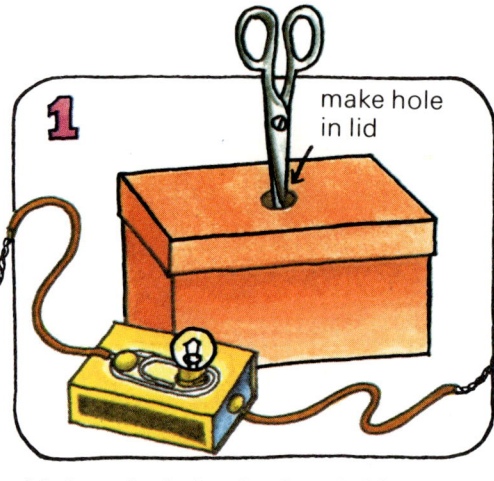

Make a hole in the box lid big
enough for the bulb to go through.
Wind the end of a piece of flex
round each of the fasteners on
the KnowHow bulb holder.

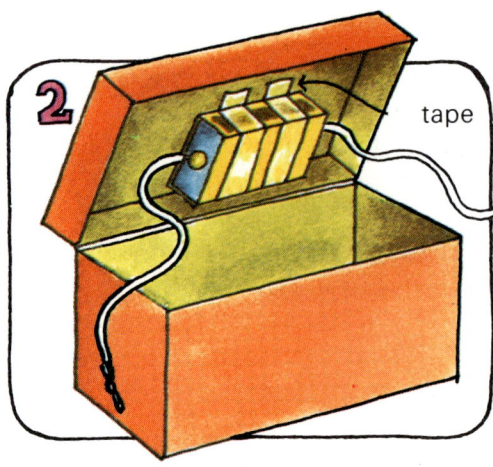

Put the bulb holder underneath
the lid and push the bulb up
through the hole. Fix the bulb
holder to the inside of the lid
with sticky tape.

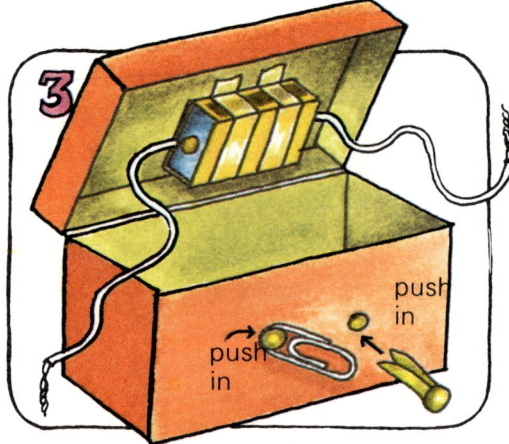

Make a small hole in the front
of the box. Hold a paper clip over
the hole and push a paper
fastener through. Push a second
fastener in near the clip.

Lay the box on its front and wind
the end of a bulb holder flex round
one paper fastener. Join the other
flex to a terminal on the battery.

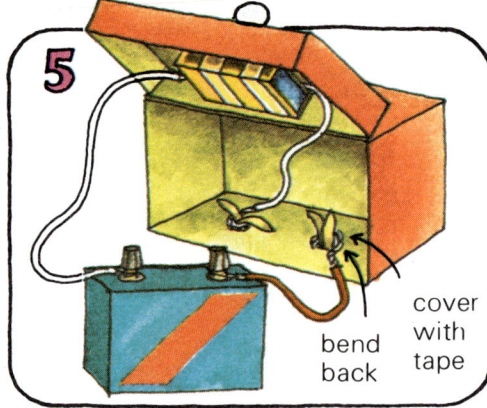

Wind one end of a third flex round
the free fastener. Join the other
end to the free battery terminal.
Bend back the prongs of the paper
fasteners and cover with tape.

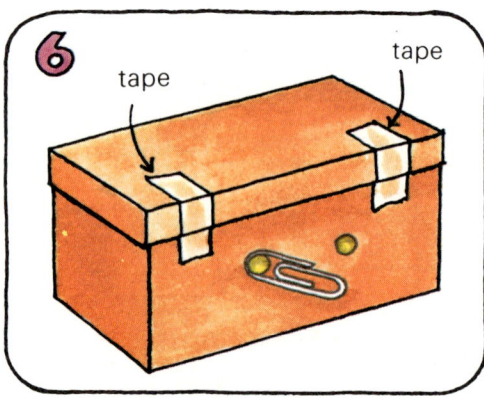

Put the battery in the box. Tuck
in all the flex and close the lid.
Stick it down with tape.

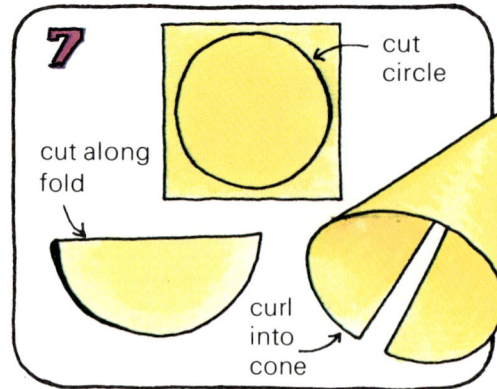

To make the shade, cut out a
circle of paper. Fold it in half
and cut along the fold. Curl one
half circle into a cone.

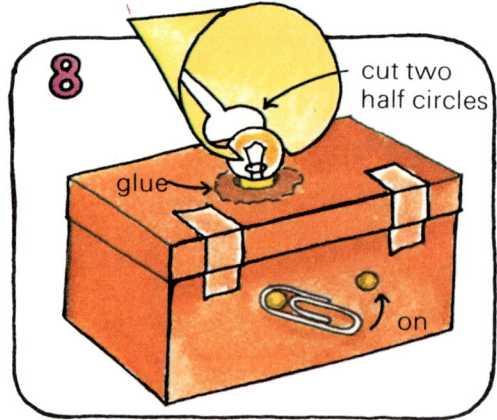

Hold the cone round the bulb in
the box and mark where the bulb
will be. Cut out two little half
circles at the marks. Curl up the
cone and glue it round the bulb.

Coloured Lights

Switch on and turn the handle on the box to make the light change colour. Try working it in the dark or use it for signals.

You will need
a KnowHow Night Light, like the one on page 14 but in a larger, tall cardboard box
cardboard
coloured cellophane
a pencil and a paper clip
paper and kitchen foil
sticky tape, glue and scissors

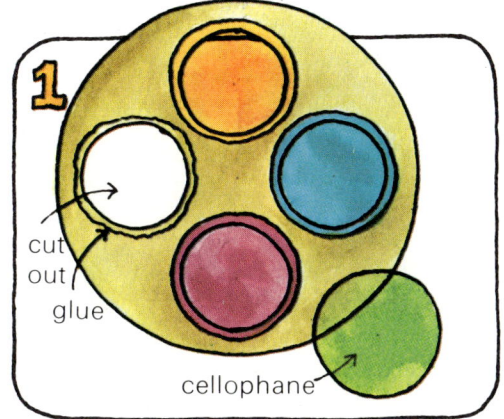

Cut out a circle of cardboard about one and a half times the height of the box. Cut out four circles and glue circles of coloured cellophane over them.

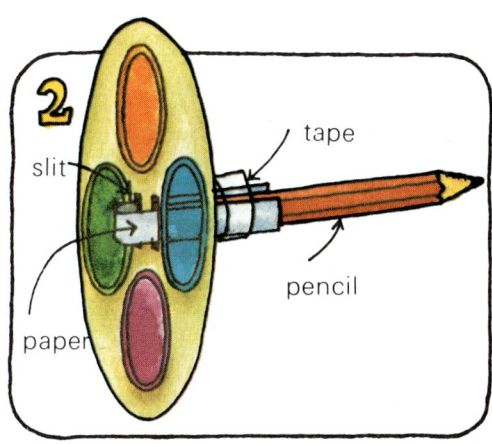

Make two slits in the centre of the cardboard circle. Thread a strip of cardboard through them and stick the ends to a pencil with tape, like this.

Make a hole through the box about 3 cm from the top. Push a pencil through. Bend a paper clip to make a handle and tape it to the end of the pencil.

Cut out a half circle of paper and snip two little circles on the straight edge. Stick foil on one side, roll it into a cone and glue it round the bulb.

Steady Hand Game

You will need

a KnowHow bulb holder (see page 10) and a 3.5 volt bulb

3 pieces of flex, each about 15 cm long, with stripped ends (see page 8)

a 4·5 volt battery

2 pieces of florists' wire, one about 40 cm long and one about 15 cm long

a cardboard box with a lid

sticky tape and scissors

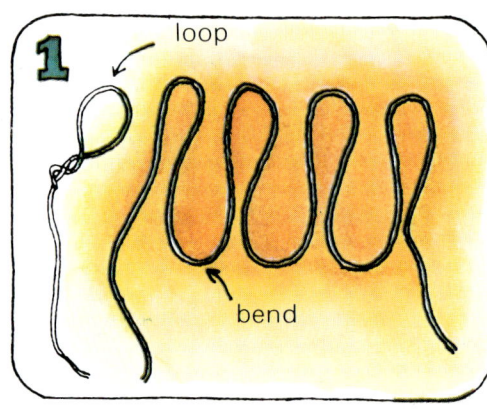

Bend the short piece of florists' wire to make a loop at one end. Bend the other piece of wire into a curly line, like this, but leave a clear path for the loop.

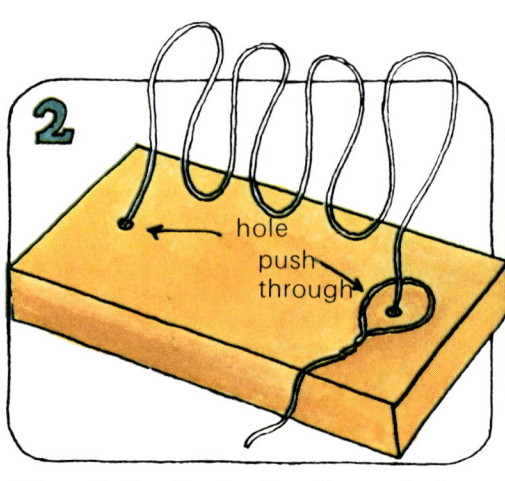

Thread the bent wire through the loop. Make two small holes in the lid of the box and push the ends of the bent wire through.

How to Play

Try to pass the loop all the way over the wire without lighting up the bulb. The more bends you make in the wire, the harder the game will be.

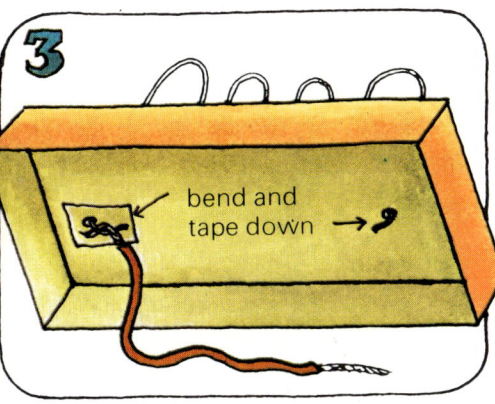

Twist one end of a piece of flex round one end of the bent wire. Bend back the ends and stick them to the lid with tape. Bend back the other end and tape it down.

Wind the ends of two new pieces of flex round the two paper fasteners on the bulb holder.

Make a hole big enough for a bulb in the box lid. Push the bulb through from the inside and stick the holder to the lid with tape.

Make a small hole in the box lid and push through an end of one flex from the bulb holder.

Join the free end of the other flex to one battery terminal. Join the flex from the bent wire to the second battery terminal.

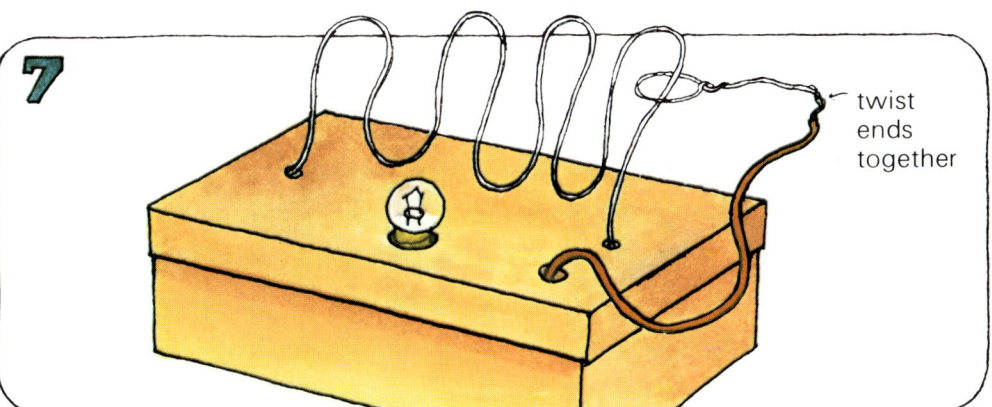

Put the battery in the box and tuck all the wires in. Put on the lid.

Twist the end of the wire loop round the end of the flex coming through the hole in the box lid. The game is now ready.

Stop-Go Traffic Lights

You will need

4 round bulb holders, each with
   a 3·5 volt bulb
a 4·5 volt battery
2 pieces of thin cardboard,
   about 20 cm square
a small cardboard box with a
   lid, big enough for a battery
3 paper fasteners and a paper
   clip
8 pieces of flex, at least 50 cm
   long, with stripped ends (see
   page 8)
1 short piece of flex about
   10 cm long, with stripped ends
sticky tape, paper and scissors
red and green poster paint

Make two holes in each piece of
cardboard, a little smaller than
the bulbs. Cut out a door at the
other end of the cardboard.

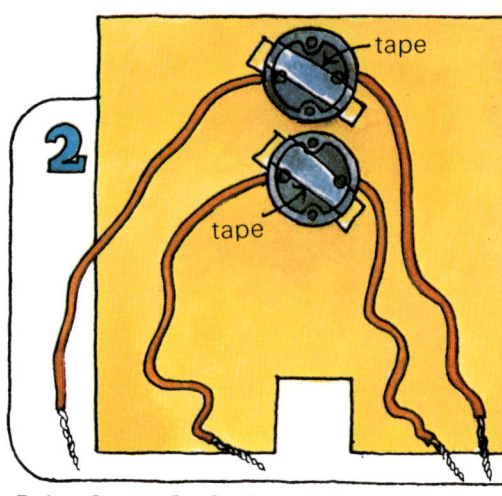

Join the end of a long piece of
flex to each of the screws on
the four bulb holders.

Push a paper fastener through the
lid of the box. Join the end of
one free flex from a top bulb holder
and one from a bottom holder
to the fastener.

Bend back the prongs of the paper
fastener and stick a small piece
of tape over them.

Push a third fastener through a
paper clip and then push it through
the box lid. Bend up one end of
the clip to make a handle.

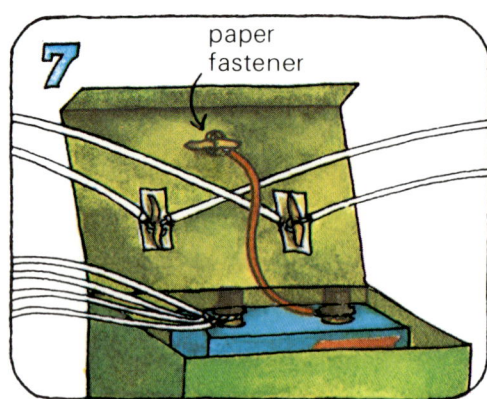

Wind a short piece of flex round
the third fastener and join the
other end to the second battery
terminal. Close the lid and stick
it down with tape.

Make a set of traffic lights for
your model cars. When one
light goes red, the other is
green. Move the switch and
change the lights.

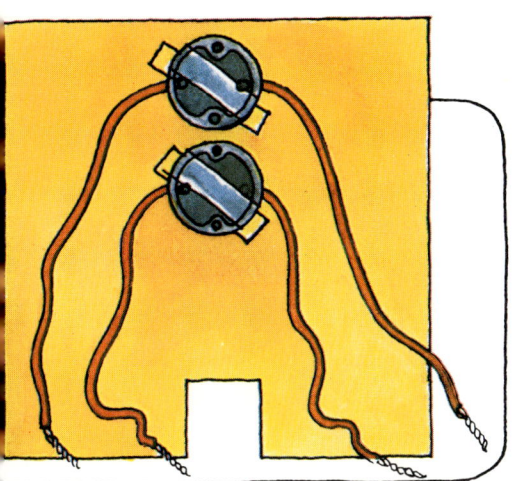

Hold a bulb holder over a hole in the cardboard and screw in a bulb from the other side. Keep it in place with sticky tape. Fix the other holders in the same way.

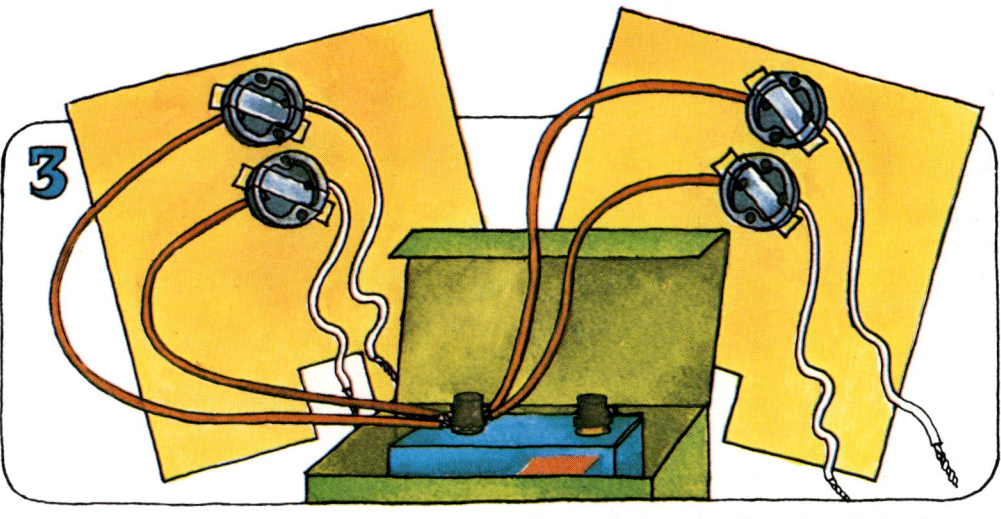

3 Put the battery in the small box. Twist the ends of one flex from each of the bulb holders together.

Hook the twisted ends of the four pieces of flex round one battery terminal and do it up. Your flex will be longer than it looks here.

5 Push a second fastener through the lid of the box. Join the ends of the two remaining pieces of flex to it.

Bend back the prongs of the paper fastener and cover them with a piece of sticky tape.

Roll up the sheets of cardboard round the bulb holders with the flex coming out one end. Stick the tubes with tape.

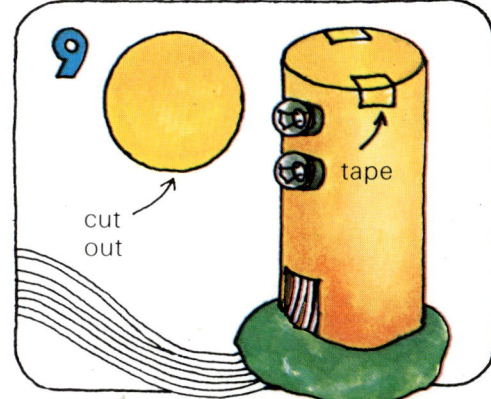

9 Stand the tubes upright and press plasticine round the bases. Cut out paper circles and stick them to the tops. Paint the bulbs of each traffic light red and green.

Morse Code Transmitters (1)

With these two transmitters you can send secret messages from one room to another, or even from indoors to outdoors. When someone presses the key of one transmitter, the bulb on the other one lights up. Then the receiver of the message can tap out a reply. Use the Morse code or make up your own signals. The transmitters are a bit fiddly to make so try to follow the instructions very carefully.

You will need

2 small, long cardboard boxes with lids, big enough for a battery
2 4·5 volt batteries
2 KnowHow bulb holders (see page 10) with 3.5 volt bulbs
5 pieces of flex for each transmitter, each a little longer than the boxes, with stripped ends (see page 8)
3 pieces of flex, long enough to stretch between two rooms
kitchen foil
10 paper fasteners
2 strips of cardboard
2 rubber bands
sticky tape and scissors

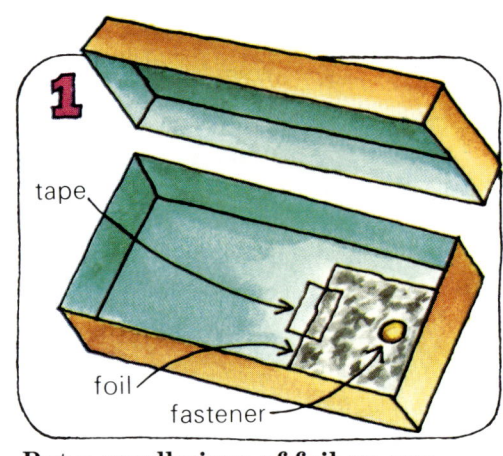

1

tape

foil

fastener

Put a small piece of foil on one end of the tray of the box. Push a paper fastener through the foil and the tray. Stick down the foil with tape on the edges.

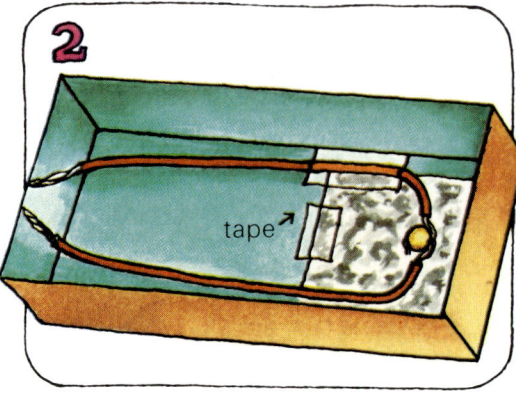

2

tape

Wind the ends of two short pieces of flex round the fastener. Fold back the prongs underneath the box and cover with tape. Stick down the flex with tape, like this.

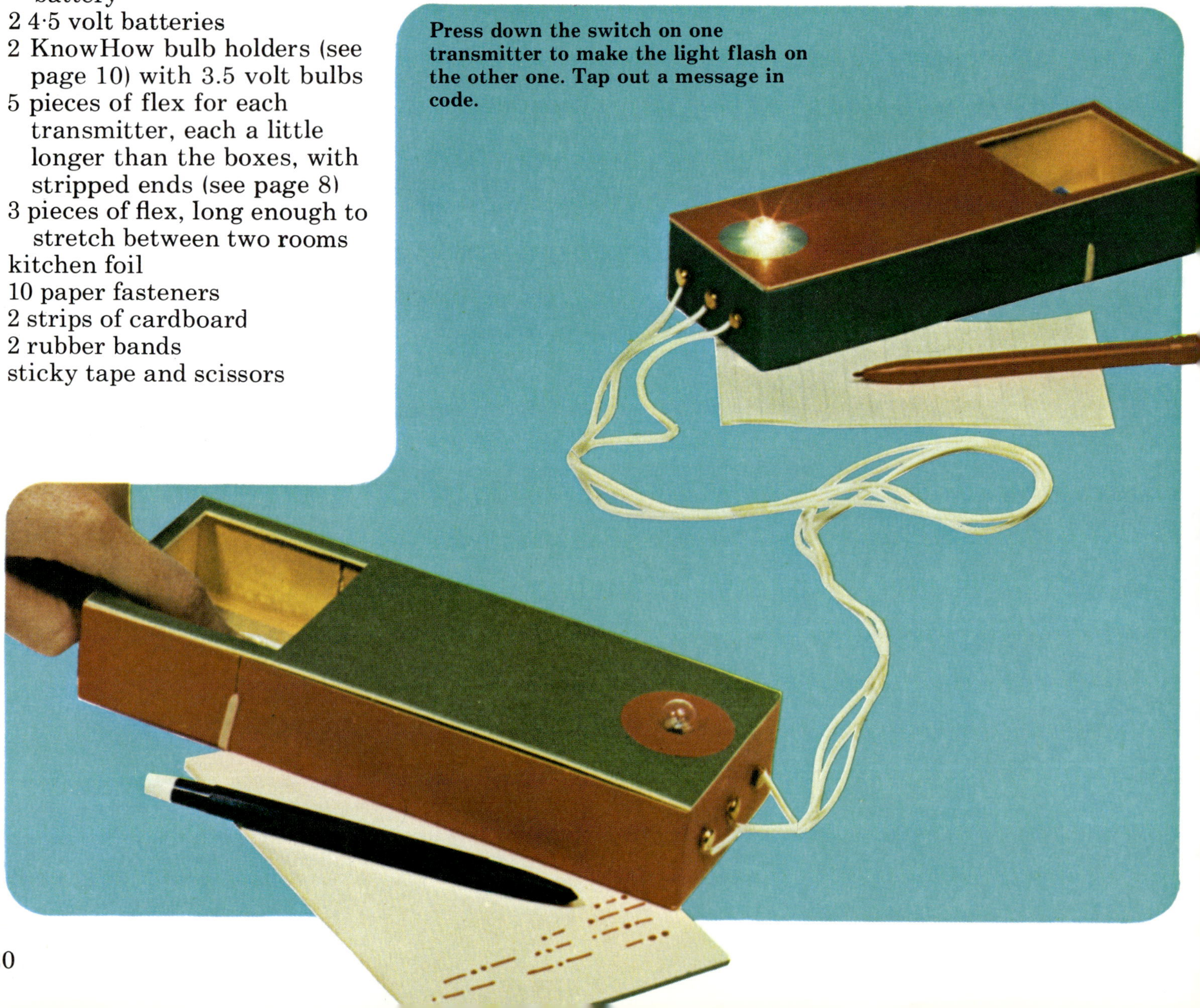

Press down the switch on one transmitter to make the light flash on the other one. Tap out a message in code.

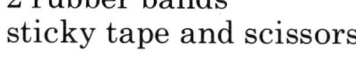

3

Push a paper fastener through the other end of the box. Mark it Terminal 1 on the outside.

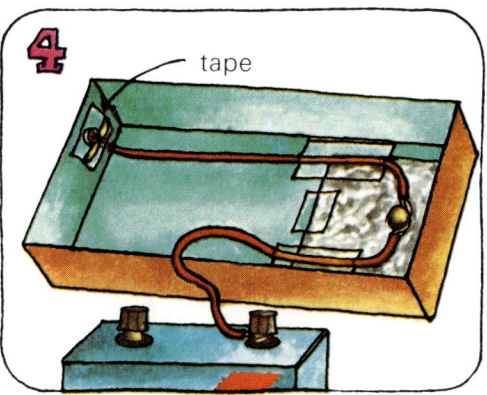

4

tape

Join the end of one flex to the terminal fastener. Bend back the prongs and tape them down. Join the end of the other flex to one of the battery terminals.

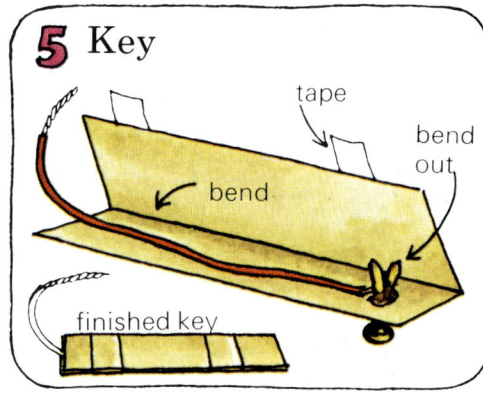

5 Key

tape
bend out
bend
finished key

Fold one of the pieces of cardboard in half, lengthways. Push a fastener through one end and join a new piece of flex to it. Tape the card together.

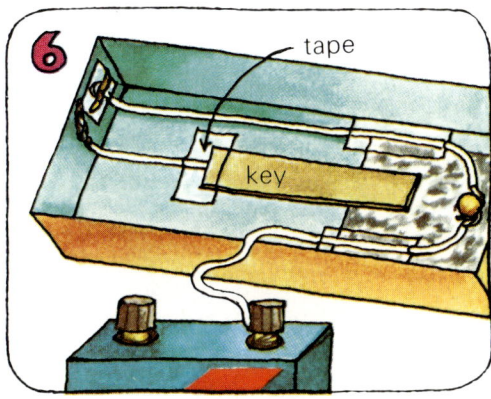

6

tape
key

Stick the key, with the fastener underneath, to the bottom of the box, with tape. Make sure that the fastener touches the foil.

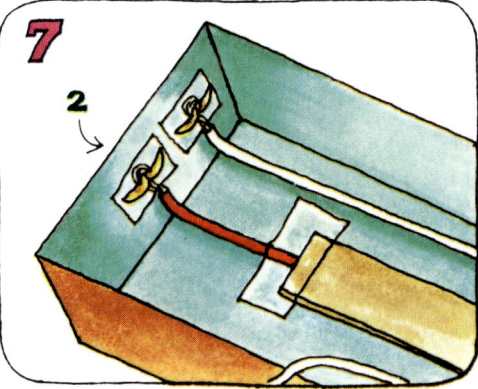

7

2

Push in a second fastener beside Terminal 1. Mark it Terminal 2. Join the key flex to it, bend back the prongs and cover them with sticky tape.

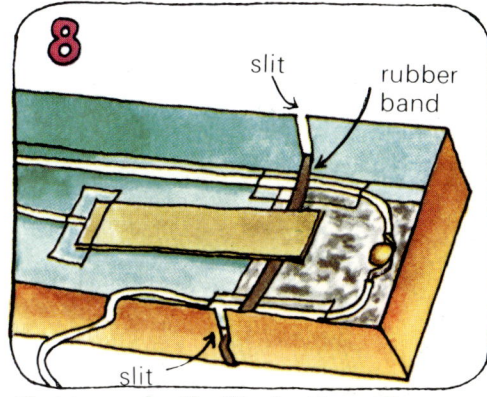

8

slit
rubber band
slit

Cut two small slits in the sides of the box, like this. Stretch a rubber band round the bottom of the box, through the slits and under the transmitter key.

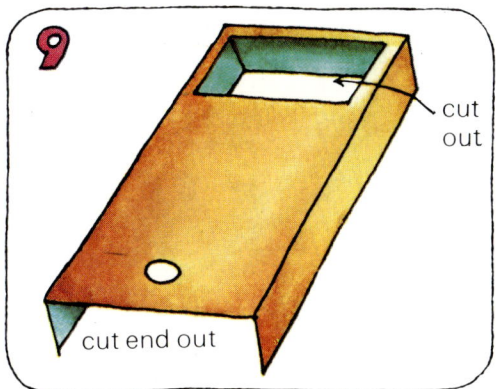

9

cut out
cut end out

Cut a large square hole at one end of the lid of the box. Cut off the other end. Make a hole big enough for a bulb to be pushed through.

The bulb on the receiving transmitter lights up . . .

21

Morse Code Transmitters (2)

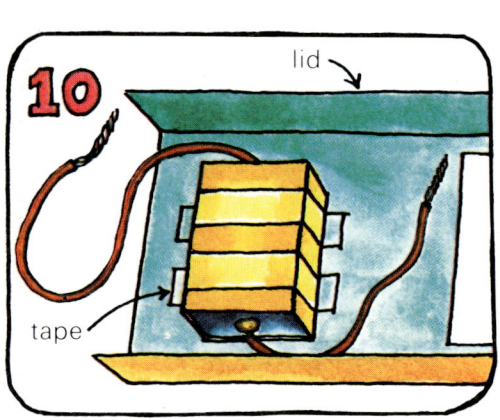

10

lid

tape

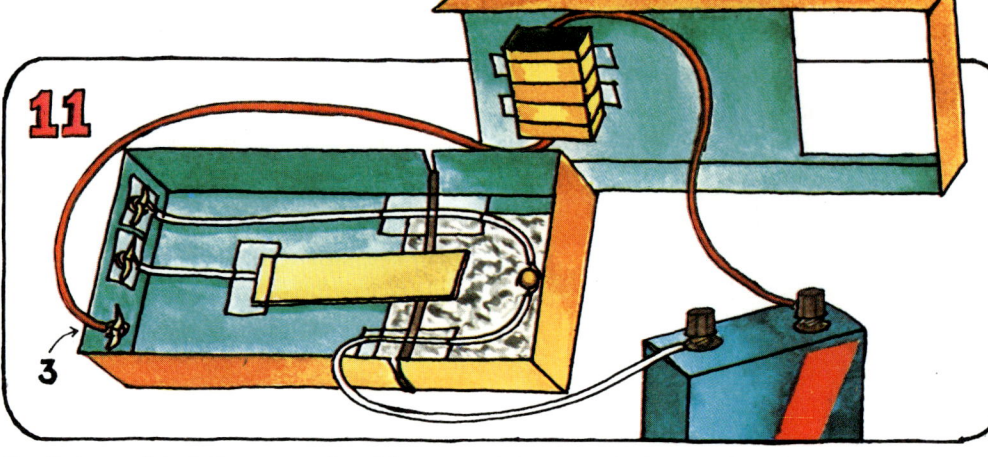

11

3

Wind the end of a new piece of flex round each fastener on the bulb holder. Push the bulb through the hole in the lid. Stick the holder in place with tape.

Push in a third fastener beside Terminals 1 and 2 at the end of the box. Mark it Terminal 3.

Join one bulb holder flex to this fastener and the other bulb holder flex to the free battery terminal.

13

3
2
1

make your flex as long as you like

1
2
3

Put the two transmitters end to end, like this. Wind an end of a long piece of flex round Terminal 1 on one box.

Join the other end of the flex to Terminal 1 on the other box. Use a flex as long as you like.

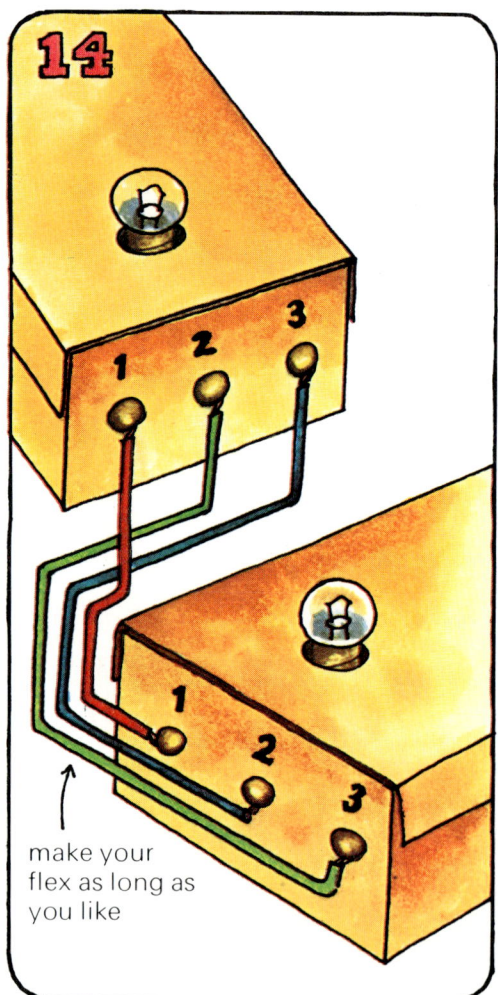

14

1   2   3

1
2
3

make your flex as long as you like

...when the sender presses the key on the other transmitter.

Join another long piece of flex to one Terminal 2 and to a Terminal 3. Put the third long flex from Terminal 3 to Terminal 2. The transmitters are now ready to use.

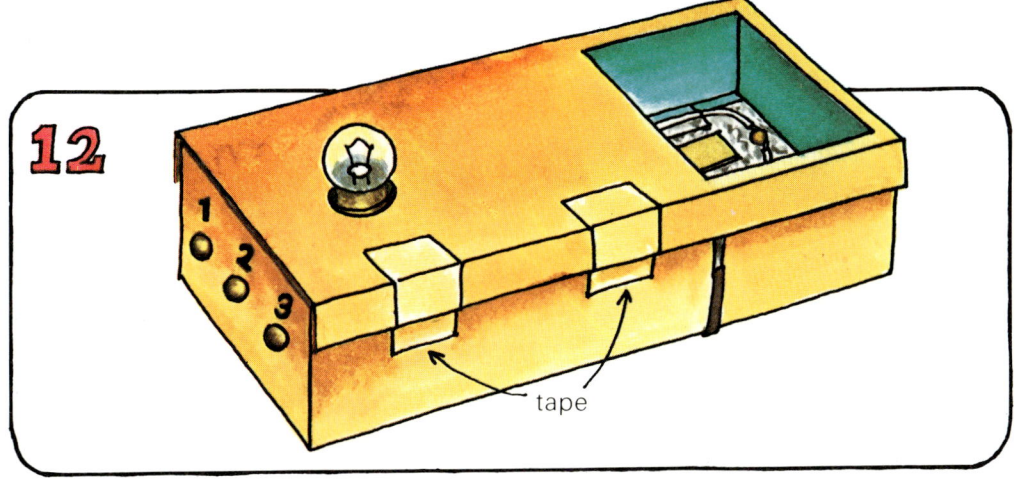

12 Place the battery in the box and tuck in all the flex. Put on the lid, with the hole over the key. Stick it down with tape.

tape

Now make a second transmitter in exactly the same way as you made the first one.

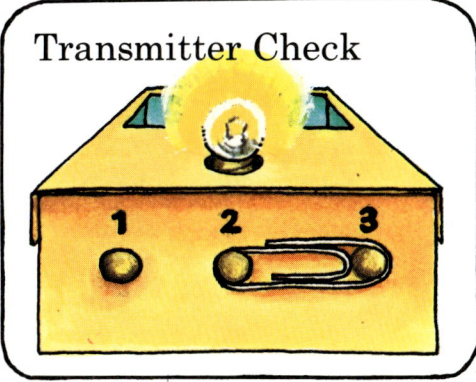

To check that the transmitter is working properly, hold a paper clip across Terminals 2 and 3 at the end of the box. Press the key and the bulb will light up.

Getting the Message

Use the Morse code by tapping out long or short flashes with the key. Make the long flashes two or three times longer than the short flashes. Each operator needs the code to send messages and to read the answers. Or you can make up your own secret code. For example, two long flashes and a short one could mean 'Danger, stay where you are'. Four short flashes could mean 'All clear, come at once'. Make the codes easy so that you can remember them.

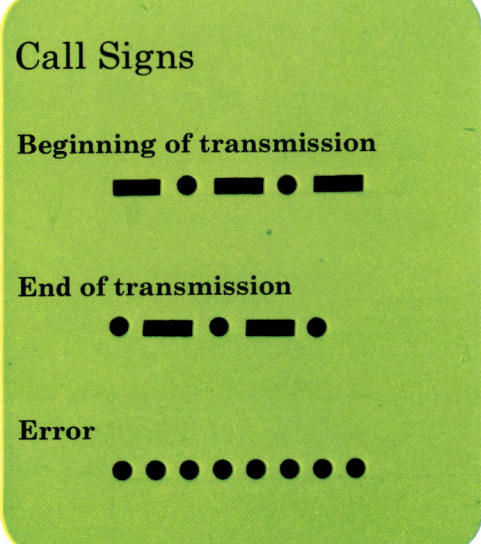

Call Signs

Beginning of transmission

End of transmission

Error

Morse Code

a ● ▬
b ▬ ● ● ●
c ▬ ● ▬ ●
d ▬ ● ●
e ●
f ● ● ▬ ●
g ▬ ▬ ●
h ● ● ● ●
i ● ●
j ● ▬ ▬ ▬
k ▬ ● ▬
l ● ▬ ● ●
m ▬ ▬
n ▬ ●
o ▬ ▬ ▬
p ● ▬ ▬ ●
q ▬ ▬ ● ▬
r ● ▬ ●

s ● ● ●
t ▬
u ● ● ▬
v ● ● ● ▬
w ● ▬ ▬
x ▬ ● ● ▬
y ▬ ● ▬ ▬
z ▬ ▬ ● ●
1 ● ▬ ▬ ▬ ▬
2 ● ● ▬ ▬ ▬
3 ● ● ● ▬ ▬
4 ● ● ● ● ▬
5 ● ● ● ● ●
6 ▬ ● ● ● ●
7 ▬ ▬ ● ● ●
8 ▬ ▬ ▬ ● ●
9 ▬ ▬ ▬ ▬ ●
0 ▬ ▬ ▬ ▬ ▬

Rollek the Flashing Robot (1)

Switch on the Robot, push it along and its eyes flash. You will find it works best on carpet. Paint Rollek or cover him with coloured paper but do not use foil. The switch will not work if you do.

You will need

a large, square cardboard box
a small cardboard box
5 empty cotton reels
cardboard
kitchen foil
3 thin wooden rods, long
    enough to go through the
    square box
2 KnowHow bulb holders (see
    page 10) with 3.5 volt bulbs
florists' wire
7 pieces of flex, 2 longer than
    the height of the square box,
    with stripped ends (see
    page 8)
a pencil
a 4·5 volt battery
coloured wire and paper
sticky tape, glue and scissors

Push a rod through the hole in the cotton reel. If it does not fit tightly, wind some sticky tape round the rod. Put a reel on either side of the first one.

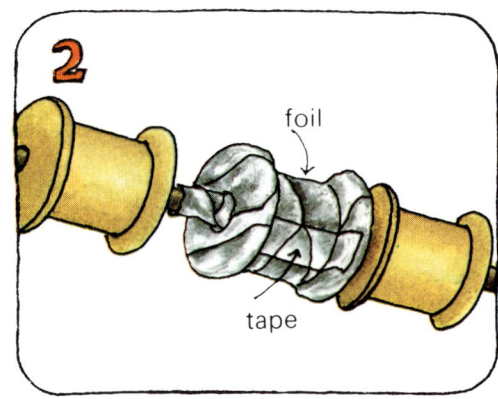

Wrap kitchen foil tightly round the middle reel and round the rod, like this. Stick two pieces of tape over the foil on the reel but not on the rod.

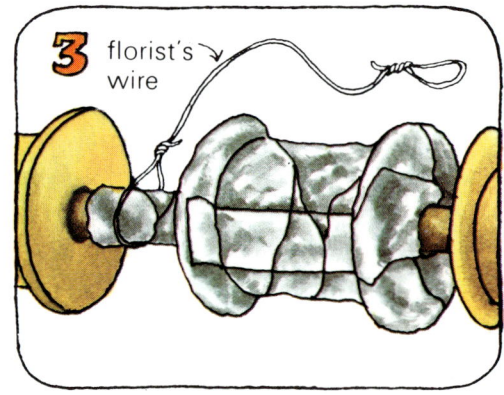

Twist a piece of florists' wire round the foil on the rod and make a loose loop. Make a small loop at the other end.

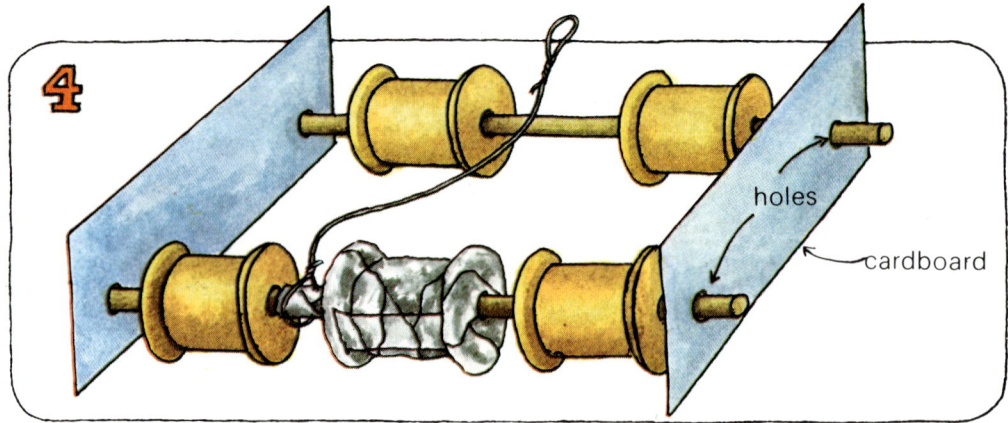

Cut out two side strips of cardboard as long as the large box. Make two holes in each strip in the corners about 2 cm from the edge.

Push the rod through the holes in the cardboard. Push a second rod through two cotton reels and through the other two holes, like this.

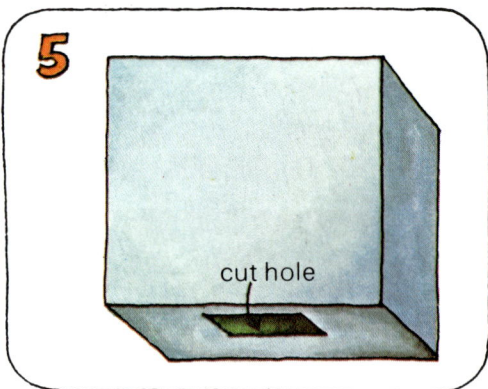

Cut a square hole in the bottom of the large box, near one end. Make it about 5 cm square.

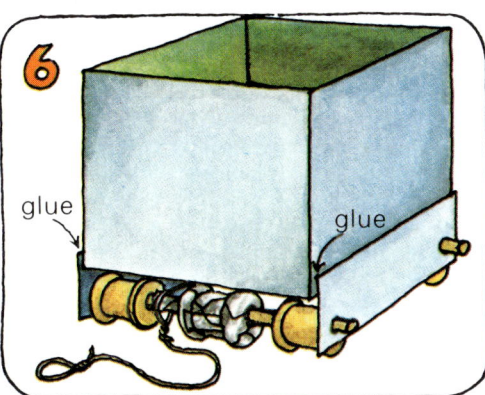

6 Glue the cardboard strips to the sides of the box so that the foil-covered reel is below the hole. Make sure the reels do not touch the box.

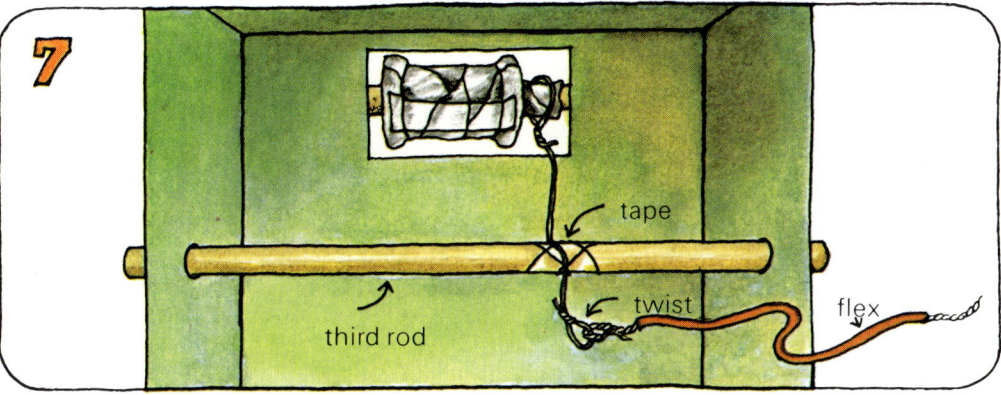

7 Push a third rod through the sides of the box, just above the hole. Pull the end of the florists' wire through the hole.

Join a piece of flex to the end of the florists' wire. Put the wire over the third rod and stick it down with tape.

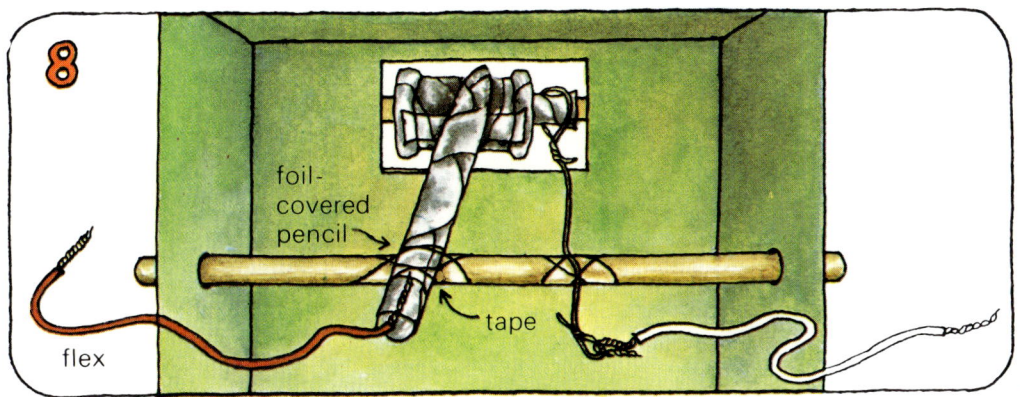
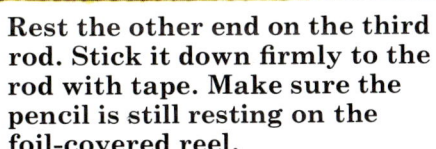

8 Wrap a pencil tightly in foil and stick one end of a flex to it with tape. Put the pencil through the hole in the box and rest it on the foil-covered reel.

Rest the other end on the third rod. Stick it down firmly to the rod with tape. Make sure the pencil is still resting on the foil-covered reel.

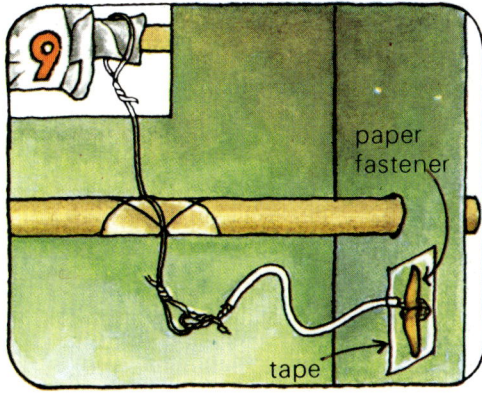

9 To make a switch, push a paper fastener through the side of the box. Join the flex from the wire loop to it and bend back the prongs. Cover them with tape.

10 Push a second fastener through a paper clip and through the box, near the first one. Join a flex to it and the other end to one battery terminal.

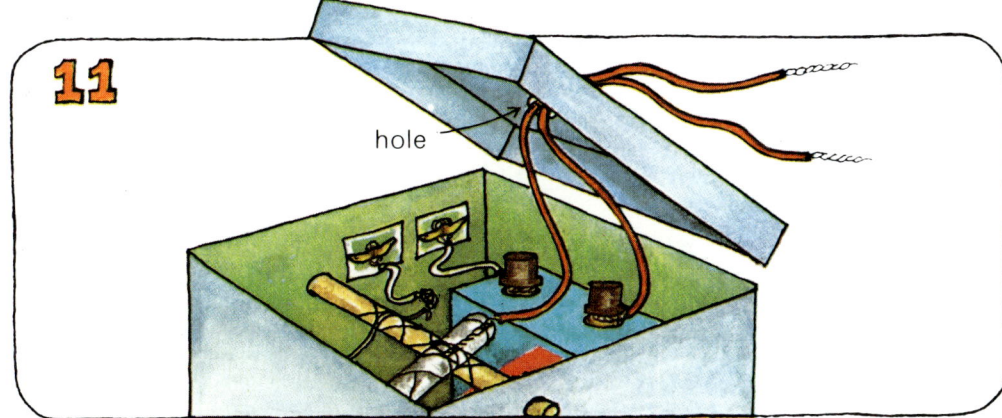

11 Make a hole in the box lid. Join one end of a long flex to the second battery terminal. Push the other end through the hole. Put the battery in the box.

Push the free end of the flex from the pencil through the hole in the lid. Put the lid on the box and stick it down with tape.

Rollek the Flashing Robot (2)

To make the eyes, join a flex to one paper fastener on each bulb holder. Join the ends of a third flex to the two free fasteners.

Make two holes in the small box, big enough for the bulbs. Push the bulbs through the holes from the inside and stick the holders in place with tape.

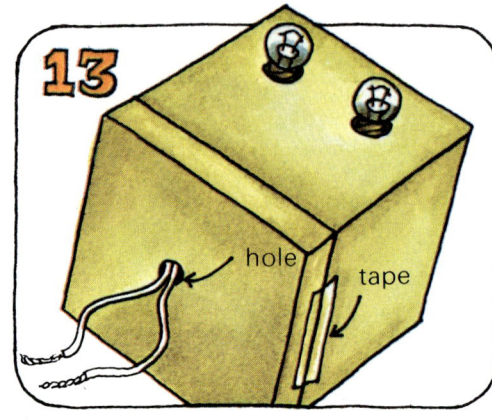

Cut a hole in the lid of the box and push the two free ends of the flex from the eyes through. Close the lid and stick it down with tape.

Push the joined flex down inside the body. Put the head over the hole and glue it to the body.

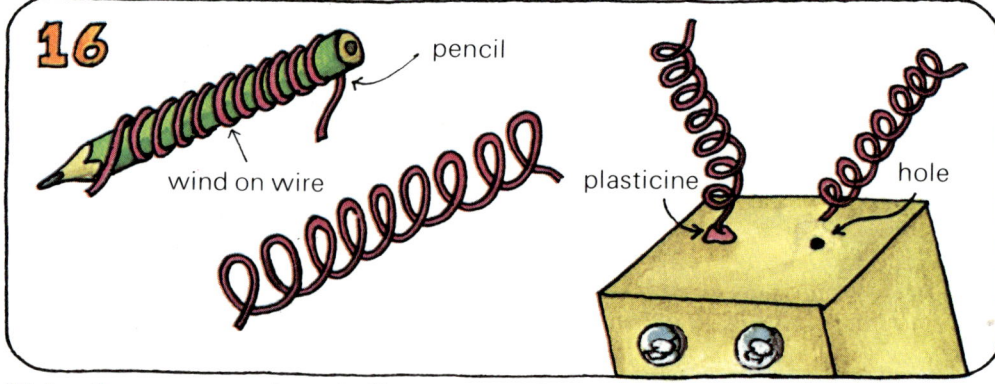

Make the antennae by winding a coloured wire round a pencil. Slide it off and the wire will stay in a coil.

Make two small holes in the top of the head. Push the ends of the antennae through and keep them upright with plasticine pressed round the ends.

For the speaker, make a circle with a strip of cardboard and stick it with tape. Make a criss-cross pattern with strips of foil. Glue it to the head.

Make two arms by rolling up two strips of cardboard and sticking them with tape. Glue them to the sides of the box.

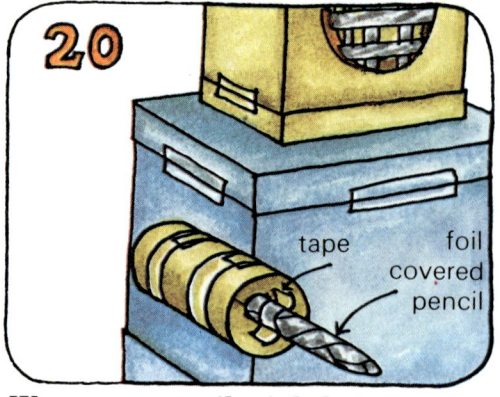

Wrap two pencils tightly in foil. Stick them with tape to the ends of the arms to make sensor probes.

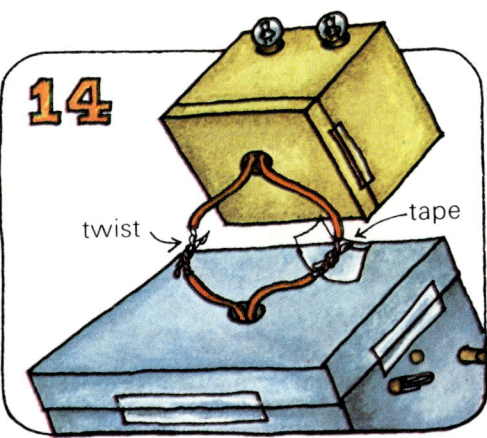

14

twist — tape

Twist a flex from the head round one from the body. Wind a piece of sticky tape round the join. Do the same with the two other wires.

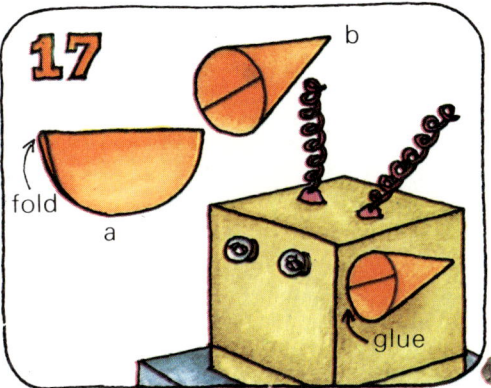

17

b

fold

a

glue

For the sound receivers, cut out a circle of paper. Cut it in half (a). Curl up each half circle into a cone (b) and glue to the head.

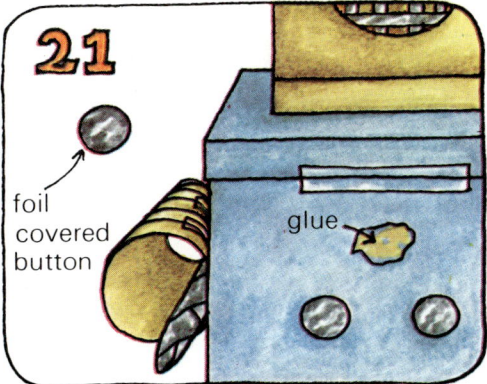

21

foil covered button

glue

Wrap three buttons tightly in foil, making one side very smooth. Stick them with glue to the front of the robot body to look like control buttons.

Switch on the Robot and push it along to make its eyes flash. Remember to switch off when you have finished playing or the battery will go flat.

Making an Electro-Magnet

You can make a magnet with an iron bolt or nail, some glazed copper wire and a battery. When the electricity from the battery flows through the wire round the bolt, the bolt becomes a magnet. Break the circuit by switching off and the bolt is no longer a magnet. The more times you wind the wire round the bolt the stronger the magnet will be. Switch off the electro-magnet when you are not using it or the battery will wear out very quickly.

You will need
an iron bolt about 5 cm long
  or a big iron nail
a piece of glazed copper wire,
  about 2 metres long
2 pieces of flex with stripped
  ends (see page 8)
a KnowHow switch (see page 10)
a 4.5 volt battery
sticky tape and scissors

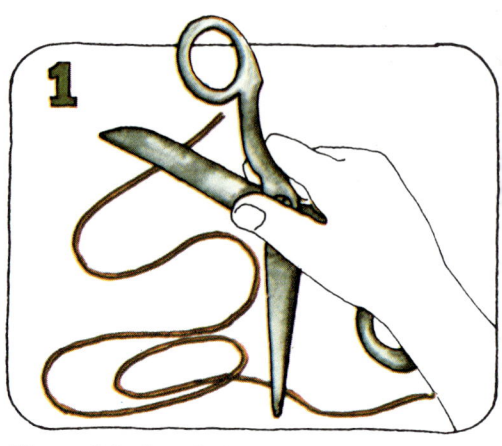

Use a blade of the scissors to scrape about 2 cm of varnish off both ends of the glazed copper wire. Do this carefully or the electro-magnet will not work.

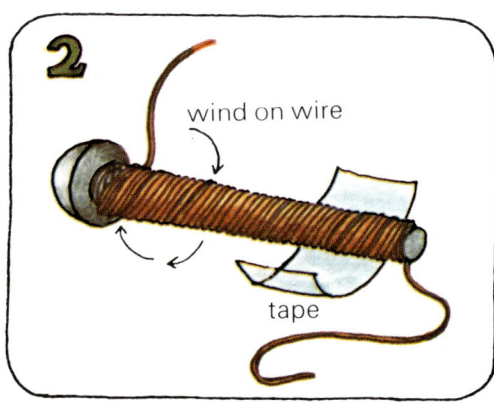

wind on wire

tape

Hold one end of the wire against the bolt or nail and wind the wire round and round. Keep the coils very close together.

wind this way

When you reach the end of the bolt or nail, put a small piece of tape on the wire. Wind the wire along the bolt back to the beginning. Keep the coils as close as you can.

Join a piece of flex to each of the fasteners on the KnowHow switch. Wind the free end of one flex round a battery terminal.

on

Twist the other flex round one wire on the electro-magnet. Join the end of the free wire on the bolt to the second battery terminal.

Switch on the electro-magnet and try picking up a few pins or small nails. Switch off and they will drop off.

Putting the Shot

You will need

an electro-magnet wired to a
   battery and a switch (see
   page 28)
a large cereal box
2 strips of stiff cardboard about
   5 cm wide and 25 cm long
a sheet of paper the same size
   as the box
a pencil and ruler
scissors and sticky tape

1

cut out top
of box

tape

Close the end of the box and
stick it down with tape. Cut out
one side and lie the box down flat.

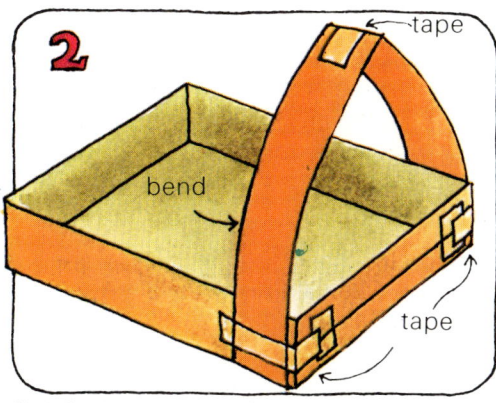

2

tape

bend

tape

Stick the strips of cardboard
one either side of the box, at one
end, like this. Bend the tops
until they meet and stick them
together with tape.

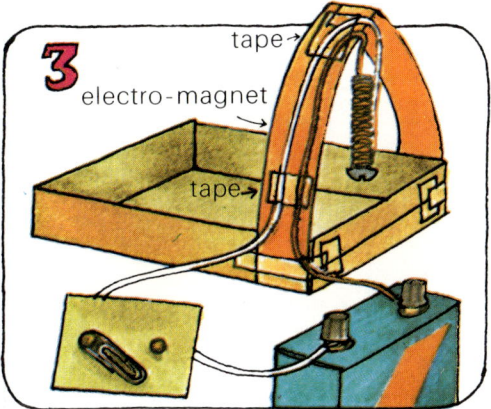

3

tape

electro-magnet

tape

Hang the electro-magnet over the
arch, so it can swing easily, and
stick the flex to the top of the
arch with tape. Tape the flex
down one strip of cardboard.

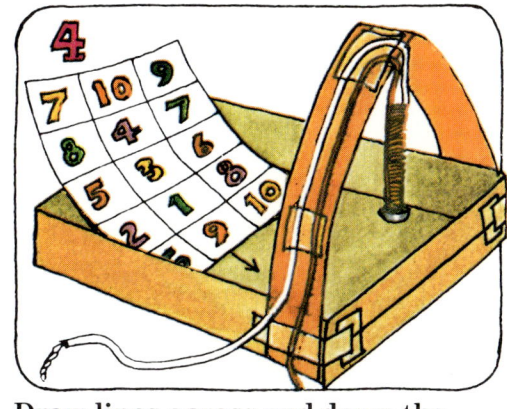

4

Draw lines across and down the
piece of paper. Write a number in
each section, putting the
higher numbers at the sides.
Put the paper in the box.

How to Play

Switch on the electro-magnet
and stick a small nail or paper
clip to it. Pull the electro-
magnet back and let it swing.
Switch off and see which
number the nail or clip drops
on. Keep the score for each
player. If the nail or clip goes
out of the box, the player loses
a point. The player with the
highest score wins.

29

Mighty Magnet Pick-Up Truck

This electro-magnet truck will pick up pins and nails, or tow a small metal car. Just wind down the electro-magnet, switch on and pick something up. Winch it up and push the truck away to the dumping ground. Switch off and drop the load. Remember to switch off when you are not using the truck or the battery will wear out quickly.

You will need

a strong cardboard box, about 20 cm long and 12 cm wide
stiff cardboard
8 paper fasteners
a cotton reel
a pencil
a piece of string about 30 cm long
a 4·5 volt battery
an electro-magnet (see page 28)
3 paper clips
2 pieces of flex about 20 cm long, with stripped ends (see page 8)
sticky tape and scissors

Cut out the side of the box. Cut out four cardboard circles for wheels. Push a fastener through the centre of each wheel and then through the sides of the box.

Cut two strips of cardboard the same length. Join them, like this, to the sides of the box with paper fasteners.

Make a hole in the end of each cardboard strip. Put a cotton reel between them and push a straightened paper clip through the holes. Bend over the ends.

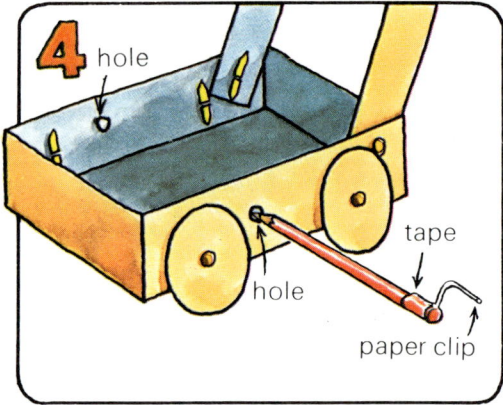

Bend a paper clip to make a handle. Stick it to the end of a pencil with tape. Make two holes in the sides of the box and push the pencil through.

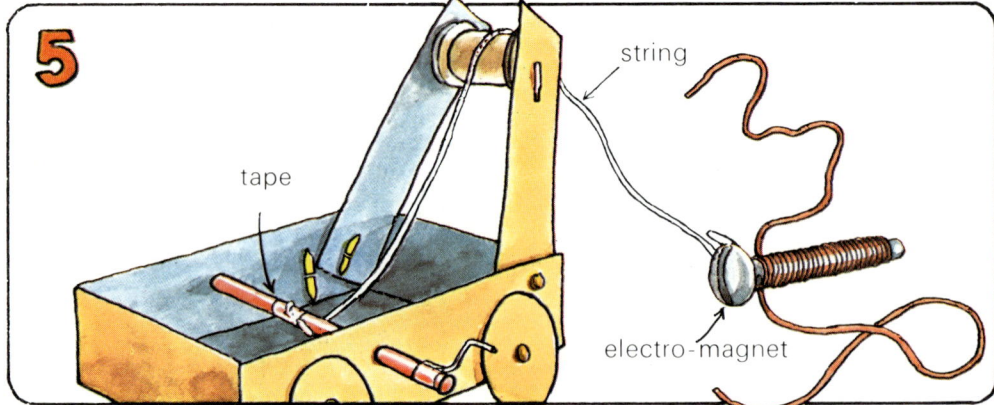

Put one end of a piece of string on the middle of the pencil and hold it in place with sticky tape.

Run the string over the cotton reel and tie the other end to an electro-magnet.

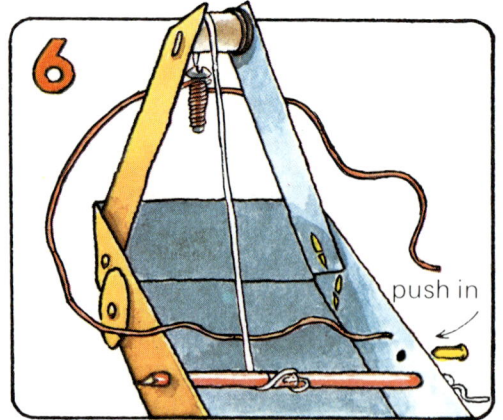

To make a switch, push a paper fastener through the side of the box. Wind one wire from the electro-magnet round it and bend back the ends.

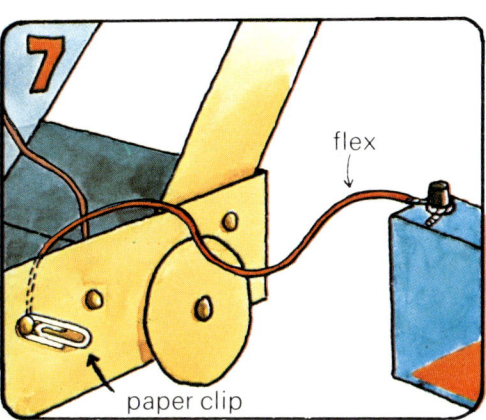

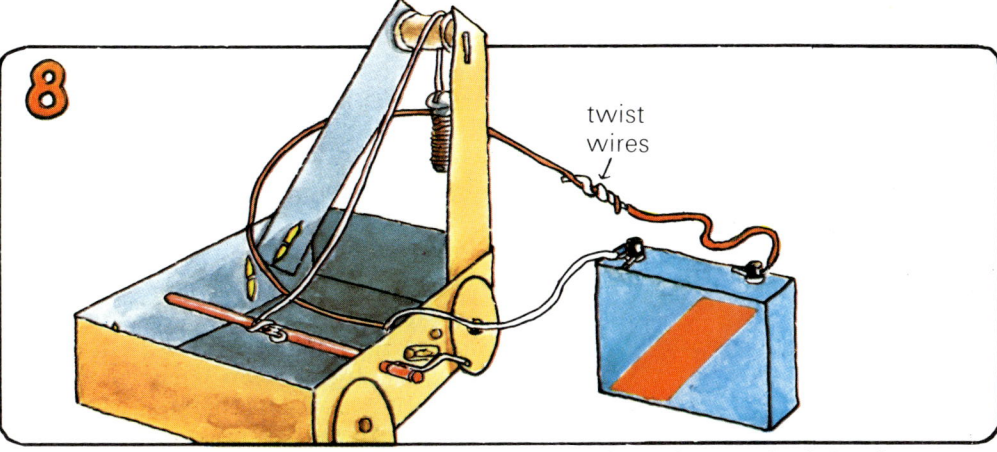

Push a second fastener through a paper clip and through the box, near the first fastener. Join one end of a new piece of flex to it and the other end to the battery.

Twist one end of a new piece of flex round the end of the second wire from the electro-magnet.

Join the other end of the flex to the second battery terminal. Put the battery in the box.

Make a driver's cab out of a small cardboard box. Cut out or paint on doors and windows. Glue or tape the box to the front of the truck.

About Electricity and Magnets

Everything in the world is made of millions of atoms. They are so small you cannot see them, even with a microscope. Each atom is made up of smaller parts, some called electrons. These electrons carry active electricity.

An Atom

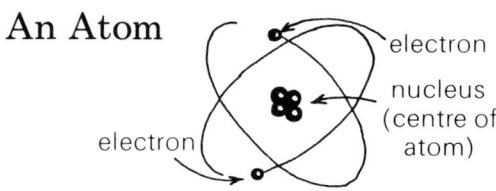

A battery makes active electricity all the time. Inside it are zinc and carbon in a mixture of chemicals. These work together to make electricity.

A Battery

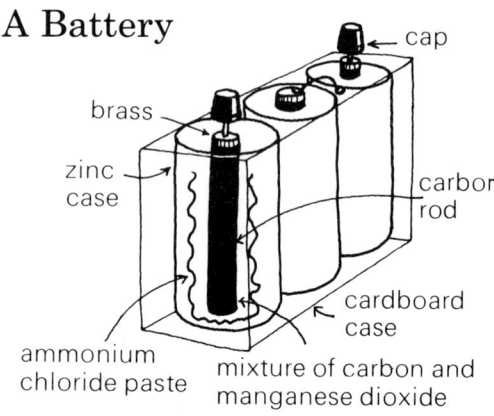

When wires are joined to the two terminals of a battery, the electricity moves along the wires. It moves from the terminal marked with a minus sign to the one marked with a plus sign. The electricity can only move when it can leave one terminal and flow back to the other. This is called a circuit.

Before you join up a wire, you have to strip off the plastic covering. Electricity cannot flow through this covering, which is called insulation. Lots of things are insulators, including sticky tape, plastic, rubber and cardboard.

The wire inside the plastic-covered flex is usually made of copper. This is because electricity can move very easily along copper. Something which electricity can flow through easily is called a conductor.

Look carefully at a bulb and you will see a very thin wire inside the glass. This wire is made of a metal which electricity cannot move through easily. Because it tries hard to flow along it, the wire becomes hot, then red hot, then white hot and gives off a white light. This happens very quickly but if you leave a bulb on for a long time, it will feel quite warm. If the wire in the bulb is too thin for the amount of electricity going through it, it gets so hot it melts.

This is why you should use a 2·5 volt or a 3·5 volt bulb with a 4·5 volt battery.

A Bulb

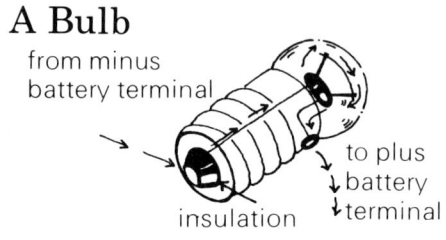

Volt is the name given to a unit which measures the amount of electrical pressure in a battery. It is named after an Italian scientist, Alessandro Volta, who invented the first simple battery in the eighteenth century.

The first magnets were discovered by the Ancient Greeks. They found that some rocks near the city of Magnesia, in Asia Minor, could attract small pieces of iron. This rock is an iron ore and is called magnetite after the city. It is also known as lodestone and was used to make the first simple compasses for ships. Now magnets are made out of steel or a mixture of metals and minerals. An electric current is passed round a bar or horseshoe-shaped piece of metal. When the current is switched off the metal is a permanent magnet.

Which Bulb Will Light Up?

Answers to page 10.

1 No. There is only one flex. This is not a complete circuit.
2 No. There are two wires on one battery terminal.
3 Yes. This is a complete circuit with a flex from each battery terminal to each screw on the bulb holder.
4 Yes. This is a complete circuit with two bulb holders. This is called a series circuit.
5 Yes. This is a complete circuit with two bulb holders. This is called a parallel circuit.

Making a Box

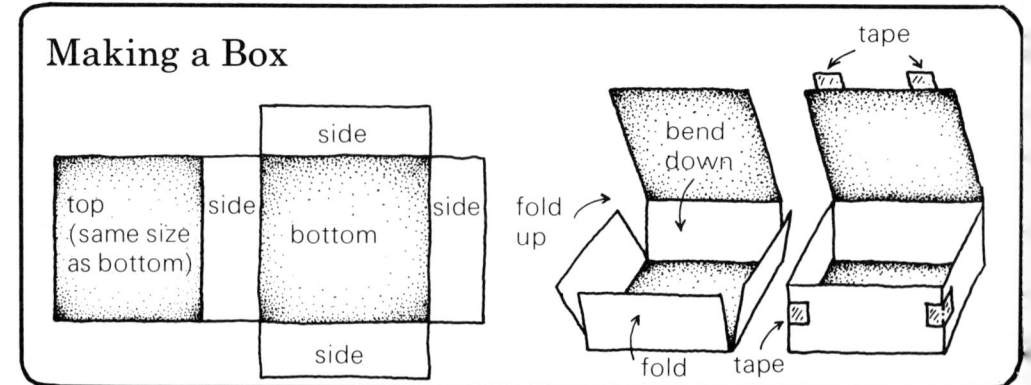

If you cannot find a box, make one out of cardboard. Use a ruler to draw the lines. The top and bottom are the same size and the sides are the same size.

Fold the cardboard, like this, to make the top, bottom and sides. Stick all the corners and the bottom together with tape.

The KnowHow Book of Fishing

Anne Civardi and Fred Rashbrook

Illustrated by Colin King
Designed by John Jamieson

Contents

Editorial Consultant:
Angela Littler

Special fish illustrations
on pages 1, 20, 21, 22, 23,
28 and 29 by:
George Thompson
Printed in Italy

First published in 1976
Usborne Publishing Ltd
Usborne House, 83-85 Saffron
Hill, London EC1N 8RT
© Usborne Publishing Ltd
1989, 1976

The name of Usborne and
the device 🎈 are Trade
Marks of Usborne
Publishing Ltd.

About This Book

This book shows you how to fish from land with bait, the cheapest and easiest kind of fishing to do.

It tells you about two sorts of bait-fishing; freshwater fishing–in ponds, lakes, rivers and streams–and saltwater fishing–in estuaries and from the seashore.

This book does not tell you about more complicated and expensive kinds of fishing, such as fly fishing, spinning and fishing from boats.

It shows you how to put floats, weights, hooks and bait on the fishing line, and the kinds of bait to use to catch different sorts of fish.

It also shows you where the fish live and feed, and where you are likely to catch them.

On page 4 we show you how to make a rod yourself. As there are lots of rods and reels you can buy, we have suggested the kinds that will be easiest to use. If you are not sure what sort to choose, ask for help in a fishing tackle shop.

Anglers use lots of special words about fishing. We have tried to explain them in the book, but if you come across one you don't understand, the list on page 32 may help you.

Kinds of Fishing

Freshwater Fishing

There are two sorts of fishing you can do in freshwater. They are called float fishing and leger fishing.

1 Float Fishing

THIS IS WHEN YOU USE A FLOAT AND LITTLE WEIGHTS, CALLED SPLIT SHOT, TO FISH WITH. THE WATER SHOULD NOT BE VERY DEEP AND YOU SHOULD FISH CLOSE INTO THE BANK.

2 Leger Fishing

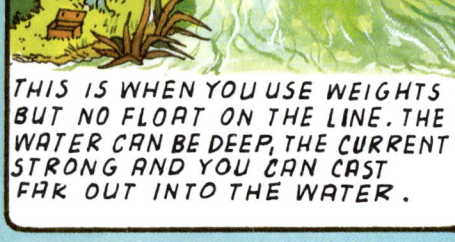

THIS IS WHEN YOU USE WEIGHTS BUT NO FLOAT ON THE LINE. THE WATER CAN BE DEEP, THE CURRENT STRONG AND YOU CAN CAST FAR OUT INTO THE WATER.

Seashore Fishing

There are two sorts of fishing you can do from the seashore. They are called sea float fishing and sea leger fishing.

1 Sea Float Fishing

THIS IS WHEN YOU USE A FLOAT AND A SMALL WEIGHT ON THE LINE. THE WATER SHOULD BE CALM AND YOU FISH CLOSE INTO THE SHORE.

2 Sea Leger Fishing

THIS IS WHEN YOU USE A HEAVY WEIGHT AND NO FLOAT ON THE LINE. THEN YOU CAN FISH FAR OUT INTO THE WATER AND WHERE THE CURRENT IS STRONG.

The Things an Angler Uses

Anglers use lots of different kinds of fishing equipment. You can make some of it yourself, such as freshwater floats, landing nets and even a simple rod. The rest you can buy quite cheaply from any fishing tackle shop.

Rods

Your rod will probably be made of fibre-glass with a cork handle and metal reel fittings. Your line is wound on to a reel which fits into the reel fittings.

Fresh water rod

sea rod

Reels

fixed spool reel

There are lots of reels you can buy. This is one of the best and easiest kinds to use.

Fishing Line

The best kind to use is monofilament line. Buy it in 100 m spools. For freshwater, the breaking strain should be about 2 kg. For sea fishing, about 8 kg.

Hooks

eye

Buy the hooks with eyes. They are the easiest kind to tie to fishing line.

Hook Lengths

Anglers often keep their hooks tied to short pieces of nylon line. These are called hook lengths. They are finer than the fishing line which makes them hard for fish to see.

Floats

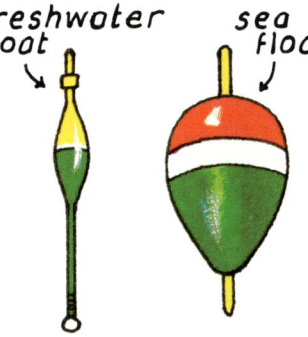

freshwater float   *sea float*

A float is fixed to the fishing line. It keeps the hook at the right depth and shows you when a fish bites. It is painted brightly on top so you can see it in the water. The part that goes under the water is dark so fish cannot see it.

Float Rings

Float rings

These are rubber rings which are used to fix floats to fishing line.

Baits

These are bits of food, such as bread, cheese, maggots, garden worms, lugworms, prawns and mussels. You put them on to the hook to catch different kinds of fish.

Landing Nets

Most anglers take a net with them when they go fishing to help them land big fish.

Weights

Anglers fit different kinds of lead weights to the fishing line above the hook. In float fishing, the weights keep the bait down and the float upright. In leger fishing, they keep the bait on the bottom.

Split shot are little balls of lead with a slit in them which are used as weights in freshwater float fishing.

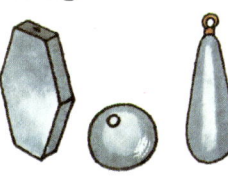

Freshwater leger weights are heavier and bigger than split shot and are used without floats.

Sea float weights are bigger and heavier than split shot. They keep a sea float upright in the water and the bait hanging at the right depth.

Sea leger weights are heavy weights used in sea fishing. The heavier they are, the further out you can cast the line.

Swivels

Swivels are small metal things which allow the hook and weights to turn round and round without twisting the line.

3

Rods and Reels

If you want a really simple and cheap rod, make the home-made one on this page. You will be able to catch little fish in shallow water with it.

To catch bigger fish you will need to buy a proper rod and reel from a fishing tackle shop. Ask the tackle dealer to help you choose the right rod.

The best kind of reel to use is the fixed spool reel. It has a metal arm which goes round and round to wind the fishing line on to a fixed spool.

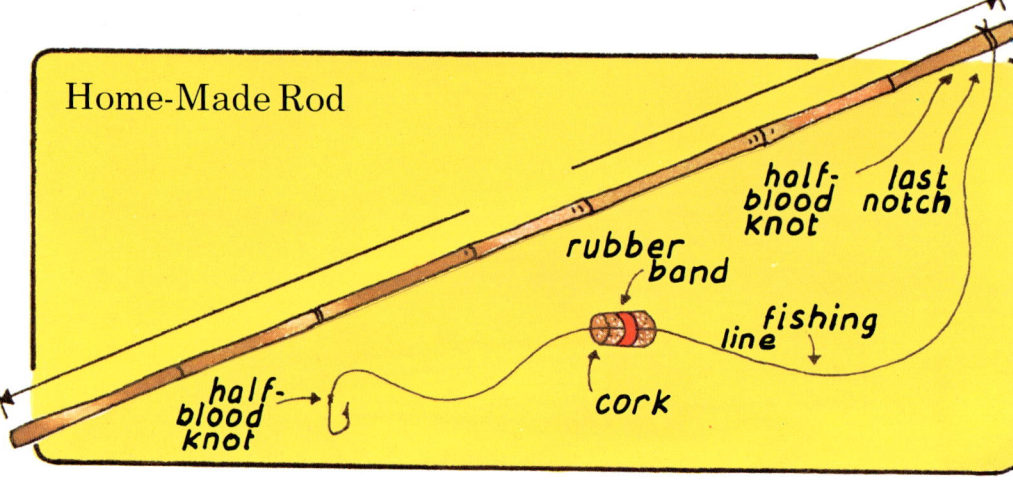

Home-Made Rod

half-blood knot | last notch
rubber band
fishing line
half-blood knot
cork

Buy a bamboo cane, about 3 metres long, from a garden shop. Tie some nylon fishing line, just over 3 metres long, below the top notch, like this.

Wind a rubber band round a cork. Fix the cork about half-way up the line, as shown, to use as a float. Then tie a hook to the end of the line.

Fixed Spool Reel — this part attaches to the rod handle
drag setting nut | reel spool | reel handle
the spool stays still
bale arm (closed)

this part spins round as you turn the handle
wind the handle this way

bale arm (open)

This is an easy reel to fish with once you learn how to use it properly. You need a stronger and bigger one for sea fishing than for freshwater fishing.

When you turn the reel handle the metal arm, called the bale arm, spins round and round, winding the fishing line on to a fixed spool.

When you open the bale arm, the reel line can run off the spool. As soon as you turn the reel handle, the arm clicks shut automatically and stops the line running off the spool.

1 Winding on the Line

thin string

Fix the reel on to the rod handle and open the bale arm. Then wind some thin string round the reel spool until it is about half full.

2

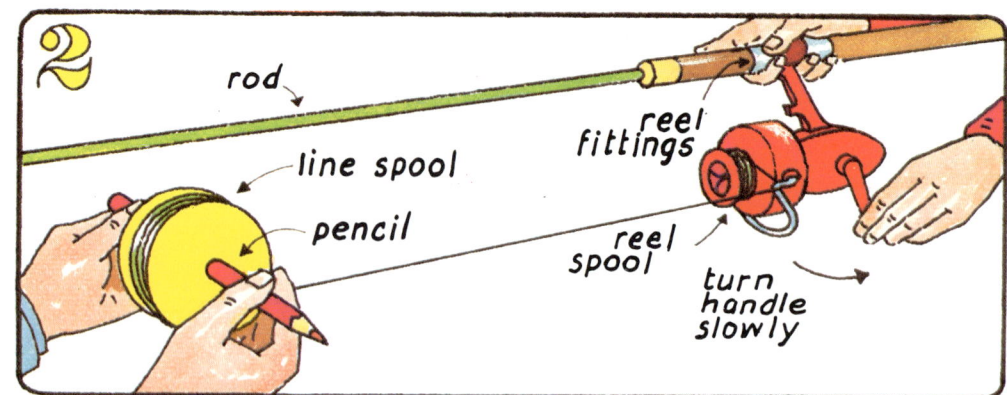

rod
line spool
pencil
reel fittings
reel spool
turn handle slowly

Tie the fishing line to the end of the string. Put a pencil through the line spool and ask a friend to hold it. Now turn the reel handle slowly to wind the line on to the reel.

Keep the line tight as you wind it on to the reel. The reel must not have too much line on it. Cut the line when it is about 3 mm from the rim of the reel.

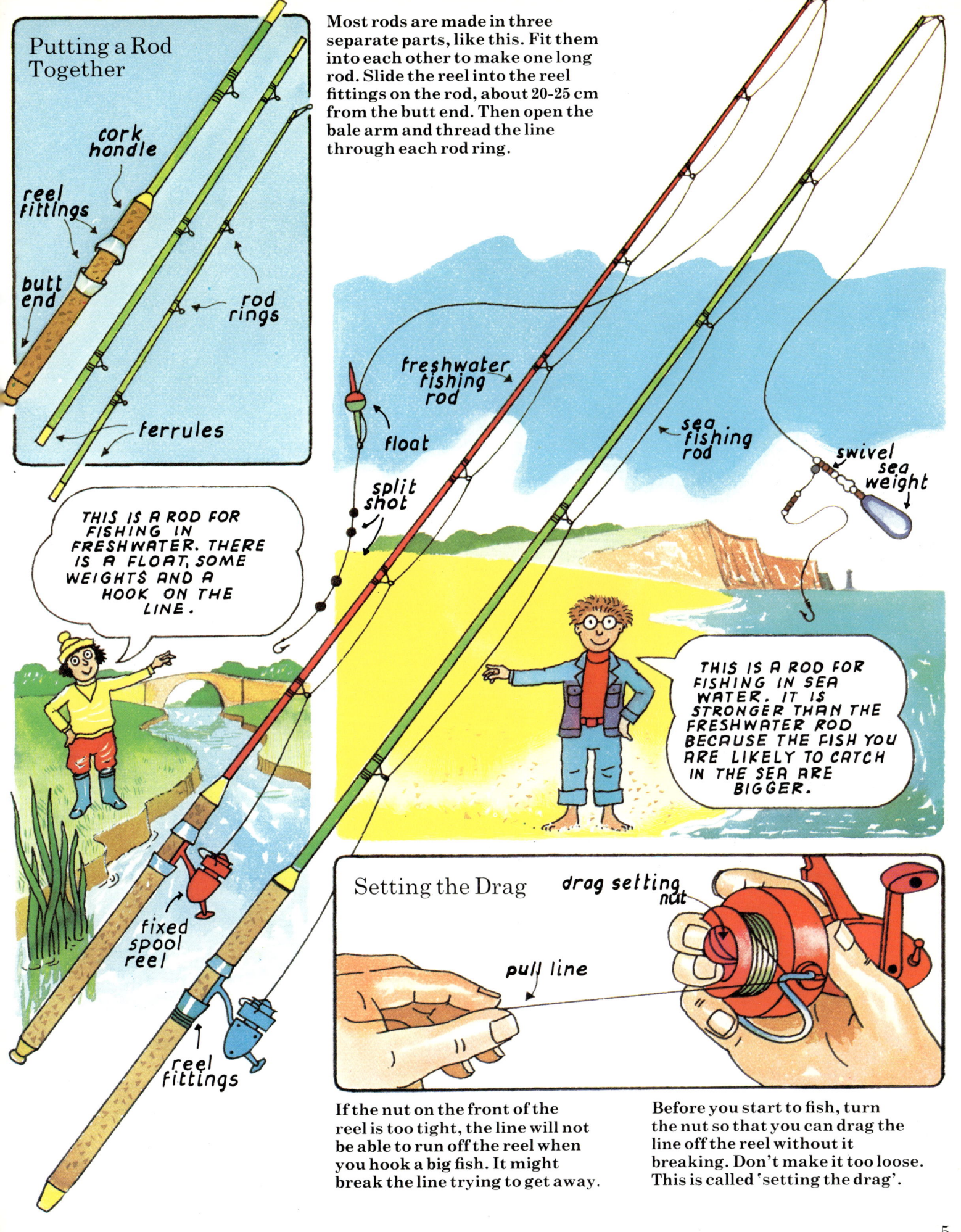

Putting a Rod Together

cork handle

reel fittings

butt end

rod rings

ferrules

Most rods are made in three separate parts, like this. Fit them into each other to make one long rod. Slide the reel into the reel fittings on the rod, about 20-25 cm from the butt end. Then open the bale arm and thread the line through each rod ring.

freshwater fishing rod

float

split shot

sea fishing rod

swivel

sea weight

THIS IS A ROD FOR FISHING IN FRESHWATER. THERE IS A FLOAT, SOME WEIGHTS AND A HOOK ON THE LINE.

THIS IS A ROD FOR FISHING IN SEA WATER. IT IS STRONGER THAN THE FRESHWATER ROD BECAUSE THE FISH YOU ARE LIKELY TO CATCH IN THE SEA ARE BIGGER.

fixed spool reel

reel fittings

Setting the Drag

drag setting nut

pull line

If the nut on the front of the reel is too tight, the line will not be able to run off the reel when you hook a big fish. It might break the line trying to get away.

Before you start to fish, turn the nut so that you can drag the line off the reel without it breaking. Don't make it too loose. This is called 'setting the drag'.

5

Knots and Hints

These are the special knots you need to know for fishing. If you use ordinary knots they will slip on nylon line and you will lose some of your tackle.

Practise tying them so that you can put all the tackle in this book together very quickly.

We have used different coloured line to make it easier for you to see how to tie them.

Simple Loop Knot

Use this kind of knot to make a strong loop at the end of the reel line or a hook length.

Double Loop Knot

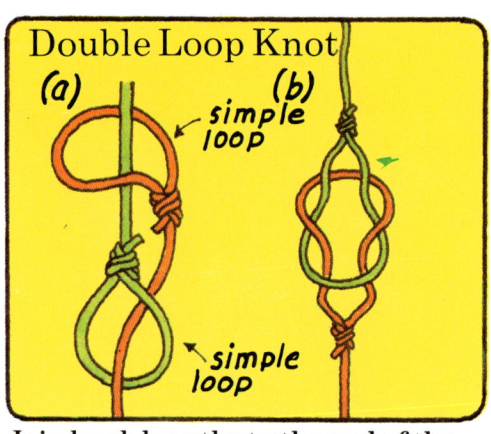

Join hook lengths to the end of the reel line with a double loop knot.

Stop Knot

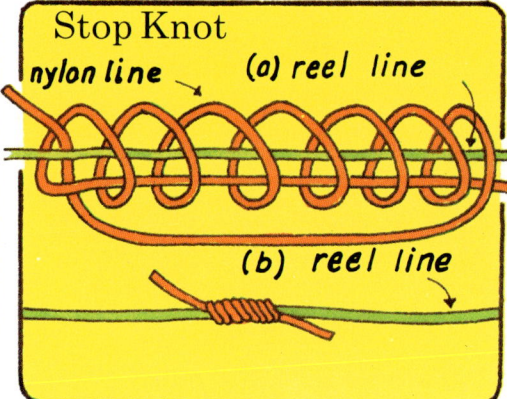

When you use a sliding float, tie a stop knot on to the fishing line above the float.

Half-Blood Knot

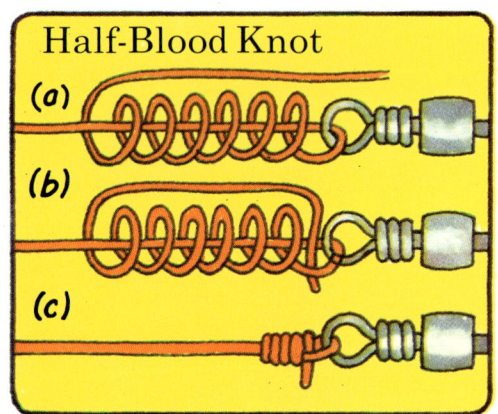

Tie quick-release swivels, barrel swivels and hooks with eyes to the line with a half-blood knot.

Blood Knot

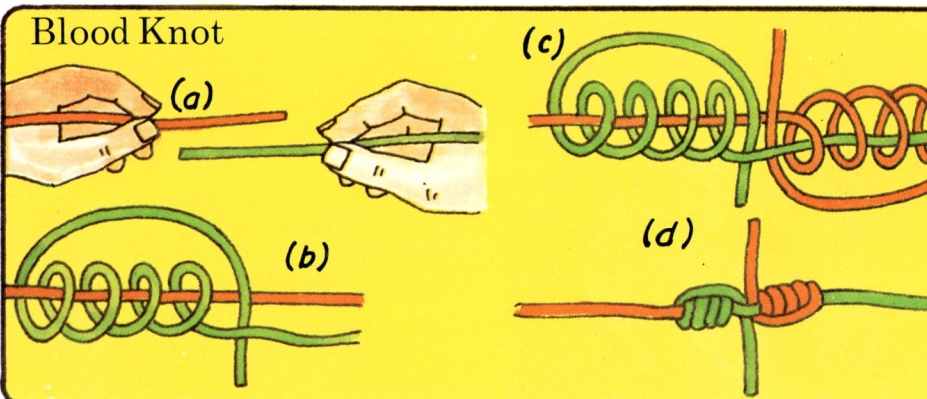

Use this knot to join two lengths of nylon fishing line together.

You can also use it to tie the fishing line to the string you wind on to the fixed spool reel.

Blood Loop

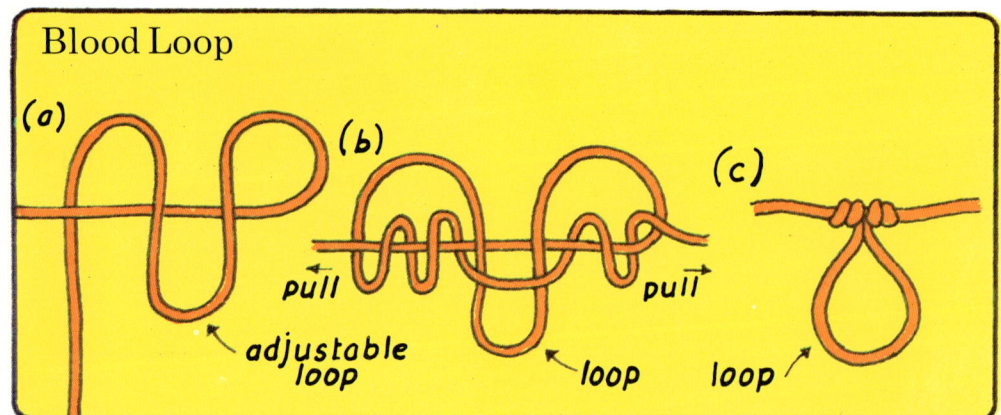

This is how you make a blood loop in a paternoster line for seashore fishing. It is difficult to tie and needs lots of practice.

The loops should be big enough to stick out from the line and to put a hook on.

Hook Lengths

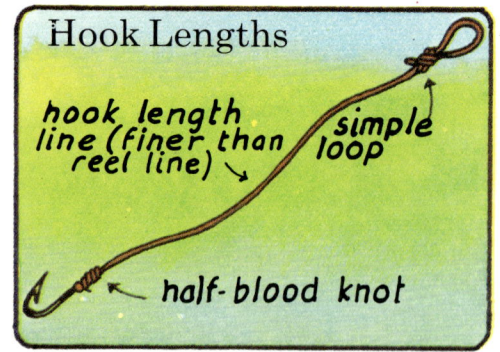

Make up some hook lengths with different size hooks. Tie one to the reel line instead of a hook. It is much quicker. Line often gets broken or tangled and you have to change hooks quickly.

Holding Fish

wet cloth

Most of the freshwater fish you catch have to be put back in the water. Always wet your hands before you hold a fish, or use a wet rag. It stops you from rubbing off the fish's scales and hurting it.

1 Unhooking – By Hand

push down on hook

wet hands

Try very hard not to hurt fish you are going to put back in the water. If the hook is in the lip or on the edge of the fish's mouth, take it out with your fingers.

Push down very gently on the hook to free the end or the barb. Then slide it out of the fish's mouth. When you unhook a big fish, lie it on some wet grass or in a wet landing net.

2 Unhooking – With a Disgorger

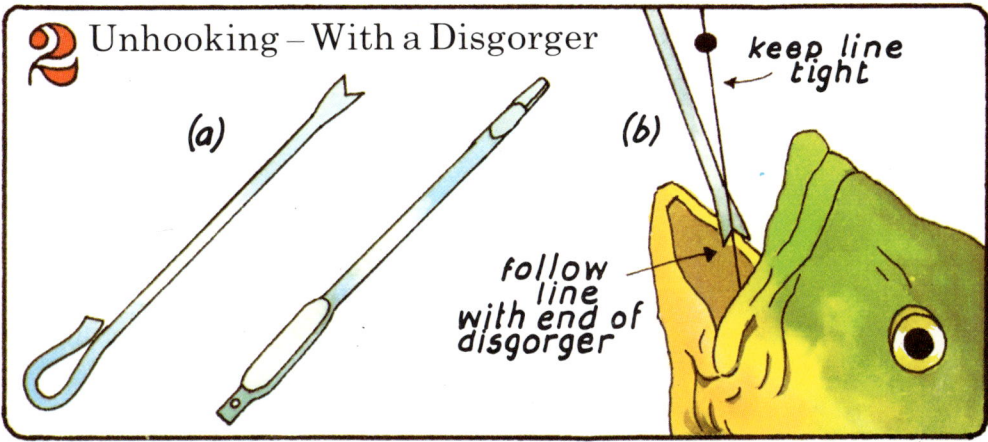

(a)

(b)

keep line tight

follow line with end of disgorger

If the hook is right down the fish's throat, use a disgorger to get it out. These two kinds (a) are the best ones to use. Buy them from a tackle shop.

Slide the disgorger down the fishing line. Then slip it on to the bend of the hook and press down gently to free the barb from the fish's throat (b).

Keeping Records

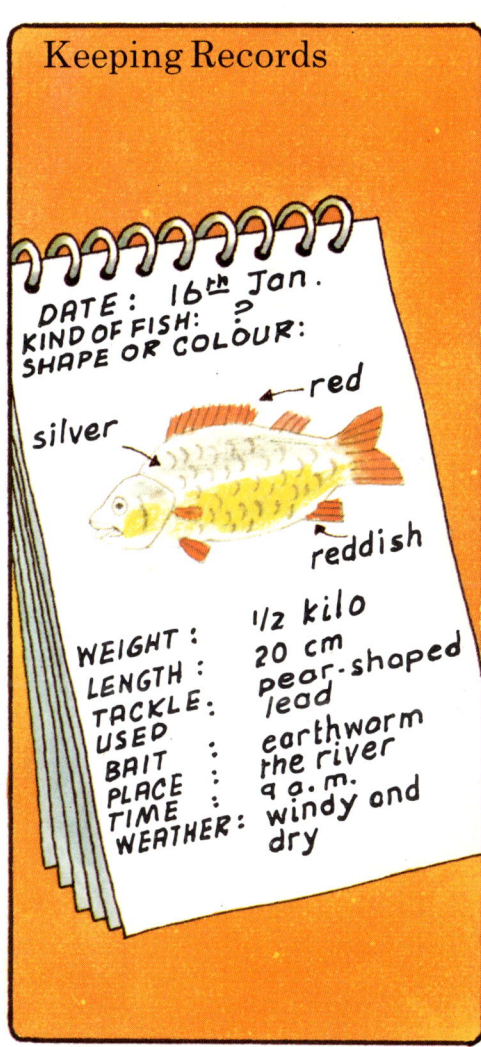

DATE: 16th Jan.
KIND OF FISH: ?
SHAPE OR COLOUR:

red

silver

reddish

WEIGHT: 1/2 kilo
LENGTH: 20 cm
TACKLE: pear-shaped lead
USED:
BAIT: earthworm
PLACE: the river
TIME: 9 a.m.
WEATHER: windy and dry

It is a good idea to keep a log book of the fish you catch. Write down the important things, such as the name, weight and length of the fish, the tackle and bait you used and the time of day. Then you will have a record of the best ways to catch different fish.

Weighing Your Catch

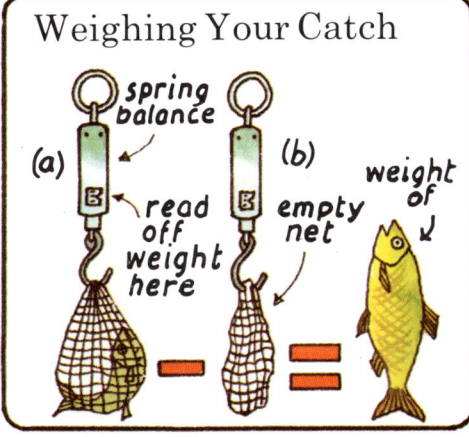

spring balance

(a)

read off weight here

(b)

empty net

weight of

Put the fish into a wet net. Hook the net on to a spring balance, like this. Read off the weight (a). Subtract the weight of the net afterwards to get the weight of the fish only (b).

Looking After Tackle

Keep your rod in a bag and your reel in a box between fishing trips. After fishing, clean off any dirt or sand. Oil all the ferrules.

Hooks must always be very sharp. Sharpen the points with a sharpening stone or sandpaper. Dry the hooks before you put them away to stop them rusting. After fishing, cut any frayed or worn bits off the reel line.

Fishing Gear

You can save money and have a lot of fun making bits of fishing gear yourself.

These two pages show you how to make some things you will find useful. They also show you what weights and hooks to buy for freshwater fishing.

You will need
For the Landing Net
2 wire coat hangers
a strong wooden stick (about 1.5 metres long)
a big net vegetable bag (ask for one at a vegetable shop)
string and waterproof tape
a hair grip or a big darning needle

For the Float Box
a plastic box with a lid
strong elastic thread
sheet sponge, waterproof glue and scissors

For the Rod Rest
a wire coat hanger and string
a strong stick and a penknife

For the Hook Box
a plastic box with a lid
sheet sponge and a cork
waterproof glue and scissors

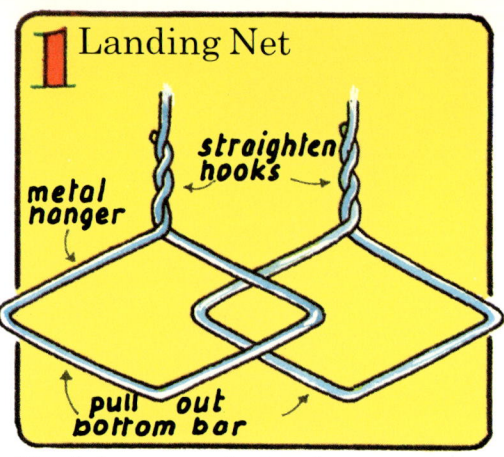

1 Landing Net

Straighten out the hooks on two metal coat hangers. Then pull out the bottom bars so that both hangers are a diamond shape.

Tape the two hangers together, like this. Then tie them to the end of the strong stick with string. Use lots of string and make sure it is very tight.

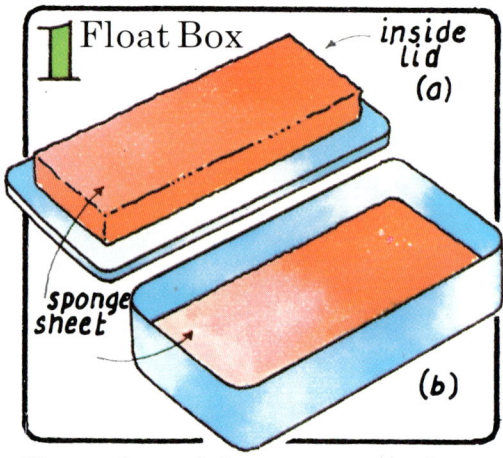

1 Float Box

Glue a piece of sheet sponge to the inside of the box lid, about 2 cm from each side (a). Glue sheet sponge to the bottom of the box as well (b).

2 strong elastic thread

Make three holes with scissors in each end of the lid. Thread a bit of elastic through each pair of holes, like this. Tie knots in the ends.

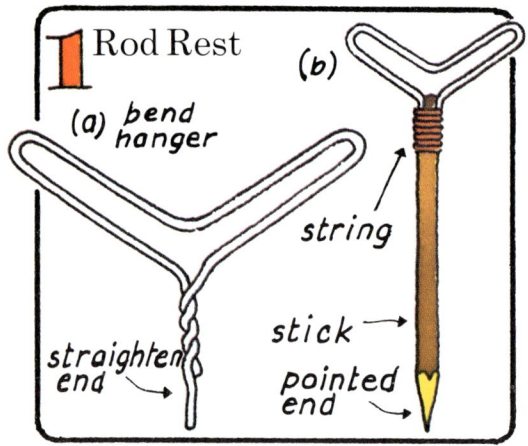

1 Rod Rest

Straighten the hook on a wire coat hanger. Bend the hanger to this shape (a). Trim one end of a stick to a point. Tie the hanger to the other end with string (b).

Always take a rod rest with you when you go fishing. You need two for leger fishing. Put your rod on them, like this, while you are waiting for a fish to bite.

Hold the rod yourself when you use a float. Only leave it on the rod rest when you put bait on the hook, hold or land a fish. Never lie your rod on the ground.

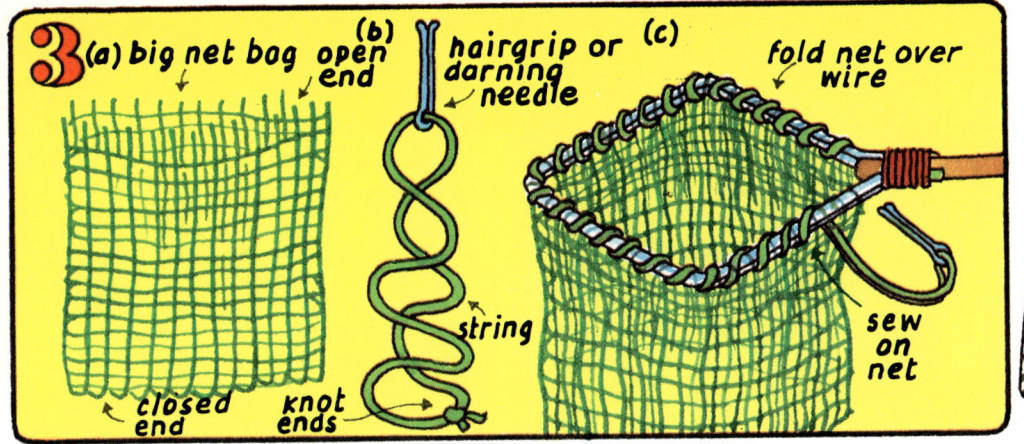

3 (a) big net bag open end (b) hairgrip or darning needle (c) fold net over wire

string

sew on net

closed end   knot ends

Cut off the top of the big net vegetable bag until it is about 35 cm deep (a). Thread string through a hair grip or a big darning needle. Knot the ends (b).

Fold the open end of the net bag over the wire frame. Sew it to the frame with the string, going over and over (c). If the net is too big, gather the edge together as you sew.

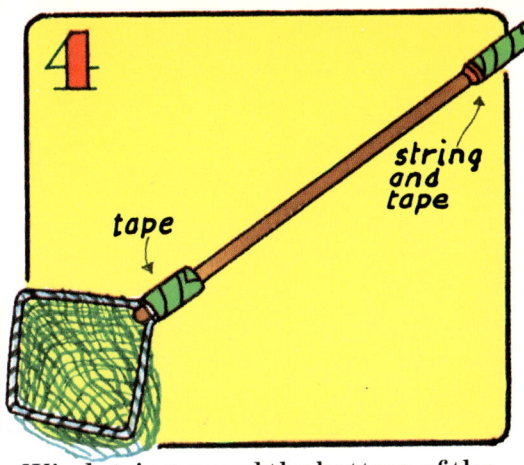

4

string and tape

tape

Wind string round the bottom of the stick for a handle. Cover it with waterproof tape. Then cover the string at the other end of the stick with waterproof tape.

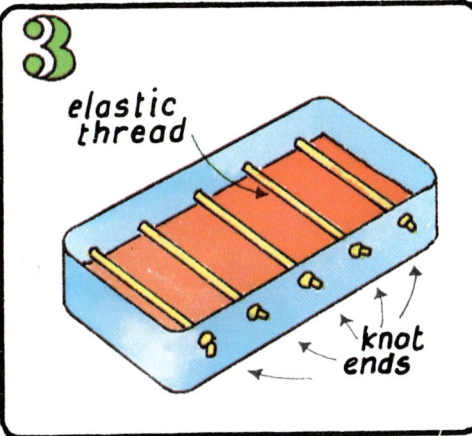

3

elastic thread

knot ends

Make five holes in opposite sides of the plastic box, as shown. Thread a bit of strong elastic through each pair of holes. Tie knots in the ends.

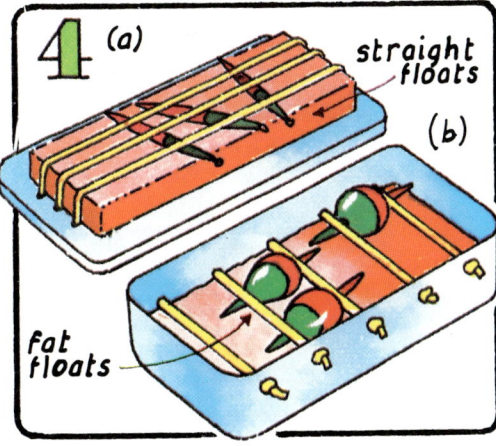

4 (a)   straight floats

(b)

fat floats

Keep your straight floats under the elastic thread on the box lid (a). Keep fat ones and long ones under the elastic on the bottom of the box (b).

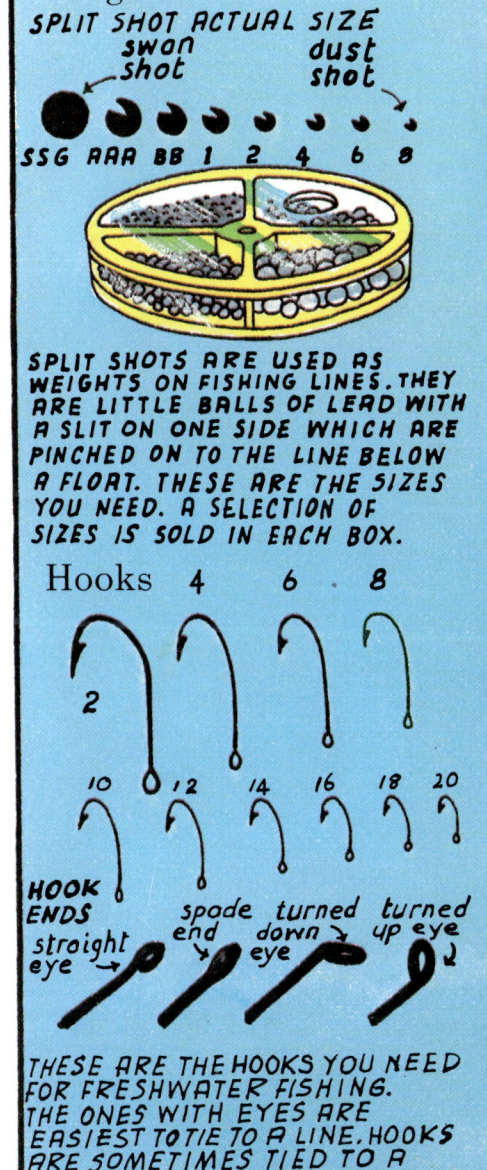

Weights

SPLIT SHOT ACTUAL SIZE

swan shot   dust shot

SSG AAA BB 1 2 4 6 8

SPLIT SHOTS ARE USED AS WEIGHTS ON FISHING LINES. THEY ARE LITTLE BALLS OF LEAD WITH A SLIT ON ONE SIDE WHICH ARE PINCHED ON TO THE LINE BELOW A FLOAT. THESE ARE THE SIZES YOU NEED. A SELECTION OF SIZES IS SOLD IN EACH BOX.

Hooks   4   6   8

2

10 12 14 16 18 20

HOOK ENDS   spode end   turned down eye   turned up eye
straight eye

THESE ARE THE HOOKS YOU NEED FOR FRESHWATER FISHING. THE ONES WITH EYES ARE EASIEST TO TIE TO A LINE. HOOKS ARE SOMETIMES TIED TO A DIFFERENT LINE FROM THE REEL LINE. IT IS CALLED A HOOK LENGTH.

1 Hook Box glue on cork sheet

lid

sponge

box bottom

Glue a piece of sheet sponge to the inside of the box lid. Glue some to the bottom of the box too. Then glue a cork to the middle of the lid, like this.

2 push hooks in sponge and cork

sticky labels with sizes

Push your hooks into the sponge and cork to keep them sharp and safe. Group them in size order. Stick labels with the size numbers above each group.

Making Freshwater Floats

These are some freshwater floats you can make. The longer they are, the more weights they need on the line below them to float upright in the water. Sea fishing floats are bigger and difficult to make. It is better to buy them.

Always glue up the ends of the float to seal them and make them water-tight. Let the glue dry before you paint the float.

You will need
2 big feathers (chicken, duck
   or turkey feathers will do)
a cork
a plastic drinking straw
a thin, wooden stick or thin
   dowel (about 15 cm long and
   as thick as a pencil)
2 wooden golf tees
a peacock quill from a tackle
   shop
a ping pong ball
fine sandpaper, a penknife
   and waterproof glue (Copydex)
thin wire and some thread
rubber float rings from a tackle
   shop (to fix the float to the
   fishing line)
scissors and a paint brush
waterproof paint (craft paints
   or special float paints)

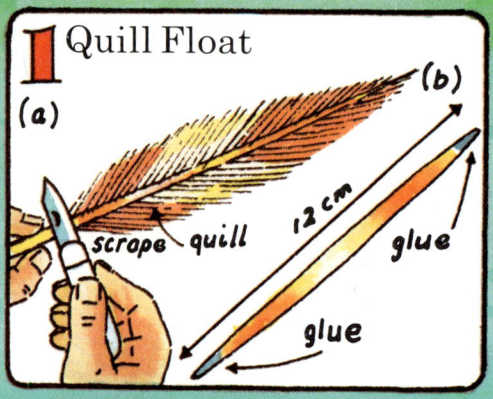

1 Quill Float

Starting from the thick end of the feather, scrape clean about 12 cm (a). Cut it off – this is the quill. Cut the thin end until it is as thin as a match. Glue up both ends (b).

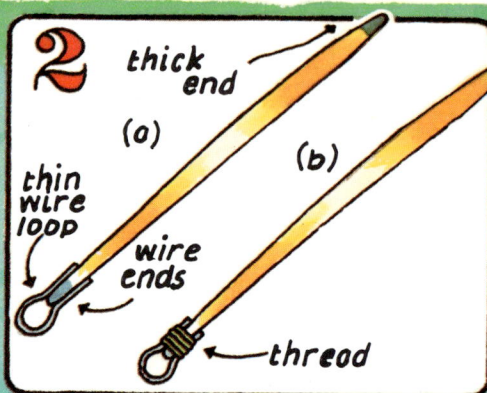

Rub the quill with sandpaper. Loop a bit of wire round the thin end (a). Wind thread round the wire ends and coat it with glue (b). This is called whipping.

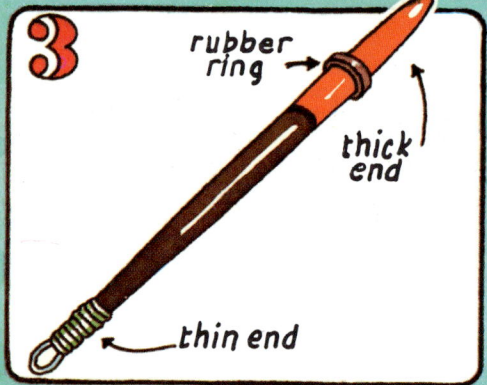

Paint 3 cm of the thick end of the quill a bright colour. Paint the rest a dark colour. Leave it to dry. Then slide a rubber float ring on to the thick end.

1 Quill and Cork Float

Make a hole through the middle of a cork with thin scissors or a knitting needle. Do not make the hole too big. The cork is for the body of the float.

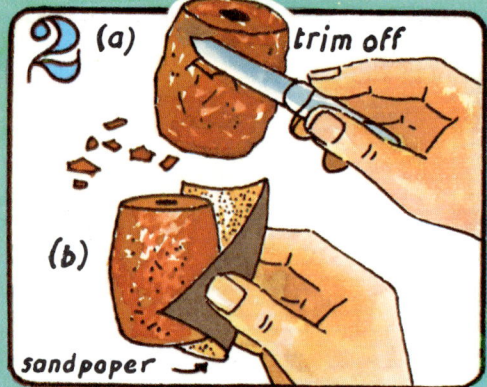

Shape the cork with a sharp knife until it is about this size (a). Then smooth off the rough corners with fine sandpaper (b).

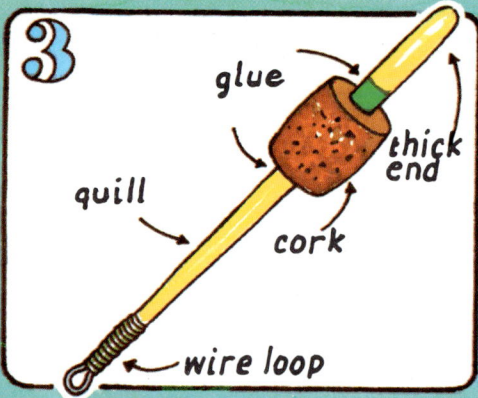

Clean off, trim, sandpaper and glue a quill as in Quill Float 1 above. Push the quill through the hole in the cork. Glue up the holes. Then whip on a wire loop.

Paint the thick end and half the cork a bright colour. Paint the rest a dark, murky colour. Leave the float to dry. Then slide on a rubber float ring.

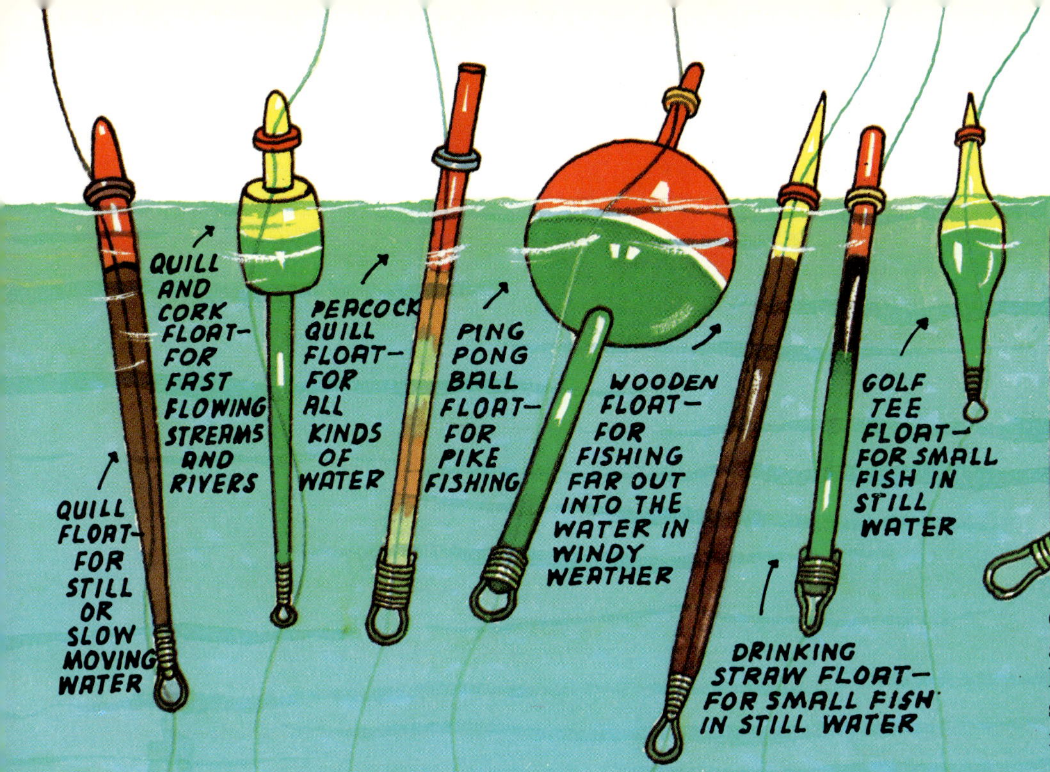

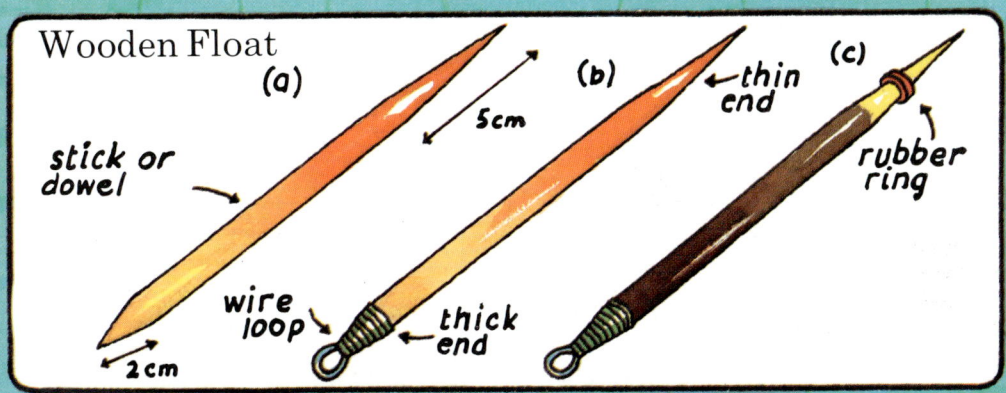

QUILL AND CORK FLOAT—FOR FAST FLOWING STREAMS AND RIVERS

QUILL FLOAT—FOR STILL OR SLOW MOVING WATER

PEACOCK QUILL FLOAT—FOR ALL KINDS OF WATER

PING PONG BALL FLOAT—FOR PIKE FISHING

WOODEN FLOAT—FOR FISHING FAR OUT INTO THE WATER IN WINDY WEATHER

DRINKING STRAW FLOAT—FOR SMALL FISH IN STILL WATER

GOLF TEE FLOAT—FOR SMALL FISH IN STILL WATER

Drinking Straw Float

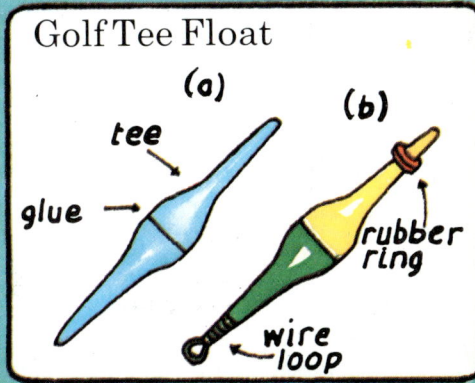

rubber ring

straw

glue

wire loop

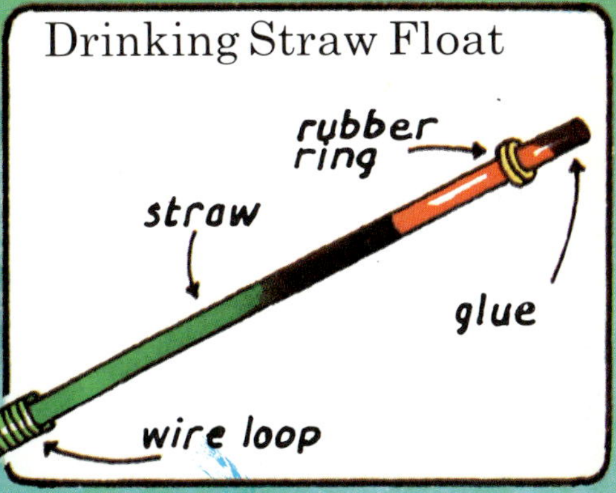

Glue up both ends of a plastic straw about 10 cm long. Whip on a wire loop with thread and glue. Paint as shown. Then slide on a rubber float ring, like this.

Wooden Float

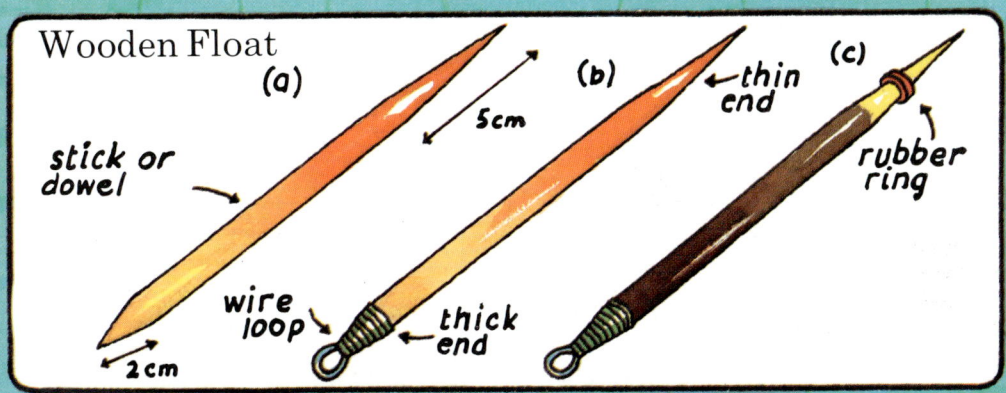

(a) stick or dowel — 5cm — wire loop — 2cm

(b) thin end — thick end — wire loop

(c) thin end — rubber ring — wire loop

Cut about 15 cm off a thin stick or piece of dowel. Use a knife to shape one end to a long, thin point. Shape the other end to a short, thick point, like this (a).

Smooth the stick with fine sandpaper. Whip a wire loop on to the thick end (b). Paint as shown and leave it to dry. Then slide a float ring on to the thin end (c).

Golf Tee Float

(a) tee — glue

(b) rubber ring — wire loop

Glue two wooden tees together, like this (a). Whip a wire loop on to one point. Paint as shown. Then slide a float ring on to the other point (b).

Peacock Quill Float

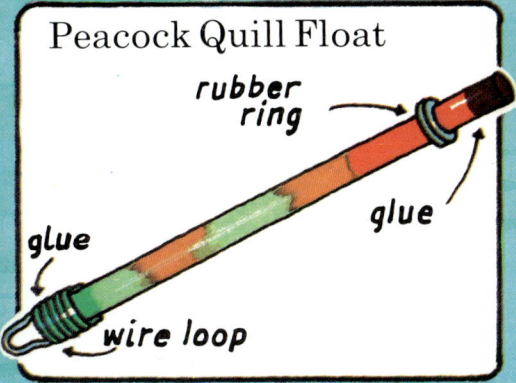

rubber ring

glue

glue

wire loop

Put glue on both ends of a peacock quill about 10 cm long. Whip a small wire loop on to one end. Paint the quill as shown. Slide on a rubber float ring.

Ping Pong Ball Float

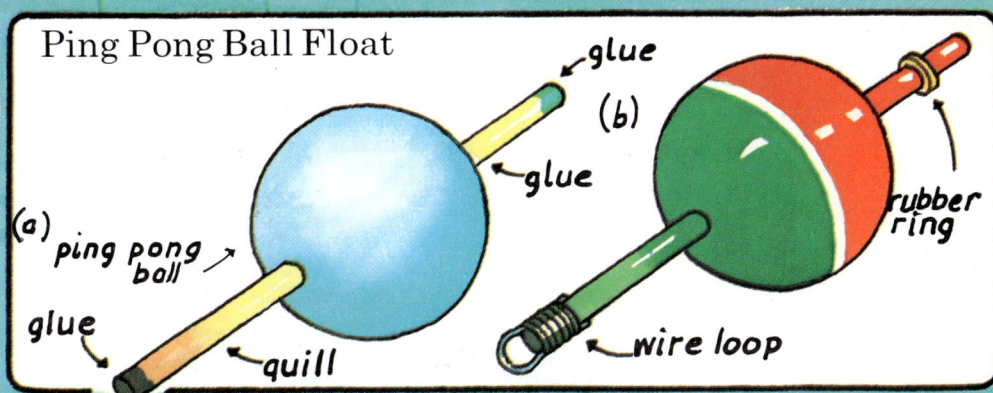

(a) ping pong ball — glue — quill

(b) glue — glue — rubber ring — wire loop

Make two holes in a ping pong ball, as shown. Push a quill, 10 cm long, through the holes. Put glue on the quill ends and round the holes in the ping pong ball (a).

Whip a wire loop on to one end of the quill. Paint the other end and half the ball a bright colour. Paint the rest a dark colour. Slide on a float ring (b).

Casting and Landing

Swinging the rod to drop the hook into the water at the right spot is called casting. It takes lots of practice. Practise in a field or garden with a small weight on the line and no hook.

The hardest part is letting go of the line at the right moment. When you get very good you will be able to get the hook and bait to the right spot every time.

As soon as a fish bites, reel in slowly and land it. If you don't get a bite after a few minutes when you are float fishing, reel in the line and cast again.

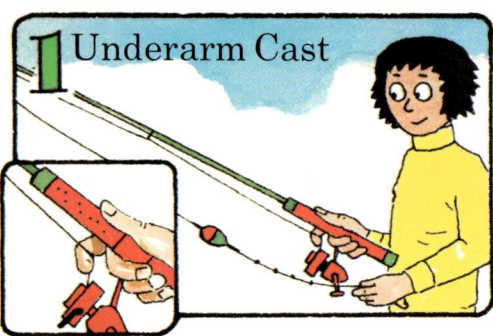

1 Underarm Cast

Hold the rod handle in your right hand. Open the bale arm of the reel and press the line against the rod with your first finger. Then hold the line in your left hand, just above the hook, as shown.

2

Gently swing out the line, lifting up your finger at the end of the swing. As soon as the hook-bait hits the water, turn the reel handle to close the bale arm.

3 wind handle to tighten line

Wind the handle until the fishing line is tight right down to the float. Use this underarm cast when you are fishing with floats.

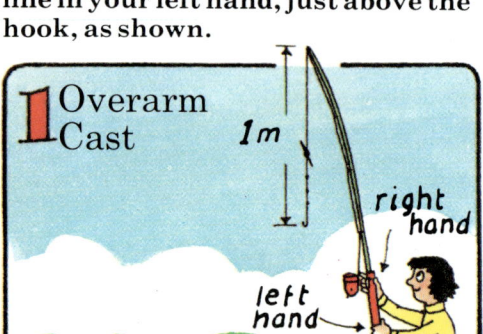

1 Overarm Cast 1m right hand left hand

Use an overarm cast when your fishing spot is far out from the bank. Pull one metre of line below the rod tip. Hold the rod up with both hands, like this.

2 swing line clear

Open the bale arm and press the line against the rod with your finger. Swing the rod back a bit. Aim at the right spot in the water and jerk the rod forwards.

3 jerk rod forwards

When your right arm is straight, lift up your first finger to let the line fly out. As soon as it hits the water, close the bale arm and wind the reel handle to tighten up the line.

1 Beach Casting 1m weight feet apart

Pull about one metre of line from the rod tip to the weight. Stand with your feet apart and your left shoulder towards the direction you are going to cast.

2 right hand left hand

Hold the rod in both hands. Open the bale arm. Press your finger against the line. Swing the rod right back. Jerk it forwards, pulling down with your left hand and pushing forwards with your right.

3

When your right arm is straight, lift up your finger and let the line fly out. When the weight has sunk to the bottom, close the bale arm and tighten the line.

Hand Landing

If you catch a little fish, you don't need a net to land it in. Just swing it straight into your hand. Hold its head and shoulders gently so that you don't hurt it.

1 Net Landing

rod tip bent
keep line tight

When you catch a big fish, use your landing net. Hold the rod upright so that the fish pulls against the rod tip. Keep the line very tight or the fish might wriggle off the hook.

2

rod tip straight

The rod tip will straighten out when the fish gets tired. Now reel in very slowly, keeping the fish just under the water. Slide the landing net under it when you get it to the bank.

1 Beach Landing

If you hook a big fish from the beach reel it in very slowly until it is partly out of the water. Then walk backwards up the beach and wait for a big wave.

2

Let the wave wash the fish safely up the shingle or sand where you can pick it up. Never try to lift it out of the water on the end of your line. You might break the line and lose the fish.

IMPORTANT!

WATCH OUT FOR TREES AND BUSHES BEHIND YOU AS YOU CAST. YOUR LINE MIGHT GET TANGLED UP IN THEM.

TRY NOT TO MAKE SHADOWS ON THE WATER. THEY SCARE THE FISH AWAY. STAND WITH THE SUN SHINING TOWARDS YOU IF POSSIBLE.

DON'T JUMP ABOUT ON THE BANK OR MAKE TOO MUCH NOISE. FISH CAN HEAR VERY WELL AND WILL SWIM OFF AT THE SLIGHTEST SOUND.

NEVER REEL IN A FISH ON TOP OF THE WATER. IT WILL THRASH ABOUT AND FRIGHTEN OFF THE FISH NEARBY.

Freshwater Baits

Most freshwater fish will eat different sorts of bait. If you don't catch any fish with one kind, try another. Baits put on hooks are called hook-baits.

Keep bread and cheese baits in a wet cloth to stop them from crumbling. Put worms in an old box with damp garden soil, vegetable scraps and tea leaves.

You are much more likely to catch a fish if you use ground-bait. This is bait you put into the water near the fishing spot.

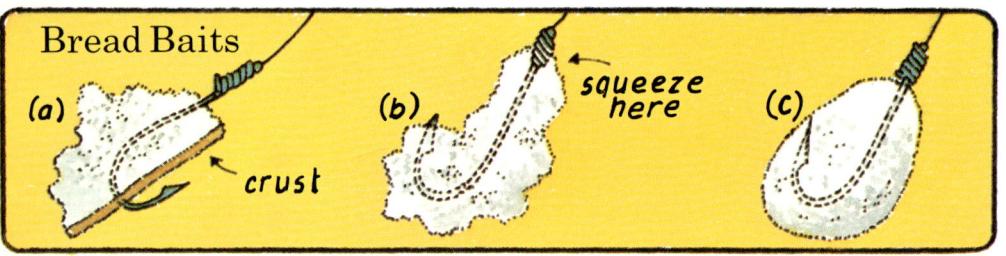

Bread Baits

(a) crust
(b) squeeze here
(c)

Nearly all freshwater fish like bread baits. Put a small bit of crust on the hook, like this (a) or press some fresh bread round the bend of the hook, like this (b).

Use lumps of bread paste. Make it by wetting some stale bread. Put it in a rag and squeeze out the water. Shape it into lumps (c). Use hook sizes 8-14 for bread baits.

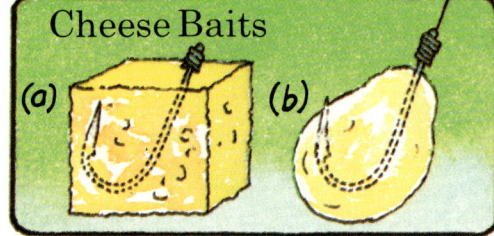

Cheese Baits

(a) (b)

Cheese is a good bait for chub. Use any fairly soft cheese, either in small cubes (a) or mixed with bread paste (b). Use hook sizes 6-8 for cheese baits.

1 Minnows

hook here

Minnows, alive or dead, make very good bait for pike, perch and eels. Hook them through the lip, like this. Use hook sizes 6-8 for minnow baits.

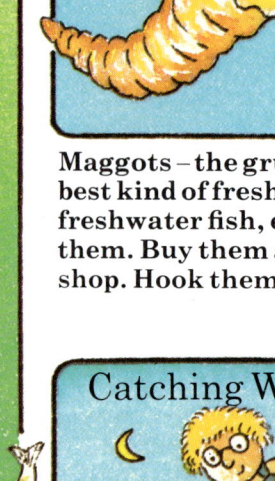

2

bread

Try catching minnows in a bottle, like this. Put it in shallow water with bits of bread in it and wait for the minnows to swim in.

Maggots and Casters

(a) (b)

Maggots – the grubs of flies – are the best kind of freshwater bait. All freshwater fish, except pike, will eat them. Buy them alive from a tackle shop. Hook them like this (a).

A Maggot's Life

1. egg 2. maggot
3. caster (chrysalis) 4. fly

You can use one or more at a time. Casters (b)–maggots which have turned into chrysalises–also make good bait. Use hook sizes 12 downwards for these baits.

Catching Worms

(a) (b)

washing-up liquid and water

Lots of freshwater fish like garden worms. Dig them up, or collect them by torchlight on the lawn after dark (a). If you pour water with a

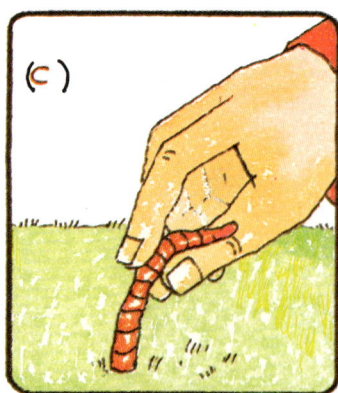

(c)

little washing-up liquid over the grass, it helps bring worms out of their holes (b). Pull them out very gently, like this (c). A whole worm is much better than half a worm.

Ground-Bait

SOME ANGLERS FIND THAT THEY CATCH MORE FISH IF THEY SCATTER LOTS OF BAIT ROUND THE SPOT WHERE THEY ARE FISHING. YOU CAN DO THIS BY MAKING BALLS OF BAIT, EACH ABOUT THE SIZE OF AN ORANGE, AND THROWING THEM INTO THE WATER WHERE YOU ARE FISHING. AS THE BALLS OF BAIT, CALLED GROUND-BAIT, HIT THE WATER THEY BREAK UP INTO BITS AND SINK TO THE BOTTOM.

IF YOU ARE FISHING IN FLOWING WATER THROW THE GROUND-BAIT JUST UPSTREAM OF THE FISHING SPOT. THEN IT WILL SINK IN THE RIGHT PLACE.

IF YOU ARE FISHING IN STILL WATER THROW THE GROUND-BAIT BALLS STRAIGHT TO THE SPOT YOU ARE GOING TO FISH IN.

Ground-bait for Flowing Water

worms added

When you fish in flowing water, use ground-bait that does not break up too quickly. Soak bits of stale bread in water and squeeze them into balls. Add bits of the hook-bait you are using, such as maggots, bits of worm or cheese.

Still Water Ground-bait

For still water fishing, use ground-bait made out of very small breadcrumbs. They will break up quickly and cloud the water. Roll a bottle over bits of stale bread to make the crumbs. Dampen them and squeeze them into balls.

Making a Wormery

(a) (b) (c) (d)

If you make a wormery, you will always have worms for bait. Dig up a patch of earth. Throw away any stones and twigs (a). Then mark the patch with sticks (b).

Mix old tea leaves, vegetable scraps and cut grass in with the soil as often as possible (c). Keep it wet and cover it with sacking (d). Lots of worms will soon wriggle into the wormery.

Hooking Garden Worms

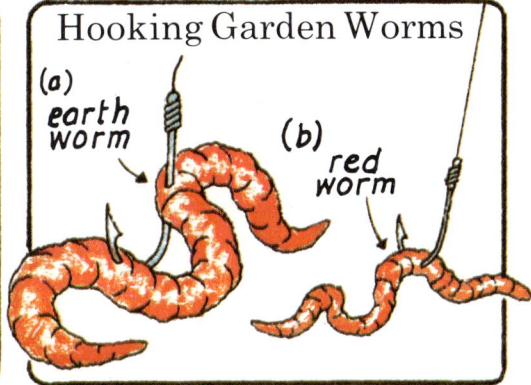

(a) earth worm   (b) red worm

Push the hook twice through a big worm, like this (a). Hook a small one through its middle (b). Use hook sizes 6, 8 or 10 depending on the size of the worm.

Freshwater Float Fishing

A float shows you when a fish bites and keeps the hook at the right depth. Use a float when the water is not very deep. The fishing line you use should be no longer than your rod or it may be difficult to cast.

Use bought floats or the ones you have made. The weights keep the float upright in the water and stop the hook-bait from rising. The amount of weights you need on the line depends on how deep and fast the water is.

First fix the float to the line and put on the weights. Then find out how deep the water is with a plummet to make sure that the hook hangs just above the bottom. Take the plummet off and put bait on the hook.

1 Fixing on the Float

float ring

wire loop

Slide a float ring on to the line about one metre from the end. Push the tip of the float through the ring. Thread the line through the loop on the end of the float.

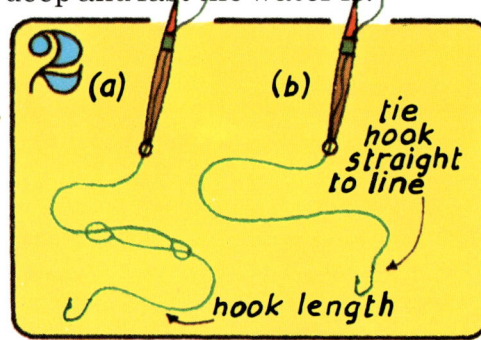

2 (a) (b)

tie hook straight to line

hook length

Tie a hook on to the end of the line. Use either a hook length (a) or tie the hook straight on to the line (b). See page 5 for hook lengths and knots.

3

lead shot (size AA or BB)

press on shot

Squeeze enough split shot on to the line to make the float stand upright in the water. Only about 1 cm of the tip should show. This is called cocking the float.

1 Setting the Float

(a) ring   (b) float

cork strip

plummet   push hook into cork strip

Now use a plummet (a) to find out how deep the water is. Thread the hook and line through the plummet ring and push the hook into the strip of cork (b).

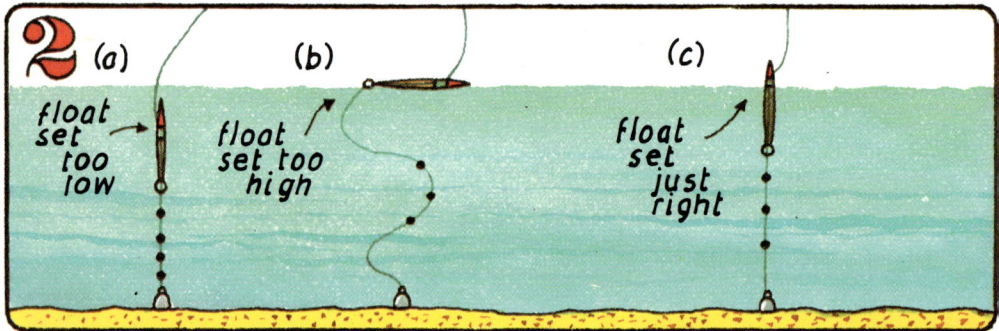

2 (a)   (b)   (c)

float set too low   float set too high   float set just right

Cast the plummet into the water. If the float goes under, it is set too low (a). If it lies flat on top, it is set too high (b).

Slide the float up or down the line, until just the tip shows above the water when the plummet is on the bottom (c). Take off the plummet and put some bait on to the hook.

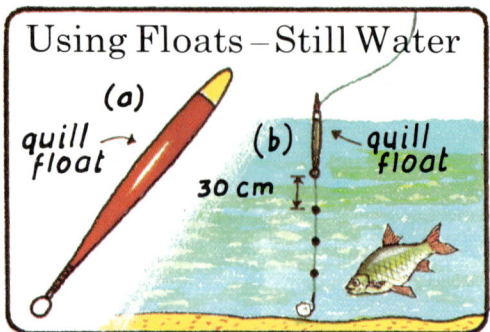

Using Floats – Still Water

(a) quill float   (b) quill float

30 cm

Use a light float such as a quill (a). Squeeze enough shot on to the line to cock the float. Space it out evenly, like this. Then set the float with a plummet (b).

Using Floats – Flowing Water

avon float (a)   (b)

peacock quill float

shot

Use a heavier float, such as an Avon float or peacock quill (a). Group the shot close to the hook so that the bait sinks quickly to the bottom. Cock and set the float.

Once you have set the float, push it up the line another 25 cm. Then the hook-bait will stay on the bottom (b). This sort of tackle is called trotting tackle.

Fishing with Trotting Tackle

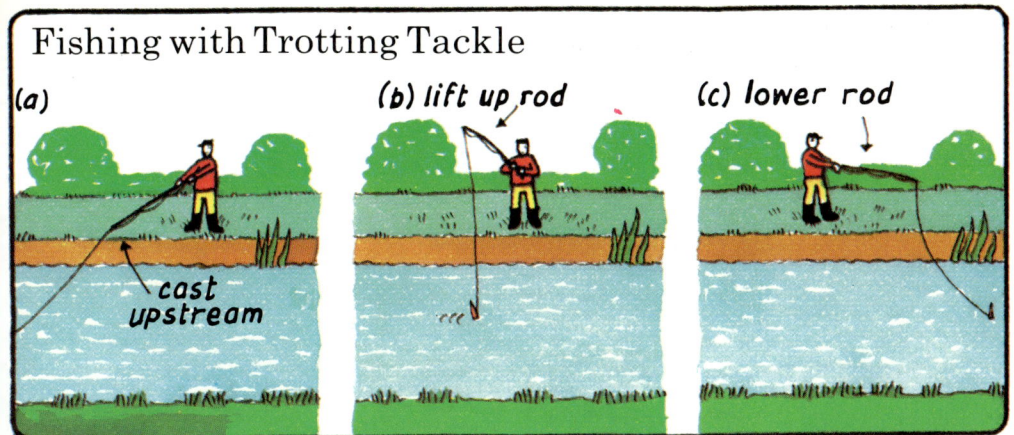

(a)

(b) lift up rod

(c) lower rod

cast upstream

Cast the tackle a little way upstream (a). Keep the line tight. Lift up the end of the rod a bit as the float comes towards you. Point the rod at the float, like this (b).

When the float goes past you, lower the rod a bit. Let it stay downstream for a few seconds (c). If you don't get a bite, reel in the line and cast again.

Windy Weather

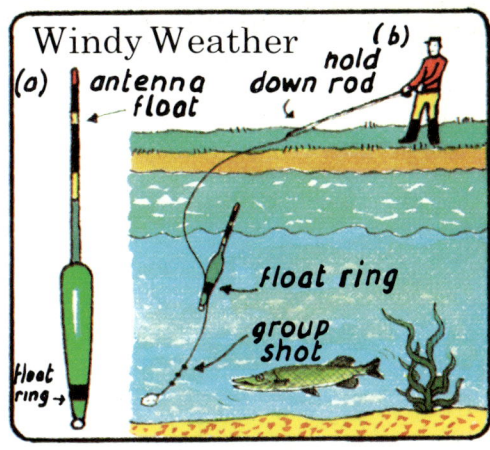

(a) antenna float

hold (b) down rod

float ring

group shot

float ring

Use an antenna float (a). Only thread the line through the float ring. Group the shot as shown and cock the float. Then set it so the bulky part is under the water (b).

1 Laying-on Method

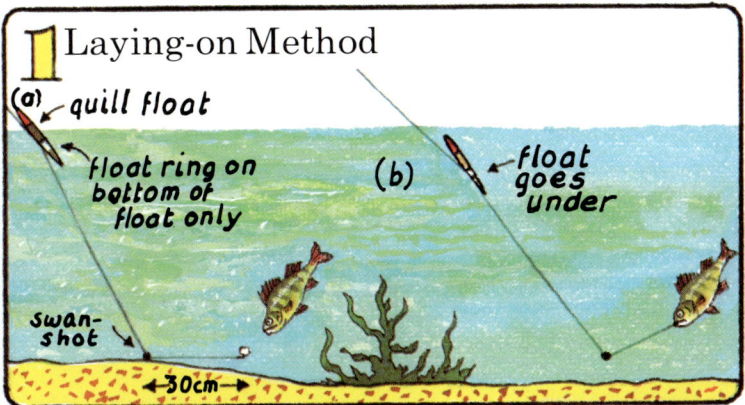

(a) quill float

Float ring on bottom of float only

(b)

float goes under

swan-shot

←30cm→

If you are not getting many bites, try the laying-on (1) or lift (2) methods of fishing. The weight keeps the bait still on the bottom. You can use the laying-on method in both still and flowing water. First cock and set the float.

Then push it up the line another metre. Cast out the line and then tighten it up until only the tip of the float shows (a). When a fish bites, the float will go under the water (b). Use the lift method in still water.

2 Lift Method

(c) float

(d) float lies flat

rubber ring

5cm

Thread the line through a float ring on the bottom of the float only. Cock and set the float so that a swan-shot just rests on the bottom (c). When a fish bites, it lifts the shot off the bottom and the float lies flat on the water (d).

Sinking Bait Quickly

group shot

Sometimes little fish swimming near the top, eat hook-bait before it sinks to where the bigger fish are feeding. Move the shot nearer the hook to make it sink more quickly.

When to Strike

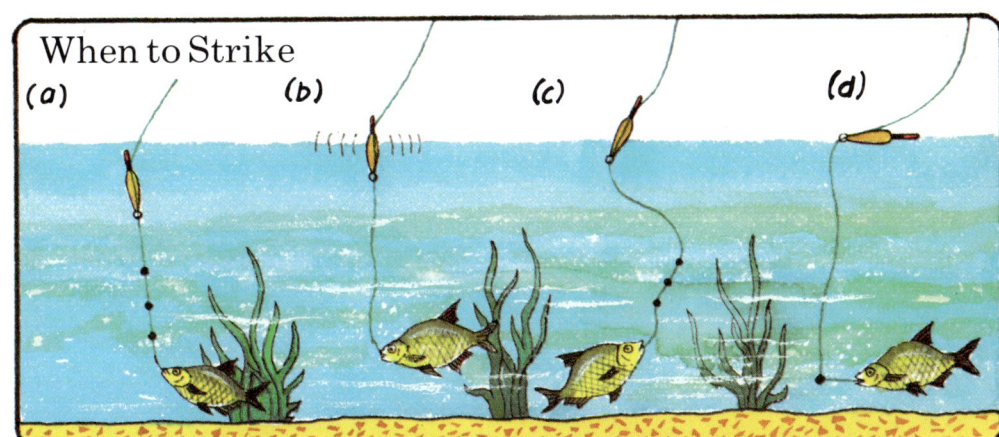

(a)   (b)   (c)   (d)

Striking means lifting up the tip of your rod quickly as soon as a fish takes the bait. As you lift it the line tightens and the hook sticks into the fish's mouth.

Strike if the float goes under the water (a) or wiggles about sideways (b). If it come right up out of the water (c) or lies flat on top (d) strike at once.

Freshwater Leger Fishing

When you fish in deep water, in a strong current or far out from the bank, it is better to use a weight but no float. This is called leger fishing. Leger weights are heavier than the ones you used with a float.

These two pages show you how to make up different kinds of leger tackle for freshwater fishing. The lead weights come in different sizes. Make sure you use one heavy enough to keep the hook-bait in the right spot.

When you have fixed the leger weight on to the line, tie on a hook, put bait on it and cast out. Let the lead settle on the bottom. Then tighten up the line. Hold the rod or use two rod rests while you wait for a bite.

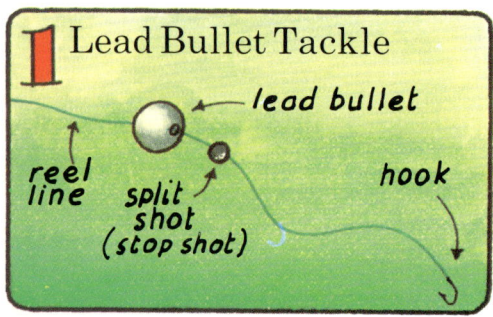

1 Lead Bullet Tackle

lead bullet, reel line, split shot (stop shot), hook

Thread a lead bullet on to the line. Squeeze on a shot, about 45 cm from the hook. The shot stops the bullet from sliding down to the bait. It is called a stop shot.

2

ball rolls along bottom

Lead bullet tackle is a good tackle for still or flowing water. It is specially good for catching chub. In rivers, the bullet rolls along the bottom until it gets downstream.

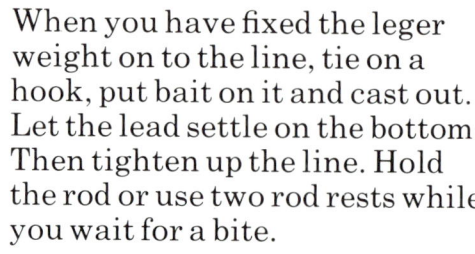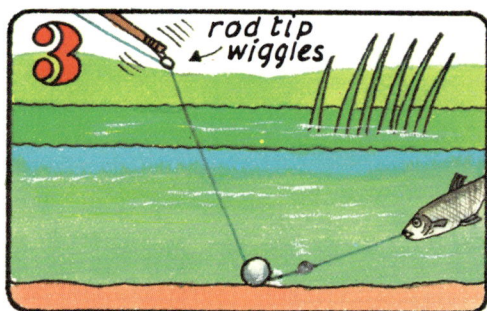

3 rod tip wiggles

When a fish takes the bait, the line slides through the hole in the lead and the fish does not feel it. Strike when you see the tip of the rod starting to wiggle.

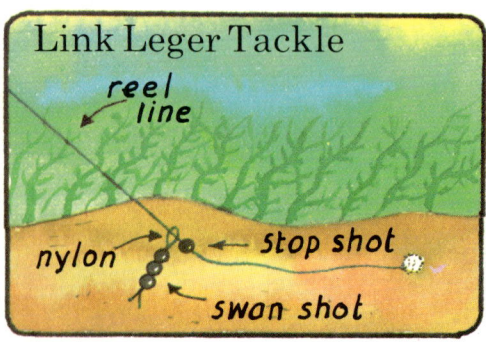

Link Leger Tackle

reel line, stop shot, nylon, swan shot

This is a good tackle to use over weedy ground. Loop a bit of nylon line round the reel line. Pinch two or three swan shot on to the nylon line. Then put on a stop shot.

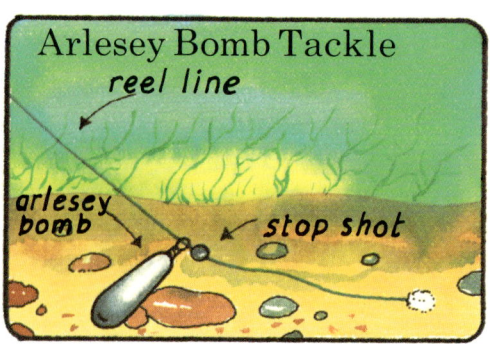

Arlesey Bomb Tackle

reel line, arlesey bomb, stop shot

This pear-shaped lead is one of the best leger weights to buy. You can use it in all kinds of water. Thread it on to the reel line and squeeze on a stop shot, like this.

Coffin Lead Tackle

coffin lead, stop shot

Use a coffin lead over a muddy bottom. The flat shape stops it from sinking into the mud. Thread the lead on to the reel line and then squeeze on a stop shot.

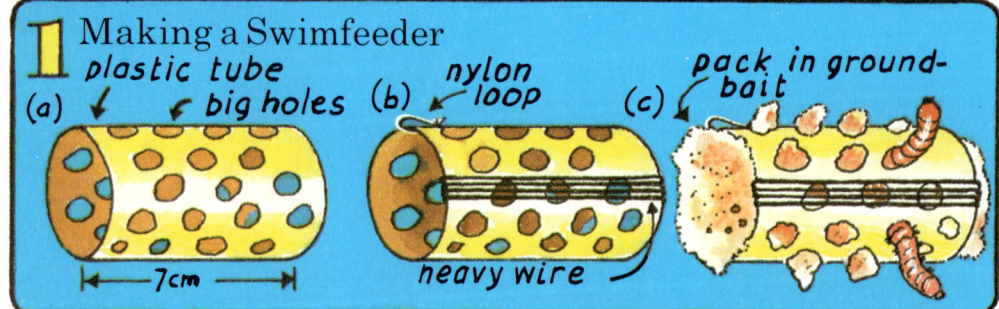

1 Making a Swimfeeder

(a) plastic tube, big holes
(b) nylon loop
(c) pack in ground-bait, heavy wire

7cm

A swimfeeder makes a good leger weight. It also puts ground-bait near the hook-bait in the water. To make one, punch big holes in a small plastic tube with scissors (a).

Wrap some lead wire round one side of the tube to use as a weight. Tie on a small nylon loop (b). Before you start to fish, pack the feeder with bread, bits of worm or some maggots, like this (c).

2

reel line, stop shot, bait

Thread the feeder on to the fishing line and squeeze on a stop shot. When you cast it into the water, the bait comes out of the holes and brings fish to that spot.

ALWAYS KEEP AN EYE ON YOUR ROD TIP OR BITE INDICATOR. IF YOU DOZE OFF OR READ A BOOK YOU MIGHT MISS A BITE OR EVEN LOSE YOUR TACKLE.

Trails

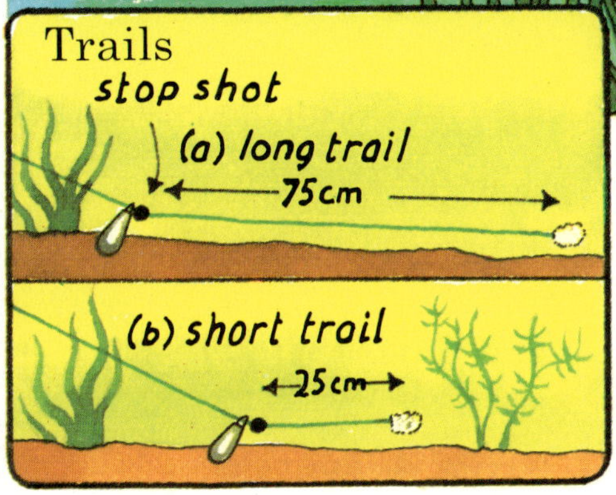

stop shot
(a) long trail
75 cm
(b) short trail
25 cm

The length of line between the stop shot and the hook is called the trail. In flowing water, it should be about 75 cm long (a). In still water, it should be about 25 cm (b).

1 Bite Indicators – Bread Ball

(a) last rod ring
bread paste
(b)
ball pulled against rod

A bite indicator tells you when a fish is biting. The simplest kind is a ball of bread paste. Squeeze it on to the line between the last rod ring and the reel (a).

When a fish takes the hook-bait, it pulls the line tight and the bread ball is pushed up against the rod (b). Strike as soon as you see this happen.

2 – Twig or Silver Paper

(a) small twig
(b) silver paper

A small twig (a) or a folded piece of silver paper (b) also make good bite indicators. Wait until they are pulled up against the rod before you strike.

3 – Swing-tips

(a) screw in
leger rod
bendy part
extra bit of rod
swing tip
(b) swing tip before fish bites
(c) swing tip when fish bites

A swing-tip is a bite indicator which screws into the top of a leger fishing rod (a). You can buy one from a fishing tackle shop.

To use it, cast out the leger tackle in the ordinary way. Reel in the line until the swing-tip hangs down (b). As soon as a fish takes the bait, the tip lifts up (c).

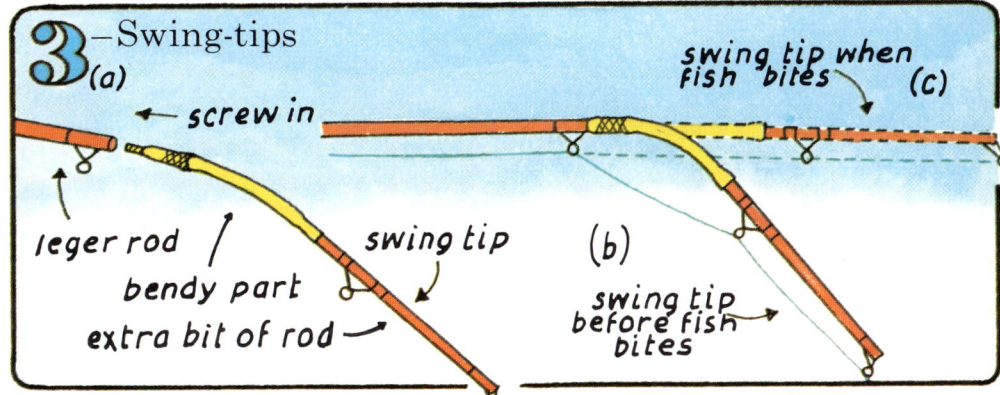

19

River and Stream Fish

These two pages show you where to find fish in flowing water, such as rivers and streams. You might find some of them in still water, such as ponds and lakes, as well. The next two pages show you where to catch fish in still water.

Chub, dace and barbel like fast flowing rivers and streams. Rudd, carp and tench prefer still water. Roach, pike and bream are found in slow running water as well as in still water. Perch, minnows, eels and gudgeon like all kinds of water.

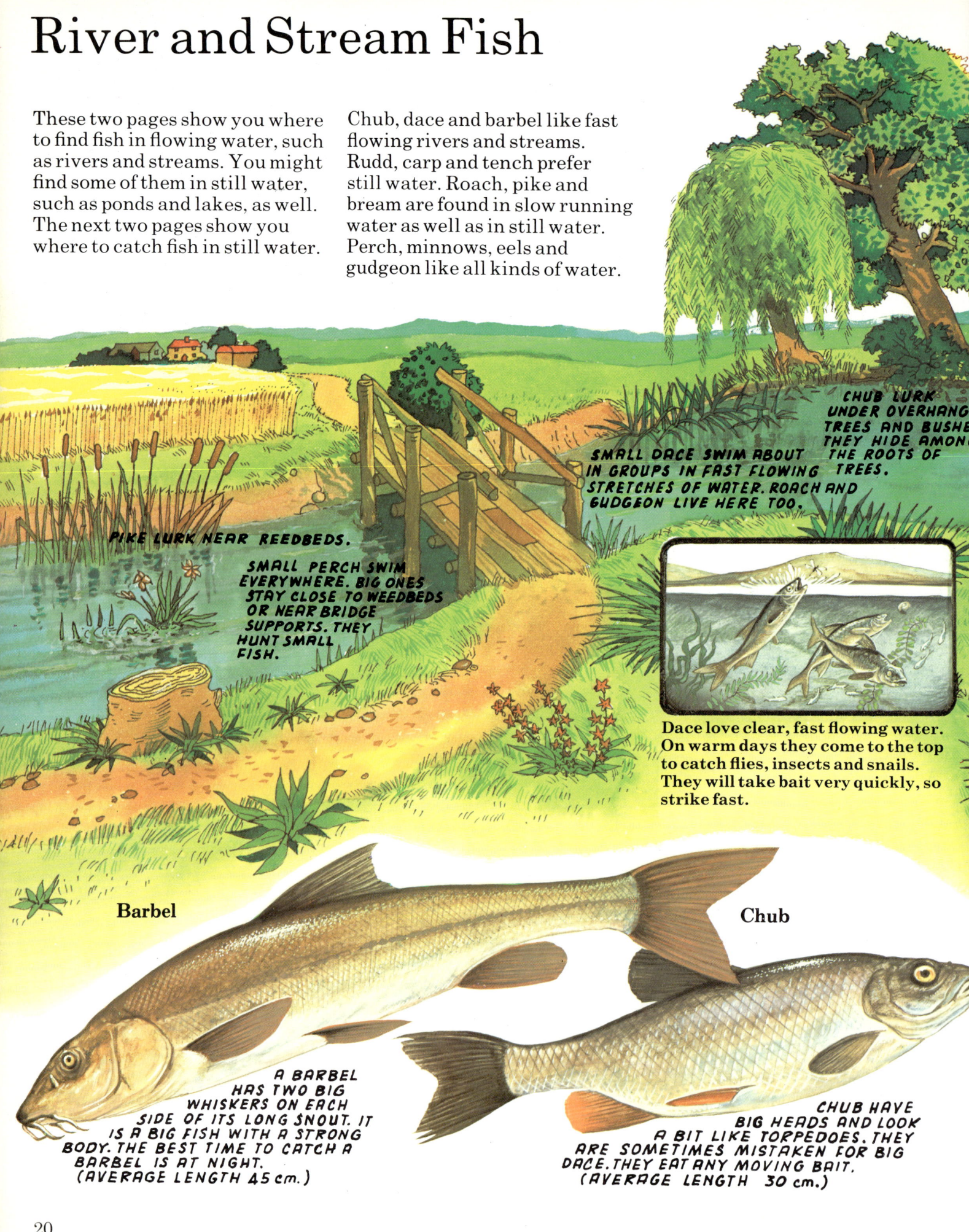

CHUB LURK UNDER OVERHANG TREES AND BUSHE THEY HIDE AMON THE ROOTS OF TREES.

SMALL DACE SWIM ABOUT IN GROUPS IN FAST FLOWING STRETCHES OF WATER. ROACH AND GUDGEON LIVE HERE TOO.

PIKE LURK NEAR REEDBEDS.

SMALL PERCH SWIM EVERYWHERE. BIG ONES STAY CLOSE TO WEEDBEDS OR NEAR BRIDGE SUPPORTS. THEY HUNT SMALL FISH.

Dace love clear, fast flowing water. On warm days they come to the top to catch flies, insects and snails. They will take bait very quickly, so strike fast.

Barbel

Chub

A BARBEL HAS TWO BIG WHISKERS ON EACH SIDE OF ITS LONG SNOUT. IT IS A BIG FISH WITH A STRONG BODY. THE BEST TIME TO CATCH A BARBEL IS AT NIGHT. (AVERAGE LENGTH 45 cm.)

CHUB HAVE BIG HEADS AND LOOK A BIT LIKE TORPEDOES. THEY ARE SOMETIMES MISTAKEN FOR BIG DACE. THEY EAT ANY MOVING BAIT. (AVERAGE LENGTH 30 cm.)

Chub are shy, so be very quiet. Four or five may hide together among the roots of a tree. They feed on frogs, small fish, caterpillars and beetles.

Although gudgeon are very small, they are fun to catch. They like clear, running water and will snap up any small worms you use as bait.

Barbel will fight hard to get away when you hook them. They swim very fast. One of their favourite places is at the bottom of a pool below a weir.

SHOALS OF BREAM LIVE IN SLOW RUNNING RIVERS. THEY LIKE DEEP WATER WITH A MUDDY BOTTOM.

CHUB SHELTER IN DEEP POOLS, AWAY FROM FAST FLOWING WATER.

CHUB HIDE UNDER OVERHANGING BANKS AND AMONG PLANTS AT THE EDGE OF THE BANK.

GUDGEON LIVE ON GRAVELLY RIVER BEDS. THEY ARE FOUND EVERYWHERE. THEY LIKE THE SAME SPOTS AS ROACH AND DACE

ON SUNNY DAYS, ROACH LIKE SHADY SPOTS. IN WINTER, THEY STAY IN DEEPER WATER.

SMALL FRY AND MINNOWS LIVE CLOSE TO THE BANK, IN SLOW MOVING, SHALLOW WATER.

BARBEL LIKE DEEP POOLS, JUST OUT OF THE FAST FLOWING WATER.

Gudgeon

Bronze Bream

Roach   **Dace**

Minnows

BIG BREAM HAVE DEEP BODIES WITH GREY-BROWN OR BRONZE COLOURED BACKS AND PALE STOMACHS. SMALL BREAM ARE SILVERY. (AVERAGE LENGTH 30cm.)

ROACH LOOK VERY LIKE RUDD. THEIR FINS ARE NOT QUITE AS RED AND THEIR THICK, UPPER LIP STICKS OUT. (AVERAGE LENGTH 30cm.)

DACE LOOK LIKE CHUB BUT ARE SMALLER, LITTLE DACE LIVE IN SHOALS. BIG ONES SWIM ABOUT BY THEMSELVES. (AVERAGE LENGTH 20cm.)

GUDGEON HAVE ONE WHISKER ON EACH SIDE OF THEIR MOUTHS. THEY SWIM ABOUT IN GROUPS. (AVERAGE LENGTH 13cm.)

MINNOWS ARE VERY SMALL FISH. THEY ARE EATEN BY BIG FISH AND USED AS BAIT BY ANGLERS. (AVERAGE LENGTH 10cm.)

Pond and Lake Fish

The fish on these two pages are found in still water, such as ponds, lakes, canals and gravel pits. Look at the picture of the lake to find their favourite feeding places. You are most likely to catch them there. Some feed near water plants, overhanging trees and bushes. Others lurk in the reedbeds.

The little pictures round the lake tell you how to catch the fish and show you some of their habits. The big pictures show you what the fish look like and what size they are.

Rudd are always hungry. If you throw bits of crust on the water, they will swim up to eat them. Put a hook through one crust.

MANY FISH, SUCH AS TENCH, BREAM, CARP AND EELS FEED NEAR FALLEN TREES OR BUSHES IN THE WATER.

SHOALS OF BREAM ROAM THE OPEN WATER. THEY FEED AS THEY GO.

PIKE AND PERCH LURK NEAR REEDBEDS AND OTHER HIDING PLACES. THEY GOBBLE UP SMALL FISH AS THEY SWIM BY.

TENCH, BREAM AND CARP LIKE MUDDY BOTTOMED PLACES BELOW LILY PADS AND WATER WEEDS.

Pike are very greedy. They lie in wait for small or sick fish, snapping them up as they swim by. They are cunning, big fish and very difficult to catch.

Perch nibble at bait before they swallow it. Your float will bob about as they nibble. Don't strike until it goes under the water.

Carp

Pike

Eels

EELS SWIM UP RIVERS FROM THE SEA. THEY CAN WRIGGLE OVER WET GRASS TO GET INTO PONDS AND LAKES. (AVERAGE LENGTH 45 cm.)

THE PIKE IS A VERY BIG FISH WITH A LONG GREENISH-YELLOW BODY AND A SNOUT FULL OF SHARP TEETH. IT CAN SWIM VERY FAST. (AVERAGE LENGTH 60 cm.)

CARP ARE BIG AND STRONG. THEY SWIM LAZILY AND LURK IN POOLS. THEY GRIND UP THEIR FOOD WITH FLAT, SHARP TEETH. (AVERAGE LENGTH 45 cm.)

CARP SOMETIMES HIDE IN POOLS BELOW OVERHANGING TREES AND BUSHES.

ROACH AND RUDD LIKE WATER WITH A GRAVELLY BOTTOM. THEY ALSO FEED ON GRUBS AND INSECTS NEAR WATER PLANTS.

MINNOWS AND OTHER LITTLE FISH STAY IN SHALLOW WATER NEAR THE BANK. THEY ARE SAFER FROM BIG FISH HERE.

Watch out for bubbles coming to the top of the water. Tench often make them as they feed (a). They are hard fighters and will thrash about or rush for weedbeds if they are hooked (b).

Bream swim about in big groups called shoals. This makes them easy to catch. They feed in the mud on the bottom of lakes and rivers.

Roach are the most common freshwater fish. They eat grubs and insects off water plants. You can catch them at all levels in the water.

Eels like eating small, dead fish or garden worms. The best time to catch a big eel is in the evening.

Be very quiet and keep out of sight when you fish for carp. Try catching them with crusts of bread.

They are very strong and cunning. Once you hook one it will struggle hard to get away. Hold on tightly to your rod and be prepared to lose a few hooks.

Tench

Perch

Rudd

TENCH ARE QUITE SMALL BUT THEY ARE VERY STRONG. THEY HAVE BRONZE AND DARK GREEN BODIES, RED EYES AND A VERY BROAD TAIL FIN. (AVERAGE LENGTH 25 cm)

THE PERCH IS A HUNTER WHICH EATS SMALL FISH. IT HAS A BIG SPIKEY MAIN FIN AND A STRIPED BODY. (AVERAGE LENGTH 25 cm)

RUDD HAVE HUMPED BACKS AND REDDISH FINS. THEIR LOWER LIP STICKS OUT. THIS HELPS THEM TO FEED FROM THE TOP OF THE WATER (AVERAGE LENGTH 25 cm)

Seashore Fishing Baits

All the sea fishing baits you need live on the seashore. The best time to find them is when the tide is out.

Try to keep all your baits alive and fresh. The fish are much more likely to take them like this. Make the drop net on this page to catch prawns for bait.

To use it, tie on bits of fish or worm as bait. Hold the string and let the net sink to the bottom of the pool. Leave it there for a few minutes. Then pull it up quickly.

Making a Drop Net

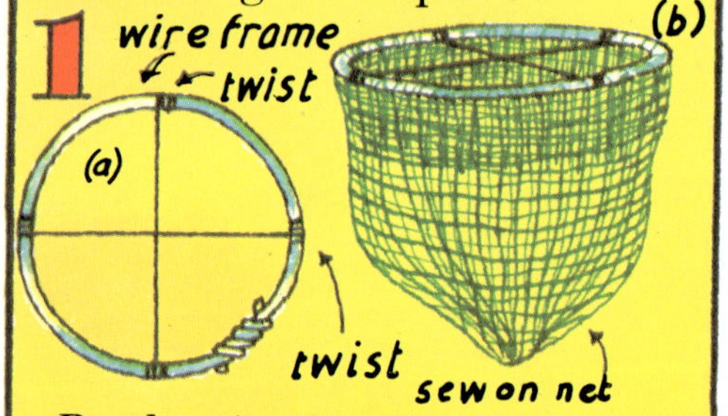

1 wire frame — twist

(a) (b) twist — sew on net

Bend some wire, 70 cm long, into a circle. Wind two bits of thin wire on to it, as shown (a). Sew a fine net bag, about 35 cm deep, to the wire frame with string.

2 (a) knot (b) knot — tie the bait on here — stone weight

Tie three long bits of string to the frame and knot them (a). Tie a stone into the bottom of the net. Before you use the net, tie bait to the thin wire (b).

Prawns

(a) (b) salt water and seaweed (c)

Prawns are good for catching bass and wrasse. They hide in rock pools under rocks and seaweed. Use your drop net (a) or poke a shrimping net under the rocks to catch them.

Keep prawns alive in a bucket full of seawater and seaweed (b). Hook a prawn through its tail, like this (c).

Crabs

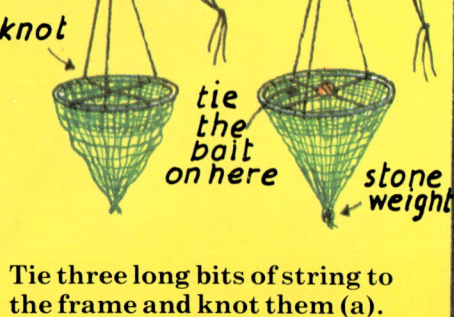

(a)

(b) thread or elastic

Codling, flounders and bass all like soft-backed crabs. These are crabs that have just out-grown their hard shells. They hide under rocks and seaweed until their new shell hardens (a).

A small crab can be used whole on the hook. Tie it on with an elastic band or some thread, like this (b). Cut big, dead crabs into little pieces.

Lugworms

(a) heap of coiled sand — small dent

(b)

(c) damp sand

(d) plastic box

Lugworms make good bait for most seashore fish. They live on sandy or muddy beaches. At low tide, you will see lots of little curly heaps of sand on the beach.

Close to each heap is a tiny dent. The lugworm lives in a tunnel between the heap and the dent (a). You can dig it out with an ordinary garden fork (b).

Keep lugworms alive in a box filled with damp sand (c). When you use a worm, push the hook through its body, like this (d).

Ragworms

(a) look under rocks

(b) wet sacking

(c) nippers

Ragworms are good bait for bass, pollack and flatfish. They live on muddy and sandy beaches. They also hide under flat rocks and thick seaweed (a).

Keep them alive in a box filled with sacking, rinsed in sea water (b). Be careful of their nippers when you bait up (c). Hold them just behind the head.

Mussels

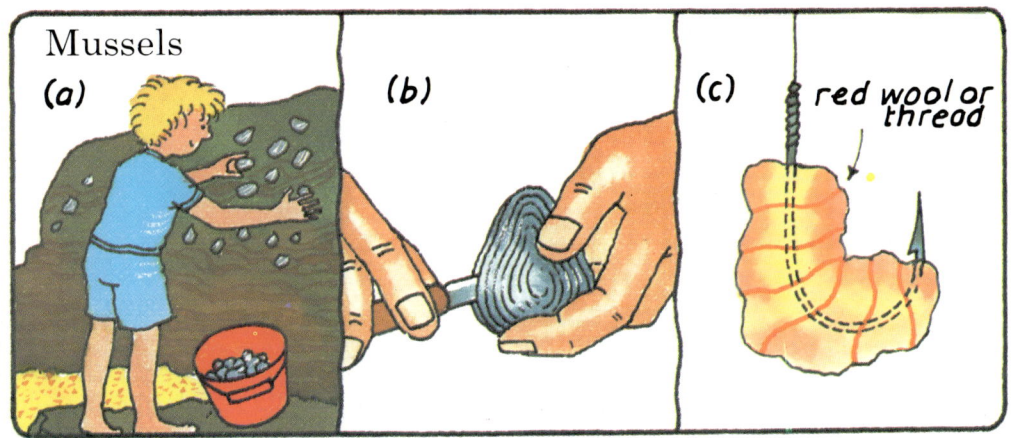

(a)

(b)

(c) red wool or thread

Codling, whiting and flatfish all like mussels. You can pull them off rocks, piers and jetties at low tide (a). Open the shells very carefully with a penknife, like this (b).

Mussels have soft bodies inside their shells. To stop them flying off the hook when you cast, tie them on with red wool or thread (c). Keep them fresh in sea water.

Other Baits

1 (a) (b)

Strips of mackerel (a) are good for catching whiting, skate and cod. Put them on the hook, like this (b). Use either fresh or frozen mackerel.

2 (a) (b)

Herring strips (a) and squid tentacles (b) make good bait for these fish too. They like them even better with a lugworm on the hook as well.

Fishing from the Seashore

Sea Leger Tackle

When you want to cast far out into the water, or fish where the current is strong, use a sea leger tackle or a paternoster tackle.

The lead weight you use must be heavy enough to keep the hook-bait on the bottom. The heavier it is, the further out you will be able to cast the line.

The reel line should have a breaking strain of about 8-10 kg. The hook lengths and paternoster lines about 6-8 kg. Page 5 shows you how to tie all the knots.

Simple Sea Leger Tackle

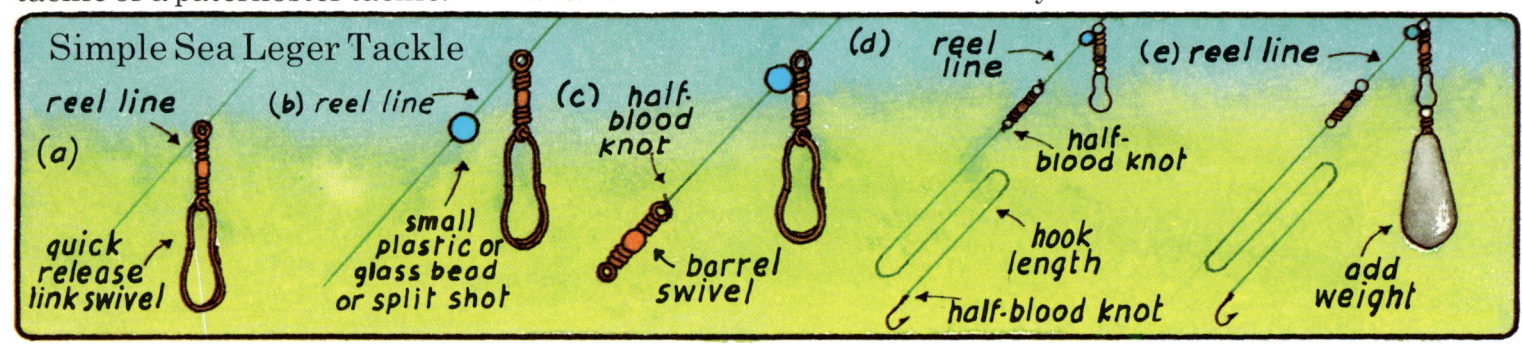

First thread a quick-release spring or link swivel on to the reel line (a). Thread a small, plastic or glass bead just below the swivel (b).

Tie the end of the reel line on to one eye of a barrel swivel (c). Tie a hook length, about 45 cm long, to the other eye of the barrel swivel.

Tie a hook to the end of the hook length (d). Then slip a weight, such as a pear-shaped lead, on to the quick-release swivel (e).

Paternoster Tackle

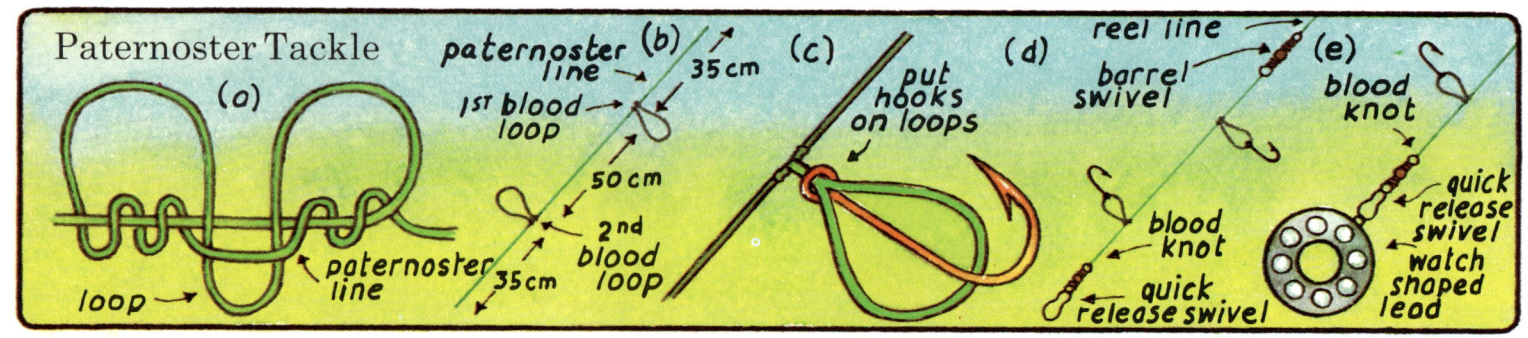

Cut a piece of nylon line, about 1.5 metres long. Tie a blood loop (a) in it. Tie a second loop about 50 cm from the first one (b). This is the paternoster line.

Put a hook on each loop. Do this by threading the loop through the eye and over the hook (c). Pull it tight. Tie one end of the paternoster line to one eye of a barrel swivel.

Tie the end of the reel line to the other eye. Then tie a quick-release swivel to the other end of the paternoster line (d). Slip a lead weight on to the barrel swivel (e).

Lead Weights and Swivels

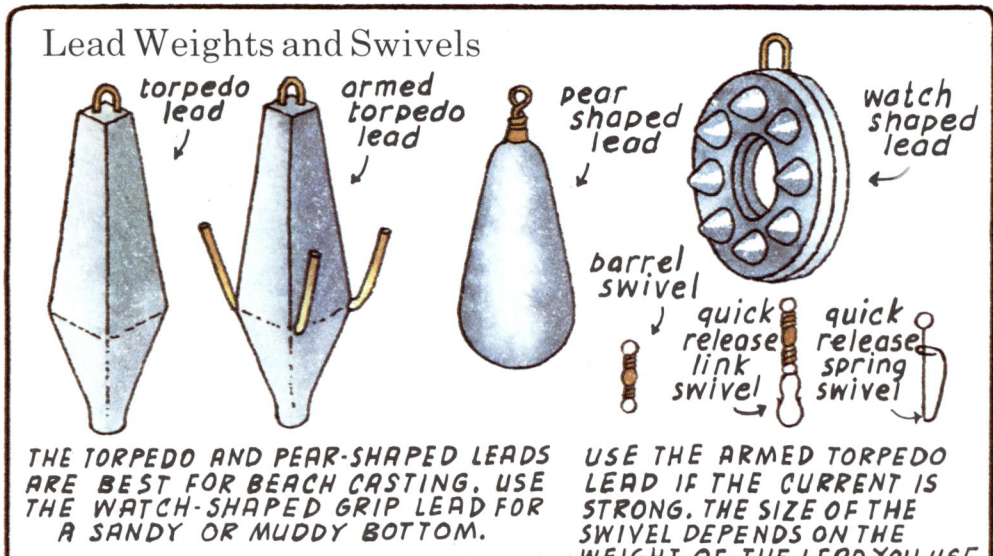

THE TORPEDO AND PEAR-SHAPED LEADS ARE BEST FOR BEACH CASTING. USE THE WATCH-SHAPED GRIP LEAD FOR A SANDY OR MUDDY BOTTOM.

USE THE ARMED TORPEDO LEAD IF THE CURRENT IS STRONG. THE SIZE OF THE SWIVEL DEPENDS ON THE WEIGHT OF THE LEAD YOU USE.

Sea Hooks

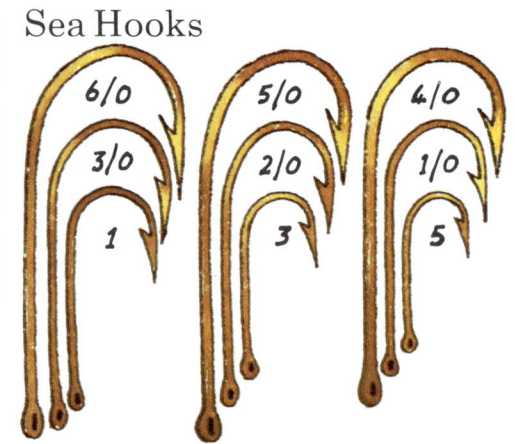

THESE ARE THE SIZE HOOKS YOU NEED FOR SEA FISHING. USE THE LARGER SIZE FOR BIG FISH, SUCH AS COD AND BASS. FO FLATFISH AND LITTLE FISH, USE THE SMALLER SIZES.

Sea Float Tackle

When the sea is calm and you do not need to cast out too far, use a float instead of a leger or paternoster tackle. It is lighter and easier to cast. Use a reel line with about a 6 kg breaking strain.

Sea floats are usually bigger than freshwater ones. The weights are heavier so that they can cock the float. Lead bullets, spiral or barrel leads are the best kinds of weights to use.

When you float fish in the sea the hook-bait does not have to stay very close to the bottom. It should hang above any rocks and reeds so that the line does not get tangled up.

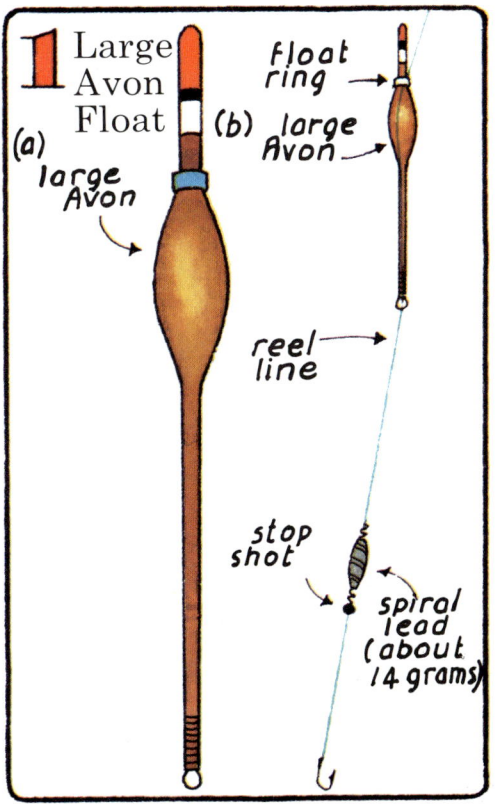

1 Large Avon Float

(a) large Avon

(b) float ring, large Avon, reel line, stop shot, spiral lead (about 14 grams)

This is a fixed float (a). A fixed float does not slide up and down the fishing line. Put it on the line, like this (b). Put a lead weight and a stop shot half-way between the float and the hook, as shown.

2 Gazette Float

(a) reel line, wooden peg, gazette float, gazette float

(b) thread line through float, drilled barrel lead, stop shot, blood knot

This is another fixed float (a). To put it on the line, take out the wooden peg. Thread the line through the middle of the float and then put the peg back into the float. Fix a weight and a stop shot half-way between the float and the hook (b).

3 Sliding Float

(a) reel line

(b) about 1 m, stop shot, sliding float, glass or plastic bead, lead bullet, stop shot, blood knot

Use a sliding float (a) when the water is deep or you want to fish quite far out. Set up the tackle, like this (b). When it is cast out, the float slides up from the bead to the knot. This stops the line from getting tangled.

When to Strike

(a) rod tip wiggles

WHEN YOU USE LEGER OR PATERNOSTER TACKLE, THE ROD TIP WIGGLES ABOUT, OR THERE IS A STEADY PULL ON THE LINE, IF A FISH TAKES THE BAIT (a). STRIKE AS SOON AS THIS HAPPENS.

(b) float moves from side to side

IN FLOAT FISHING, THE FLOAT MOVES ABOUT FROM SIDE TO SIDE AND THEN GOES UNDER THE WATER (b). WAIT UNTIL IT HAS COMPLETELY DISAPPEARED BEFORE YOU STRIKE.

Seashore and Estuary Fish

The best times to go seashore fishing are in the early morning, early evening and the two hours before and after high tide. Lots of different fish swim inshore to feed then.

These are some of the seashore fish you might catch. Look at the four pictures on the right. They show you where the fish live and feed. You are most likely to catch them there.

Flatfish is another name for plaice, flounder and dab. They are called flatfish because of their flat shape. Codling is the name for a young cod.

Cod

Whiting

Pouting

Plaice

COD AND WHITING LIKE COLD WATER. TRY CATCHING THEM IN WINTER. (AVERAGE LENGTH OF COD 45 CM; WHITING 30CM; POUTING 20 CM.)

Bass

Flounder

FLAT FISH SPEND A LOT OF TIME ON THE SEA BED HALF-BURIED IN THE SAND.

BASS ARE STRONG, HARD-FIGHTING FISH. THEY LIKE WARM WATER. (AVERAGE LENGTH 30 CM.)

Dab

(AVERAGE LENGTH OF PLAICE 30CM; FLOUNDER 25CM; DAB 20 CM.)

Pollack

POLLACK SPEND MOST OF THE DAY CLOSE TO THE BOTTOM LURKING AMONG THE ROCKS. AT NIGHT AND AT DAWN, THEY FEED MUCH HIGHER UP IN THE WATER. (AVERAGE LENGTH 25CM.)

Mackerel

Conger Eel

CONGER EELS CAN GROW TO ENORMOUS SIZES. THEY HAVE STRONG, THICK BODIES WITH SNAKE-LIKE HEADS. YOU ARE MOST LIKELY TO CATCH THEM WITH FRESH BAIT.

MACKEREL ARE FAST, POWERFUL LITTLE FISH. SHOALS OF THEM COME IN CLOSE TO THE SHORE DURING WARM WEATHER. (AVERAGE LENGTH 25 CM.)

Ballan Wrasse

DANGER! Weever

Mullet

MULLET HAVE POINTED HEADS AND SMALL MOUTHS. TRY CATCHING THEM EARLY IN THE MORNING. (AVERAGE LENGTH 25 CM.)

WRASSE LIVE AMONG ROCKS COVERED IN THICK WEED. THEY ARE FOUND CLOSE TO THE SHORE IN THE WARMER MONTHS OF THE YEAR. (AVERAGE LENGTH 25 CM.)

THIS IS THE ONLY DANGEROUS FISH YOU MIGHT FIND. IT LIES HALF-BURIED IN THE SAND WITH ONLY ITS POISONOUS SPINES STICKING OUT. (AVERAGE LENGTH 17CM.)

Estuary Fishing

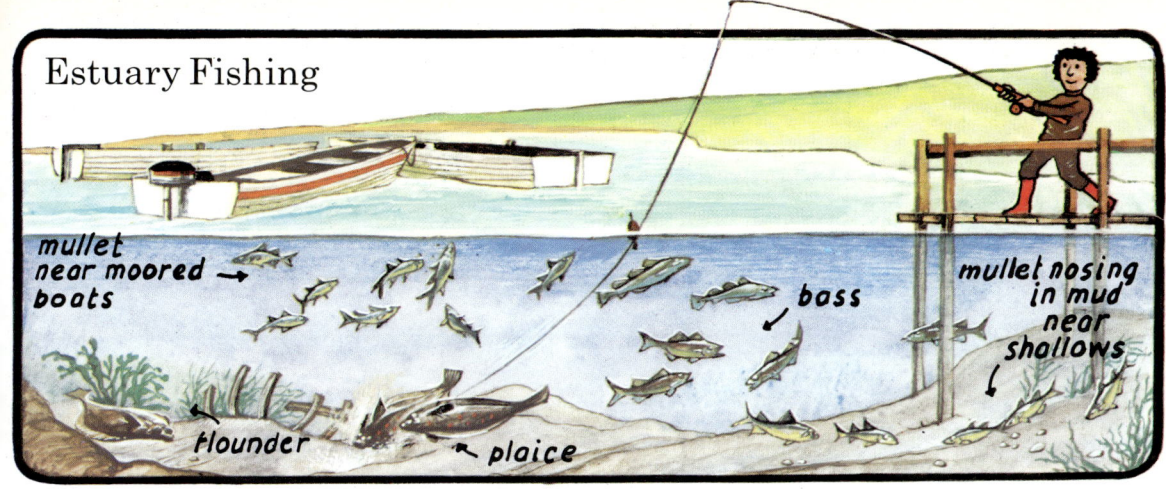

mullet near moored boats →

bass

mullet nosing in mud near shallows

flounder

plaice

An estuary – the part where a river flows into the sea – is a very good fishing spot for bass, mullet, plaice, dab, flounder and codling. Mullet like nosing about in the mud in shallow water. They also swim in shoals near moored boats, picking up scraps of food which have been thrown overboard.

You are most likely to catch cod, pouting, whiting and flatfish when you fish from the beach. They swim in close to the shore to find crabs, worms and shellfish. You might also catch bass as they swim into the surf to hunt for crabs and sand-eels. You need to cast your tackle out about 45 metres when you beach fish.

Beach Fishing

open beach

bass in surf

whiting

bass chasing sand eels in the surf

flounder chasing prawn

plaice buried in the sand

cod eating hermit crab

Rock Fishing

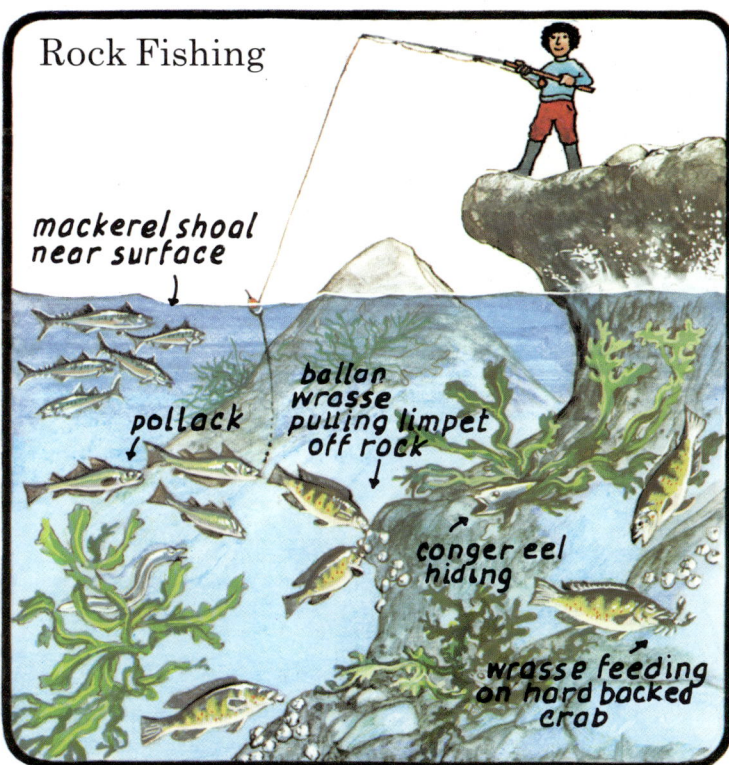

mackerel shoal near surface

pollack

ballan wrasse pulling limpet off rock

conger eel hiding

wrasse feeding on hard backed crab

Find a rocky platform over the sea, when you go rock fishing. You will be able to see far out and there will be deep water within easy reach. Wrasse, mackerel, pollack and conger eels all feed in rocky bays. Be careful of a conger. It is very strong and has a mouth full of sharp teeth.

Pier Fishing

pouting

whiting

cod

conger eel in hiding place

flounder buried

When you fish from a pier or jetty, drop your tackle straight down beside its supports. Flatfish, cod, whiting and pouting stay close to them, searching for food hidden in the seaweed. Conger eels hide between rocks and at the bottom of the pier legs among thick seaweed.

29

Do's and Don'ts

Before you go fishing, check the weather forecast. It is not much fun getting caught in a gale or thunder storm.

Always tell someone where you are going and what time you think you will be home. Take something to eat and drink if you will be away all day.

It is a good idea to go fishing with a friend. Then there is always someone about to help if anything goes wrong.

Permits and Licences

Fishing from the seashore is free for everyone. Fishing in freshwater is usually private and may cost you a little. Before you start to fish find out if you need a rod licence or fishing permit. You will probably need both. The local tackle dealer or fishing club will be able to sell them to you or tell you where to get them.

In most places you are not allowed to fish during some months of the year. It depends on what part of the country you are in and what kind of fish you want to catch. Ask the tackle dealer about this too.

Find out which fish you have to put back into the water and which ones you can keep.

What to Wear

woollen hat

thick pullover

waterproof coat with hood

bag for food, drinks, waterproof trousers and fishing tackle

gloves with fingertips cut off

heavy jeans

thick woollen socks

rubber boots

THESE ARE THE SORT OF CLOTHES TO WEAR FOR FISHING IN COLD OR BAD WEATHER. THEY WILL KEEP YOU WARM AND DRY. TAKE A PAIR OF WATERPROOF TROUSERS WITH YOU IN CASE IT RAINS. IN VERY COLD WEATHER, WEAR GLOVES WITH THE FINGER-TIPS CUT OFF. THEN IT IS EASIER TO USE TACKLE. IN BRIGHT SUN, WEAR POLAROID SUNGLASSES. THEY CUT DOWN THE GLARE FROM THE WATER WHICH COULD GIVE YOU A HEADACHE.

1 The Tides

Before you fish in the sea, an estuary or the tidal part of a river, find out the times of high and low tide. Get a tide table from a fishing shop or club.

2

In most places there are two high tides and two low tides every 24 hours. The times change slightly every day. Make sure you do not get cut off by an incoming tide.

3

The two hours before and after high tide are usually the best time to fish. This is when the fish come near the shore to feed. Low tide is the best time to collect bait.

The Country Code

1 Don't

It is very important to look after fishing places. This picture shows you what might happen if you don't.

Never leave rubbish about or break down trees or bushes. Don't throw away bits of nylon line or any old hooks.

They can easily kill or hurt birds and little animals. Close gates behind you and try not to damage lake or river banks.

2 Do

These are some of the things you should do. Remember to put fish back in the water if you are not going to keep them.

Don't just throw them back. Put them in your landing net and lower them gently into the water.

Move about very quietly so you don't disturb any other anglers nearby. Always read your fishing permit carefully and follow all the rules.

Angling Clubs

If you join an angling club, you will get plenty of chances for good fishing. It costs very little to become a member.

Some clubs own stretches of water. They arrange fishing and matches for their members. Beginners get help and lots of fishing tips.

Ask at a tackle shop or local library for the names and addresses of nearby clubs. Ring up the Secretary or just go along.

Anglers' Words

Baiting up – putting bait on the hook before you cast your fishing line into the water.

Breaking strain – the weight a fishing line can take without breaking. The thicker the line, the more weight it can take.

Casting – swinging the rod and line to put the bait into the water in the right place.

Cocking the float – making the float stand upright in the water by putting weights below it on the line.

Downstream – the part of a river or stream where the water is flowing away from you.

Fixed spool reel – a reel with a metal arm which winds line on to the spool.

Ground-bait – balls of bait made of bread, maggots or worms which you throw into the water near your fishing spot to attract the fish.

Hook-bait – bait which you put on the hook to make the fish bite.

Hook length – a piece of nylon line with a hook on the end which is joined to the reel line.

Reel line – the fishing line which you wind on to your reel.

Setting the drag – making sure the nut on the front of the reel is loose enough to let the line run out without breaking when you hook a big fish.

Setting the float – sliding the float up or down the line so that the hook-bait hangs below it at the right depth.

Split shot – small lead balls which you squeeze on to the line to cock the float or anchor leger tackle.

Stop shot – a split shot which you put on the line to stop a leger weight from sliding down to the hook.

Striking – quickly lifting up the tip of your rod when the fish bites so that the hook sticks in the fish's mouth.

Swim – the area of water you cast into.

Tackle – the name for all the gear you use to fish with.

Trail – the length of line between the weight and the hook in leger fishing.

Upstream – the part of a river or stream where the water is flowing towards you.

Index

The KnowHow Book of Jokes and Tricks

Heather Amery and Ian Adair

Illustrated by Colin King
Designed by John Jamieson

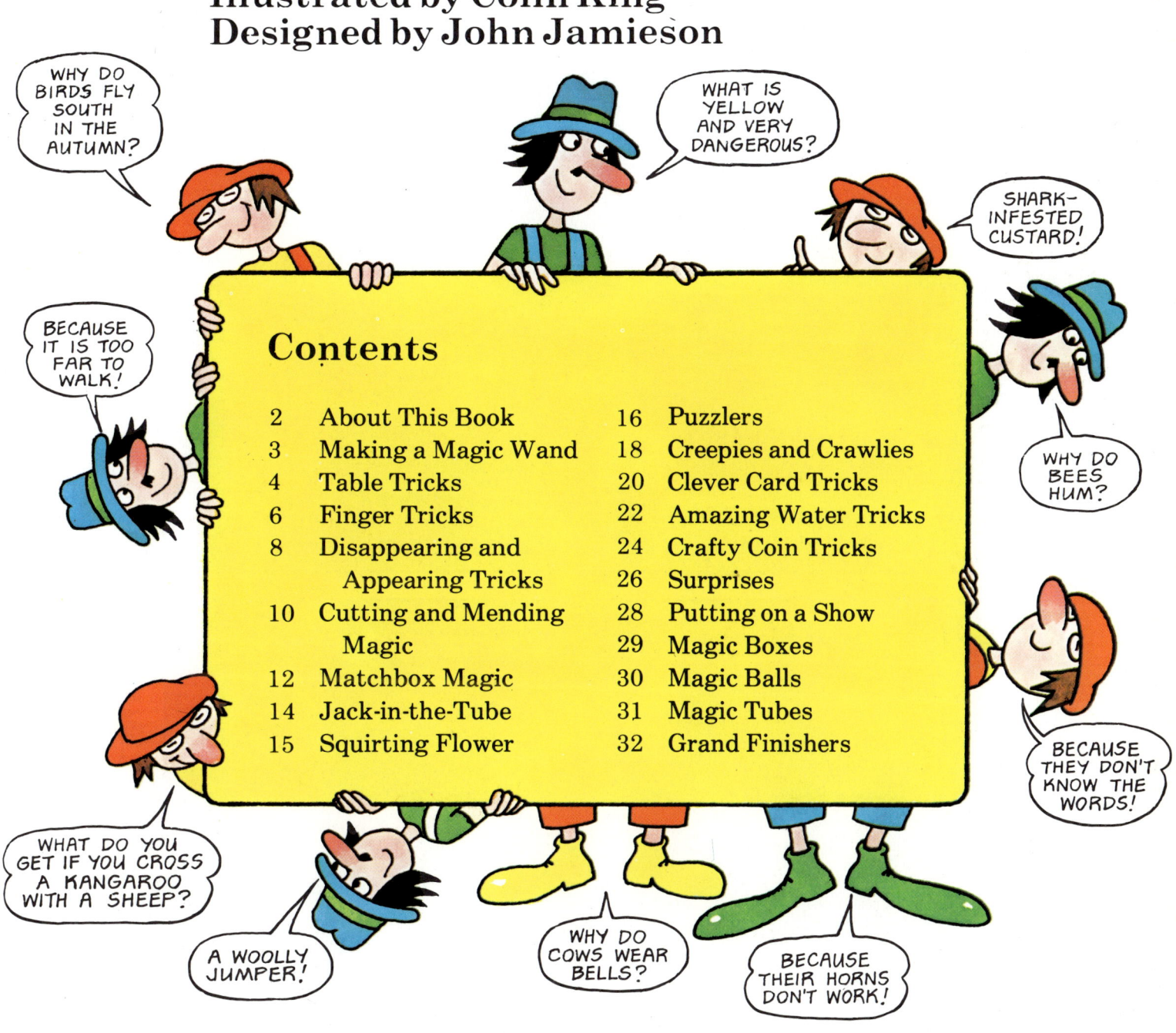

WHY DO BIRDS FLY SOUTH IN THE AUTUMN?

WHAT IS YELLOW AND VERY DANGEROUS?

SHARK-INFESTED CUSTARD!

BECAUSE IT IS TOO FAR TO WALK!

WHY DO BEES HUM?

Contents

BECAUSE THEY DON'T KNOW THE WORDS!

WHAT DO YOU GET IF YOU CROSS A KANGAROO WITH A SHEEP?

A WOOLLY JUMPER!

WHY DO COWS WEAR BELLS?

BECAUSE THEIR HORNS DON'T WORK!

Special Contributor:
Peter Howarth

Cover Illustration:
Neil Ross

Usborne Publishing Ltd
Usborne House
83-85 Saffron Hill, London EC1N 8RT

Printed in Italy

©Usborne Publishing Ltd 1989, 1980

About This Book

This book is for everyone who likes tricks, magic, conjuring, surprises and jokes. It is full of magic secrets on how to do very quick, easy tricks as well as more difficult ones which need lots and lots of practice.

At the end of the book are five special pages about putting on a show for your friends. They tell you how to be a real magician and how to make the things you will need.

There are lots of things you can make for magic tricks and surprises. All you need are cardboard boxes, bottle tops, matchboxes, string, glue, paper, paint and a pack of playing cards.

You will also need a big box to keep all your magic in. Magicians always keep their tricks a secret and never tell anyone how they do them. You will have to keep this book secret, too.

With the startling and surprising tricks, be careful who you play them on. Some grown-ups may not think they are funny if you give them a nasty shock.

Tips and Hints

All the best tricks look like magic because of the way you do them. All your movements should be very big and impressive. Stare at what you are doing and pretend you can really do magic.

The important thing is to practise all the tricks lots of times in secret. Then when you do them in front of people, they will look like real magic.

It helps a trick if you say some magic words. We have made up some special ones. They are ZIXEE SOXEE ZABADEE ZUT but you can make up your own if you like. Try to think of funny words which are not real words but sound magical.

Remember never to do the same trick twice in front of the same people – even if they beg you. If you do, they may guess how you do it and spoil the magic. The best magic is secret.

Making a Magic Wand

A wand is a useful thing to have when you do magic tricks. You can wave it when you say the magic words or push it through things to show they are empty.

You can buy a wand from a magic shop or make one of your own. Here are two easy ways of making wands. The wooden one will, of course, last much longer.

If you point your wand at something, the people watching will look at it. Then you can do a trick without them noticing the secret part.

Paper Wand

Cut out an oblong of stiff black paper, or paper painted black, about 30 cm long and 10 cm wide. Roll it round two pencils (a) and glue the edge to make a tube.

When the glue is dry, shake out the pencils. Cut two strips of white paper, each about 2 cm wide and 8 cm long. Glue one to each end of the wand, like this, (b).

Wooden Wand

To make a wooden wand, you need a piece of thin stick or dowel, about 30 cm long. Paint it black or glue on black paper. Paint the ends white or glue on white paper.

Sticky Wand

"MY MAGIC WAND STICKS TO MY HAND!"

The Secret

Push a pin into the wand (a). Hold the pin between your fingers (b) so no one can see it. Pull out the pin secretly and no one can do the trick.

1 Balancing Wand

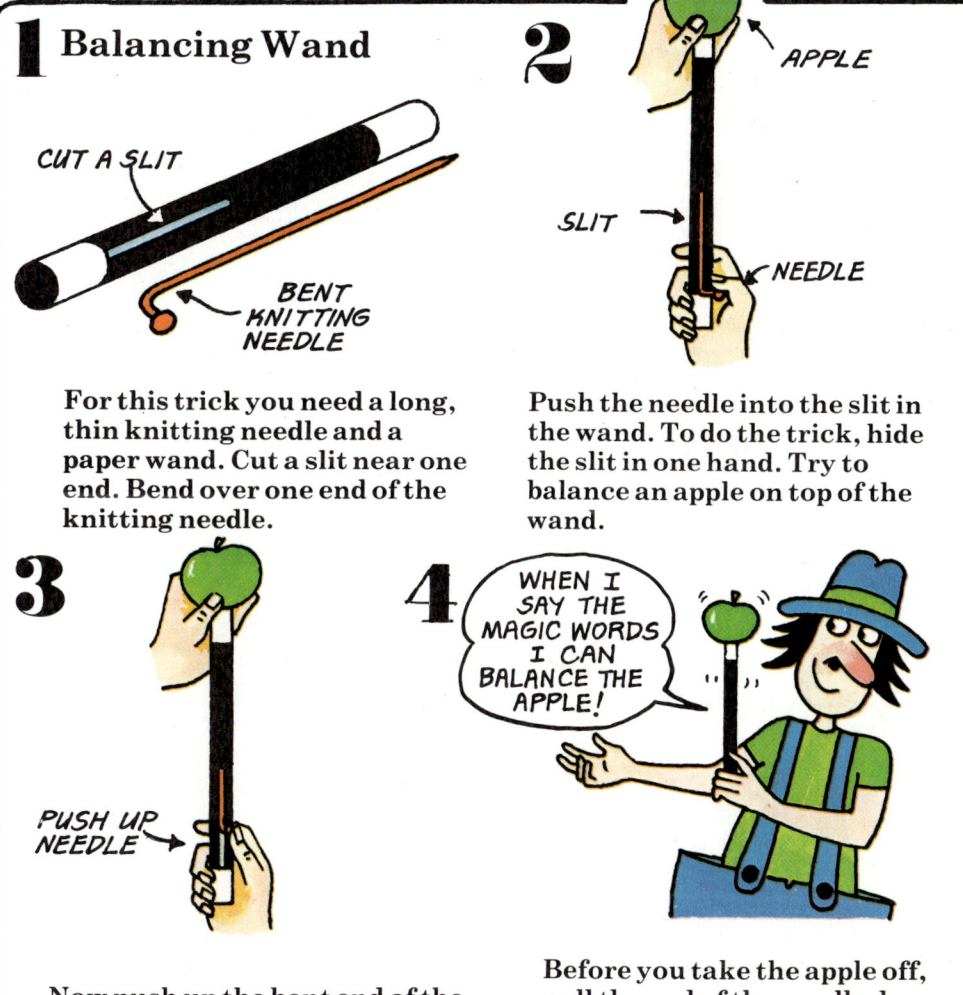

For this trick you need a long, thin knitting needle and a paper wand. Cut a slit near one end. Bend over one end of the knitting needle.

2 Push the needle into the slit in the wand. To do the trick, hide the slit in one hand. Try to balance an apple on top of the wand.

3 Now push up the bent end of the needle so the point sticks into the apple. Wave the wand and the apple will stick to it.

4 "WHEN I SAY THE MAGIC WORDS I CAN BALANCE THE APPLE!"

Before you take the apple off, pull the end of the needle down again so the point disappears. Then you can show everyone the tip of the wand.

When does an astronaut have his mid-day meal? At launch time!

Table Tricks

Here are some good tricks you can play while you are sitting at a table having a meal.

For the Table Napkin Creepy
You will need
an empty cotton reel
a candle
a table knife
a strong rubber band
a thin stick, about 10 cm long
a small paper table napkin
scissors
a matchstick and sticky tape

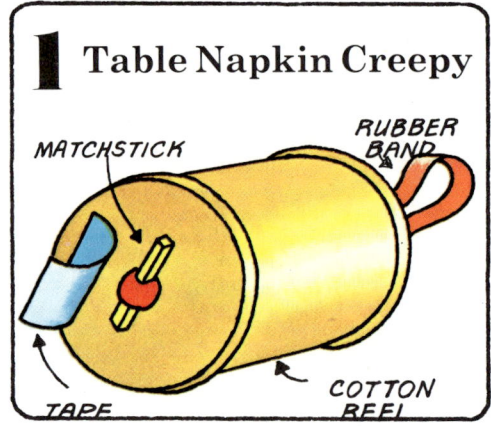

1 Table Napkin Creepy

Push the rubber band through the cotton reel. Push a bit of match stick through the loop at one end. Stick the match stick to the reel with a bit of tape.

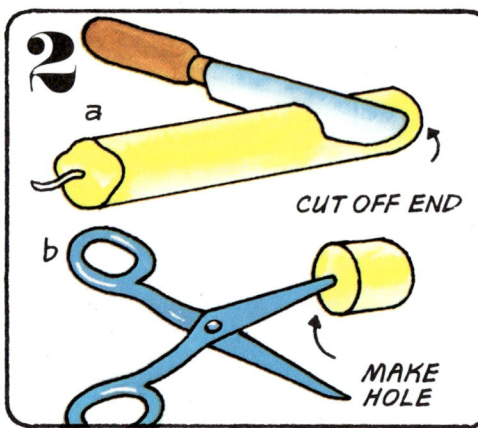

Cut a ring, about 1 cm wide, off the end of a candle with a table knife. Make a hole through the middle with scissors.

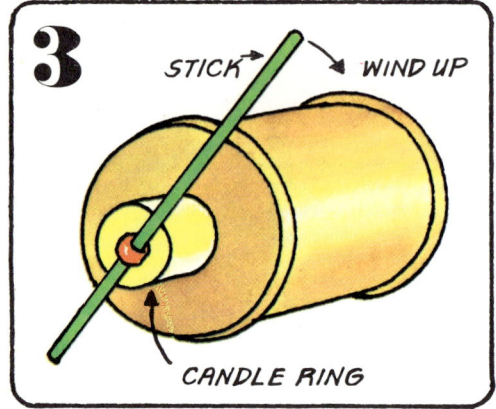

Push the free end of the rubber band through the candle ring. Then push the stick through the loop. Wind the stick round about 20 times.

Put the cotton reel on the table when no one is looking. Drop a small table napkin over it. Leave it to creep along very slowly. Someone will soon notice it.

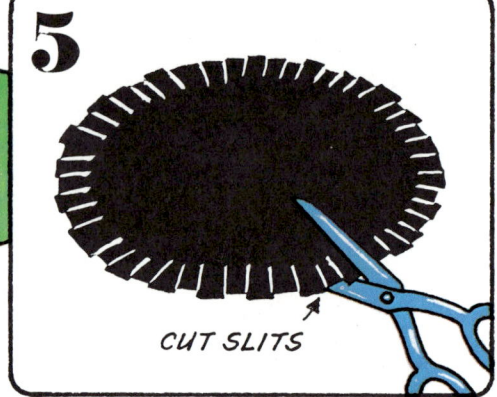

To make an even creepier Creepy, cut a circle, about the size of a saucer, out of very thin black cloth. Snip the edges all the way round. Put it over the cotton reel.

Floating Sugar Lumps

Cut out a neat square from a piece of white plastic sponge. Put it in a bowl of sugar lumps. When someone drops it into a cup of tea or coffee, it will float.

Empty Spoon

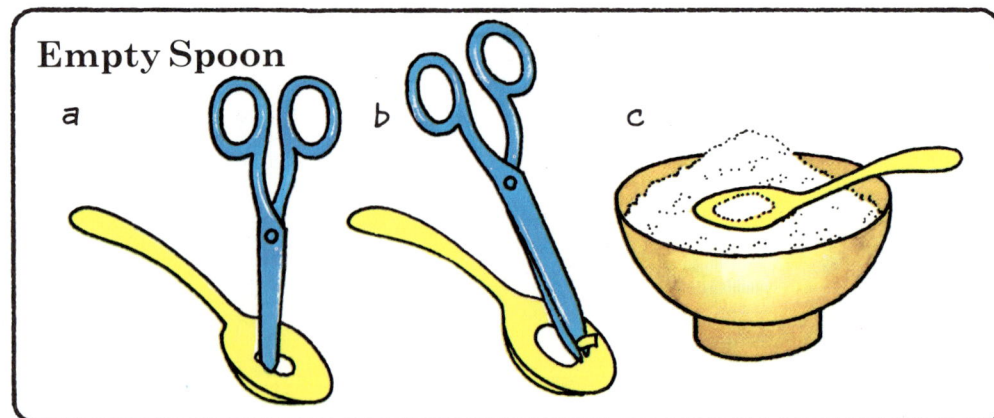

Make a hole in the bowl of a plastic spoon with scissors, like this (a). Cut out a big hole as neatly as you can (b) with scissors.

Put the spoon down on some sugar in a basin (c). It will look as if it has sugar in it. Anyone trying to spoon up the sugar will get a surprise.

Which English king invented the fireplace?   Alfred the Grate!

Ready-Sliced Banana

1 How It Looks

HERE IS AN ORDINARY BANANA.

2 *WITH MY MAGIC WAND I SLICE IT IN BITS WITHOUT CUTTING THE SKIN.*

3 *WHEN I PEEL THE BANANA IT IS SLICED INTO BITS!*

The Secret

a — **BIG NEEDLE**, **THREAD**

b

c

d

Push a piece of strong thread, about 20 cm long, through the eye of a big needle. Push the needle through one flat side of a big banana (a).

Pull the needle out, leaving the thread under the skin. Now push the needle back through the same hole and under the next flat side (b). Do this all round the skin (c).

When you get round to the first hole, pull the two ends of the thread. This will cut the banana inside the skin. Make more cuts down the banana inside the skin (d).

Magic Straw

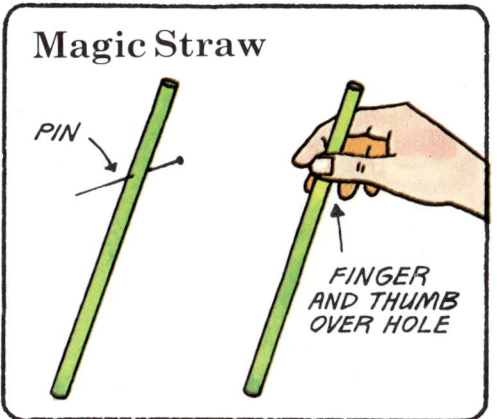

PIN

FINGER AND THUMB OVER HOLE

Singing Glasses

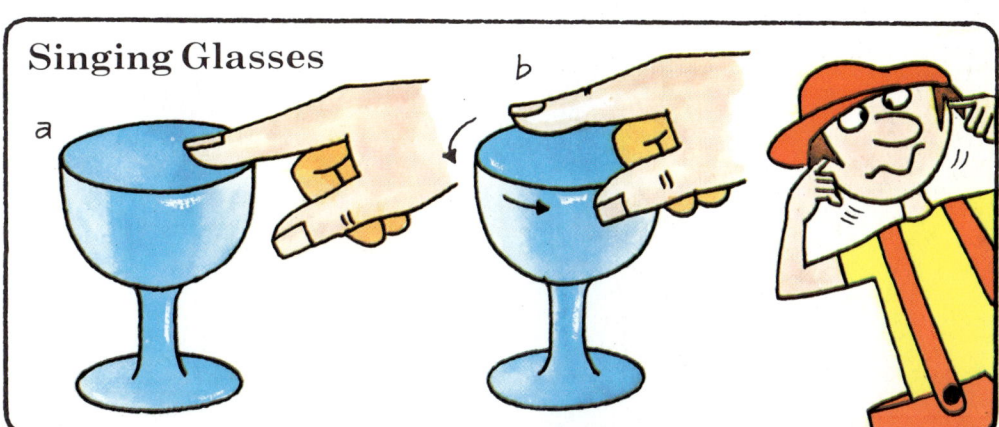

a

b

Make a hole in a drinking straw with a pin. When someone tries to drink with it, they will just suck up air. When you drink with it, put your fingers over the holes.

Why do witches fly about on broomsticks?

You can make a glass sing a long whining tune. Just put a little water in the glass. Dip one finger in the water and rub it gently round the top edge of the glass (a).

¡Because vacuum cleaners are too heavy!

If it does not work at once, try rubbing harder or more gently. Keep your finger just on the rim (b). Thin glasses work better than thick ones. Try lots of different ones.

Finger Tricks

These Finger Tricks are great fun to do. When you play them, you can pretend you are hurt. With the Wounded Finger, just wear the bandage until someone notices. Then pretend you are very brave.

The Wand Through Head Trick needs a bit of practicing. Try it secretly in front of a mirror until it looks right. You can pull the wand out of your head again. Just hold the wand in place with your other hand. Then slide the paper back along the wand.

Wounded Finger

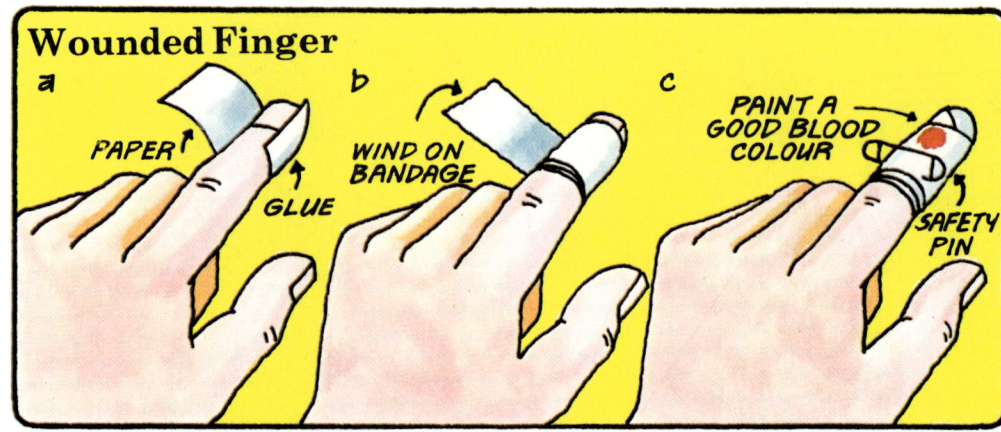

Wrap a piece of white paper round one finger (a). Stick it with glue. Wind on a short piece of bandage, going over the top of the finger as well (b). Pin the end.

Paint one bit of bandage a good red colour. Put on a bit of brown to look like dried blood (c). Slide off the bandage. Put it on secretly before you fool someone.

Which Wounded Finger?

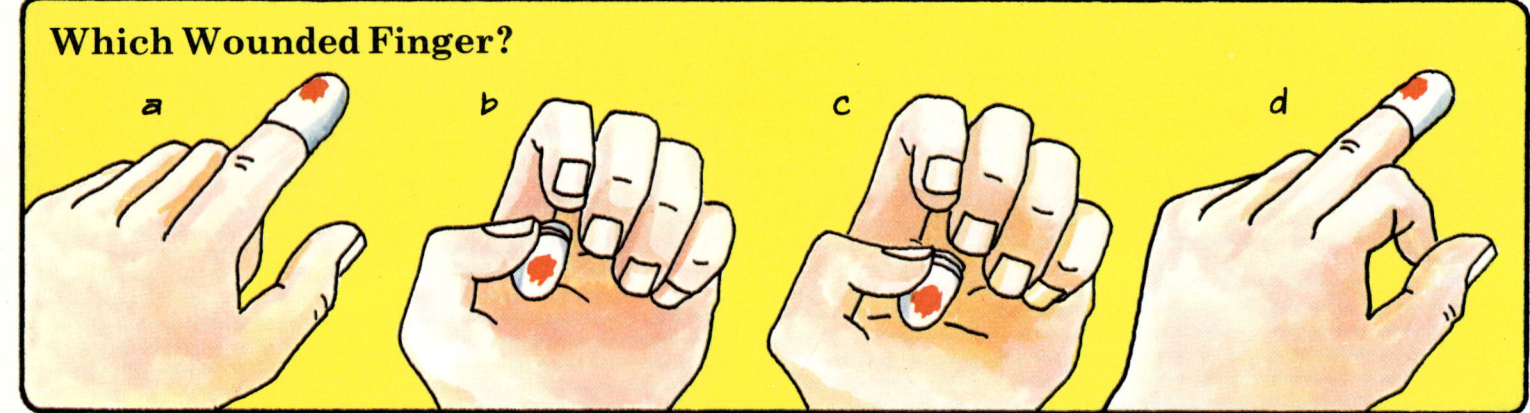

Make a Wounded Finger bandage just big enough to go on the top of one finger (a). To change it to another finger, bend the finger over into your palm (b).

Hold the bandage with your thumb and slide it off (c). Slide the bandage on to the next finger. Open your hand to show that a different finger is hurt (d).

Practise sliding the bandage off and on quickly. You can move it to all your fingers, one at a time. Pretend you cannot remember which finger has the wound.

Shaky Hand

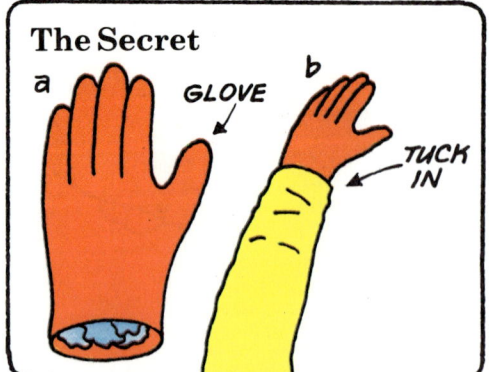

Hold out your hand to shake hands with someone. When they take it, off it comes.

The Secret

Stuff the fingers and palm of a glove with paper tissues or bits of rag. Make sure the fingers look full and fat (a). Hold the glove by the open end. Pull down your sleeve to hide your hand (b).

Which trees do fingers and thumbs grow on? ¡Palm trees!

Missing Finger

Pull on a woollen glove, putting two fingers into one space. This leaves an empty glove finger which you can wiggle about in a horrible floppy way.

1 Living Finger

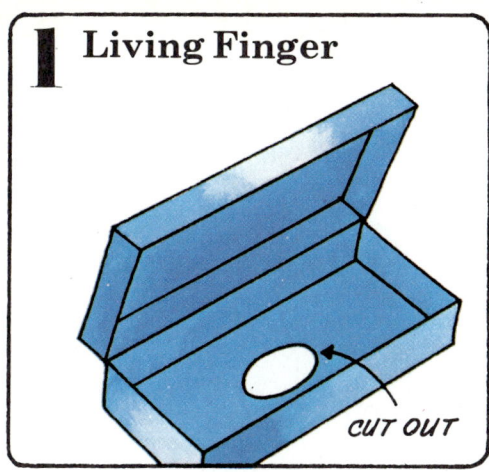

CUT OUT

Find a small cardboard cigar or chocolate box with a hinged lid. Cut a hole, big enough for your finger to go through, in the bottom of the box.

2

COTTON WOOL

HOLE

Glue cotton wool to the bottom of the box. Put it round the hole but not over it. Close the box before you show anyone the Finger.

3

Hold the box in one hand, like this. Then, as you open the box, quickly push one finger through the hole and bend it over. Keep it still and then wiggle it.

String Through Finger Trick

IT DOESN'T HURT MUCH IF I DO IT SLOWLY!

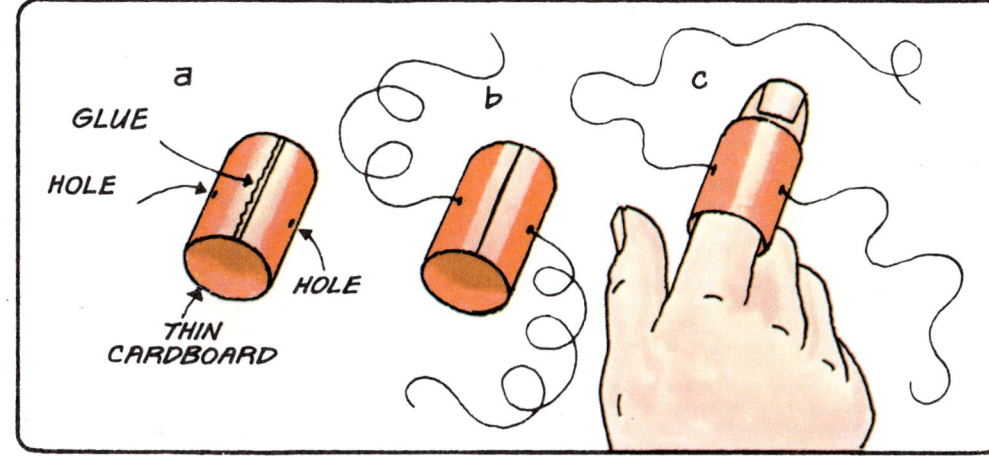

a

GLUE

HOLE

THIN CARDBOARD

b

c

HOLE

Cut out a piece of thin cardboard about 7 cm long and 4 cm wide. Roll it into a tube and glue the edges together (a). Make a hole in each side of the tube.

Push a piece of string, about 50 cm long, through the holes (b). Slide the tube on to one finger (c). Slowly pull one end of the string. Then pull the other end.

Wand Through Head Trick

Before You Start

WHITE PAPER

MAGIC WAND

GLUE

For this trick you need a black wand with white ends. You also need to wear long sleeves. Wrap a bit of white paper round one end of the wand. Glue down the end.

1

Hold the end of the wand which has the paper on it. Put the other end to your head, behind one ear. Make sure the back of your hand is towards the people watching you.

2

Now push the bit of paper very slowly along the wand so that the wand looks as if it is going into your head. The end in your hand slides up your sleeve.

What's worse than a giraffe with a sore throat?   A centipede with sore feet!

Disappearing and Appearing Tricks

Vanishing Water

Make this magazine a magic one and use it to make water vanish. When you have done the trick, put the magazine down so it is upright and pour out the water when no one is looking. You can use the magazine lots of times for making other things appear or disappear.

The magazine should be thick but floppy and make sure there are no holes in the plastic bag.

Before You Start

Spread glue on the top edges of a small plastic bag. Press the bag to an inside page of a magazine. Close the magazine and press the pages together. Leave to dry.

1 How It Looks

HERE IS AN ORDINARY MAGAZINE. YOU CAN SEE THE INSIDE AND THE OUTSIDE.

2

I ROLL IT INTO A CONE AND STIR IT WITH MY MAGIC WAND.

1 The Secret

OPEN THE BAG WITH WAND

Roll the magazine into a cone. Push one end of a magic wand into the pages where the plastic bag is. Waggle the wand round to open the top of the bag, like this.

3

I POUR IN SOME WATER AND SAY THE MAGIC WORDS.

2

POUR WATER INTO BAG

Pour about half a cup of water into the bag. If you pour in just a very little and then a bit more and then a bit more, it will look like quite a lot of water.

4

I UNROLL THE MAGAZINE AND THE WATER HAS DISAPPEARED!

3

HOLD UP MAGAZINE

Unroll the magazine and hold it up by the top corners. Show the inside and outside. Close it and put it down so it stands upright or the water will run out.

1 Vanishing Coin

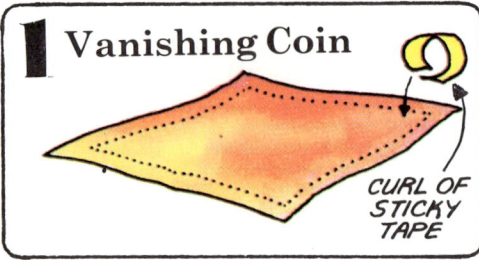

CURL OF STICKY TAPE

Make a small curl of sticky tape, like this, so the sticky side is outside. Press it down in the corner of a small scarf or coloured handkerchief.

2

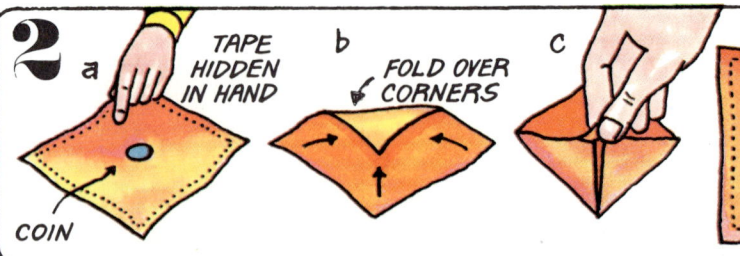

a TAPE HIDDEN IN HAND
b FOLD OVER CORNERS
c
d

COIN

Cover the sticky tape with one hand and ask someone to put a small coin on the scarf (a). Fold over the corner and press the tape down on to the coin (b).

Fold over the other three corners, like this (c). Pick up the first corner, covering the coin with your hand (d). Show that the coin has disappeared from the scarf.

What sort of lighting did Noah put in the Ark? ¡Flood lighting!

8

Empty Tube

Use a big empty tube to make things appear out of the air. This trick cannot be done too close to other people or they will see how it works. When you have finished the trick, stand the tube up on end so no one can see where things come from.

You will need
2 sheets of stiff black paper, or paper painted black, about 25 cm long and 25 cm wide
glue
coloured tissues or thin paper

1 How It Looks

HERE IS AN ABSOLUTELY EMPTY TUBE. YOU CAN SEE THERE IS NOTHING IN IT.

2

I SAY THE MAGIC WORDS AND SUDDENLY, LOTS OF THINGS APPEAR!

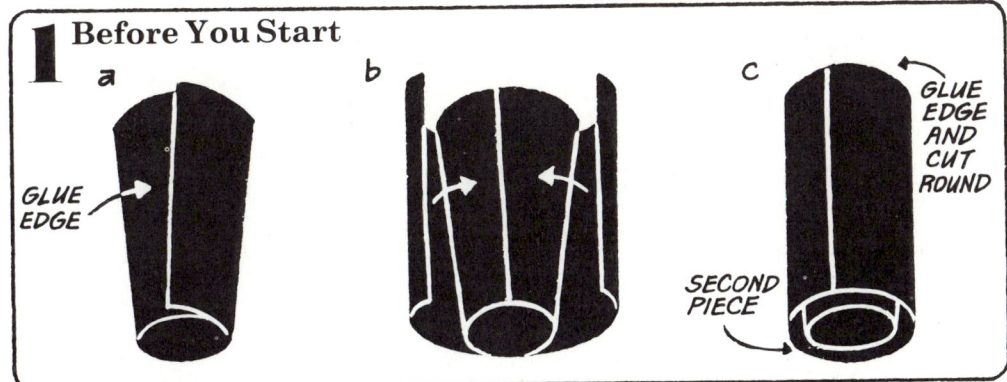

1 Before You Start

a

GLUE EDGE

b

c

SECOND PIECE

GLUE EDGE AND CUT ROUND

Roll one piece of black paper into a tube. Make it slightly wider at one end (a). Stick the edge with glue. Spread glue round the top of the wider end.

Wrap the second piece of paper round the first tube (b). Glue the edges exactly together to make the second tube straight. Cut off the bits at the top (c).

2

TUCK IN THIN PIECES OF PAPER

To get the trick ready, push small bits of coloured tissue or thin paper down between the two tubes. Hold this end towards you so no one can see the secret space.

1 Making Biscuits

a

GLUE

b

THIN BISCUITS

Open a thick, floppy magazine or comic in the middle. Glue the pages together on each side and bottom (a). When the glue is dry, put some biscuits in one side (b).

2

a

b

To do the trick, let everyone see you put some things, like bits of coloured paper and pencils, into the magazine. Close the magazine.

Now say the magic words or wave your wand. Open the magazine again and tip out the biscuits. Be careful to hold the other side so the things do not drop out.

What's green, hairy and goes up and down? A gooseberry in a lift!

Cutting and Mending Magic

Here are two easy ways to cut string in half and then make it into one piece again. All you need are pieces of string and a pair of scissors.

For the Tearing Trick, you will need two small paper handkerchiefs, which look exactly alike, and some glue.

When you do the tricks, look at your hands as if you really expect some magic to happen. And remember to say the magic words each time.

Short Cut

1 How It Looks

HERE IS A PERFECTLY ORDINARY PIECE OF STRING. I CUT IT IN HALF.

2 I SAY THE MAGIC WORDS AND IT IS IN ONE PIECE AGAIN!

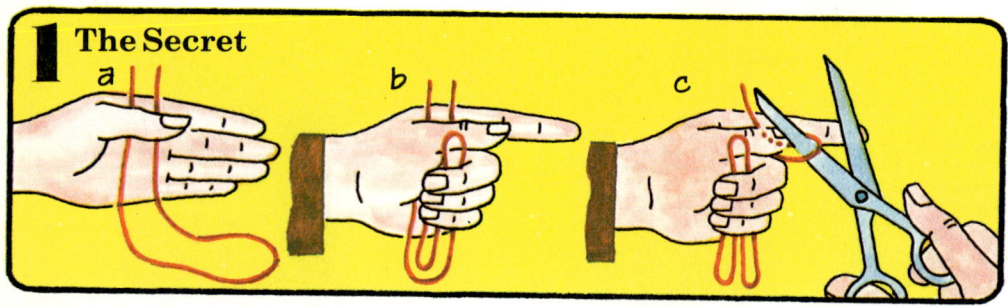

1 The Secret

a

b

c

Hold the ends of the string in one hand (a). Bring up the loop and hold it with your fingers (b).

Hook one blade of the scissors under one string near the end (c). Pretend you are hooking the loop.

2

Pull the string up above your hand so it can be seen. Cut the string very slowly and obviously.

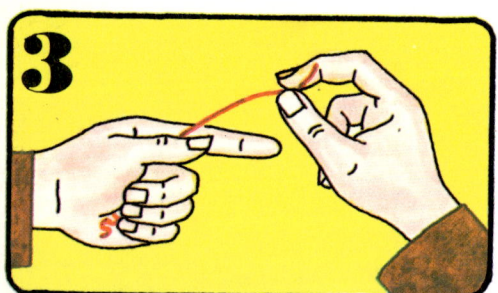

3

Hold one bit of the string you have cut. Push all the rest of the string into your hand and hold it.

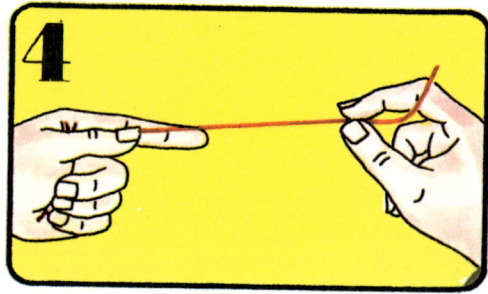

4

Say the magic words. Pull the string very slowly out of your hand to show it is in one piece.

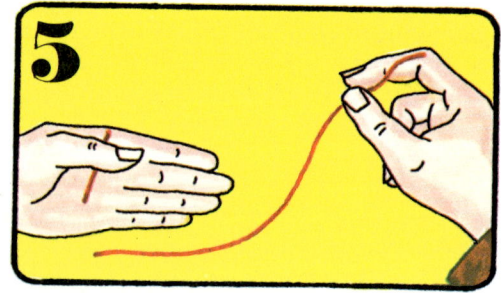

5

Keep the short cut-off string in your hand. Hide it in your pocket when no one is looking.

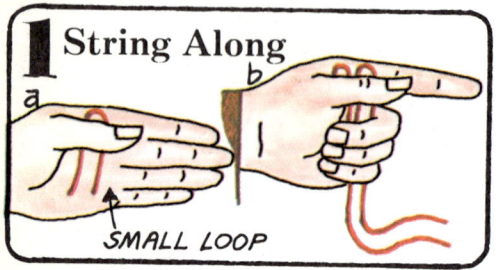

1 String Along

a

b

SMALL LOOP

Hide a short loop of string in your hand (a). Let everyone see you hold a long piece (b).

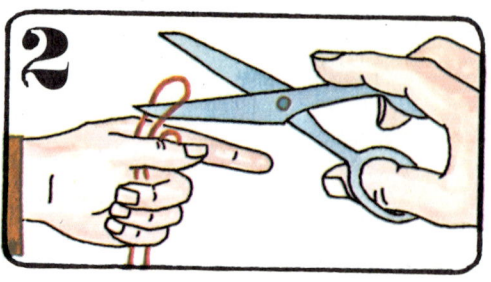

2

Hook one blade of the scissors under the short loop and pull it up a bit. Cut it in half.

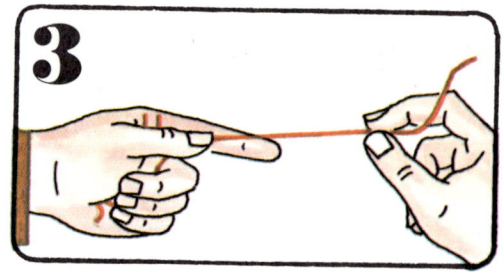

3

Push all the string into your hand. Hold one end of the long piece and pull it out. Hide the short bits.

What is an astronaut's watch called? A lunartick!

Tearing Trick

Before You Start

Put two paper handkerchiefs, which look exactly the same, on top of each other. Drop a bit of glue on to one corner (a) and stick them together.

Fold the top hanky backwards and forwards to pleat it into a strip (b). Pleat the strip (c) to make a neat square in one corner. The trick is now ready.

Not a Knot

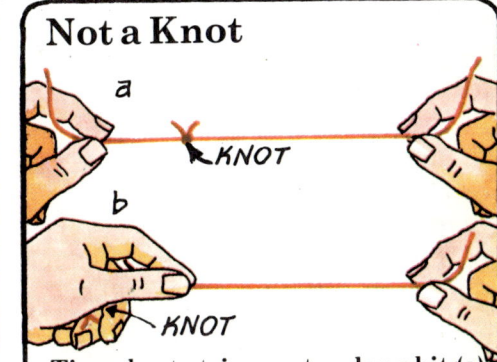

Tie a short string on to a long bit (a) so it looks like two bits tied together. Put all the string in one hand. Pull out one end, sliding the knot along and hiding it in your hand (b). The knot has vanished.

How It Looks

1 HERE IS A PAPER HANKY. I TEAR IT INTO VERY SMALL BITS.

2 I PUT THE BITS INTO MY HAND. NOW I WHISPER THE MAGIC WORDS.

3 SLOWLY, VERY SLOWLY, I PULL THE HANKY OUT OF MY HAND!

The Secret

FOLDED HANKY

TEAR IN STRIPS

BITS IN HAND

UNFOLD HANKY

Hold the paper handkerchief in one hand with your thumb over the folded-up one (a). Hold the top of the hanky with the other hand and tear it into strips (b).

Tear the strips into bits. Put all the bits into one hand (c). Hold your hand up to your mouth and whisper the magic words.

Take hold of the top corner of the folded-up hanky. Pull it slowly out of your hand so it unfolds (d). Hide the torn-up bits in your other hand so no one sees them.

If pig skins make good shoes, what do banana skins make? ¡sɹǝddᴉ๐ls poo◕

Matchbox Magic
Small Change

1

HERE IS AN EMPTY MATCHBOX.

1 The Secret

MATCHBOX TRAY

CUT OUT

Take the tray out of the box. Cut a narrow slit in the bottom of one end of the tray.

2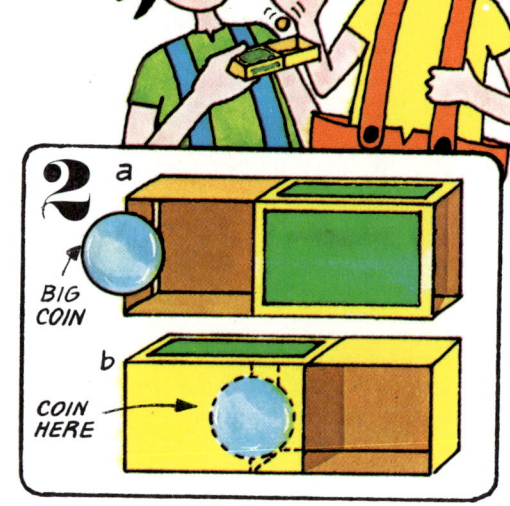

JUST DROP IN A VERY SMALL COIN.

2

a BIG COIN

b COIN HERE

Hold a big coin on the tray (a). Push the tray into the cover so the coin is held inside (b).

3

I CLOSE THE BOX, OPEN IT AGAIN AND TIP OUT A BIG COIN!

3

DROP IN SMALL COIN

Show someone that the box is empty and ask them to drop in a small coin.

4

TILT BOX

COIN SLIDES INTO HAND

Tilt the box so the small coin slides out of the slit in the tray and into your hand.

5

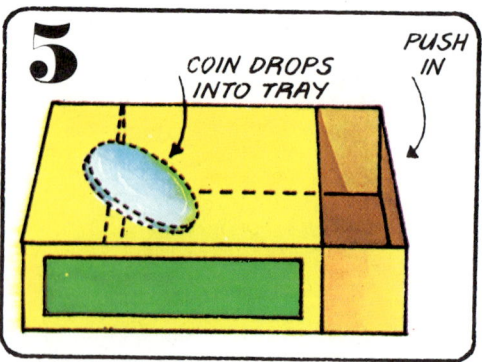

COIN DROPS INTO TRAY

PUSH IN

Push in the tray. The big coin drops into the tray. Hide the small coin in your hand.

6

OPEN BOX TO SHOW COIN

Say the magic words. Open the matchbox again and tip out the big coin into your empty hand.

Obedient Matchbox

JUST CALL 'STOP' AND I WILL STOP THE MATCHBOX ANYWHERE ON THE STRING!

Hold the string with the box loosely. The box will slide down. When it reaches the end, hold the string up the other way. To stop the box, pull the string tight.

Before You Start

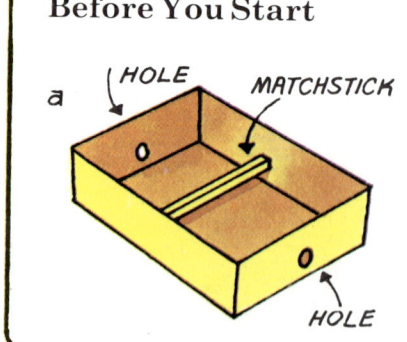

a HOLE   MATCHSTICK

HOLE

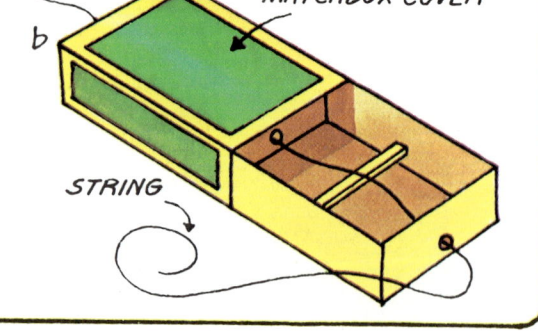

b MATCHBOX COVER

STRING

Take the tray out of a matchbox. Make a hole in each end of the tray. Break one end off a matchstick so it just fits into the tray. Jam it into the tray.

Push a piece of string through one hole, over the matchstick and out through the other hole. Slide on the matchbox cover (b).

What's a good place for water skiing? ¡A sloping lake!

More Matches

1 HERE IS A FULL BOX OF MATCHES.

For this trick you need a box of safety matches which looks exactly the same on both sides of the box.

2 I SHAKE OUT ALL THE MATCHES.

Hold your hand over the box so that no one can see the other side.

3 I OPEN THE BOX AGAIN, AND IT'S FULL OF MATCHES!

Close the box and secretly turn it over in your hand. Do not shake it or the matches will rattle.

1 Before You Start

CUT OUT

Take the tray out of the box. Cut out the bottom very neatly. Pull off any bits of paper.

2 GLUE IN

Push the bottom half-way up into the tray. Glue it all the way round. Leave the glue dry.

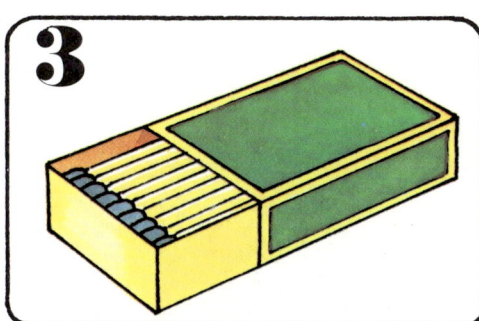

3

Fill one side of the box with matches. Turn the box over and fill up the other side.

Colour Changes

You can use the More Matches box to do other tricks. Here is a simple one. You can probably think of some of your own to do.

Remember never to let anyone look very closely at the box or they will see how you do the tricks.

1 PUT IN RED

Before you start, put a piece of blue paper or cloth in one side of the box. Turn the box over. Show that it is empty. Put in some red paper or a bit of cloth.

2 PULL OUT BLUE

Close the box and secretly turn it over. You can do this by waving it about and saying the magic words. Open the box and the red paper or cloth has turned blue.

Rattling Boxes

1 HERE IS A FULL BOX OF MATCHES. I CLOSE THE BOX AND SHAKE IT BUT IT DOESN'T RATTLE!

2 HERE IS AN EMPTY BOX. I CLOSE IT AND SHAKE IT. STRANGE, IT DOES RATTLE!

The Secret

For this trick you need three boxes of safety matches—one full box, a half-full one and an empty one. Jam some extra matches into the full one so the box does not rattle when you shake it.

Put the half-full box up your left sleeve and hold it there with an elastic band round your arm. When you shake the empty box, the box up your sleeve makes the rattling noise. When you shake the full box, make sure you hold it in your right hand or the one up your sleeve will rattle.

What has a bottom at its top? A leg!

13

Jack-in-the-Tube

Push down the head of this jack-in-the-tube and leave it to pop up again. If it takes a long time to jump, tap it very gently on the end.

You will need
3 small cardboard tubes
a ping pong ball
5 long, thin rubber bands
2 long, big-headed pins
sticky tape and scissors
thin paper and paints

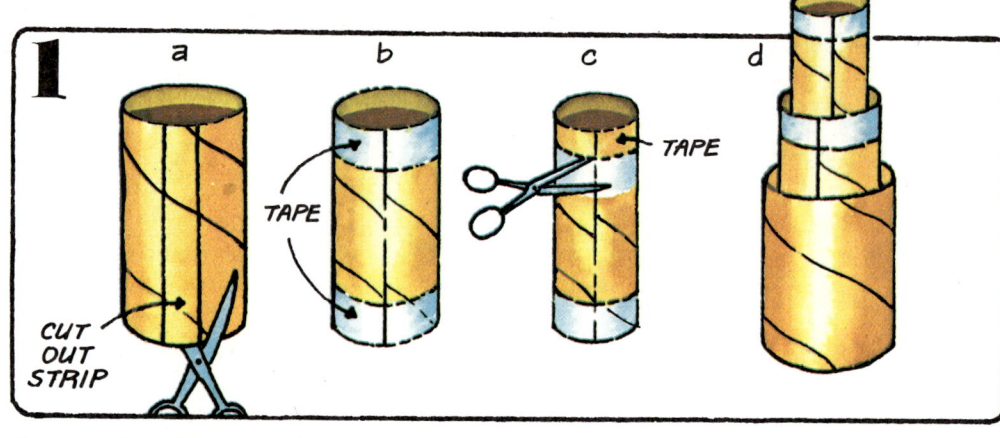

1

Cut a strip, about 1 cm wide, out of a cardboard tube (a). Hold the cut edges together and stick them with tape (b).

Cut a strip, about 2 cm wide, out of a second tube. Stick it with tape. Cut about 2 cm off the top (c). Put the three tubes together (d) to make sure they slide easily.

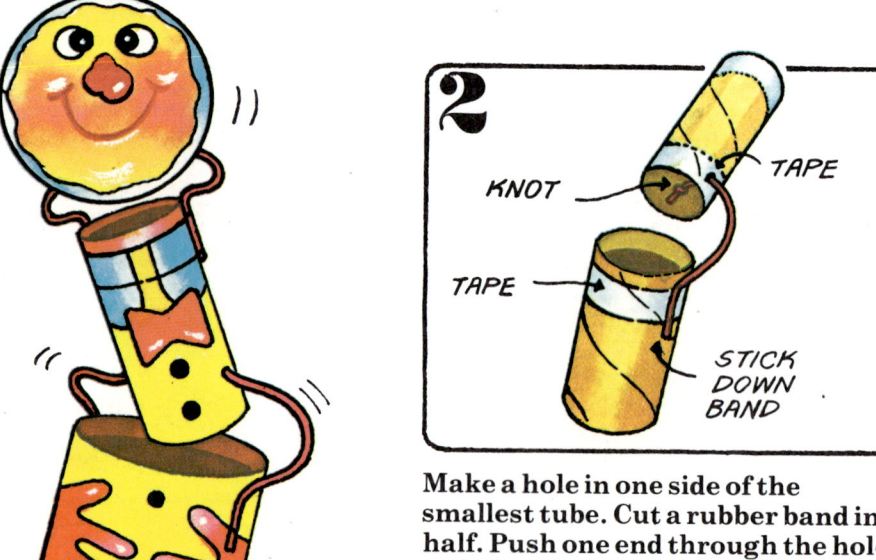

2

Make a hole in one side of the smallest tube. Cut a rubber band in half. Push one end through the hole and tie a knot. Tape the other end to the second tube.

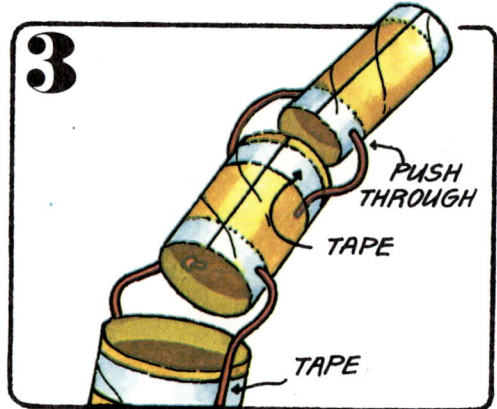

3

Join the second tube to the third tube in the same way. Now join the other sides of each tube with rubber bands. The tubes should be about 2 cm apart.

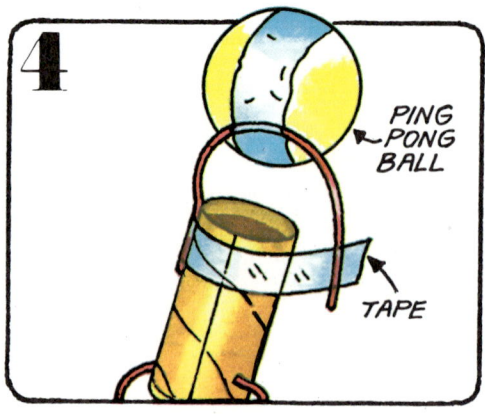

4

Cut another rubber band in half. Tape it to the top of the smallest tube with tape. Tape the ping pong ball to the rubber band.

5

Push pins into the ping pong ball for the eyes. Paint or colour the face. Paint the tubes or cover them with coloured paper.

Man: Hey, you're not allowed to fish in that river.

Boy: I'm not fishing. I'm teaching my pet worm to swim!

Squirting Flower

Put this flower in your button hole. When someone is close enough, squeeze the tube to make it squirt water.

You will need
an empty plastic tube with a
  screw-on top
a plastic drinking straw
a coloured plastic bag
a paper clip
waterproof glue, such as Bostick 1
thin thread
scissors

WOULD YOU LIKE TO SMELL THIS LOVELY SCENT?

WOULD YOU LIKE TO SMELL MY PLASTIC FLOWER?

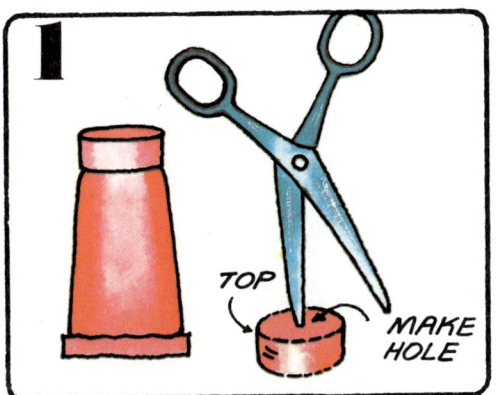

1

TOP

MAKE HOLE

Take the top off the plastic tube. Make a small hole in the top with scissors, like this.

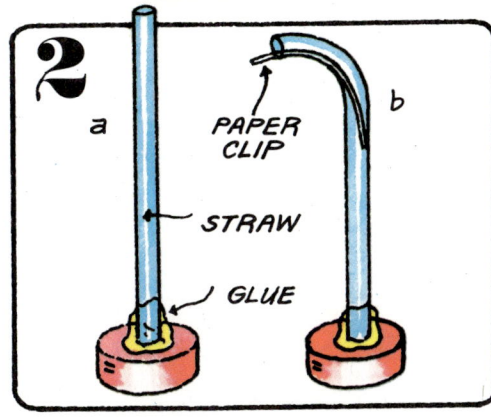

2

a

PAPER CLIP

b

STRAW

GLUE

Push one end of a plastic straw into the hole. Glue it to the top (a). Straighten out a paper clip. Bend over one end and push it into the top of the straw (b).

Scent Bottle

a

PLASTIC BOTTLE

MAKE HOLES

Make about six small holes in the bottom of an empty plastic bottle with one blade of the scissors, like this.

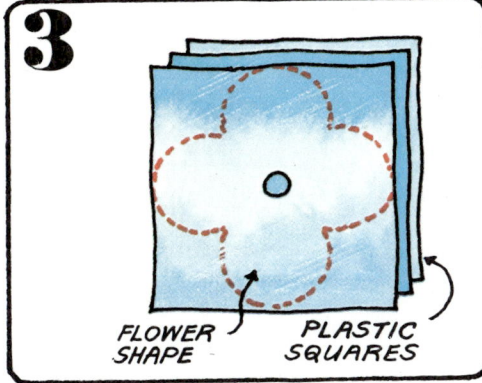

3

FLOWER SHAPE

PLASTIC SQUARES

Cut three squares from a plastic bag. Put them together and cut out a flower petal shape, like this. Cut a small hole in the middle of each shape.

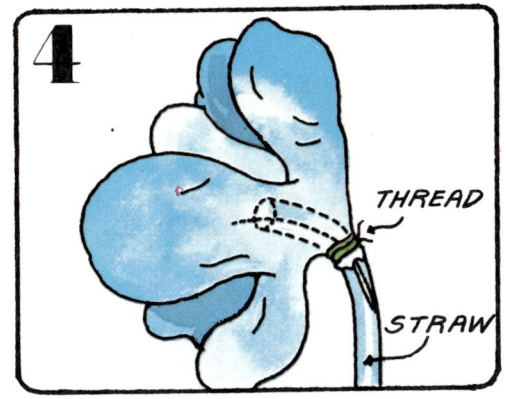

4

THREAD

STRAW

Push the top of the straw through the holes in the flower shapes. Tie them to the straw with thread. Pour some water into the plastic tube and screw on the top.

b

PUT ON TOP

FILL WITH WATER

Fill the bottle to the top with water. Screw on the lid very quickly. No water will come out if you hold the bottle upright. But when someone takes off the lid, just watch . . .

What was purple and tried to conquer the world? Alexander the Grape!

Puzzlers

Magic Seesaw

Set up this seesaw and make it go up and down as many times as you like. Be careful not to touch the cups as you do it.

You will need

a strong ruler or flat piece of
    wood about 35 cm long
2 empty yoghurt pots or paper
    cups
a matchbox
a jug of water

Before You Start

Put the middle of the ruler on the matchbox, like this. Put a pot or cup on each one. Make sure they balance each other exactly.

How It Looks

1 I PUT MY FINGER IN ONE POT AND THE SEESAW GOES DOWN. WHEN I TAKE IT OUT AND PUT IT IN THE OTHER THE SEESAW TIPS THE OTHER WAY.

2 I POUR THE WATER OUT OF THE TWO POTS. NOW COMES THE DIFFICULT PART.

3 IF I TRY VERY HARD I CAN MAKE THE SEESAW GO DOWN WITHOUT TOUCHING THE POTS. IT'S VERY DIFFICULT TO DO. I HAVE TO GET VERY CLOSE AND THINK HARD AT ONE END AND THEN THE OTHER.

The Secret

When you dip your finger into the water in a cup, the seesaw goes down. Anyone can do this. When you put your finger in an empty cup, bend down very close to it and pretend to try very hard. Then groan a little as if it is difficult. When you groan, blow gently into the cup and it will go down. Then groan and blow gently into the other cup. Be careful not to touch the cups. This looks like real magic.

Spooky Straws

Cut a drinking straw in half. Put the bits down, like this. When you put a finger between them and say the magic words, they move apart. When you speak, blow gently at the same time down your finger.

Linking Clips

1

For this trick, find two envelopes which look the same. Glue them back to back. Link up seven paper clips and drop them into one of the envelopes. Close both flaps.

2

To do the trick, open the empty envelope. Drop in seven clips and close the flap. Secretly turn the envelopes over, saying the magic words. Open the flap and tip out the linked clips.

If a buttercup is yellow, what colour is a hiccup? Burple!

Paper Chase

1 Before You Start

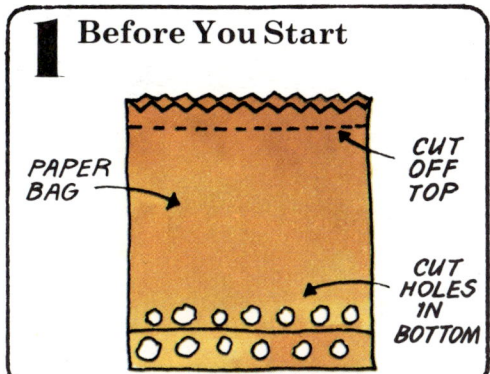

PAPER BAG

CUT OFF TOP

CUT HOLES IN BOTTOM

Find two small paper bags which are the same size and colour. Cut about 1 cm off the top of one bag. Cut some holes in the bottom of the bag, to let air through when you blow in it.

2

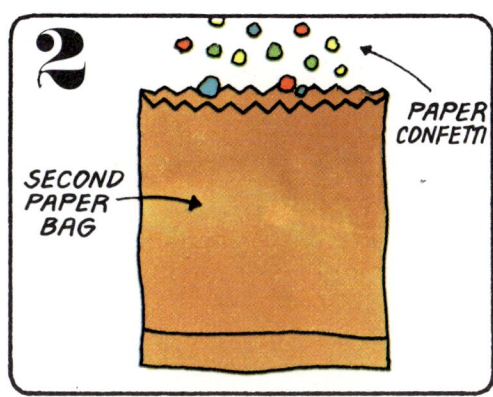

PAPER CONFETTI

SECOND PAPER BAG

Cut up lots of bits of coloured paper to make confetti. Put the bits into the second paper bag. When you do the trick, this bag bursts but not the one with the holes in it.

3

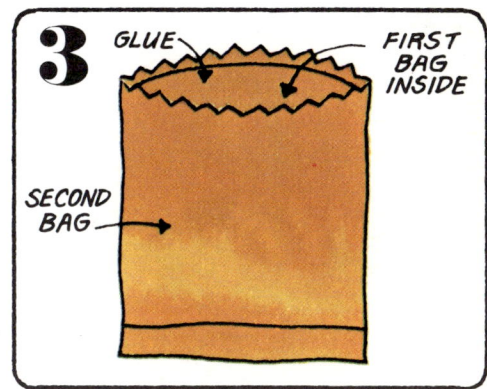

GLUE

FIRST BAG INSIDE

SECOND BAG

Push the first bag into the second one. Glue the edges of the two bags together round the tops. Make sure the inside bag is very smooth. When you have done the trick, quickly crumple up the bags.

1 How It Looks

THIS IS AN ORDINARY PAPER BAG. YOU CAN SEE IT IS EMPTY. I PUSH IN A COUPLE OF PAPER TISSUES.

2

I BLOW UP THE BAG AND THEN SAY THE MAGIC WORDS.

3

WHEN I BURST THE BAG THE TISSUES HAVE TURNED INTO COLOURED CONFETTI!

Knotty Problem

1

WATCH ME TIE A KNOT IN THIS HANDKERCHIEF.

2

I FLIP IT ONCE, TWICE AND A THIRD TIME AND THERE IS THE KNOT.

The Secret

a   b   c

Tie a knot in a corner of a hanky. Hide the knot in one hand (a). Flip the hanky upwards, twice (b). The third time, drop the knot and grab the other end (c). Practise until you can do this very quickly.

What are the best things to put into a fruit pie? Your teeth!

Creepies and Crawlies

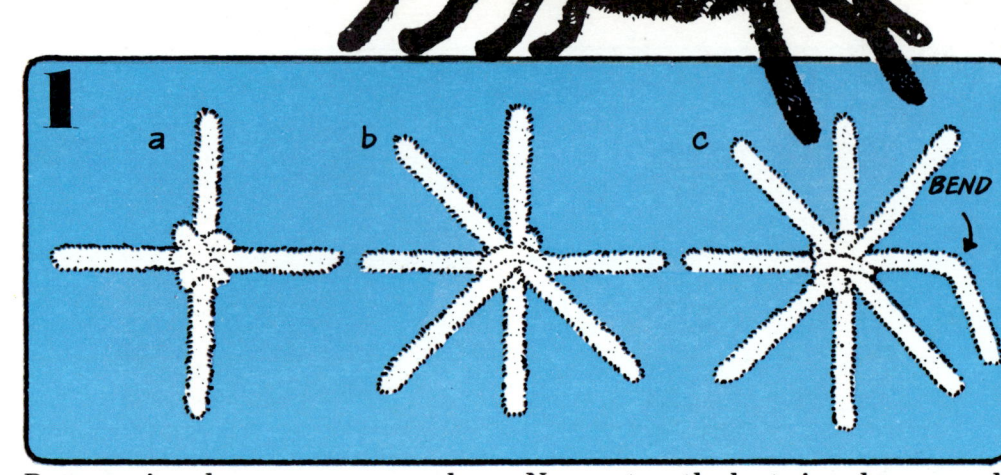

Climbing Spider

This monster spider climbs down its thread and up again. Hang it up in a dimly-lit room and no one will notice how you work it. The nastier it looks the bigger the horrible surprise.

You will need
6 pipe cleaners
cotton wool
2 small buttons and 2 pins
thin black thread
a paper clip
glue and black paint

1

a **b** **c**
BEND

Put two pipe cleaners across each other, like this. Wind a third one round them to join them together (a). Join on a fourth cleaner with another one (b).

Now put on the last pipe cleaner and fasten it on (c) to make the eight legs of the spider. Bend over all the legs.

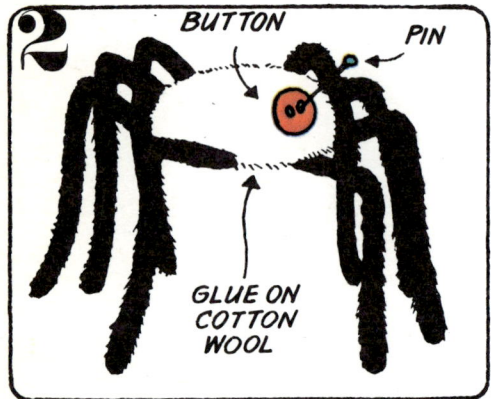

2 BUTTON PIN
GLUE ON COTTON WOOL

Glue a lump of cotton wool to the middle of the legs to make the body. Paint the whole thing black. Pin on two bright buttons to make the eyes.

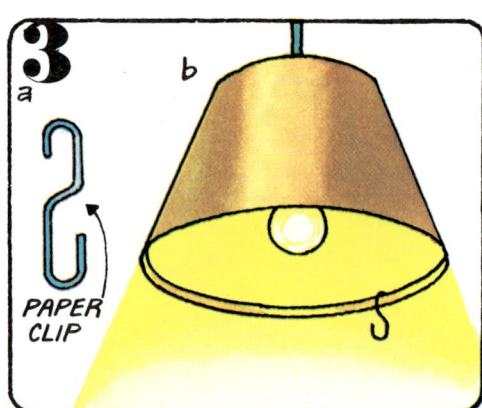

3 **a** **b**
PAPER CLIP

Bend a paper clip, like this, to make a loop at each end (a). Hook one end on to the frame of a lamp shade, on the inside (b).

4
PULL THE THREAD

Tie a very long piece of black thread to the top of the spider. Hook the thread over the paper clip. Pull the end of the thread to make the spider go up and down.

Crawlies

You can make lots of nasty crawlies out of coloured plasticine. Roll out a long pink bit to make a wriggly worm. Shape some brown plasticine to look like a slug, with bits for its horns. On a lettuce leaf or in a plate of salad these nasties will look quite real and will put anyone off their food.

Caterpillars

Cut a pipe cleaner into four bits to make caterpillars. Paint them yellowy green or in yellow and green stripes. When the paint is dry, bend them into wriggly shapes.

How do you know when it's raining cats and dogs?   ¡ǝlpood ɐ uᴉ dǝʇs noʎ uǝɥM

Flying Bat

This bat flies across a room at great speed. Make it look as horrible as you can. It will look best in a fairly dark room.

You will need
a sheet of stiff black paper, or
   white paper and black paint
a piece of black paper, about 8 cm
   long and 4 cm wide
2 pipe cleaners
a small curtain ring
very thin nylon string or fishing
   line, about 8 metres long
glue, sticky tape and scissors

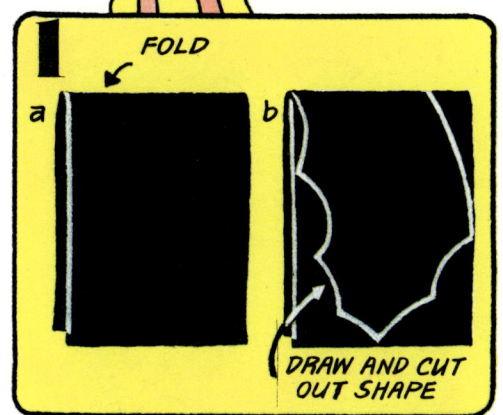

Fold the sheet of paper in half (a). Draw the shape of a bat's wing on one side (b). Cut out the shape but do not cut along the folded edge. Open out the paper.

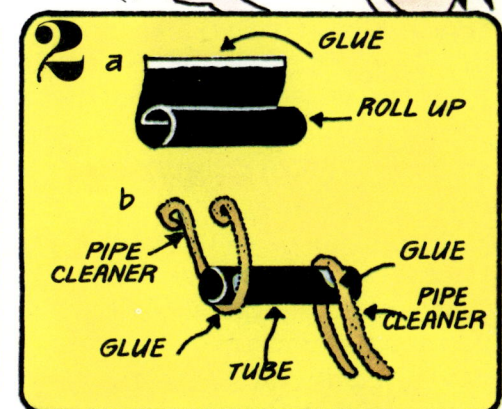

Roll up the small piece of paper to make a tube. Glue the edge (a). Bend a pipe cleaner round one end for the eyes and one round the other end for legs (b). Glue on.

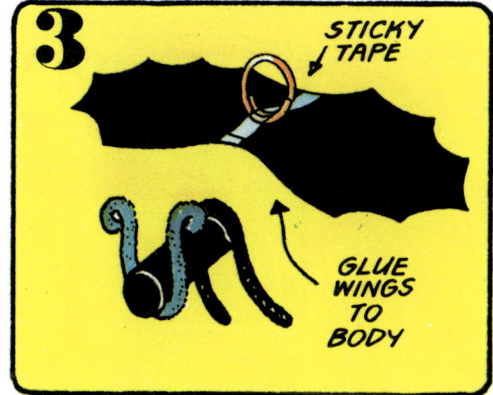

Stick the curtain ring upright to the middle of the wings with tape. Glue the wings to the body, like this. Paint the pipe cleaners black and bend them a little.

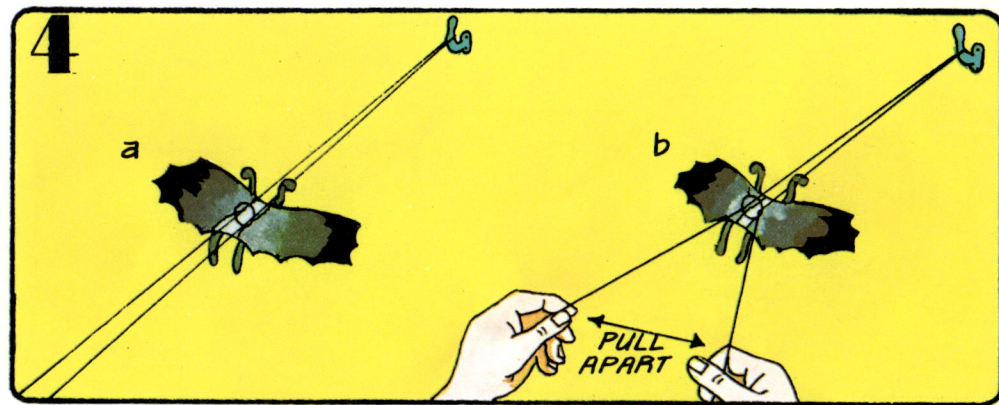

Hook the middle of the nylon string on to something high up in a room, perhaps near a door. Slide the ends of the string through the ring on the bat (a).

Hold one end of one string in each hand. Slide the bat down close to your hands. Now pull the strings apart as quickly as you can. The bat will fly along them (b).

Flies

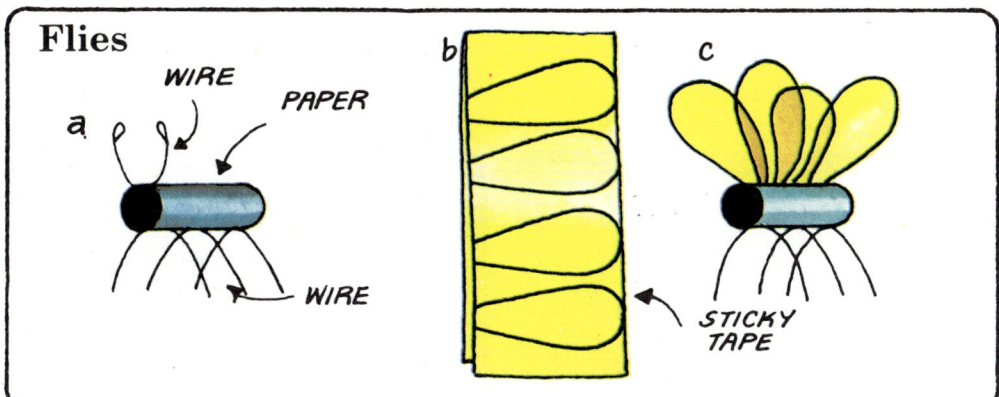

Make a little roll of paper and glue the edge. Cut some short bits of very thin wire. Glue them on to make legs and antennae (a). Paint the paper black. Leave to dry.

Fold over a piece of sticky tape so the sticky sides are together. Cut out four oval shapes (b) and glue them on as the fly's wings (c). Everyone hates flies.

Wasps

Make another fly but before you glue on the wings, wind a pipe cleaner round the body. Paint it in yellow and black stripes. Then glue on the wings.

What did one eye say to the other eye? Something has come between us that smells!

19

Clever Card Tricks

There are hundreds, or even thousands, of card tricks. Some are very difficult and need lots of practice. Here are some easy ones which are fun to do. All you need is a pack of ordinary playing cards.

When you are doing card tricks, talk at the same time if you can. It stops people thinking about what you are doing and puzzling out your secrets.

With the Pick a Card tricks, ask the person to look very hard at the chosen card. While they are staring at it, they will not notice what you are doing.

Crazy Card

When you do this trick make the card follow the wand. Move the wand up and down slowly, then quickly, then in little jerks.

The Secret

Hold some cards like this, your fingers towards people watching. Hold your wand over the cards. Then move your thumb up and down. This will move one card.

Reading Finger Trick

Hold out some cards and ask a friend to pick one (a) without you seeing it. Take it, like this (b) and rub it with one finger. Say you are reading it.

Put the card back in the pack and hold it together neatly (a). Now lift off some cards. The one that comes face up is the card you rubbed with your finger (b).

The secret is that when you rub the card, you bend it a little. When it is in the pack, it holds the cards apart and you can lift them off at the right place every time.

Magic Sevens

This is a really magic trick. It comes right every time you do it but there is no explanation why. You need 21 cards. Any 21 will do but make sure they are all from the same pack.

Put down three cards in a line (a). Add a second card to each one in the line, then a third, until you have used them all (b). There will be seven cards in each row.

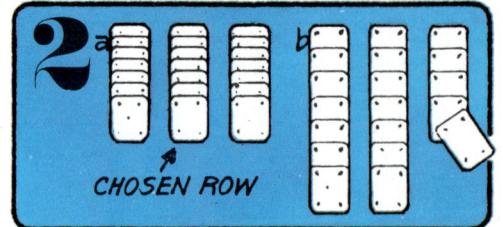

Ask someone to choose a card but keep it a secret. Ask which row the card is in. Pick up that row and put it between the other rows (a). Put out the cards again in the same way in three rows of seven (b).

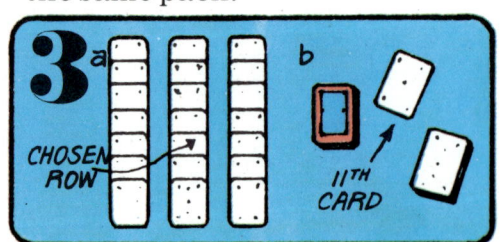

Ask which row the chosen card is now in. Put that row between the other rows (a). Keeping the cards in the same order, turn them over. From the top, count out ten cards. The eleventh is the chosen one.

Why did the chicken cross the road? ¡suoseəɹ ʍoɟ ɹoℲ

Pick A Card

Fan out some cards (a). Ask a friend to pick one and look at it, without you seeing it. Take half the pack in your right hand and look, secretly, at the bottom card (b). Ask a friend to put back the picked card, face down, on the cards in your left hand (c). Put all the cards together. Turn them over, from the top, one at a time. The card after the one you looked at will be the picked card (d).

Pick Another Card

Before you do this trick, divide a pack of cards into red and black ones (a). Put the two halves together again. Fan them out, face down, and ask someone to pick one.

Hold one edge of the fan towards the person so they take a card from one end (a). Ask them to put it back. Move the fan round so it goes in at the other end (b).

Turn the cards over and hold them up so no one else can see them. If the picked card is red, it will be among the black cards. If it is black, it will be with the reds.

1 Card Through Cards

Hold a pack of cards in one hand. Pick off the top two cards, holding the edges exactly together so they look like one card. Let everyone see which card it is.

2

Put the two cards down on top of the pack. Slide off the top one (a) and put it at the bottom of the pack (b). Let everyone see very clearly what you are doing.

3

Give the pack a good bang with one hand (a). Say that this is to bang the bottom card up to the top again. Pick off the top card and show it is the same one again (b).

What do you get if you cross a kangaroo with an elephant? Huge holes all over Australia!

Amazing Water Tricks

Tricky Tumblers

Playing with water is good fun but be careful where you do these tricks. Hold the glass over a big, empty bowl or put a deep tray on top of a table.

Use a thick drinking glass which will not break easily, or better still, an unbreakable one, if you can.

When you do these tricks, turn the glass over as quickly as you can. You will have to practise them a few times first.

1 Clever Cloth

Put a piece of thin cloth over a glass. Let it flop over loosely. Pour in some water, through the cloth, until the glass is full.

2

Stretch the cloth tightly over the glass. Hold it down with one hand. Turn the glass upside down very quickly. Hold it straight and the water will stay in.

1 Sticky Paper

Fill up a glass with water, almost to the top. Put a piece of stiff, thick paper over the top of the glass. Hold it down with one hand.

2

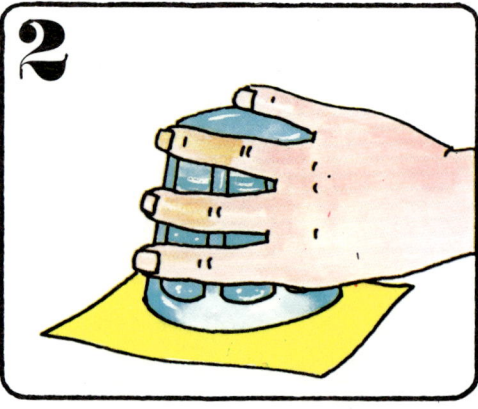

Hold the glass with the other hand and turn it over quickly. Take away the hand holding the paper. The paper will stick to the glass and keep the water in.

1 Air Magic

Put an empty glass down on a sheet of stiff, colourless plastic. Draw round the glass with a ball point pen (a). Cut along the line with scissors (b) to cut out a circle.

2

To do the trick, hide the plastic circle under the piece of stiff paper. Fill up the glass. Hold the circle under the paper and put it over the top of the glass.

3

Make sure the circle is exactly over the top of the glass. Hold the paper down with one hand and turn the glass over with the other.

4

Peel the paper off very slowly and carefully. The plastic circle will stick and hold the water in. From a little distance, it will look like magic.

When is it bad luck to be followed by a black cat? When you're a mouse!

Coloured Water Magic

This trick will really puzzle people but do not let them come too close when you do it. Practise it a few times first so you get it just right.

You will need a glass with lines or ridges on it, a small square scarf or coloured handkerchief, and some pieces of stiff, coloured plastic or acetate. If you can find lots of different colours, you can make the trick last much longer.

How It Looks

1 HERE IS A GLASS OF GREEN WATER I COVER IT WITH MY MAGIC HANDKERCHIEF.

2 I LIFT OFF THE HANDKERCHIEF AND THE GREEN WATER HAS TURNED INTO ORANGEADE!

Hold up a glass full of coloured water. Drop a bright scarf or handkerchief over it.

Lift off the scarf and the water has changed colour. Cover the glass and change the colour again.

1 Before You Start

STIFF COLOURED PLASTIC — CUT TO FILL

Cut out pieces of coloured plastic so that they just fit tightly in the glass. Cut about 1 cm off the top. Each piece should slide in and out easily but stay upright.

2 THIN NYLON LINE

Make a small hole in the top of each plastic shape. Tie a short piece of nylon line or thin white thread to each shape.

3 WATER — PLASTIC SHAPES

Push all the shapes into the glass so they stand upright. Hang the strings over one side, towards you. Pour in enough water to fill the glass nearly to the top.

1 The Secret

Hold up the glass. Be very careful that the shapes are flat towards the people watching. If they are sideways on, they will show. Drop the scarf over the glass.

2 PICK UP THREAD

With your finger and thumb, pick up a thread through the scarf and lift it up. Hide the shape in the scarf. Cover the glass again and take out another shape.

3

When you have taken out all the shapes, drink the water to show it is real. Or make the trick longer by putting back the shapes. This needs a bit more practice.

What's worse than finding a maggot in an apple? Finding half a maggot!

Crafty Coin Tricks

Vanishing Coin

1

Ask a friend to sit down facing you and hold out one hand. Hold a coin between your fingers and thumb. Press it into the friend's hand but keep hold of it.

2

Lift your hand above your head. Then press the coin into the hand again. The third time ask the friend to grab it. But the coin has vanished. Show your empty hand.

The Secret

When you raise your hand the third time, drop the coin on to the top of your head. Pretend you are still holding it and press the friend's hand hard with one finger.

Magic Spinner

1

Hold a big coin upright on a table with one finger, like this. Now rub that finger with a finger of the other hand. Explain that you are working up the magic.

2

Now quickly rub your finger along towards the nail. Lift up both hands and the coin spins away.

The Secret

When you do the last rub of your finger, whizz your hand away and just catch the edge of the coin with your thumb. This is to make it spin. Practise it in secret.

Detective Work

1

Put three small bottle tops, all exactly the same, down on a table. Give someone a small coin and ask him to hide it under one top while you look the other way.

2

When the coin has been hidden, stare very hard at each top. Then pick up the one hiding the coin. You will be right every time.

The Secret

Before you do this trick, pull out a hair from your head. Glue about 3 cm of it to a coin, like this. When the coin is under a top, look for the hair sticking out under it.

What cake tried to conquer the world? Attila the Bun!

Dissolving Coin

1 HERE IS A COIN AND MY MAGIC SCARF.

2 I HIDE THE COIN IN THE SCARF.

3 NOW I PICK UP A GLASS OF WATER.

4 I PUT THE SCARF OVER THE GLASS AND DROP THE COIN IN.

5 I TAKE AWAY THE SCARF AND YOU CAN SEE THE PENNY.

6 I COVER THE GLASS AGAIN WITH THE SCARF AND SAY THE MAGIC WORDS...

7 WHEN I TAKE AWAY THE SCARF THE COIN HAS *DISAPPEARED!*

1 The Secret — TILT GLASS — DROP COIN

2 COIN UNDER THE GLASS

3 COIN HIDDEN IN HAND

When you cover the glass with the scarf, tilt the glass a little. Drop the coin so it hits the outside of the glass and falls into your hand.

Before you take the scarf away, make sure the coin is under the glass. It will then look as if it is in the glass.

When you take away the scarf again, hide the coin in your hand. Hold the glass up with your fingers and thumb. You can put the coin in your pocket or hide it later.

How does an elephant get down from a tree? Stands on a leaf and waits for autumn!

Surprises

This is a very good trick. People can stand quite close without seeing how you do it. But it needs lots of practice. Follow the instructions and do the trick several times in secret to get it right.

Before you start, crumple up four bits of tissue paper into balls. You also need two saucers.

When you do the trick, hold the saucers upside down, with your thumbs on top and fingers underneath. Pick up the paper balls between your fingers so they are hidden under the saucer. Do not turn the saucers over during the trick.

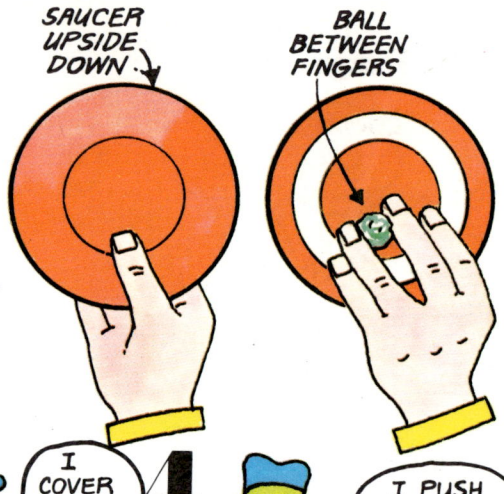

SAUCER UPSIDE DOWN.

BALL BETWEEN FINGERS

1 HERE ARE FOUR BALLS OF TISSUE PAPER AND TWO SAUCERS.

Put the four balls on the table in a square, like this. They should be about 20 cm apart. Pick up the two saucers with your thumbs on top and fingers underneath.

2 I CAN COVER ANY TWO BALLS AT A TIME, LIKE THIS OR ANY OTHER WAY.

Cover two balls with saucers, then two more several times. The last time, secretly pick up ball 1 in your right hand. Slide the left saucer over the empty place. Put the right saucer over ball 2 and drop ball 1.

3 I COVER TWO BALLS AND PICK UP THE THIRD BALL.

Leave both saucers on the table and pick up ball 3 in your left hand. Pass it to your right hand.

4 I PUSH THE BALL UP THROUGH THE TABLE AND SAY THE MAGIC WORDS.

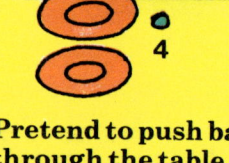

Pretend to push ball 3 up through the table. Knock on the underside of the table, pretending it is very hard to get through. Secretly hide the ball in your right hand.

5 I LIFT UP THE SAUCER AND THERE ARE THE TWO BALLS.

Pick up the saucer in your left hand to show the two balls underneath it. Pass the saucer to your right hand, which is hiding ball 3.

6 I COVER THE TWO BALLS AND PICK UP THE FOURTH ONE.

Put the saucer in your right hand over the two balls and drop ball 3 beside them. Now pick up ball 4.

7 I PUSH IT UP THROUGH THE TABLE AND SAY THE MAGIC WORDS. I LIFT UP THE SAUCER AND THERE IT IS.

Pretend to push ball 4 up through the table. Hide it in your right hand. Lift up the saucer with your left hand to show three balls. Pass the saucer to your right hand. Put it over the three balls and drop ball 4 beside them.

8 I NOW PULL THE LAST BALL DOWN THROUGH THE TABLE AND PUSH IT UP BESIDE THE OTHER THREE. I LIFT UP THE SAUCER AND THERE THEY ARE!

Put your hand under the table. Pretend to move ball 4 from under the empty saucer and push it up under the other one. Lift up the saucer to show the four balls. Pick up the other saucer to show there is nothing under it.

How does a sparrow with engine failure land safely? ¡By sparrowchute!

Night Pinger

This is a good trick to do at night. Put the Pinger in a cupboard in a bedroom or under a bed. It will go on working for a very long time. As the peas take up the hot water, they grow bigger. Then they push out of the cup and drop on to the tray.

You will need
2 plastic cups or pots
a tin tray or big baking tray
a big cardboard box
dried peas or beans
glue

Glue the cups, end to end, like this. Fill the top cup with as many dried peas as you can push in.

Put the tray in the bottom of the cardboard box. Stand the cups on the tray. Pour hot water into the top cup. Close the box and wait very patiently for the pings.

Clothes Line

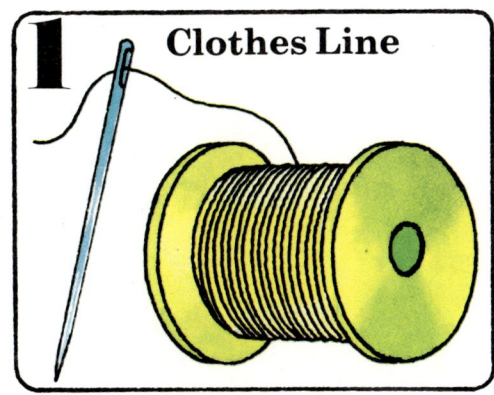

Push the end of the thread on a reel of coloured cotton through the eye of a big needle.

Push the needle through the sleeve of your jersey or shirt from the inside. Pull off the needle, leaving a bit of thread hanging on the outside.

When someone says "You've got a thread hanging" and pulls it, the thread just gets longer and longer. Make sure the reel can unwind easily but stay hidden.

Cardboard Flapper

Pass the Flapper to a friend or send it in an envelope through the post.

You will need
a big paper clip or piece of strong, bendy wire, about 12 cm long
a rubber band
a strip of cardboard, about 12 cm long and 8 cm wide
a small square of thick cardboard
sticky tape

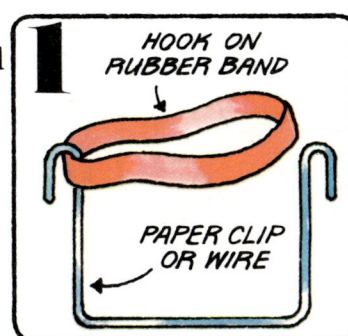

Bend the paper clip or wire into this shape. Bend over the two ends. Hook the rubber band across the top.

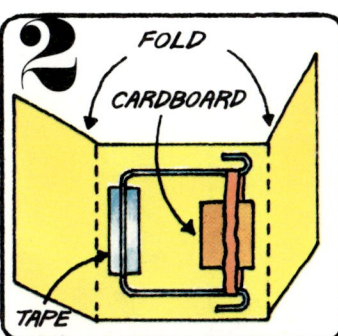

Fold the cardboard in three, like this. Stick one side of the clip to the middle fold of the cardboard. Slide the small cardboard square between the band.

Wind the cardboard square round and round about 20 times. Fold over the two flaps of the cardboard strip to stop the square unwinding. The Flapper is ready.

What do you get if you cross a mink with a kangaroo?   A fur coat with big pockets!

Putting on a Show

When you are good at doing magic, try putting on a show for your friends. On the next four pages are things you can make before a show. You can use most of the other tricks in this book as well.

Before a show, practise all the tricks lots of times in front of a mirror. Then you can see exactly how they look.

Write out a list of your tricks and put it on the table. It will remind you in which order you have decided to do them. Put all the things you need on the table. Have a box beside it so you can drop things into it when you have done the tricks. Start and end the show with two of your very best tricks. Arrange the others so each one looks very different from the last. Do not do two which look a bit alike.

If you find it easy, talk to the audience while you are doing the tricks. If this is hard for you, put on a record or radio music programme, just loud enough for people to hear.

It is a good idea to have an assistant to help you and hand you the things you need. Choose a friend who will keep your magic tricks a secret.

Making Mistakes

When you are putting on a show, don't worry if a trick goes wrong. Just pretend it is part of the show and no one will notice. It is a good idea to have a whistle or something which makes a noise. This startles the audience and you can go on to the next trick. Or you can do a quick trick. Here are two you can have ready if you need to cover up a mistake.

You will need a table to do your tricks on. Cover it with a cloth if you have one. Before the show arrange the chairs for the audience. Make sure everyone sits in front of the table and not too close to it. If you can, put a light near the front of the table and just to one side. The light should not be too bright.

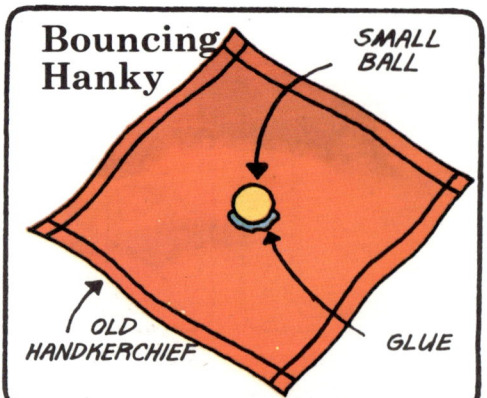

Bouncing Hanky

SMALL BALL

OLD HANDKERCHIEF

GLUE

Glue a small ball to the middle of a handkerchief. Pull out the hanky. Pretend to wipe your face and drop it on the floor. It will bounce back up to your hand.

Big Sneeze

HANDKERCHIEF

BIG JAGGED HOLE

SNIFF

Cut a large jagged hole in an old hanky. Pull it out of a pocket and pretend to sneeze into it. Hold it up show how strong your sneeze was.

Doctor, doctor, I've got only 59 seconds to live. Hold on, I'll be with you in a minute.

Magic Boxes

You can use this magic box for making all sorts of things appear – or disappear – by magic.
You will need
a cardboard box about 28 cm long, 16 cm wide and 8 cm deep
a piece of cardboard the same size as the lid of the box
a piece of cardboard the same size as the end of the box
a piece of black card, or card painted black, the same length as the box and about 5 cm wider
2 elastic bands
4 paper fasteners
paints, sticky tape and scissors

Cut one end off the box (a). Paint the inside black. Cut two long strips out of the lid, leaving a strip down the middle (b).

Put the lid on the box. Stick it down all the way round the edges with tape (c).

Fold the piece of black cardboard in half, lengthways (a). Push it into the box, like this (b). This makes a secret space at the back of the box.

Stick the large piece of cardboard to the side of the box with tape to make a door. Stick the smaller piece of cardboard to the top of the box to make a flap.

Push a paper fastener through the door and another through the side of the box (a). Push a third fastener through the flap and a fourth through the box back (b).

Hook a rubber band over the door fastener and the side one. Hook a band over the flap and back fasteners.

Put small scarves, handkerchiefs or lots of small flat things into the secret space in the box. Close the door and the flap. Hook up the rubber bands.

Unhook the rubber bands. Open the door and show people the inside of the box. Put your hand into the space in the front to prove that the box is empty.

Close the door and hook up the band. Say the magic words or wave your wand. Open the flap and slowly pull out the things you have hidden in the back.

What do you call a strange thing which falls into a chip pan? An unidentified frying object!

Magic Balls

This trick needs quite a lot of practice or people may see how you do it.

Use strong, thin black or brown thread. If you can get it, colourless nylon thread is best.

If the box is thin cardboard, tear it up at the end to prove there are no balls in it.

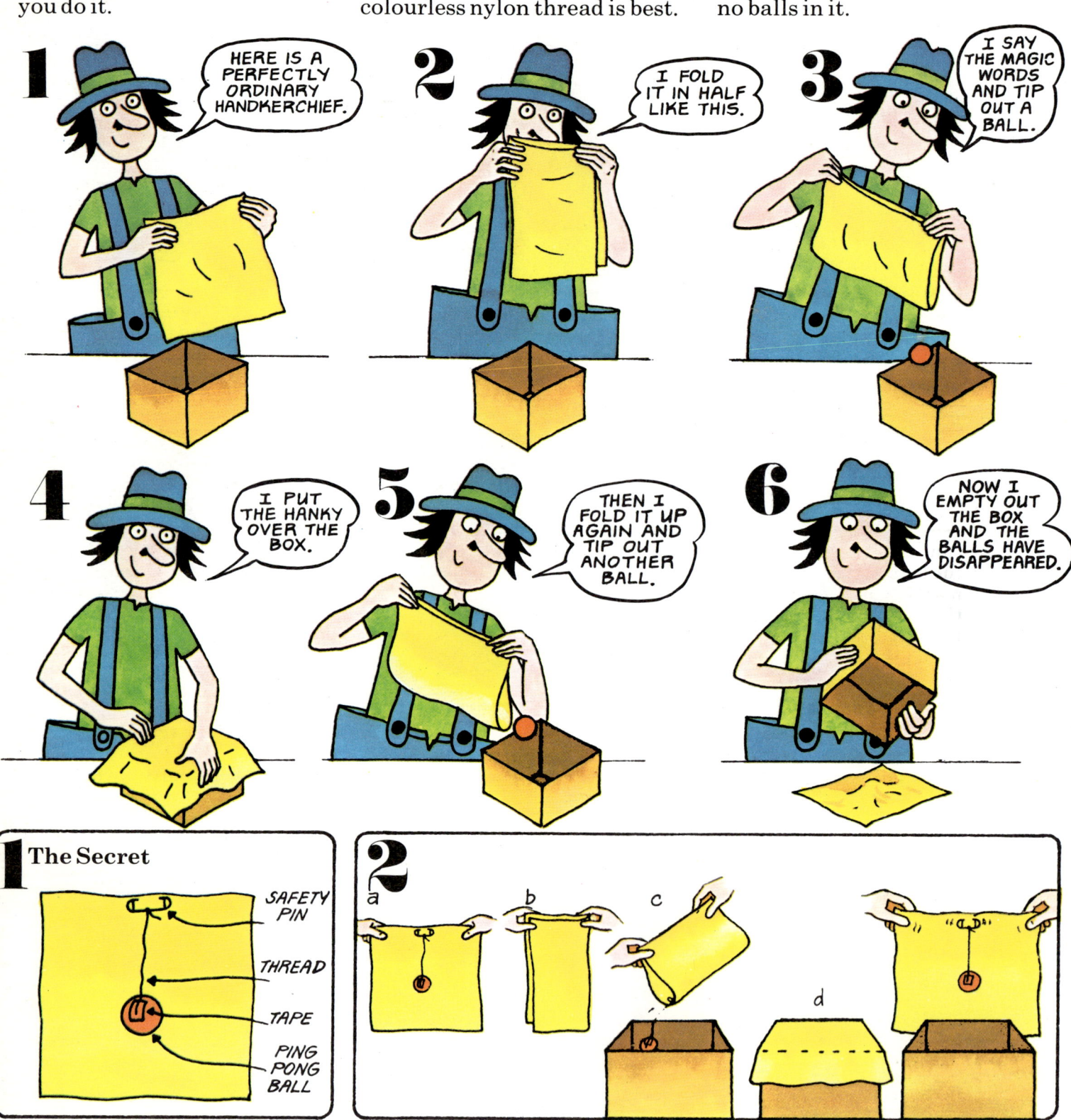

1 HERE IS A PERFECTLY ORDINARY HANDKERCHIEF.

2 I FOLD IT IN HALF LIKE THIS.

3 I SAY THE MAGIC WORDS AND TIP OUT A BALL.

4 I PUT THE HANKY OVER THE BOX.

5 THEN I FOLD IT UP AGAIN AND TIP OUT ANOTHER BALL.

6 NOW I EMPTY OUT THE BOX AND THE BALLS HAVE DISAPPEARED.

1 The Secret

SAFETY PIN

THREAD

TAPE

PING PONG BALL

Stick the end of a piece of thin, strong thread to a ping pong ball with tape. Tie the other end to a safety pin. Put the safety pin in the hem of a big handkerchief.

2 a b c d e

Hold up the hanky with the ball towards you (a). Fold it in half (b). Tip out the ball into the box (c). Let the hanky fall over the box (d).

Pick up the two corners nearest you so the ball is still towards you (e). You can tip out the ball in the same way lots of times. Then show the box is empty.

What do you do to a blue banana? Cheer it up!

30

Magic Tubes

You can make lots of things appear out of these magic tubes. Remember to pull a tube down when you are taking one off. And push it up from the bottom when you are putting it on again.

You will need

a small tin without a lid

2 sheets of thin cardboard or thick paper, big enough to roll round the tin

a paper clip and sticky tape

coloured ribbons or long strips of thin, coloured paper

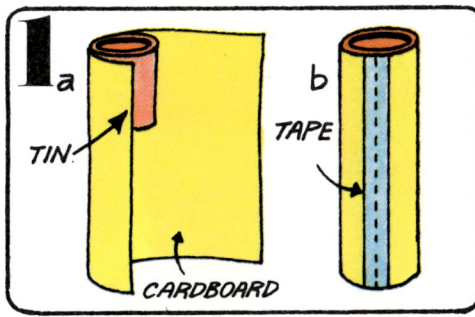

Put the tin down on a sheet of cardboard or paper (a). Roll the sheet loosely round the tin to make a tube. Stick the edge with tape (b).

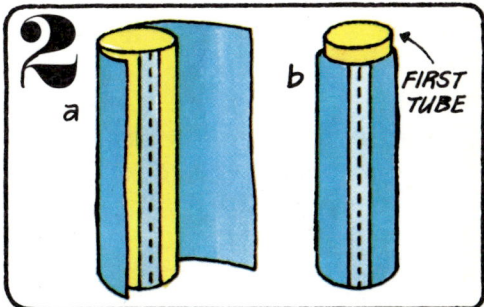

Roll the tube up in the second sheet of cardboard to make another tube. Stick the edge with tape. The first tube should slide easily inside the second one.

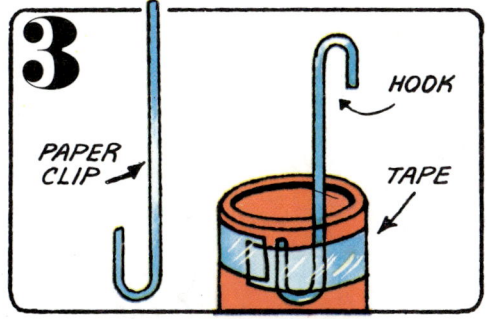

Straighten out one end of a paper clip. Stick the loop end to the top edge of a tin with tape, like this. Bend over the straight end to make a small hook.

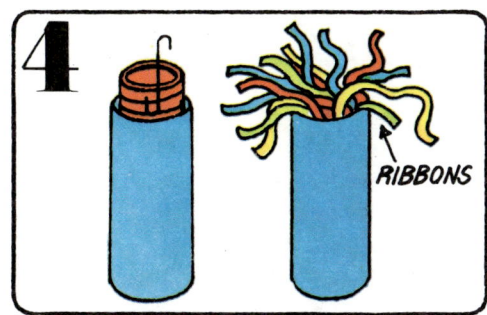

Slide the first tube into the second one. Put the tin into the top of the tubes. Make sure the paper clip hooks on to them. Fill the tin with ribbons or long strips of paper.

The Secret

Keep the hook towards you. Hold the outside tube and slide the inside one downwards. Show that it is empty. Now slide it up inside the outside tube. Hold the inside tube at the top and slide the outside one downwards. Show that it is empty. Slide it on again from the bottom. Hold both tubes in one hand and pull the ribbons out of the tin.

How It Looks

1 HERE ARE TWO MAGIC TUBES.

2 I SLIDE OUT THE INSIDE ONE.

3 YOU CAN SEE IT IS EMPTY. I SLIDE IT BACK INSIDE THE OTHER ONE.

4

5 NOW I SLIDE OFF THE OUTSIDE TUBE.

6 THE OUTSIDE TUBE IS ALSO EMPTY.

7 I SLIDE IT BACK ON TO THE INNER ONE.

8 I SAY THE MAGIC WORDS AND THE TUBES ARE FULL OF RIBBONS!

What do you get if you cross an elephant with a mouse? Huge holes in the skirting boards!

Grand Finisher

This is a very good trick to do as the last one in a show. You need a helper ready in the audience. He should pretend he does not know what you are going to do. Before you start this trick, ask for a volunteer from the audience. Your helper must get up very quickly before anyone else offers to help.

A few days before the show, find an old shirt for your helper to wear. Write in big letters, with a brush and paint, 'The End' across the back of the shirt. Leave the paint to dry.

1 I AM NOW GOING TO TAKE OFF THIS VOLUNTEER'S SHIRT. FIRST I UNDO THE BUTTONS ON HIS COLLAR AND SHIRT FRONT.

Ask your helper to sit down on a chair or stool. Stand behind him and undo the buttons on his shirt collar and shirt front.

2 I NOW UNDO THE BUTTONS ON HIS CUFFS.

Now undo the buttons on your helper's shirt sleeves.

3 I SAY THE MAGIC WORDS AND GIVE THE SHIRT A GOOD PULL.

Take hold of the shirt collar. Say the magic words. Give the shirt a good pull upwards.

4 I SAY SOME MORE MAGIC WORDS AND OFF COMES THE SHIRT!

Say some more magic words. Pull the shirt again. Keep on pulling and it will come right off from under the helper's coat.

5

Turn the shirt round so the audience can see what is written on the back. Everyone will then know the show is over and will clap while you bow.

The Secret

1

Before the show, put the shirt round your helper, so that it hangs down his back. Do not put his arms into the shirt sleeves.

2

Do up the collar button and the top two front buttons. Put the sleeves down his arms and do up the buttons.

3

Put on the helper's coat and do up the buttons. Make sure that the shirt looks as if it is on properly and that sleeve ends show under the coat.

What do you get if you pour boiling water down a rabbit hole? ¡ʎuunq ssoɹɔ ʇoɥ ∀